SPIRAL

William L. Story

Cover Art by Neil Jackson

Spiral
Third Cove Press
ISBN-13: 978-0615902050
ISBN-10: 0615902057

Forward

SPIRAL is completely a work of my imagination. None of the characters or events have counterparts in real life. Even the criminal characters of Italian ethnicity in this novel, commonly referred to as the Mob, Mafia or La Cosa Nostra, have been driven to virtual extinction by law enforcement. They once thrived in Boston's North End and even though today Italian criminality enjoys a sort of romanticism or cachet kept alive by motion pictures, television series, and other works of fiction, its heyday is over and its numbers are few. At least, that's what we are led to believe...

W.L.S.

Chapter One

Bobby Ellis, better known to his friends as Chug because he could chug or swill a beer faster than anyone alive, had no way of knowing who the four women sitting in the corner booth were.

If someone had told him that the real good looking one with the silver fox fur beside her was the wife of the number two man in Boston's organized crime hierarchy and that the older one next to her was that man's mother, Chug, if he believed what he was told, would have grabbed Frankie Ricciardi's elbow and marched back to the stolen, idling Chevy outside with Leo Santos waiting behind the wheel.

What the hell, there was such a thing as using common sense and picking your shots.

Probably, though, he wouldn't have believed they were who they were. Wives and mothers of Mafioso chieftains hung out in the North End in their own little private room of some *ristorante* with a name like *Angela's* or *Gina's*. Not in a franchise restaurant (although one of the better franchises) stuck in a high-traffic cluster of highways in the suburbs.

Those highways were one reason Chug and Frankie had picked this place. They could lose themselves in any of several directions.

They were wearing phony 'staches and baseball caps pulled low, one with a B for Chug who was a Red Sox fan, and one with the Yankees NY logo for Frankie who fancied he might look just a bit like

Derek Jeter with a little Sly Stallone in his younger days thrown in. They also wore jackets that were too large with a couple of sweaters under to make them look heavier than they were.

Fortunately, the weather was chilly.

The four women had been coming to this restaurant every Tuesday afternoon for years. They sat in the same booth and ordered the same food. They each had two cups of coffee, one with the meal and one after.

They would chat, complain that they could no longer smoke cigarettes in a restaurant, and then leave together in a black Lincoln Town Car. The number two man's wife drove.

The reason they came to this place was that years earlier, on this very site sat a take out hamburger joint where the wife of the number two man worked and served a burger, large order of fries and a Coke to the number two man who at the time was just a skinny but very Italian-looking *bel ragazzo*.

He had thought she was *molto bella* too and one thing led to another. Today, the site still held a very special place in her heart and she could remember exactly the order she had served him and one or two other details about their first encounter.

Besides the four women and the help, only five other people were in the restaurant: two guys in their late thirties, who, from the look of their suits might be businessmen or salesmen. And a young married couple with a child about two or three whose face was smeared with ice cream.

This was just what they had planned on. Light mid-afternoon crowd but with the receipts still in the register from a busy breakfast and lunch business, a lot of it cash from college students (not that college students didn't use credit cards) in nearby Medford and Somerville.

They weren't planning on a major killing. Just a few low-risk bucks. But, hey, they weren't the James brothers and, as far as Chug was concerned, this wasn't a career move.

Chug fingered the nine-millimeter in his jacket pocket. No problem getting the guns. Even in Massachusetts with its strict gun control laws, guns were about as hard to get as a cold in December.

The plan was simple. Walk in, hats pulled low, make sure no cops were having a cup of coffee at the counter, and go right to the register. Frank would stick his piece under the nose of the store manager while Chug covered him.

After filling a bag with the cash, back out to the Chevy, which they'd drop in a strip mall a half a mile away, and switch to a Ford Taurus. They'd split the take at Frankie's.

Chug felt himself sweating and not just from the two sweaters under his jacket. He was more hyped than he thought he'd be, hyped the way he used to be when he had played schoolboy hockey.

He eyed the customers. No problem with the marrieds, who looked like churchgoers to Chug, and little kid. No problem with the four women. No problem with the two guys unless they turned out to be plain-clothes cops or FBI agents, which, Chug figured, wasn't too likely.

The help were the usual assortment. None of them looked like potential heroes.

The only one who might have a heart attack was the old dame. And me, Chug thought. He smiled inwardly. Damn adrenalin.

Chug and Frankie exchanged a glance and drew their pieces.

As he pointed his in the general direction of the dining room, Chug heard Frankie, in a voice a little strung out, tell the guy at the register to open it and hand him all the cash.

Chug was also conscious, in a kind of slow motion, surrealistic way, of the two guys staring at him and sitting very stiffly; of the mother hugging the little kid to her; of the two women who were facing him, the old one with her mouth shaping an O of shock and then the lips just kind of sagging. The other woman, the good looking one, looked really pissed, as though she might pick up the shaker of sugar and throw it at Chug. Instead, she said in a clear, loud voice, "You sonsabitches."

The two women with their backs to Chug slowly shifted around and stared dumbly. One was the sister of the number two man's wife and the other was a friend of the wife.

What happened next wasn't planned. The angry looking woman reached for the silver fox fur. Maybe she thought Chug was going to ask for it, which he wasn't. She grabbed it to her quickly and Chug wasn't even aware of squeezing the trigger of the nine but the damn thing went off anyway.

"Jesus," he heard himself say through the ringing of the shot in his ears.

He saw Frankie looking at him and mouthing something.

The bullet had hit the old lady whose sagging lips stiffened in surprise and pain. A red splotch blossomed on her shoulder near her collarbone and she slumped in her seat as though someone had shoved her.

Frankie, screaming obscenities, grabbed Chug's arm and they ran out to the Chevy leaving a wounded crime boss's mother and a cash register full of money behind.

Leo fishtailed from the parking lot with a big screech of the tires, cutting off a Honda Civic loaded with college students who screamed and whipped collective fingers at them.

"Easy, Leo," Chug said who sat in front beside Leo. "Nice and easy. Just drive normal."

"Who the hell are you to be giving advice?" Frankie said. He was in back and swiveling around, looking to the left, the right, and back from where they had come.

"How'd we make out?" Leo asked.

"How'd we make out?" Frankie said. "How'd we make out? We didn't. We got zilch. Chuggy, boy, here got nervous or something and pulled the goddamn trigger. Shot an old lady. What'd you think, she was drawing on you?"

Chug gave Frankie a look.

"Easy, Frank. Don't start loading on me. You want to have it out, I'm ready anytime."

Frankie leaned back in his seat and muttered but kept it low.

Chug peeled his phony 'stache and took off his hat. He slipped off his jacket and one of the sweaters. Frankie did the same. Chug tossed his stuff into the back seat and Frankie stuffed them in a plastic trash bag.

They kept their guns.

Leo, now driving civilly, pulled into the strip mall and found a spot.

Leaving the plastic bag in the Chevy, they walked, not together, to the Taurus. When they got to it, Frankie was still muttering. He opened the front door to get in beside Leo.

Chug grabbed his arm and twisted it up behind Frankie's back. "Get over it, Frank."

He spun Frankie to the back door and shoved him inside. Then he got in front with Leo.

In the distance, they heard sirens and then a police car flashed past in a blur of blue lights.

They picked up Route 93 and drove toward Boston. Frankie sat silent for a while but as they approached the Zakim-Bunker Hill Bridge he started to mutter again.

Chug leaned over the seat and looked at him.

"Frankie, I gotta tell you something. I know where you're coming from, it makes you feel any better. My fault, okay? No getting around it. But, guess what? Right now all I can think of is that woman I shot. You know what I mean? The look on her face."

Chug held Frankie's gaze and Frankie blinked and looked away.

"So you're pissed. Too bad. Be as pissed as you want but just zip it."

Chug reached over the seat and tapped Frankie softly on his cheek with the flat of his hand and gave him a smile.

They rode in silence until they dumped the Taurus in a parking garage and then walked to a T station and went their separate ways.

Chapter Two

He stared into the muzzle, 9 millimeters across, all the way down the rifled grooves to the blunt nub of the bullet. Saw it explode and spiral its way out until, in a split second, it found the soft, white flesh of the old woman and opened a red blossom on her shoulder.

It sat on the table across from him, an ugly looking little mother, in his estimation, as it awaited his decision on its fate. Some guys, he knew, got off on guns, savored looking at them, touching them, talking about them, reading about them, cleaning them and, of course, most of all, *firing* them. Frankie was one of those guys.

Frankie had got them from someone he knew in New Hampshire, a Browning for himself and some kind of Colt for Chug.

"These are good pieces, Chug," Frankie had told him, his face swollen with appreciation of the brace of nines. "Very definitely not junk."

Chug eyed the Colt. He ought to take a trip to the Charles and chuck it, just a casual stroll over the Longfellow Bridge at night and a quick flip of the wrist when no one was looking. Bye, bye.

He turned his gaze from the Colt to the dollar bill held submerged in bleach by a small pebble in a half-pound margarine tub. It was the day after the fiasco and he sat in his kitchen in a shaft of late afternoon March sunshine slanting through his window. His body ached and his mind was cottony from not getting much sleep. He had taken off yesterday, the day of the debacle, and today, the day of recrimination, from his part time job with a florist, pleading an upset stomach.

He stared at the bill, breathed bleach fumes, and tried not to think of the old woman he had shot, her sagging face and body. The red splotch.

He stared some more at the dollar bill which for three hours had sat in the half-pound margarine tub in an inch of bleach. Chug pulled out the bill and inspected it. He blotted it with a paper towel and then smoothed it with the flat of his hand. The results weren't what he wanted but weren't unexpected. Except for being rather limp and stinking of bleach the bill was as good as new.

At his sink, he blotted the bill again on another paper towel and washed the traces of bleach from his hands. He once again examined the bill carefully and then put it down. On a piece of plain white paper, in the upper left, he wrote the date and the word 'bleach.' Beside that, he wrote 'negative.'

Next, he'd try various acids, maybe start with muriatic.

Paper was the problem with funny money, especially now with the special threads and other things built into the bills. He figured if he could wash the ink out of a low denomination bill today's photocopiers could put a high denomination in its place that would be passable. Maybe. A pipe dream, actually, he conceded but something to do and worth a shot. You never knew.

Definitely a better idea than what yesterday had turned out to be. He played the scene over again, trying to focus on when the gun had gone off, the trigger pulled by some strange force because *he* had not pulled it. When the good-looking woman had reached for her fur, his eyes and hand had followed her. He was sure of it. And he sure as hell didn't see her as any kind of threat, didn't think she was reaching for some little feminist snub-nose. Maybe a cell phone, now that he thought of it, but he wasn't thinking of that at the time.

Still, the Colt had gone off somehow and hit the old woman.

He thought of her and his throat tightened but after he had seen reports of the screw-up on last night's and this morning's news the whole thing became a lot more than a matter of conscience. The shooting had gotten a fairly big play because the woman had been elderly and white but mainly because she was Florence Scarlata, mother of William Scarlata.

Chug definitely knew who he was and it didn't comfort him at all.

What the hell had she been doing in a restaurant like that? It made no sense for her to have been there but he couldn't very well get on the horn to William and say, "Geez, what the hell was your mother doing in a classless joint like that?" As if William would say, "Wasn't your fault. How would you know she ate there?"

The news had said she was in Mass General in stable condition, which didn't sound too bad, except at her age you couldn't be sure. But Chug knew that didn't mean William Scarlata wouldn't be mightily pissed off.

And he couldn't blame him. He'd be more than pissed off if someone hurt his widower father now in a nursing home.

Chug lit a cigarette, put a couple of Fenway Franks in a greased pan and prepared two rolls with mustard and relish. He popped a can of Bud and drank some while he waited for the dogs.

He eyed his clock, a little electric thing that was supposed to look old fashioned but it buzzed and its pendulum swung too fast. By the time he ate his dogs, Ellie should be home.

He picked up the *Herald* and read for at least the third time the account of yesterday. It was on page three. Like the TV news, it provided a description of the gunmen that gave Chug a little relief. It had his height between five-ten and six-one. He was actually five-eleven. But his weight had been pegged somewhere between 200 and 220, comfortably over his 180. The sweaters had done their job.

He thought of William Scarlata, of what he knew of him. He didn't know him personally, although he had seen him once or twice in the North End, the long-time headquarters of Boston's Italian mob. Mainly, he knew about William Scarlata from the newspapers and from street talk.

William Scarlata. A.K.A. Will Scarlet. Just one of the Merry Band robbing from anyone they could, rich or poor.

William Scarata was probably fifty, fifty-one, Chug thought. Tall, thin, good shape. Mean looking. Chug knew he wasn't the Godfather but he was right up there.

He took a deep gulp of beer, right down to the bottom of the can, in fact, and got another from the fridge.

He poked the dogs as they sizzled in the grease. A little trail of black smoke wiggled up from the pan. The stove didn't have a vent of fan. For that matter, the two rooms in Southie that Chug called home didn't have much at all in amenities except for some fairly upscale techno entertainment gear. An iPod hooked in and out of a stereo and Rod Stewart was singing *Maggie May*. Chug's dad had liked Rod Stewart and because of that so did Chug. There was also a forty-two-inch high def TV and a good laptop.

Framed sports pictures and posters hung on the walls, a medley of Red Sox, Patriots, Celtics, and Bruins.

Chug turned off the heat under the dogs and turned to a shelf with a framed picture of his mother and father leaning against a '70s Ford in bright summer sunshine. He didn't know where the picture was taken but he always had liked it, the way his parents looked in it. Another framed photo showed him and his brother Jimmy with their Mom and Dad when Chug was about nine or ten.

He picked up the picture of his mother and father. His mother had been gone for almost ten years now. It had been quick. An aneurism. A triple A the doctor had called it. Strange, but he couldn't remember what other two *A*s stood for.

He put the picture back onto the shelf, brushing his fingers over the image of his mother and thought of Florence Scarlata. Then he thought of her son and tried to push him out of his mind, or, more precisely, thoughts of what William Scarlata did and was likely to want to do to whoever shot his mother. The word was that William Scarlata was in charge of enforcement for the wops. Chug winced as he thought of an ice pick in his ear.

He eyed the Colt again and leveled a curse at it and Frankie. But when he thought of William Scarlata he admitted he might just need the ugly little sucker.

He pulled his cell phone from his pocket, punched Ellie's speed dial number, listened to five or six rings, and waited until he got her voice mail before shutting off. She was probably home but maybe in the shower.

He thought of Ellie. They had known each other for over three years and she wanted to marry and he was leaning to it but now he had something else to think about. If they did, she'd be Ellie Ellis. They both thought that was funny.

If he could get the ink out of a dollar. Funny money could be the way to go if you didn't get too greedy.

He went back to the stove and looked at the dogs but no longer felt hungry.

The stink of bleach still assailed his nostrils. He went to the table his stereo sat on and opened the drawer where he kept his stash of snow in a little tin that had started life as an innocent carrier of breath mints.

He spread a line on the table beside a Boston speaker, pulled a straw from the drawer, and vacuumed up the line into his nose. The rush hit him and he flowed with it and rode on its wave, letting it drive away the annoying thoughts of Frankie Ricciardi and the more sinister, reptilian thoughts of William Scarlata.

He collapsed on his sofa and wallowed in euphoria. Rod Stewart, in his gritty voice, was now singing *You're in My Heart*. He thought of Ellie and sang with Rod. "You're in my heart, you're in my soul . . . you're my lover, you're my best friend." His voice faded and he knew that the euphoria was going to have a short life this time. He could feel it slipping already, being pushed aside by the replay of Florence Scarlata's look of shock as the bullet punched her and she bled a quickly spreading crimson blossom.

He looked over at the kitchen table, at the Colt lying on its side where at this angle its black nine-millimeter muzzle was pointing directly at him.

He phoned Frankie at his place.

"Look, Chuggy, the thing is that Colt was only a nine. An ACP. Not a lot of power there. Cops don't even use them much anymore. Not enough stopping power. All the bad guys use tens. At least."

Chug wanted to ask what an ACP was but that would just get Frankie going on and on about guns like he was some kind of expert. That was the thing with Frankie. He liked to throw out these bullshit terms, half of which he didn't even understand. He also wanted to say, Hey, Frank, we're bad guys and we used nines.

Instead, he said, "Yeah, Frank, wonderful it was only a nine. See, the thing is that this is an old woman. I shot an old woman. If I shot her with a goddamn BB gun that would be bad enough. I don't think it takes much *stopping* power to hurt an old woman."

There was a pause and then Frankie said, "Hey, Chug, you think this is smart? I mean talking on the phone like this?"

"Cut the CIA crap, Frank, huh?"

"Yeah, well, anyway, we gotta get together, Leo too, and see what we're gonna do."

"Yeah, Frank, we gotta do that."

He looked at the bleach-dampened dollar bill. Stupid.

"Something else, Frank. How much dough was in that register? I mean everyone pays with credit cards, for chrissake."

"We've been through this, Chug. I told you, I've been in that place and seen—with my own eyes— plenty of people pay cash. But that's neither here nor there now, is it?"

There was a pause and then Frankie continued.

"But what's still here is my bills and this shitty economy, know what I'm saying?"

"Yeah, I think I do, Frankie, and no deal. That's it for me. I gave it a shot."

He regretted the choice of words but Frankie didn't pick up on the comment.

"Hey, Chug, I always say if you don't succeed, try again."

He wondered why he had even called Frankie.

"Look, Frank, I'll call you in a couple of days. Let me do some thinking."

"Jesus, Chug, that was Will Scarlet's mother," Frank said for about the fifth time. "Talk about heavy duty."

"Yeah. Heavy duty."

Sometimes on summer evenings, maybe after a movie, Chug and Ellie would drive to a small park north of Logan Airport and watch plane after plane coast in for a landing. In certain warm weather conditions, the park was directly under the landing path and they would conjecture where the plane was coming from, especially those whose foreign logos they could read, and talk of where they might go themselves someday.

Now, it was still March but the wind direction was right for planes to glide in over Chug's head as he sat alone in his Explorer, engine running and heater on low, in that same park.

The sun was setting and the planes were lined up in the northwest sky, their lights on as they approached Logan, moving so slowly, it seemed, in the distance that they would surely just simply fall before reaching their destination. But as they got close and came in low, waffling slightly from side to side and their jets whining, their speed became obvious.

Chug had left his apartment, the smell of bleach and burned hotdogs and the remnants of failed cocaine still in his head and the Colt nine millimeter tucked in his belt, and driven to the airport. He drove past terminals, compelled by the germ of a not thought-out impulse to grab a plane for somewhere distant.

But just as certainly as he knew he couldn't get on a plane with the Colt, he also knew he couldn't get on one without Ellie. And he knew he couldn't just fly away from the image of a shocked and bloodied Florence Scarlata.

So he had driven from the airport and now found himself sitting under a flight path, smoking cigarettes and trying to sort things out, trying to formulate where to go and what to do.

He watched a jumbo jet approach, everything about it defined and improbably large in the spotlight of the sun's final rays. His eyes followed it as it made its touchdown. Its engines screamed as they kicked into brake mode.

He thought of the people on the plane. Happy families returning from vacation, probably a returning honeymoon couple or two, some successful business types, no doubt.

He thought of himself and Ellie and what tomorrow now held for them was even more important than his worries about Florence Scarlata and her son.

He played his options out in his mind and how each played out with Ellie. He flicked a cigarette out the window and counted the airplanes lined up in the sky.

Then he drove from the park back to Southie through the Ted Williams tunnel. For a moment he played with the idea of driving into the North End, looking up William Scarlata and saying, "Hey, you sonovabitch, here I am. What are you gonna do?"

He laughed at that and drove to a bar with shamrocks on the windows lit up by neon beer signs.

Inside, a couple of guys shooting pool nodded at him as he walked to the bar and grabbed an empty stool.

"Chug, my man, what's goin' on?" the man behind the bar said. He reached down and pulled up a dripping bottle of Bud and placed it in front of Chug. He and Chug bumped fists.

"The usual, Danny. Which means nothing. Hey, Dan, one cave woman says to another cave woman, 'What's your boyfriend use that big old club for?' The other one says, 'Beats me.'"

Danny smiled. "How's your Dad, Chug?'

"He's hanging in there. Thanks for asking. He's one tough old guy."

Chug nursed his beer and watched the TV over the bar for a few moments. A cable sports channel was showing highlights of spring training games. As he watched, Chug became aware of his hunger.

He signaled Danny, ordered a cheeseburger and fries, and tilted his now empty bottle.

Danny caught him checking in the mirror a couple of guys at a table near a window. One had his sleeve pinned to his shirt.

"That's Tommy O'Shea," Danny said, voice low. "He's been over a year rehabbing at an Army hospital in Texas, I think. Lost the arm but got really screwed up internally from shrapnel. I guess he was lucky, though. Was in a Humvee but everyone else was killed."

Chug nodded and regarded Danny, a guy in his early sixties who'd been a marine in Nam and was himself shot up pretty bad during Tet.

"I don't really know him," Chug said. "I mean, I mainly remember him as a little kid when I was in high school. Who's the other guy?"

"An Army buddy from down South somewhere."

Danny put the fresh bottle of Bud on the bar in front of Chug. Chug regarded it a moment and then said, "Hey, Danny, send whatever they're drinking to their table on me, huh?"

In the mirror, Chug watched Danny deliver the drinks. Tommy O'Shea and his friend looked Chug's way and Chug flipped them a little salute.

Then he watched the game of eight ball and listened to the clack of pool balls for a couple of minutes until his burger and fries came.

He attacked them greedily as he watched the cable sports channel.

When he finished eating, he pulled out his cell phone and punched Ellie's number. He got her voice mail and then remembered this was the night of her real estate course.

He felt for the Colt to make sure it was not showing and then swiveled around on his stool to watch the game of pool.

After another night of bothered sleep, Chug stood on the porch of a three decker in Lynn with the vase of a floral arrangement slippery in his hand. Lynn was about as far north of the city as they delivered. The doorbells were all painted over and the names printed on white tape below the mailboxes were blurred and faded. Both doors were locked. This was the kind of neighborhood he hated delivering to and for this very situation.

He looked at the name written on the envelope stuck into the plastic wand that jutted from the vase. Maria Fuentes. He put the vase onto the porch deck, checked the phone number on the envelope and punched it into the cell phone.

After five rings a woman answered.

"Hello," Chug said. "Maria Fuentes?"

"Who is this?" A crusty voice.

"Is this Maria?"

"Yes."

"Maria, this is Bradford Brothers Florist. I've got a beautiful floral arrangement for you."

"Who?"

"Bradford Brothers. I've got some nice flowers for you."

"Wait a minute."

At least she had answered. Chug leaned against the porch railing, which didn't feel all that secure. An old died up sponge mop leaned against the railing with Chug. Two green plastic chairs sat on either side of a small green plastic table with an ashtray filled with a mountain of cigarette butts on it.

He couldn't count the times you'd ring a bell and no one would answer. Then you'd call with the cell phone and get no response. The procedure then was to find a neighbor you could leave the arrangement with, place delivery tags in mailboxes, and hang them on doorknobs. Finally, you'd phone back to leave a message. What would very often happen? The recipient would answer and you'd have to trudge back to the neighbor to retrieve the flowers.

Chug was glad Maria Fuentes was home. This didn't look like the kind of neighborhood where neighbors were neighborly or if you left the arrangement with someone else it would find its way to the intended recipient. The street was lined with three deckers whose angles were no longer plumb and whose porches were sagging. The street gutters were gardens of plastic trash and cigarette filters.

If it were in Boston, it might be the kind of neighborhood he'd like to avoid, unless it was

Southie. But it was Lynn, a semi tough city but he didn't feel too uncomfortable. Didn't feel as though he needed the nine, which was back at his place in a bureau drawer covered with his underwear.

He heard the right hand door open and a woman about thirty-five dressed in a loose robe stood there with suspicious eyes and disheveled hair. Kind of hard for hair to look messed when it's dreadlocks or cornrows, Chug thought, although he wasn't too sure of the difference between the two.

"Maria? These are for you," Chug said, handing the arrangement to the woman. "Beautiful, aren't they?"

He loved to watch the expression on a woman's face when she received flowers. Maria Fuentes didn't disappoint.

The suspicion snapped from her eyes and she smiled a luminous smile of startling white teeth.

"For me?" she said. "Who sent me these?"

Chug smiled. "I don't know. There's a card."

Maria Fuentes reached for the flowers but Chug pulled them back. He felt like kidding and now Maria looked as though she could use a little kidding and would appreciate it.

"Wait a minute," he said. "How do I know you're Maria Fuentes? Got any ID?"

She laughed. "I'm Maria. I promise."

Chug handed her the flowers.

"Who would send me these?" she asked again.

Chug shrugged. "I bet a lot of guys would."

"Thank you so much" Maria Fuentes said. "I need to sign something?"

21

"No. You're all set. Enjoy the flowers," Chug said. He gave her a smile and returned to the delivery van.

On his trip sheet he put a check beside Maria Fuentes's address, which had been his last delivery for this load. Now he'd head for the Ted Williams tunnel and back to the shop to load up again.

Maria Fuentes was still on the porch. She had put the arrangement down and was reading the card. He gave her a little blip of the horn and she waved as he drove away.

That's what he liked about this job. It wasn't as though he was handing people a summons. He gave them flowers and made them smile.

He checked the time on the dashboard clock. It would be just about noon when he got back to the shop. As he drove he listened to a sports talk show on the radio but wasn't really tuned in.

Be something if he got an arrangement to deliver to Mass General for Florence Scarlata. He thought about that and wondered how she was. He'd like to be able to see her, to see that she was doing all right. But he didn't know if he could look at where she was wounded, taped up. She was probably on painkillers and he tried to shake that thought from his mind. He imagined handing her a bouquet of flowers and seeing her face light up.

"For me?" she'd say.

"For you," he'd say. "Beautiful, aren't they?"

Maybe William Scarlata would be there visiting his mother. He'd nod at Chug and Chug would nod back. See, I'm not such a bad guy. I sure as hell didn't mean to shoot your mother. What kind of person you think I am?

He tried to concentrate on the talk show, an analysis of the starting rotation for the Red Sox this coming season.

It was too bad he couldn't make a living delivering flowers. It was a job of no stress and no pressure. Just spend the day making people smile and listening to sports talk although more and more he was listening to a couple of NPR stations at Ellie's urging. He found himself liking those shows. Smart people who made a lot of sense, even though he didn't always agree with them. They didn't rant and rave the way a lot of talk show hosts did.

He'd been delivering flowers part time for close to two years now, since he got laid off from what had been a pretty good job as a manager of the electronics department at Sands department stores, a victim of the economy.

He helped around the shop a little in the early morning before starting deliveries. Filled buckets with water. Some flowers required warm water, some cold. He had to put a kind of white powder in some of the buckets but not in others. It didn't require a degree from MIT.

He had to admit, though, that the girls in the design room were pretty creative and artistic when they made the arrangements. And they were fast.

Pretty soon he'd be starting his other part time job with a landscaper who paid him under the table. His head spun sometimes at the crazy hours chopped and mixed between the two jobs but so far he could pay the bills but sometimes just barely.

He liked the landscaping too, the physicality of it and being outdoors. He'd tell Ellie, "It's like going to a gym, in a way, know what I mean? And I get paid."

Using his own cell phone, not the shop's, he punched some numbers doing a good job of keeping his eyes on the road.

"Doctor Winters' office."

"Hi, it's me."

"Hi, you," Ellie Robinson said.

"What are you doing?"

"The usual. Smiling at patients and making reminder calls for appointments. How 'bout you?"

"Not much. Driving back to the shop. I'm making a reminder call right now. See you tomorrow night."

"Oh, thanks for the reminder. I totally forgot," Ellie said with a laugh

"You forgot?"

Ellie laughed louder. "What do you think? Hey, I gotta go."

"Okay," Chug said. "Love you."

"Love you too."

He zipped through the Ted and made his way to the parking lot behind the shop on Mass Ave. Two of the five shop vans were there. They were all the same, green Honda Odysseys with Bradford Brothers Florist in gold lettering on the sides. They all had a lot of mileage but still rode pretty good.

"You made good time, Chug," Mike Bradford, his boss, said when Chug walked through the back door.

One time Ellie had called the shop and asked for Chug instead of Bobby and he had to explain the nickname. He had wowed them with a demonstration using a plastic tumbler filled with water from the cooler.

"Yeah, everything went pretty smooth."

"That's what we like to hear. Write everything up on this table, please," Mike said.

Chug checked the table. There were eight pieces, three of them large funeral baskets.

"Okay, let me grab my lunch first," Chug said, heading to one of the coolers near the front of the store where he had stored his submarine sandwich with everything on it (but light on the hots), a small bag of chips, a chocolate bar and a bottle of spring water. He'd eat in the van while driving.

Three women stood behind designer tables snipping and stripping stems and jamming them into vases or pieces of green oasis foam. A garden of color sprouted on the floor in front of them, buckets and buckets of flowers.

Chug had known the names of some of the flowers before he had started work at the shop. Flowers that everyone recognized like roses and daisies and tulips. But now he recognized varieties he had never heard of before. Larkspur, hypericum, stock, iris, bells of Ireland, eucalyptus.

"Hey cutie," Paula Euvino said. "What's cookin'? How's the world of floral delivery?"

"It's hell," Chug said, flashing her a smile. "You can't even imagine."

"Like in here. I caught a rose thorn while stripping a stem. It hurts. Want to see it? Want to kiss it?"

"Watch out for her, Chug," Maddie Cramer said. "She's trouble."

Paula was about Chug's age and cute. Maddie was neither but was very nice in Chug's opinion.

"Hey, I caught a thorn, too," Maddie said and held up her hand. "You kiss her hand and you have to kiss mine."

"At least one of us is a lady, Chug" Anna Jankowski said. "I didn't get stabbed by a thorn but you can kiss my hand anyway."

The three women laughed.

"We won't tell Ellie," Paula said.

"Okay, if that's the case," Chug said and made a mock move toward the three women.

He got his lunch from the cooler and went back and wrote the addresses on his trip sheet. One was for a place on Beacon Hill. Chug liked going there. It would be nice to live among bricks and cobblestones and windows with real wooden shutters. The recipient probably wouldn't tip, though. Few people did but the big bucks people, especially old-money Brahmins never did.

A year ago just before St. Paddy's day, he delivered to a low-income housing place in Chelsea. When he went into the apartment he nearly gagged on the cigarette smoke. An elderly woman in a wheelchair and tubes from a tank running into her nose handed him a twenty after he set the arrangement on a table for her.

"Thank you very much," Chug had said, "but I can't take this."

"Sure you can. Go buy yourself a couple of Guinness."

Just before he loaded the van he looked back to see Paula Euvino pucker her lips at him.

As he headed toward Brighton, he munched his sub, savoring the cold cuts, cheese, and oil. The bag of chips was open and he crunched a couple at a time. Bright sunshine splayed cheerfully across the windshield and reflected off the dash. Small favors, he thought. Couldn't take a rainy day.

The three funeral baskets were going to Matthews' Funeral Home in Brighton, a place that they delivered to a lot. Most places, they left the baskets or sprays in the flower room but at this place, if there was no wake, they brought them right into the showing room.

"Go there first, Chug," Mike had told him. "There's a four o'clock wake. They go in the Lodge room."

By the time he got to the funeral home he had just finished his chocolate bar and was swishing spring water around his mouth. Ellie told him to swish water and chew sugarless gum after he ate if he couldn't brush. When he finished swishing, he popped a stick of gum into his mouth. The gum would also help kill the smell of the onions, he hoped.

He parked in the lot at the rear of the funeral home and unloaded the first basket. In the Lodge room, a middle age man in a dark suit was bent over the casket and doing something with what Chug thought was a small brush to the face of another middle age man who lay uncomplaining in the casket.

The man with the small brush looked at Chug and said, "How you doing?"

"Hi," Chug said. "Where do you want this?"

"How many pieces you got?"

"Two more."

"All baskets?"

"Yeah."

"Just leave them there. We'll set them up."

27

When Chug brought in the third basket, the man had finished his detailing and was standing, head cocked at a slight angle, admiring his work. Then he reached down and adjusted the dead man's tie.

Chug looked at the guy in the casket. Rosary beads were wrapped around his hands. An American flag was folded on the casket, a shiny mahogany one. The room reeked of lilies.

The man turned to Chug and smiled. "How's Mike?"

"He's fine," Chug said.

"Tell him I said, hi."

"I will."

The man eyed the arrangements Chug had brought in.

"And be sure to tell the girls that the flowers look great. As usual."

"I'll be sure to do that."

Whatever the man had been using was clutched in his hand and Chug tried to make out what it was. A brush? Scissors? He couldn't tell.

Back in the van, he checked his trip sheet.

Funeral directors made a ton of money, he thought, but it was a hell of a way to make a living.

Chapter Three

William Scarlata sat by himself in his office which was actually just a small room on the third floor of a brick building right around the corner from Hanover Street. Smells of Italian cooking, garlic and olive oil, hung in the air but William Scarlata was oblivious to them. He was drinking a glass of red table wine, something he rarely did before evening. But he had just returned from the hospital where he had visited his mother and his usual flat line nerves were bumping up and down.

His mother was doing well enough, but after much prodding from William, her doctor had admitted that any bullet wound was a concern and in someone Florence Scarlata's age complications could set in.

To William, she looked, lying in her bed with needles stuck in her arms, frail and white. Her eyes looked as though she had been punched.

William Scarlata was no stranger to what people looked like when hit by bullets; indeed, he knew the effects quite well, having over the years on occasion been the one with his finger on the trigger. The big difference was that, when he pulled it, the victim wasn't lucky enough to end up in the hospital.

It was quite some time, however, since he had done work of that sort. Now, either some of his own in-house people or subcontractors did his disposal work. In this case, though, if he found who put his mother in the hospital, he would deal with that person himself. In his own way.

From his window, he could glimpse a slice of Hanover Street with its usual clogged traffic, and some of the roofs of the North End, a very old part of Boston. Paul Revere's house still stood there, an artifact that amused William but did not particularly interest him. He had never been inside it.

He watched a Volvo double park and a fashionably dressed young woman run into an Italian bakery, probably for some canolis to take back to her waterfront condo where she'd serve them to yuppie friends tonight and gush about how quaint the North End was with its old Italian ladies dressed in black and the old Italian guys sitting in the Prato playing cards. It's so *old,* so old-worldish, almost like being in *Italy.*

That was the problem with the North End. Volvos and yuppies taking over. Young Italians moving out.

It bothered the old Italian ladies and men who had lived here all their lives or since they were little and had come from Napoli or Roma or Sicilia. For them, the North End was a connection to old ways and old places. It bothered William Scarlata's mother. And it bothered William. This was his home. Born and raised here. This is where he did business.

Pretty soon the whole neighborhood would be taken over by computer wizard types and their brainy, slender wives and their Northern European cars and their little fairy dogs leaving dog shit all over the sidewalks. If pressed, William Scarlata would admit that most of them did pick up after their dogs.

Sometimes William Scarlata felt as though his world was falling apart between the yuppie dog shit and the Feds who had made all kinds of major busts the last few years that sent long-time fixtures of Mob power packing off to serve long time. And in the bargain they had made them look like pathetic old men.

Not that William hadn't moved up the power ladder as a result. Still, it was scary. Had to keep the office swept for bugs which he learned to do himself.

Then there were the Columbians. While it was true that Mario Cotoni and William Scarlata still called the shots on most of the illicit business in New England, those goddamn spics, or whatever they were, were sending their own men up here to have direct involvement in the traffic. And those guys didn't scare off. They'd just as soon laugh at the old magic words like *Mob, Mafia,* or *Cosa Nostra* that at one time would make any sane person run for cover. Laugh or match any muscle you'd care to flex.

There was a slight knock on the door.

"Come on in, Lou."

Lou Russo, a short, heavy-set man, male-pattern baldness well established, jovial looking, came in. He always reminded William, for some reason, of a butcher. Which he was. But he didn't slice up steaks and chops.

Lou Russo sat across from the desk near the window, resting his right ankle on his left knee.

"How's your mother, Will?"

Only a few people called William Scarlata 'Will.' Lou Russo was one. Mario Cotoni, the only man who outranked William Scarlata, was another. His mother called him William or *Guglielmo* and his wife called him Bill. Most everybody else called him Mr. Scarlata.

William Scarlata nodded. "She's gonna be okay. Thank you. Helluva thing, huh, Lou? Women go to a restaurant to relax, spend some time with friends and some punk probably trying to feed a habit . . ." His voice trailed.

His lips and face were taut, an indication of his struggle with his mother's situation. Then he forced a smile and looked at Lou Russo.

"You want some wine?"

Lou Russo waved his hand, a gesture that said no.

"I want who did this to her, Lou,' William Scarlata said, getting right to the point. "I want that sonovabitch."

"You got any idea?"

William Scarlata shook his head and squeezed his lips together.

"No. Nothing beyond the descriptions were in the papers. Just a couple of ordinary-looking guys. Losers. Dumb but not so dumb. Knew that baseball caps and phony 'staches—I'm sure the 'staches were fake—along with people panicking would make them hard to describe. No surveillance cameras. You believe that?"

He shook his head.

"I'll get the word out. Someone'll know who these guys are. Usually they're their own worst enemy. They can't keep their mouths shut."

"Yeah, that's good, get the word out, but if that don't do it I'm ready to sweeten the deal. By whatever it takes. But I want to hold off on that 'cause I don't want any bogus tips just for the dough. That's important. I want the real guy. Christ knows we got enough people out there with their ears to the ground who owe us or want to kiss ass."

Lou Russo remembered some previous people William Scarlata had wanted and had got and he remembered what he had done to them. With most it had been nothing personal. Strictly business. But, Jesus, when you thought of what he did sometimes.

"When you get the sonovabitch, Lou, don't hurt him. Just bring him to me."

Lou Russo nodded. He understood.

"What you got in mind, Will, you don't mind me asking?"

For a long moment William Scarlata said nothing and Lou Russo thought that maybe he hadn't heard.

Then he said, "Well, you know, Lou, I'm not sure. I guess I gotta give it a lot of special thought. I mean, as far as I'm concerned whoever did this went beyond anything anyone's ever done to me before. We're not talking money or business or any of the usual kinds of screwings."

He sipped his wine.

"This is blood. My mother's blood."

William Scarlata's eyes welled a little and he looked away from Lou Russo as he blinked. He started to say something but his voice broke. He got up, went to the window and looked down at the street for a long moment.

When he got control of his voice, he turned and said, "I guess I gotta give this a lot of thought, Lou, wouldn't you say?"

He sat down again and topped his wine glass. He looked into the red wine as though trying to read something. Then he looked at Lou Russo and smiled thinly. "But whatever I do, Lou, is going to be something very special."

Chapter Four

It had turned exceptionally cold for almost mid March and the time of the raid had been picked at the last minute because of that. Everything would be buttoned up tight and cozy inside. Lieutenant Billy Wilkins knew that between the kerosene heater hissing away and the stereo (Jesus, it had to be about a thousand watts per channel) Ramon and the boys would have no notion of anything outside. Their tropical blood congealed at forty degrees and they wouldn't have their antennae out the window on a dare.

From across the street in his unmarked Ford, Wilkins noted with satisfaction that the windows of Ramon's flat were glazed with frost, another bonus of the cold. Orange light strained to get through and looked almost festive. If he put his window down, Wilkins could feel as much as hear the beat of the stereo, just the bass notes beating a jungle rhythm.

He pushed the light button on his watch. He was due inside in ten minutes.

He thought of them: Ramon, the leader, the brains of the four. Wilkins called him Roman, at first to his face and in good humor until it became obvious that Ramon found it unfunny. Philippe, well fed and well dressed, strangely out of place in the fast lane this crew traveled, more natural in a 40s movie, sort of a Spanish Sydney Greenstreet sitting under a slowly turning fan.

It would bother Wilkins a bit to bust Ramon and Philippe. He rather liked them, had gotten to know them pretty well in the six months he had been setting them up. As it turned out, the bust could have been sooner, or he could have gotten them on bribery of a police officer, but they were trying to go higher and net more fish. There wouldn't be any more fish, though. But this would still be a pretty good bust. But probably not the headline grabber with maybe a column in *Time* he had hoped for.

It wouldn't bother him at all to bust Luis and Miguel. They were scum. The snake brothers, he had thought of them as, both for their slender, reptilian appearance and their shifty, furtive manner. If the knife in the ribs had ever come from anyone, he figured it would have been from them.

Wilkins tapped a cigarette from the pack on the seat beside him, the little subconscious voice nagging him to quit.

Everything should be in place by now. All the plain clothes dicks and the black and whites. It was funny. Wilkins always thought of the patrol cars as black and whites, TV talk, even though in Boston they were white with a blue stripe. That was probably because in the little back woods Georgia town where he was originally from the sheriff's cars were black and white.

He took out his snub-nose .38 and checked the cylinder. The entire cop world, it seemed, had long switched to nine or ten-millimeter automatics but Billy Wilkins still liked a revolver. Checking the .38 was a reflex action, something to do, more than an actual check. It was loaded and he knew it. Under his crew neck sweater and button down shirt, the bulletproof vest felt heavy and stiff. Sweat was beginning to prickle.

He took three quick drags on the cigarette and then flicked it out the car window.

It was time to go in.

Inside the third floor walk up flat one street off Huntington Avenue, Ramon Mendez moved his head in time to the beat of the stereo and watched Philippe Leon's oozing body splayed over the edges of a cheap aluminum lounge chair. The yellow and white plastic webbing was frayed and ripped in several places. Philippe's fat ass bulged down and almost touched the floor. The lounge chair belonged on a beach of nice white sand and blue tropical water which was where Ramon wished he was right now instead of freezing to death in New England. Back home, this time of year, the sun would be nice and high and the breezes toasty. But he was making a bundle. They all were. He'd put up with the cold for that.

Philippe was wearing a little smile that Ramon knew had nothing to do with the music or probably anything else in range of his senses. Philippe always seemed to be enjoying a private joke, seemed on the verge of a belly laugh. He was a thinker, Philippe was, with his nose always in some book or other.

In the next room—once a dining room when the place had been respectable—Luis and Miguel Orantes were talking softly and blowing some weed, passing the joint back and forth. They looked satisfied, like a pair of lizards sunning themselves on a rock. Well they should. The four had just received a nice shipment of assorted candy, stuff to appeal to a range of tastes, ecstasy for customers of all types, with a street value that Ramon couldn't comprehend anything had a right to command. He thought of his father working the sugar fields. All those hours, all those years. There was no way Ramon was going to be like his father. One day's work with the stuff he trafficked made more than his father made in a year. Ten years, maybe. It was enough to make you laugh. Or cry.

He, Philippe, Luis, and Miguel had put in some time down in Miami but things were crazy there. It was too rushed, too thick with competition so they decided to find someplace else. Philippe had suggested Boston because he knew some people in one of the colleges. Between their connection to a steady line of quality stuff and the student population in Boston just screaming for good times, they figured they'd found heaven.

Except for the winter, which took its time dying. Maybe he'd be around long enough to see that greenhouse effect that Philippe always talked about. Boston would be like Miami then, Philippe said, except for one little problem. It would be under water. Who could understand stuff like that? That was the problem with Philippe. Always reading about things that made no sense, just made you worry, but in Philippe's case it just made him smile that little twisty smile or laugh with his big belly shaking.

Ramon looked at his watch. Time for Wilkins to get here. A business expense was what he was. A greedy cop, willing—eager, actually—to let you do your business, to look the other way if you slipped him a little something on a regular basis. Cops like that weren't hard to find. You just had to be careful not to let them cross you.

Ramon leaned his head back on the recliner chair and concentrated on the music. He had to go to the bathroom but didn't want to get up because Philippe would probably take over the chair. First come, first served on the chair, the most comfortable piece of furniture they had. Jesus Mary, with all their money they could fill the place with recliners except they never got around to it. But tomorrow he would. He'd call a furniture place and have three big, comfortable recliner chairs delivered and throw that piece of junk Philippe was in the hell out. Better get something heavy duty for Philippe's fat ass.

Now what was Philippe doing? What'd he want? He had shifted in his lounge chair and was smiling at Ramon. He crooked a thick finger, the flesh dented with a jeweled ring. That was Philippe's style. If he had something to say, you had to go to him like he was a Spanish grandee.

What Ramon wanted to say—but didn't—was, you want to talk to me, you fat shit, you come over here. Instead, he tilted his recliner shut with his legs and went to Philippe.

He looked down at the still smiling Philippe. Ramon wanted to ask, Wha' you smiling at? You always smiling about something even when there's nothing to be smiling about? When I smile, I smile 'cause I'm happy or there's something funny going on.

Look at Luis and Miguel. They never smile except maybe when they thinking they maybe goin' put a knife in someone.

Now Phillipe, Jesus still smiling, beckoned for Ramon to bend down so that he could talk directly into his ear. Phillipe spoke in Spanish and what he said was about Billy Wilkins.

Chapter Five

Leo Santos slipped the needle into the space next to his big toe, pressed the plunger, and almost immediately slid into euphoria. He floated on pleasure-tinted clouds and thought how easily life's shit could be turned to chocolate ice cream with just a little press of the needle.

He smiled at the image and then grinned at Rui Lobao across from him who was also drifting around his own clouds.

Leo started laughing at his metaphor. It was hilarious and certainly worth sharing with Rui who everyone but his parents, old-world Portuguese, called Roy.

"This is good shit, Roy . . ." Leo had to pause because he had unintentionally added a wrinkle to the metaphor that made it almost too funny to bear: good shit turning life's shit to ice cream.

He started to explain but couldn't because he was laughing too hard. He practically had to clutch his stomach.

Rui laughed too, if not a sharer of the humor, then a sharer of bliss, momentarily bonded to Leo by a drug-induced camaraderie.

For several moments they laughed until the image's humor was squeezed out of Leo. It wasn't so funny after all. The image of shit was actually shitty, he thought.

And life's shit . . . well, it was real. You always came back to that.

They were in Roy's place, three rooms of clutter, stink, and cockroaches in East Boston, mainly an Italian enclave like the North End, but, like the North End, with more and more non Italians moving in.

Leo and Roy had done some time together at the Essex County Jail, the one in Middleton, thank God, not the old Salem Jail, which he had heard, you want to talk about life being shitty, would have made a hole like Rui's place look like Donald Trump's penthouse. Some guys he knew who had done time in Salem Jail and in Walpole State Prison said they rather go back to Walpole.

Still, that didn't mean Middleton hadn't been bad enough. He remembered his first day there. He had thought he was badass. Okay, he *was* badass. He had been a tough kid growing up and going through vocational school that no one gave any grief to. He'd gone to jail wearing a pair of fancy sneakers that cost him about a buck ten when the meanest looking freak he'd ever seen, like someone out of a prison movie, came up to him and said, "Give me your sneakers."

Just like that. "Give me your sneakers."

A bunch of other dudes, from the same movie, stood around grinning, waiting to see what Leo would do. Hoping he'd do something, maybe thinking he was the new guy in jail played by Clint Eastwood or Charles Bronson, strong as King Kong and as skilled in the martial arts as the old Jap guy in "The Karate Kid."

Leo might be badass but he wasn't stupid. He gave the guy his sneakers and a look he hoped said, don't think this means you own me, and don't any of you think this isn't where I draw the line.

It never came to any more but every time Leo saw the guy wearing his sneakers he got mightily pissed off. After a while, the mean-looking guy started to look less mean but Leo never demanded his sneakers back.

Leo wondered why he was thinking about Middleton Jail. He never had depressing thoughts when he took the stuff he took. Maybe he needed more. How long had it been? That was the thing with this junk, you kind of lost track of time.

The thing that was bothering him slipped around furtively until it finally broke through and stood in front of him.

He looked at Roy, smiling and lying back on an old sofa, stirring a little to Bryan Adams playing on the stereo. Obviously, he was still in the clouds.

A groan ripped from Leo and his lip curled in an Elvis-like snarl.

"What?" Roy said, after a moment's pause, the time it took for the groan to cut through the clouds.

"You remember the guy who took my sneakers back at Middleton? What the hell was his name?"

"I remember him. Connors. Phil Connors. They called him Gorilla. Jesus, you're not still thinking about him, are you?"

Leo lay back in his chair, a big stuffed thing he figured Roy got at Wal-Mart. He stared at the wall.

"Huh?" Roy said after a moment. "You still letting that bother you?"

Leo muttered something.

"That was a long—"

"Not Connors. William Scarlata. Will friggin' Scarlet."

"Who?"

"William Scarlata. Jesus, don't tell me you don't know who William Scarlata is."

"I know who he is," Roy said, a little miffed that Leo would think him so ill informed. "They call him Will Scarlet. Why do they call him that?"

Leo really didn't know the allusion except that it had something to do with Robin Hood. He couldn't figure it. Robin Hood and his men were supposed to have been good guys, at least sort of.

"I gotta watch out for William Scarlata because of a screw up that wasn't even my fault."

That got Roy's attention. Someone like William Scarlata was much more interesting than Gorilla Connors an animal who'd rip your ears off. He'd heard that William could get you to rip your own off trying to convince him that you were really all right.

Roy lay back and waited for Leo to tell him more. You prodded Leo and he'd probably just shut his mouth. Besides, Roy wasn't finding it too easy to talk. He felt good but kind of cottony still.

He watched Leo who was curling his lip like some kind of animal and muttering under his breath. Roy thought that was funny and almost started to laugh when Leo said, "Why'd he shoot at women? The guy's got a habit he's gotta feed. Thing is, though, you gotta be cool."

Although what Leo was saying wasn't making much sense, it was interesting and Roy waited, pretty sure Leo would answer his own question and also tell him who shot at women and had a dependency problem as if Leo didn't.

Leo muttered some more and then just sat and brooded.

Finally, Roy asked, "Who you talking about?"

"Chug. I'm talking about Chug, okay?"

"Who's he?"

"You don't know him."

"I know I don't know him," Roy said. "That's why I asked who he was."

Caution nudged Leo and then whispered in his ear, Keep your mouth shut.

Roy drifted on his chemical currents for a few moments, assimilating what Leo had been saying. Eventually, the comments synchromeshed with what he had heard and read lately.

He sat upright. "Jesus Christ, you know who shot William Scarlata's old lady? This Chug dude, huh?"

The caution that had been loitering around Leo was now replaced by fear that jumped on his gut. He looked at Roy and then looked away.

He thought of Chug whose fault all of this was and then thought, No way I take a fall for him.

Chapter Six

Sylvia Scarlata unhooked the back of her dress and stepped out of it with that little subconscious gratefulness she always felt when dressing or undressing didn't necessitate messing her hair. She sat on the edge of the bed and finished undressing. She reached under her pillow, pulled out her nightgown and slipped it on.

Then she went to her dressing table where she applied various cleansers to her face as she eyed her husband in the mirror. They had just returned from a suburban restaurant (one of several at which William Scarlata either held a large interest or owned outright) before which they had visited his mother at the hospital. She wished that on *the* day she had gone to one of those restaurants rather than indulging in the sentimental journey the place of the shooting represented.

"It could have been me too, you know," she said, picking up on one of several themes of conversation they had been having for most of the evening and, for that matter, since Florence Scarlata had been shot.

"I mean, it's bad enough your mother got shot but the sonovabitch could have got me." Sylvia wiped the blue from an eyelid. "Or any of us."

That hadn't come out quite the way she wanted it to. This was touchy ground and she knew it. She couldn't make it sound as though she was glad her mother-in-law had been shot rather than herself but her fright and anger, undiminished since the shooting, made her talk more forcefully to her husband than she normally would. And because he had done little or nothing to discourage her, she continued registering her feelings, which she knew were fanning his own.

She eyed her husband in the mirror. He had removed his suit, tie, and shirt and, in his underwear, was hanging them in his closet. He was a good-looking man—better looking than a lot of Hollywood stars, Sylvia thought—dark hair, a full head of it, just starting to silver. He had the lean body of a conditioned athlete which he worked hard to maintain at a gym. Sylvia thought he looked like one of those Latin tennis players, wiry and muscular, that you see in movies or read about who are always having affairs with rich, beautiful women they're giving tennis lessons to.

She still loved him and loved the power he yielded and the deference yielded to him and, because of him, to her. She knew full well who he was and what he did, although some of the logistics of his business she could only guess at.

"I don't like the morphine," he said. "I'm glad they're taking her off it. She says the pain's better."

He went into the bathroom off the bedroom and Sylvia heard the electric toothbrush. He brushed his teeth the way he did everything, thoroughly and unrushed.

He came from the bathroom and lay on the bed after folding down the covers. Outside, a cold rain, on the verge of sleet, sizzled on the window.

When Sylvia finished her ablutions, she stood and faced her husband. She was still a beautiful woman and she still possessed a schoolgirl's body, as taut and trim as her husband's. He eyed her but without lust. She knew he was thinking of his mother, that her being shot had outraged him, preoccupied him.

She lay on the bed beside him and made a show of reading a book she was mildly interested in, a biography of a movie star. William Scarlata lay quietly for a short time, staring at the ceiling before turning onto his side and pulling the covers over him.

Sylvia gave the book a few more minutes before shutting out the light beside the bed. His breathing told her that her husband was not yet asleep.

"You know what I was thinking about?" she said. "I was thinking about the time on Revere Beach, years ago, we had just met, when that guy mouthed off at me. I was in the car and you were buying some subs or something and him and his buddies went by and he said something real raunchy, I can even remember what. You remember that?"

William Scarlata remembered. He had just started working for Milano Corso who used to control Boston, odd stuff, a little of this, a little of that, a little muscle. Milano saw in him a gutsy, strong kid with a cool head who did what he was told.

When he came back to the car, though, and Sylvia told him what the guy had said to her, he lost his cool head.

For a moment they lay quietly, remembering, listening to the rain.

"I thought you were going to kill him," she said.

She rolled onto her side, toward him, her hand touching his shoulder.

When he had come back to the car with the two submarines and a couple of Cokes, the guy, early twenties, and his buddies were maybe a hundred feet up the sidewalk.

William Scarlata had left the food with Sylvia, ran after the goons, spun the foulmouth around, removed a couple of his teeth, bent his nose, vibrated his ears, and, for good measure, planted a knee in his groin.

Foulmouth's friends, recognizing someone out of control but in control, wisely scattered.

Sylvia savored the recollection. Since that long ago incident, she always felt her husband could and would protect her from insults and harm. And, over the years, his power had only grown.

But now this. This brush with a bullet. Like something you saw in a movie. The shot, the splotch of blood. Sylvia replayed the scene many times in her mind and could easily imagine the bullet ripping into her, paining her, *disfiguring* her.

She squeezed his shoulder. "Bill, if you ever find this guy who shot your mother, I hope you do to him ten times what you did to that guy at Revere Beach."

"Not *if,* Syl. *When.* It's just a matter of time. And I got something in mind that . . ." William Scarlata let his voice trail.

He thought of the guy back at Revere Beach and many others over the years he'd treated far worse. But for whoever shot his mother, what he had in mind would make any punishment he had ever inflicted on anyone seem very kind.

Chug and Ellie Robinson were eating pizza and drinking beer at her kitchen table, not too many miles as the crow flies from where William and Sylvia Scarlata were bedding down.

A radio on the counter was playing Country and Western, Ellie's favorite kind of music. A pretty zippy number was on, maybe a banjo or mandolin churning out notes at a good clip.

Chug bobbed his head in time and then looked at Ellie and winked. He picked up his glass of beer, tilted his head and with a flick of his wrist the glass was empty.

Ellie smiled and gave a little laugh as she always did when he chugged a beer like that. "You jerk."

Chug went to the fridge and came back to the table with a couple more beers.

"Hey," Ellie said, "I'm still working on number one here. I savor my beer."

"Who said one's for you? What's that mean, *savor*?"

"Well, you wouldn't know, would you? At least with beer."

She watched him pour his beer into the glass. Good-looking lug. A lot of hair if a little unkempt. "Takes you longer to do that than to pour it down your throat. And you can pour it down your throat as fast as I could spill this glass onto the floor."

"Quite a talent, huh? Think I should try to get logged into the Guinness Book of World Records?"

"I do. I think you should. I'll be your agent. I'll take you on tour."

He regarded her evenly and thought how she was the best thing he had going and hoped he hadn't screwed it up.

She bit into her pizza, daintily actually, and sipped her beer. He liked the way her hair was cut, short and elfish. Her lips were pouty and full, her face was pretty, her body was thin except where it counted. She was twenty-eight, two years younger than he was.

"So what's on your mind?" she said.

"What do you mean?"

"Whenever you chug a beer like that, it means you got something you want to tell me. To unload. And, the flowers. I mean, I know you work for a florist but I don't get flowers all that often."

Chug had brought a nice arrangement that Maddie Cramer had made for him. It sat in the middle of Ellie's table.

The Country and Western number finished and the rain pelting the window replaced its sound. The view outside that window, if it had been daytime and over 230 years earlier would have revealed a scene of carnage where colonial militia and British troops slaughtered one another at battles on Breed's Hill and Bunker Hill.

Today, a 221-foot granite monument marked the site and the pride of many locals in the area was still in, among other things, a code of silence about its members who walked unlawful paths. Others said that the code was a thing of the past.

"I'll have to keep that in mind. I don't want to be too readable," Chug said even as he resisted the urge to chug another beer.

"So how's work?" he said.

"How's work? It's wonderful. It's a job, Chug. I mean how exciting can working for a dentist be? That's why I'm studying real estate. Even though the market is what it is."

She looked at him, tilted her head and smiled.

"Come on. What's up? I know you. You've got something cooking."

He looked at her smile. It was gorgeous. A great advertisement for the dentist she worked for although he had nothing to do with it. And now Chug knew he was about to erase it.

"Hey, that rain's really coming down, huh?"

"Yeah, it is. That's what's been bothering you, I can tell. The rain. Come on, Chug, spill it."

He nodded and then he had to force the words out and wondered whether he should.

"El, I gotta tell you, I stepped in something and I'm in real deep.

"Uh, oh," she said, tone light, hoping it wasn't really serious.

"Been reading the papers, watching the news?"

She shrugged a, Yeah, of course.

He chugged another beer.

"Hey, hey, slow down. What's going on here? You're making me nervous."

"You've heard, I assume, of William Scarlata? Will Scarlet."

She looked at him evenly a moment and then said, "Oh, Jesus, Chug, don't tell me . . ."

"It was an accident."

She put her hands to her ears and stomped a little tap dance on the floor. "Stop it, stop it. Just stop it."

She looked at him. "I don't know you. I don't know who you are. I mean, what the hell were you even doing there? From what I read, this was a two-bit robbery. Where do we even go from that?"

Her voice was high and quavering, on the edge of breaking.

She swept her pizza and beer glass onto the floor and then looked at him, just staring, eyes filling, then blinking back the flood that was ready to burst.

"You're still feeding your nose, aren't you? That's why you did this. I thought you were through with that crap. But, oh no, you need some quick dough to feed your habit so you get involved in a cheap heist. That's bad enough but you top it off by shooting an old woman who just happens to be a Mafia don's mother. Sweet Jesus."

"What can I say?"

"What can you say? That's it? What can you say?"

Chug picked up her pizza and dropped it into the sink. He picked up her beer glass and mopped up the beer with paper towels.

He sat down and looked at her. "It wasn't just for . . for what you said. Times are tough. I mean I don't earn a hell of a lot delivering flowers. I gotta pay the rent."

"Oh, come on, will you. Times are tough. Give me a break. How many times have we talked about you moving in with me and giving up your place? Now I know why you don't want to. You want to be able to do your little drug thing without me around to tell you cut it out."

"Okay, okay. I don't justify it. Question is, what do I do? I gotta tell you, El, the worst thing about all this is how I feel about that woman. And I'm not yanking your chain when I say that."

She kept nodding her head in little rapid shakes. "Yeah, that's noble, it really is, but it's also gotta be on your mind that you've got both the cops and, I imagine, Will Scarlet looking for you. You probably better hope the cops find you before he does."

They sat through a long pause. A mournful vocal was playing now. Ellie patted her eyes with a napkin.

"I'm sorry," she said. "I'm sorry I said that."

He smiled. "No, you're right. Hell of a choice, huh? Some hard time or a cement jacket."

She stared at him a moment and then said, "I thought that you were through with that kind of thing. Ohmigod, Chug, you promised me you were on the straight and narrow. But, oh no, you step it up a notch. Armed robbery. At least I assume this is the first time you've ever done this."

"It is. And it'll be the last"

"How did you ever get involved in something like this? At least I hope it wasn't your idea."

"It wasn't. It wasn't my idea but I've got no one to blame but myself."

"So what the hell *are* you gonna do?"

"Not sure. Gotta talk with the guys who were with me."

"Who are they?"

"Probably better that you don't know."

She got up, went to the sink and looked at her mangled piece of pizza. She shoved it into the disposal and washed it down.

"You ruined my night. You know that, don't you?"

She dabbed at her eyes.

He got up and came to the sink.

"I said the worst thing about this is how I feel about shooting that woman. Maybe that's not quite right. The worst thing is that I'm worried sick about how it'll affect you. I mean how you'll feel about me."

She looked at him.

"What are you looking for? Forgiveness from me? You want me to say, 'Hey, Chug, I know you're sorry so it's okay.'?"

"No. I don't expect that."

"What do you expect?"

She started to walk away from him but he held her arm. She looked at his hand but didn't try to pull away.

He pulled her close and they hugged a long time, listening to the rain and another mournful Country and Western song.

Chug felt that his life had become an out of control spiral, with the police closing in on one side, Will Scarlet on the other, and with Ellie slipping away.

Chapter Seven

C. Trevor Whitehead—the C was for Chauncey—stared at the young dead man stretched in front of him. Revulsion and fascination tugged this way and that. A small, dark hole in the man's forehead surprised him with its neatness but all too easily he was able to imagine what the back of the head looked like.

"That him?" the man with Whitehead asked, a detective with the Boston Police Department.

"I believe so." Whitehead's voice quavered.

"You *believe* so."

Whitehead stared searchingly. Death had a way of altering appearance, especially sudden, violent death. Besides, he had seen the dead man only in poor light when he was alive.

"It's him. Paul somebody-or-other. I'm not sure of his last name."

The detective nodded to the morgue attendant who slid Paul somebody-or-other back into his chill. He directed Whitehead with a touch to his elbow.

As they walked, Whitehead sniveled a little and dabbed at his eyes with a none too clean handkerchief that looked as though it had probably begun its career from a rather expensive box.

"S'matter, Mink? This guy mean something to you?"

Everyone called C. Trevor Whitehead 'Mink,' most—except for the police—because they didn't know his real name.

The origins of the name 'Mink' were unknown, except maybe to Whitehead himself who, when questioned about it, would only shrug. The cops, though, had a couple of theories: A reference to his expensive but somewhat feminine tastes. Or an allusion to his slinky manner. Perhaps both.

Like the handkerchief that he was stuffing back into his pocket, C. Trevor Whitehead had begun life auspiciously enough, although not quite as auspiciously as the 'C. Trevor' would indicate. His mother had had a theory that if you gave someone an elegant name you increased that person's chances of an elegant and prosperous life. She had in mind that maybe her son would one day be Secretary of State or Chief Justice of the Supreme Court. Or at least a CEO someplace.

He never lived up to those expectations and the only thing he learned for certain at the expensive mostly-boys prep school his parents sacrificed to send him to was that he liked boys.

In a way, he did profit from his training as a business major at college in Boston. But the business he started for himself had to disappoint his parents. Being entrepreneurial but essentially lazy and hedonistic, he combined business and pleasure by peddling himself in territory near the Boston Common. Certainly not the road to riches but it kept the wolf from the door so to speak. AIDS, of course, was a worry but he was as careful as he could be.

One thing led to another and he kept his ears open and learned to trade nuggets of information to the police in exchange for favorable treatment when he was scooped in various nets by the Common, the South End, or near the Fens.

Mink was used to seamy things but, although big-city violence was all around him, his experience of it was mainly in the abstract. Seeing Paul somebody-or-other lying cold and pale with his forehead drilled was more than unsettling.

It also made him wonder how it affected his relationship with the police. He had told the police about a fairly big drug deal that was supposed to go down this very evening and had provided the location in the South End.

Paul was to have been the recipient of a distributable amount of quality cocaine according to what Mink had been able to piece together from pieces of conversation, some of it admittedly disjointed, that he'd heard at a bash of drugs and gay love in a lovely old brick condo in the South End.

The voices had been low and he looked asleep or out of it so he wasn't supposed to hear. He heard but wasn't able to tell who the speakers were.

Now poor Paul wouldn't be the recipient of anything but a few hollow prayers and an early grave. And the cops now had the murder investigation of another lowlife on their hands to add to the list of investigations that went nowhere and didn't distress too many that they did. Except it would have been easier and made better PR to make a nice clean drug bust.

It wasn't Mink's fault that Paul had his brains scattered maybe because of the drug deal or maybe by a jealous lover. But the cops counted on him for hard, reliable information and it wouldn't take too many glitches for his stock to sink.

Mink and the cop whose name was Donovan now stood ready to leave the morgue.

"Hey, Donovan, I didn't know this would happen. I mean the drug bust getting screwed up. But maybe it's more . . ." Whitehead groped for a word. "Maybe it's more useful to get a tip on a murder."

It seemed obvious to Whitehead that a murder was more heinous than the passage of drugs and that the police, whose job was to fight evil, would therefore be grateful to him for providing the clue that a murder victim was about to be involved in a drug transaction. Maybe there was no glitch. Maybe his stock would actually rise.

Donovan was lighting a cigarette. "Mink, no offense, but another fag gets dusted who gives a shit? It's like with the blacks. I mean officially we check it when they blow each other's brains out but you think anyone really cares? Happens too often for one thing."

Whitehead was thinking that if he had a wire on he'd own this guy after what he just said.

"Geez, Donovan, how about at least a little political correctness. I mean we've got a black president and--have you heard?—that gay marriage is now legal in more than just Massachusetts."

Donovan looked at C. Trevor Whitehead the way someone might look at a toilet plunger or rat poison. It did useful work but was essentially disgusting. You didn't want to touch it.

It wasn't that he was bad looking. He had refined, sensitive features and a slender, almost athletic body. He was dressed in expensive designer clothes, tight jeans that showed off his nice little can. Donovan could understand why other gays would find him appealing.

But, of course, there was a dissipation that coarsened the vitality of his youth. Donovan guessed that Mink was twenty-three or twenty-four but looked almost ten years older.

"Look, Mink, my man," Donovan said, "you hear anything about who might have plugged old Paulie there, we're interested."

You might not like the gays, Donovan was thinking, but you couldn't ignore them. Mink was right, they had a lot of political clout so you couldn't give the impression you didn't care when one of them bought the farm. And there was no point in antagonizing Mink.

What made him so useful was that he was familiar with and accepted in a number of circles besides the gay community. He seemed to be regarded as a likeable character in a number of the neighborhoods.

Donovan knew that Mink heard things from many sources, ranging from college students he still mingled with on occasion to the characters involved in legal and illegal gambling. Mink was a hopeless gambler.

"Donovan, what I like about you is you're all heart, man, know what I'm saying?"

The 'fag' remarks were stinging a bit even though Mink was used to them. Maybe because the term was used less and less.

"I can tell you're practically crying about Paul."

What the hell was his last name? French, Mink thought. LeBlanc, LeBelle, something like that. Poor little frog. He pictured the neat hole in the forehead again and felt his stomach do a somersault.

Donovan looked at him and blew a stream of smoke practically up Mink's nose

Mink smiled and said, "Hey, one of your guys got burnt the other night. Over near Huntington Avenue."

"Oh yeah? When did you hear that?"

"I don't know. A couple of days ago. Your guy was standing there with his thumb inserted and all the troops outside ready to come in like Delta Force. One of them got wind of your guy—Wilkins I hear his name was—and cleaned out all the goodies except for a couple of joints."

Donovan put a hand on Mink's shoulder and squeezed hard.

"I ought to . . .Did you hear about it before or after the fact?"

"Donovan, give me break, huh. Strictly after. If I knew about that before it goes down, don't you think I tell you? I know which side my bread is buttered on."

"How'd you hear about it?"

"Something like that the word gets out."

Donovan dropped his cigarette and stepped on it carefully, working it with the toe of his shoe.

"Listen to me, C. Trevor Whitehead, let me think for one minute that you're holding out on me on something like this and we got enough to send you where your cute little bum'll get more blasting than an artillery range."

Mink wiggled his rear and said tauntingly, "Is that a threat or a promise?"

"Listen, make sure you remember exactly what our arrangement is. I let you do your thing, you know what I'm talking about, only if you feed me what I can use. That's all you got going."

Donovan had grabbed and twisted Mink's jacket. Abruptly, he let it go and turned and walked away.

"Oh, I love it when you get angry," Mink called after him in his best fruity falsetto. "It's so manly."

He kicked the cigarette butt Donovan had dropped. Donovan, you bitch, he thought.

Then he thought, Paul you stupid frog, what'd you have to go and get shot for?

Chapter Eight

"I got a friend thinks he knows who plugged Will Scarlet's old lady," Tilly Tillotson said.

C. Trevor Whitehead looked up from the *Globe* on his lap. He'd been reading about the Celtics loss to the Knicks. He wasn't particularly interested in the Celtics except as a vehicle for betting but it was important to know their ins and outs to make betting more predictable.

Certainly, most of them weren't physically attractive unless you felt like cozying up to a giraffe.

C. Trevor gave Tilly an interested expression. The shooting of William Scarlata's mother had assumed dimension. It was talked about. And it was especially fascinating to conjecture the fate of the perp when Will Scarlet got his hands on him.

C. Trevor sipped his coffee and took another nibble from his blueberry muffin. The thing was, though, that nearly everybody knew someone who knew someone who knew who shot Florence Scarlata.

C. Trevor and Tilly were sitting in a Dunkin Donuts looking out at Boston Common scrubbed by late morning sunshine, the bare trees and the bundled passers-by tossed by a cold March wind. March had definitely come in like a lion, C. Trevor thought.

"Word's out Will Scarlet'll pay to get this guy," Tilly said.

"How much?"

"Don't know. Heard different figures. Fifty large, maybe."

They were talking low in the guarded tones appropriate to any discussion of William Scarlata or his associates even though they sat by themselves near the window. A couple of scruffy refugees from the wind huddled at the counter, bent over steaming coffee mugs like the devoted at prayer. Their rum-berried noses inhaled the steam as though it were incense.

C. Trevor ran his finger around the edge of his coffee mug absently and thought of fifty grand and what good use he could put it to. With any kind of luck he could parlay that into a pretty good stake.

He looked at Tilly who, from his dreamy expression, also seemed to be thinking of fifty big ones. Goddamn Tilly would go through fifty K in about two snaps of the fingers, C. Trevor was thinking, sucking it up his nose. Well, fifty K might take more than two snaps.

His real name was Howard, Howard Tillotson, but everybody called him Tilly. Sometimes C. Trevor called him Johnny, after the fifties singer, Johnny Tillotson, that practically no one remembered. C. Trevor was a bit of a trivia buff and was especially strong on fifties music even though it was long before his time.

Tilly, a tall, skinny guy with an equally anemic mustache frequently breakfasted with Mink Whitehead, the two having met a few years ago at the now defunct Wonderland dog track in Revere. They still occasionally took the T together to Suffolk Downs. Tilly was not at all bothered by Mink's sexual preferences even though they were not his own.

"Your friend tell you the guy's name?" Mink asked.

"Yeah, he told me," Tilly said with a look that said, But that's as far as it goes.

"Your friend bullshitting you?"

Tilly smiled and shook his head. "No way."

"How's he know?"

"Says he got it from a good source. Says the guy was in on the heist just trying to pick up a few bucks to feed a habit."

"Sounds shaky."

"You wouldn't say that if you knew my friend."

"He gonna turn the name over to Will Scarlet?" Mink asked with a slight smile, thinking that he was probably listening to a load of horseshit. Hundred to one at least there was anything to this. Still, Tilly had come up with stuff in the past, some of it pretty good. That dropped the odds but by how much?

"He says he wouldn't do that."

Mink watched a guy chase a baseball hat snapped from his head as though it had been spring loaded. It blew onto Tremont Street and the guy had to stop at the curb and watch his hat get pounded by traffic.

"Not for fifty thousand?"

"Mink, that's the way this guy is."

C. Trevor Whitehead finished his muffin and thought about getting another. It'd be something if old Tilly really had the name of the guy who shot Will Scarlet's mum. Hey, sometimes the improbable happened. Hell, it happened all the time.. You'd read about it. Something like some old lady would win the lottery by having her pet dog or cat pick out the winning numbers with its paw. Or somebody would be digging in their yard to plant tomatoes and uncover a letter written by George Washington. All the time people stepped in shit only to have it turn to gold. Trouble was, it was always someone else, someone you read or heard about.

The guy whose hat blew off dashed onto Tremont Street at a slight traffic lull and retrieved the cap which hadn't been hit by any car after all. All those cars and not one had hit it. What were the odds there?

"So what say you tell me the name?" Mink asked. No sense beating around the bush.

"C'mon, Mink, huh."

"I'm serious."

"Hey, what do I look like, some fink who'd turn a guy into a fate worse than death?"

"Thanks a lot. You think I'll go running to Will Scarlet?"

"Then what do you want the name for?"

"Tilly, I'm just curious, is all."

Tilly leaned back and folded his arms across his chest. He looked at Mink, then out the window, then back at Mink. "Mink, you know better."

"What the hell you tell me you know the guy's name for?"

"I shoulda kept my mouth shut. I was just talkin'."

A gust of wing shook the window and raised a little cyclone of debris and swirling road sand that glistened prettily in the sun.

"The poor bastard must be scared out of his mind," Mink said.

"Wouldn't you be? I mean we're talking more than just getting your knees busted.

Mink tried to imagine what Will Scarlet would do to the person who shot his mother. He thought of some awful things and then thought they'd probably be just for starters.

"You want another coffee or donut?" he asked Tilly. Tilly had finished some kind of donut that to Mink looked like giant crinkled French fry.

"You gonna get any more?"

"Yeah. You want any?"

"Get me another coffee."

"You want another one of those things? What do you call those, anyway?"

"A French cruller." Tilly reached for his wallet.

Mink raised his hand. "I got it. Have a big time on me."

Mink ordered two more coffees, a blueberry muffin, and a French cruller. The two bums at the counter smelled. He thought if he ever hit the skids he'd make sure at least he took a shower and changed his underwear every day.

"So you gonna tell me that guy's name or what?" he said when he sat back down with Tilly.

"You buy me a cuppa coffee and a cruller and I gotta tell you that guy's name?"

Mink blew the steam off his coffee. Dunkin Donuts insisted on giving you coffee hot enough to remove wallpaper. He was thinking he'd really like the name. Of course, first you'd have to make sure it was bonafide. He was also thinking of long term as opposed to short-term advantage. Fifty K, these days, while nothing to sneeze at, wouldn't make you one of the rich and famous. It would buy a pretty nice set of wheels but that was about it.

No, it might make more sense to parlay the name into something more enduring. You had to think of the long haul. Of course, first he had to get the name off Tilly who could, at times, be one stubborn bastard. Right now looked like one of those times.

But Tilly had an Achilles heel. Actually, a lot of them when you thought about it, but one especially. An Achilles nose, I suppose you could say, Mink thought. Too bad, because Tilly was no dummy. He had actually graduated from U Lowell with an engineering degree but had long since cooked his brains.

He blew some more steam and tried a sip of coffee. Still too hot. Mink thought if he drank this down fast he wouldn't have to have his teeth cleaned. Melt the tartar.

"Till," he said, "you know what I'm thinking. I'm thinking I might be able to help this guy out."

"I'm serious," he added quickly when he noticed Tilly's expression. "I got an idea."

"I can't wait to hear it."

"I don't have everything worked out but it could be worth both our whiles."

"Yeah? How?"

"Not here. Let me work it out and I'll talk to you later."

Mink took a tentative sip. "But I'll need that name."

Tilly was still giving him the stone face.

"Tilly, you know my word, right? I say something and you can take it to the bank."

Honesty was more a pragmatic than ethical thing with C. Trevor Whitehead. He lived by dealing information and it had to be accurate.

Tilly gave him a grudging nod.

"I swear to God you give me that name and I don't give it to Will Scarlet or anyone associated with him. Don't even give me the name until I do a little checking and I tell you what I got in mind. Then, if you're not satisfied, that's the end of it and no hard feelings."

"What's in it for me?"

This was typical Tilly. If he actually had the name, he could cash it in but Mink knew he'd never turn someone in to a horrible fate, not even someone he didn't know.

"I give you some yummies. Good stuff. A lot."

Tilly took a deep draw of coffee and tried to look cagey but Mink knew he had him. He didn't seem at all bothered by the scalding coffee. Leather lips and false teeth, probably.

Tilly finished the coffee and stood with the half-eaten cruller in his hand. "Come on, let's take a walk where we can talk."

"Sit down. Cool it. Give me a couple of days."

Mink blew some more steam, took a couple of sips, and to himself hummed "Send Me the Pillow that You Dream On" which had been one of Johnny Tillotson's biggest hits.

Chapter Nine

The two patrol cops bent over the twisted figure sprawled on its side in the alley next to the Richdale milk store in East Boston. Because the body was still warm, they had put in a call for an ambulance as well as for detectives even though they had no doubt this guy was now standing in front of St. Peter. Looked as if his neck was broken and in general as if he probably had a few internal injuries as well.

"Probably put up a pretty good fight," one of the cops said. "I mean, he's a tough-looking sucker. Or was."

They had responded to a call from a woman who was coming out of the Richdale when a man ran into the alley being chased by two others. Practically knocked loose the bag containing a half gallon of 2% milk, a quart of diet Coke, two packs of Merits, some cheese crackers, and five scratch lottery tickets which she'd scratch while eating the crackers, drinking some Coke, smoking some Merits and watching an NYPD Blue re-run. She loved cop shows and loved NYPD Blue especially if Jimmy Smits was on. He was her favorite TV cop. A hunk.

"Didn't take his wallet," one of the cops said. He knelt down and pulled the wallet half sticking out a back pocket.

He leafed through it. The other cop crouched and held his torch on the wallet. A twenty, a five, and three ones. No driver's license and no credit cards but surprisingly, the ID card that came with the wallet had been filled out.

"Whadda you got?" the cop holding the light said.

"A name anyway. This guy filled out the little card that comes with the wallet. You know, like you do when you're about nine years old. That's about it, though. No license or credit cards."

"You think he was a retard?"

The cop holding the wallet shrugged.

"What's his name?"

The cop looked again. "A Portugee. Leo Santos."

Lou Russo was mourning his hair. He had been brushing his teeth and shaving and for some reason when he looked into the mirror and caught sight of the shiny expanse on top of his head depression over the loss of his former luxuriant black curls overwhelmed him.

Christ, it had been years. He started balding in his early twenties and the process had been fairly rapid. You'd think you'd get past it, he told himself. Well, you *did* get past it. But not entirely and every once in a while the feeling got kind of fierce. He remembered how Tina Santisi loved to run her fingers through his hair and tell him he looked like a rock star. Jesus, he hadn't seen Tina in, what, thirty years?

Those morons Mickey the Harp Ianucci and Sal the Dogcatcher Manfredi had bollixed up royally. He knew that's what had really set him off. Funny how he could be grieving his long gone hair when he had to deal with the fact that those *incompetents,* sent out to get information, ended up killing the source of that information.

One thing was for sure, he wasn't going to tell William Scarlata what had happened. This was only a temporary setback. Still, it would have been nice to hand Will the name of the idiot who shot his mother.

He wondered what Will would do to him. The usual—a bullet in the head, garroting with piano wire—would be too good. Too quick. Will had used a wood chipper once, *Fargo* style. Hired it from a rental company and hosed it clean afterward. Once, he even used a crematory oven. Arranged it through Bernardo Tranfaglia the funeral director. He remembered they had wanted some information as well as retribution. They had tied the poor bastard up and started to feed him into the oven feet first when he stunk the place up and spilled the beans simultaneously. When they had gotten what they wanted, they pushed him in the rest of the way anyway. But not too quickly. Even for Lou, that had been a bit much and he winced at the recollection.

He looked at himself in the mirror again and thought once more of Tina Santisi running her fingers through his hair.

Chug had been experimenting with muriatic acid when Frankie Ricciardi called him on his cell. He had doused the edge of a dollar bill in the acid and waited for the ink to disappear and leave him with perfect paper. The acid sat on the bill for several minutes and nothing happened except that the paper got a bit limp.

Then Frankie called and told him about Leo and they arranged to meet at a sports bar near Fenway Park which was where they were now but in a booth not at the bar.

"Question is," Frankie said, "how'd they know Leo was with us? And if they got Leo, how long do we have."

Frankie looked around as if expecting someone to walk up to the booth and riddle them.

"I think maybe you're getting ahead of yourself. We don't know who got Leo. When you say 'they' you mean Will Scarlet, right?"

"Duh. Yeah. Who else?"

"Well, why'd they kill him and leave him in an alley? Doesn't seem like the way they'd do things."

"There was a witness. They couldn't hang around. You read the papers? It was in this morning's *Herald*."

Chug hadn't read about it.

"Look," Frankie said, "I think we gotta assume it was Will Scarlet's boys got to Leo and probably got our names. So where do we go from here?"

"Where do *I* go, Frankie? I'm the one who pulled the trigger, remember? You're off the hook, far as I can see. You're golden."

"I don't feel too cool hanging around waiting to see how Will Scarlet reads this. Besides, we're buds. We go back."

The waiter came back to their booth with a couple of draft beers. "You guys ready to order?"

"Yeah, the turkey club with fries," Chug said. He was starved.

"Same," Frankie said, then when the waiter left, "All right, I'll ask again. We're do we go from here?"

Chug took a sip of his beer.

"I'll tell you, Frank, I'm not too thrilled with the idea of running away with my tail between my legs."

"Will you talk sense. We've got the cops *and* Will Scarlet after us. Whadda ya wanna do, sit around and see who comes calling first? By the way, you get rid of that piece?"

"No. I'm gonna hang onto it for a while."

"You ever hear of such a thing as ballistics?"

"Right now I guess I'm more concerned with Will Scarlet. I figure maybe I'll need it seeing I'm not exactly into the martial arts."

"Florida looks pretty good right about now," Frankie said. "Escape the cold and Will Scarlet. I say we hit the road first thing tomorrow. Tonight even."

Chug shook his head. "You go ahead if you want. I need a couple of days at least."

"A couple days? Chug, we're in a situation, you know what I'm saying?"

"Yeah, we are definitely in a situation. At least I am. But I'm not pulling up stakes and leaving here forever. I mean there's Ellie. There's my father. I'll go for a little while to let things cool."

"Chug, no offense, but are you on something right now? Don't sound to me like you're thinking straight."

"That's the way it's gonna be. You can do what you want. Something else, I don't think Florida's a good idea. Will Scarlet'll be looking in Florida, anywhere where it's warm. That's the first place people run to and it's where he's got connections. I say go north. Canada. Maybe just New Hampshire or Maine. He wouldn't expect that. And I don't think he's too connected in the White Mountains."

"Canada might be okay," Frankie said. "We'll freeze but there's good hockey."

The waiter put their turkey clubs on the table. "Can I get you guys anything else?"

Chug moved his beer mug. "Two more."

"We'll take my car," Frankie said.

"That's fine. I was thinking of maybe dropping my car off at the Logan Express on the North Shore. It's on the way if we go north by Route One to Ninety-five. That way, if they find it, it looks like I hopped a plane to somewhere. Like Florida."

Chug finished his beer.

"Or maybe I just leave it at my place. That way it looks like I've gone nowhere. I gotta think about it."

"Logan Express will cost you. Eleven bucks a day, I think it is," Frankie said.

"Yeah, well, like I say, Frank, far as I'm concerned, this is just to get away for a little while and get a chance to think things out without looking over my shoulder every two seconds. Paying Logan Express eleven a day for a couple of weeks is the least of my worries."

"Chuggie, I go north, I'm not coming back here any too quick so don't count on me to get you back."

Chug squirted a long stream of ketchup over his fries, handed the bottle to Frankie, and attacked his sandwich for a few seconds.

"Chug, you know something, I'll be up front here. I don't know about you but I'm really scared. I mean really scared. This is Will Scarlet we're dealing with here. To be honest, I don't think you get it."

He looked searchingly at Chug to see if he *was* getting it.

"You ever watch 'The Sopranos' or any of those Mafia movies? They may be movies but I think that's the way it is. Will Scarlet gets a hold of us and . . . Jesus, I don't want to even think about it."

"Yeah, Frankie, I think I get it all right. I made a mess for myself, there's no doubt about it. I'm gonna be careful but, well, you know . . ."

The waiter put their two beers on the table.

Chug picked up his and grinned at Frankie.

"Want a race?"

"Do I want a race? No, I don't want a race. I want to get my ass out of here. It's all well and good to say you don't want to run away with your tail between your legs, but you gotta use some common sense. These guys play for real."

Chug looked at Frankie and felt tired.

"Oh, I know that, Frankie. I really do."

He thought of his father and Ellie and Florence Scarlata, tilted his glass toward his lips and in less than two seconds set it down empty on the table.

Chapter Ten

Lieutenant Billy Wilkins regarded C. Trevor Whitehead evenly, his distaste masked, he felt, rather skillfully. He didn't much care for informants.

Ryan Donovan who had set up the meeting had told him Whitehead—"Call him Mink"—would not say what he had in mind but that he knew about the thwarted bust near Huntington Avenue and had "a deal" but would only talk with the cop involved in that aborted raid.

Wilkins opened a fresh pack of Marlboros, offered one to Mink, who took it, and extracted one for himself. Not supposed to smoke in the station but no one ever said anything. He snapped his lighter, held it across his desk for Mink, and then sucked the flame into his own cigarette. Lesson One: Establish rapport.

"Ryan Donovan says you wanted to see me. Says you're pretty reliable."

"No kidding? Donovan said I was reliable?"

"He did. 'Very reliable' is what he actually said."

"Honest to God?"

"No. He said you weren't reliable at all," Billy Wilkins said, the sarcasm slipping from his mouth against his better judgment. "That's why I'm sitting here listening to what you've got to say. Says you knew about a soured bust. How'd you hear about that, you mind telling me?"

Mink shrugged. "Word gets out, know what I'm saying?"

Wilkins nodded. He decided not to press it.

He took a big drag on his cigarette and played with the smoke a little, letting some out his nose and the rest in a long, cool stream from his mouth as though he had all the time in the world and was pleased as hell that he was about to have a nice little chat.

"See, what I was thinking," Mink was saying, also playing with the smoke, letting it out as he talked, "is that I might be able to get you set up again in making that bust."

"Oh, how might you be able to do that?" Jesus, what a little twit.

"I'm assuming your cover has been blown. I mean, I know it must take a long time to establish a cover."

Wilkins nodded and took another drag on his cigarette. Lesson Two: Be non-committal. Let them do the talking. At least up to a point.

"So what I'm thinking is it be really nice if you had a guy who was an established user and buyer—I mean known for it—work his way into where you were when things fell apart. No offense, by the way."

Billy Wilkins felt like slapping C. Trevor 'Mink' Whitehead around. It was almost too much to have this fink, a fruit to boot, privy to his screw up. But he had to hear him out. Besides, I wasn't a buyer, Wilkins was thinking. My cover was I was a cop on the take.

"And you know such a person and he'd be willing to help out his local police. What's he, born again or something?"

"Well, see, the thing is I don't really know if he'd be agreeable but I think he might be. I'll get to that. What I gotta find out is if things can be worked out on this end first, then I go to him."

"What things are you talking about?"

"Well, like protection, mainly."

"Hell, someone helps us out, works undercover with us, naturally we protect them as far as we can, but no guarantees."

Mink waved his hand. "No, no. I don't mean that. I mean if he helps you out can you work out one of those deals where you give a guy a new identity, immunity for past misdeeds, new name, social security, move him to another part of the country? Stuff like that?"

"Sounds like you're talking about witness protection."

"Whatever. But I mean couldn't you work it for someone who, you know, did a deal like I'm talking?"

Billy Wilkins snuffed out his cigarette even though it had a lot of life left in it, but that was part of his cutting down strategy until he quit.

"Okay, Mink, just what kind of deal *are* you talking about? Spell it out, will you?"

Mink thought for a moment. He wanted to make sure he phrased this right. "I know a guy who's in real deep, okay, who could use the kind of setup like I just described."

"In real deep how? With the law?"

"Well, yeah. Armed robbery's pretty deep, I guess. Shooting someone in the process." Mink Whitehead laughed. "Attempted armed robbery, I should say."

"Look—"

"Wait a minute. This guy's in even deeper than that and this is why I think he'd do anything to get out."

Billy Wilkins stood and said, "Listen, before this goes any further, you've gotta understand—"

Mink Whitehead held up his hand. "I know who shot William Scarlata's mother," he said in a dramatically hushed voice. He'd talked with Tilly Tillotson again and, while not yet getting the name of the shooter, he'd gotten the name of Tilly'source. He'd done some checking around and was very sure the guy was solid. Sure enough to get him in here and try to shore up his own bona fides with the cops.

Even if the guy proved not to be the shooter, he'd just say the dude wanted no part of a deal with the cops. If the police pressed things and said they wanted the name or they'd get Whitehead for withholding evidence on a felony, he'd give the name and let the bum do his own denying. In any event, Mink figured he couldn't come out looking too bad. At the very least, he'd come off as a cooperative guy who thought he had some good news and tried his best. But his gut told him that Tilly's source had the goods.

Billy Wilkins reaction wasn't quite what he expected. Wilkins said, "Sure you do. Beat it. Get out of here and stop wasting my time."

Mink felt the anger rise. Son of a bitch. Who the hell are you? He pushed the anger down and imagined himself as Di Niro in 'Taxidriver', the scene where Di Niro is rehearsing saying 'Are you talking to me?' putting an inflection on a different word each time.

"You hear what I just said?" The inflection was on 'hear,' said very cool, in control, in charge, voice not raised. "I said I know who shot Will Scarlet's old lady. This guy's gotta be beside himself, know what I'm saying, afraid he's gonna end up with an ice pick in his belly button, floating in Boston Harbor. You give him a deal, he's gonna be very cooperative, very useful. But, hey, you do what you want."

Mink Whitehead started to get up. He felt he had played that well. He might be into the cops but he'd be damned they'd own him and talk to him like he was just some little snitch they'd just as soon dump on when they didn't need him. He took enough of that from Donovan.

"Look," Billy Wilkins said, "don't get so hot under the collar. Okay, let's say you do know who plugged Will Scarlet's mother. This guy's obviously no big-time dope dealer if he's involved in a penny ante holdup."

Billy Wilkins went for another Marlboro. Frig it.

"So you're saying, what, we set him up so that all of a sudden he's a big shot buyer and seller? You think the guys I want don't see through that in about two seconds flat? You know what I'm saying? This guy, a two-bit buyer and user, tries to come across as major league and he's gonna stink so bad they'll flush him down the toilet."

Wilkins lit the Marlboro.

"Besides, it's not all that easy setting up what you got in mind. For one thing, there's the problem of seeding this person with dough. That's not done lightly. And don't forget, there's the small matter of us looking the other way with a guy who's committed a felony."

Billy Wilkins puffed his cigarette and toyed with his lighter. "Look, why don't you just give us the name? What you've got in mind is off the wall."

"Well, see, it's like this. I don't actually have the name but I can get it. The guy I'll go through, believe it or not, has his own little code. He wouldn't turn someone in to Will Scarlet for anything. He'll go along with you guys if he thinks this person can get a deal."

"Tell me, Mink, what's in this for you?"

"Come on, will you," Mink said. "What, do you get a kick making me spell it out? I get information and I deal it. You know that. It's that simple. I'm not looking for the citizen of the year award. Just trying to get by."

Billy Wilkins nodded. He'd never get used to the Boston accent. Whitehead had pronounced 'award' as 'a wad.'

"I'm just thinking," Mink said, "that here's a pretty desperate guy. Someone says to him, here's a chance to get away, new name, all that kind of thing, if you just do a little job, I think, if he's got half a brain, he'd jump at it. Hey, it was just a thought."

"What makes you think this guy's still around here? Good chance he's already long gone, don't you think?"

"That I don't know."

"Best thing is for you to get the name from your pal and give it to us. This person is better off with us than with Will Scarlet. If his name is out, Will Scarlet will find him."

Mink shook his head. "I won't be able to get the name without guarantees. I know my friend. It won't happen."

Billy Wilkins snubbed out his cigarette. "Tell you what. Maybe we can find something. Let me talk to some people. I'll get in touch through Ryan Donovan.

Mink Whitehead stood. "Okay. But I wouldn't wait too long. I don't want to sound dramatic or anything, but if Will Scarlet gets hold of this guy . . ."

He let the statement dangle, filled, he felt with implication.

"By the way," Mink said, "just curious, but what's that you're carrying, a .38?"

"It is. Why?"

"No reason. Like I say, just curious. I noticed it when you came in. I thought most cops carry nine or ten millimeter automatics now."

"They do. I don't."

"Hmmm." Mink Whitehead nodded at Billy Wilkins and left, thinking he had just dealt with a real thick Southern hillbilly, someone out of the past. He could tell Wilkins thought he was dirt. Rednecks like that gotta have someone to look down on. Must be tough on them now that they had to be at least halfway nice to blacks and gays.

Lieutenant Billy Wilkins had another Marlboro smoked nearly down to the filter as he sat and thought about what C. Trevor Whitehead had told him. Besides being unworkable, Whitehead's proposal was laughable. It really was.

But . . .

But maybe it was time to throw the book aside. What he had in mind was probably laughable too. Like something out of a direct to video movie. Still, it was worth thinking about.

SPIRAL

The funny part was if it worked maybe he'd have that write up in *Time* after all.

Chapter Eleven

"Bobby," Chug's father said to him, "a man don't have any dignity without his pants on."

Robert Ellis senior lolled loosely in a wheelchair by a window that looked out on a highway that fed into Boston from the north. It wasn't exactly scenic. The room was stifling and smelled of age and of bowels and bladders gone loose.

Chug looked at his father's thin, white legs, nearly hairless, sticking from a sparse robe. They were covered almost to his knees with elastic stockings.

"Don't they let you wear your pants?"

Chug felt anger rising in him. Who the hell knew what went on in these places? You heard horror stories all the time.

"Sometimes. But I have . . . accidents. So usually they don't let me." Mr. Ellis seemed to ponder that sadly.

At least his father's legs couldn't be cold, Chug thought. He wished he could afford one of those nice nursing homes with a fancy name like Oakdale or Meadow Glen that had game rooms, a nice view, and thermostats that worked. When you had to rely on Medicare, you ended up in a hole like this sweating to death and not even having the dignity of wearing your pants.

"I'll speak to someone," Chug said. "About your pants."

"Won't do any good."

Chug felt his father was probably right. After a pause, he said, "Dad, I might be going away for a little while. Not too long."

"They'll tell you I can have my pants but they won't let me have them. They're bastards."

Shifting gears, Chug said, "You been watching the Celtics? Or the Sox at spring training? I think they're gonna have another good year."

He watched his father's face for a glint of the old interest in sports, times they had spent together at the Garden or Fenway Park before his Dad, all his life a hard-working guy who enjoyed tipping one after a day toting U.S. Mail, had been leveled by a stroke.

His father looked at Chug vaguely. His eyes were watery, it seemed to Chug, almost constantly. Sometimes he wondered if it was the watery condition you saw in the eyes of a lot of older people or if his father was crying.

"Yeah, I been watching them. Not much else to do. Where you going?"

"Florida probably. Get away from the cold." His conscience tweaked him for the lie in the farfetched event William Scarlata would check his father out.

"How's your appetite? You eating okay?"

"Yeah. I eat okay but most of the time I'm not hungry. I'd like a beer once in a while. Can you get me a beer? Boy, a nice cold bottle of Bud would hit the spot."

"They won't let you have beer, Dad. You know that."

His father nodded. "What do they think, I'm gonna get drunk? Maybe they think it's bad for my health. Bobby, you go away you be careful."

"Don't worry about me, Dad. Just a little getting away. A little vacation."

"That's good. You hear from Jimmy lately? I haven't heard from him in a long time. Christ, you'd think he could call his old man once in a while. Sometimes I think I've got only one son."

"He's busy, Dad. He works hard. I hear from him every once in a while." Actually, very seldom, Chug thought. But I don't do a lot to keep in touch either. He wondered how these things happened because he and his brother had a good sibling relationship growing up.

They sat about another twenty minutes of stilted fragments and half sentences about things they went over every time Chug came to the nursing home. They watched cars speed to and from Boston, watching traffic now probably the most entertainment Chug's father got these days.

Chug liked to think he got involved in the attempted robbery and was trying to get the ink out of paper bills so that he could get his father out of this place to somewhere he could at least watch squirrels scamper up oak trees.

But he knew that was only partially true. Delivering flowers and working for the landscaper were stopgap and he was having a hard time feeding the demon. But he was through with it. He had slipped only twice since shooting the poor old woman.

The radiator hissed some steam at him and he got up, patted his father's thin shoulders and kissed the top of his head which still had a good supply of hair on it.

He spoke to the woman at the desk about his father's pants before he left but felt like it was talking to a manikin.

Ryan Donovan found C. Trevor Whitehead walking up Beacon Street not far from the Bull and Finch Pub with its big Cheers flag flying proudly and, despite the cold, a small gaggle of sightseers lined up on the sidewalk probably pretending that Cliff, Norm, Sam or Rebecca was about to walk in. The place was the biggest attraction in Boston besides Old Ironsides, he had read.

He beeped the horn. Whitehead got into the unmarked Crown Vic that might just as well have had police written all over it.

"Going to Cheers to have a pop with Cliffy?"

C. Trevor Whitehead looked contemptuously at the small crowd. "As a matter of fact, I'm just heading over to Newbury Street."

"I'll give you a lift."

Donovan pulled into traffic.

"I got a message for you from Billy Wilkins. He says tell your boy he'd like to see him."

William Scarlata looked down at his mother.

Complications. That's how the doctor had put it. He wasn't unaware that the doctor was afraid of him. That they all were. The doctors, the nurses. He caught them looking at him and then quickly looking away.

"We're doing all we can," the doctor had said. "But a woman her age." He had said something about clots and circulation.

Her face, which looked as though it had been punched, looked as though it had been punched again.

Her eyes were shut and her breathing, although assisted, seemed labored. It was if she had just run a race. She didn't know that her son was there.

He didn't blame the doctors.

Lou Russo said he was closing in and he knew, if Lou said it, it was true. Lou was no yes man.

A priest was hovering. He had been making his rounds through the intensive care unit.

The priest looked at the name at the end of the bed. "Is she Catholic?"

William Scarlata nodded. Too young to be called Father. Not more than a kid, actually.

The priest went to the side of the bed, bowed his head and prayed. When he finished, he looked at William Scarlata and said, "I'll remember her at Mass."

"Thank you, Father.

After the priest had gone, William Scarlata kissed his mother's forehead and held her hand for several minutes.

Outside the hospital, William Scarlata got into the silver Cadillac waiting for him near the front entrance. A thin young man who worked at and succeeded in looking like someone from a *Godfather* film sat behind the wheel.

"I want to go to Tranfiglia's, Joey," William Scarlata said.

"Oh, Jesus, Mr. Scarlata, I'm really sorry."

For a moment, William Scarlata thought his driver was expressing reluctance to drive him to Tranfiglia's funeral home as though he had some other business.

He caught himself just as he was about to lash out. "No, no. It's not my mother." Not yet. "I got some other business with Mr. Tranfiglia." He thought of a coffin, lined and pillowed, its occupant lowered, still alive into his grave.

Bernado Tranfiglia—William Scarlata with a somewhat uncharacteristic touch of humor referred to him as a grief specialist—had buried many secrets over the years for the folks who controlled Boston's organized crime.

He was stocky but kindly looking and at sixty-three wanted very much to move to Florida where at least the old folks he'd deal with were still alive and where, when the meat wagon came in, which was probably pretty often when you thought about it, someone else would handle the arrangements.

But his two sons wanted no part of the trade when their father left it and so Bernardo, being unwilling to sell off a lucrative business started by his grandfather and trapped by the fact that grieving families preferred dealing with him directly, hung on and contented himself with short trips to warm, sunny places.

When William Scarlata confronted him in the office of the funeral home that actually had a view, rather obscured, admittedly, of Boston Harbor, he made the same assumption that William's driver had and arranged his features into that expression that had long since become second nature, an expression that said, I'm so sorry but it's the will of God and I'll do all I can to make everything as easy as possible.

His expression was still mournful as William Scarlata said, "I'm going to need you to arrange a little something for me, Mr. Tranfiglia. Not just yet but I want it set up and ready to go when I give the word. Naturally, you'll be adequately taken care of."

As realization hit that this visit wasn't to arrange the burial of Florence Scarlata, the mournful features slowly deadpanned. Bernardo Tranfiglia had the feeling he wasn't going to like this. He was getting too old to do anything the law might disapprove of. Certainly too old for a stretch in prison. He'd seen enough movies about and heard enough about the horrors perpetrated by prison inmates on new arrivals of any age.

He entertained a decidedly unpleasant vision of himself spread-eagled and naked surrounded by leering, lusting non-Caucasians.

But even more unpleasant and much more immediate was a vision of a thwarted, angry William Scarlata. And so he found himself saying, "Certainly, Mr. Scarlata. Anything I can do to be of service."

William Scarlata had seated himself in a comfortable brown leather chair across from Bernardo Tranfiglia's desk. "How many funerals do you handle a week?"

Bernardo Tranfiglia's expression became guarded, as though he were talking with an Internal Revenue Agent. Even though he actually handled a few strictly cash funerals, it wasn't that easy to hide the money. A funeral was really not much more than the sale of the casket and the casket wholesalers kept careful records. Still, he had done fudging every now and again.

"Varies. Some weeks could even be none. Others..."

He spread his hands. "Five. Six, maybe."

William Scarlata was sure it could be higher but it didn't matter. "What I'm getting at is what I have in mind could be short notice and I'll need for you to have a wake in progress with a funeral coming up.

"I see," Bernardo Tranfiglia said, although he didn't see at all.

"See, what I want is for you to have a casket ready to be buried. What you'll have to do is, the morning of the funeral, after the family is gone and is on the way to the cemetery, you'll have to remove the deceased and put someone else in the casket."

Bernardo Tranfiglia tried to keep the distress from his face and voice. "Put someone else in the casket?"

"Yes."

"What will I do with the original person?"

"I'll get to that." William Scarlata had thought this out on the drive from the hospital. It wasn't that complicated but he knew he would have to lead Tranfiglia gently by the hand.

"I have to tell you that this person to be put into the casket will be alive."

Bernardo Tranfiglia tried to repeat the word 'alive' but it stuck. William Scarlata held his gaze. After a moment, he managed to ask, "Will this person be conscious?"

"Yes. But he will be securely tied and gagged. He will not be able to move or scream."

Bernardo Tranfiglia wanted to ask who was this victim of the most awful fate he could imagine. But he didn't dare and, even more, he didn't want to know. It wasn't hard, however, to figure that it was probably whoever had shot William Scarlata's mother.

He wished he had sold his business and was sunning himself on a beach where his only worries were checking his moles for signs of melanoma. Not listening to this man calmly explaining something he wanted done that would consign them both to hell. No, William Scarlata was already in hell. He was the devil incarnate.

There was no way out.

In a voice that surprised him with its evenness, he asked, "What will I do with the deceased person?"

"You'll have to cremate that person. That won't present a problem, will it?"

Bernardo Tranfiglia shook his head. Only a relatively minor problem, nothing to refusing William Scarlata.

"I recall a previous time that we used the crematory," William Scarlata said. "So I presume you could use it again. No questions, no complications. You handle it."

"Very well."

"If there are any problems on that end, you let me know. I understand there are probably forms and so on but I think we can persuade whoever we have to that they have nothing to worry about."

Bernardo Tranfiglia nodded.

William Scarlata stood. "Do you have any questions?"

"I don't think so."

"As I say, the notice may be short. If you are not running a wake when I contact you, we can hold things at our end for a time. You don't go longer than a week without a wake do you?"

"Not usually." He hoped it wouldn't be his own wake. Bernardo Tranfiglio felt his heart pound and that telltale throb at his temples. He knew his pressure was high.

When William Scarlata was gone, he took a pill from a bottle in his desk and for good measure washed it down with a stiff pull on another bottle from the same drawer.

Then he vowed that when this was over, he'd sell out and move far away to where he could scorch himself in the sun, family business or no family business.

Chapter Twelve

Mickey the Harp Ianucci sat in the middle seat of the GMC Denali with Rui Lobao as Sal the Dogcatcher Manfredi drove slowly on back streets of East Boston.

"Roy—they call you Roy right?—you gotta do better than that," Mickey the Harp said. He had his arm on Rui's shoulder in a friendly way but Rui was shivering as though he had malaria and he thought he was going to be sick.

"Honest to God, I can't remember the guy's name except it was funny."

"Yeah, I know. You said that about a million times. The guy had a funny nickname. We just want to know it so we can have a laugh."

Mickey's big hand squeezed Rui's shoulder where it joined his neck and needles of pain shot up his neck and down his arm.

"You know your problem, don't you, Roy? You're a dope fiend. You were floating when your buddy Leo told you that name and you can't remember it."

"I'm trying to remember. What else can I do? If I knew it, don't you think I'd tell you?"

Mickey gave another hard squeeze and then patted Rui's head.

"Yeah, I think you'd tell us," Mickey the Harp said, whose mother's name had been Gallagher and who could pass for black Irish as well as Italian.

"So, you know what we're gonna do? We're gonna ride around 'til you remember. No rush. We got all night."

"Hey, you hungry or anything, Roy?" Sal Manfredi said, looking at Rui via the mirror. We can take a spin to Revere Beach, maybe Kelly's, get some seafood or something. Look at the waves."

Rui's shivering increased. He was dying for a hit. Anything. Even a cigarette would help but he didn't dare ask.

"Too bad about Leo Santos, huh?" Sal said. "We just wanted to ask him his friend's name but he had to be uncooperative. You're not uncooperative, are you Roy?"

Rui thought of Revere Beach. There were plenty of lonely places where they could toss him into the water, which would be mighty nippy. He said, "Look, I came to you guys originally, didn't I? I told you what I knew, that a guy I know knows who nearly offed Mrs. Scarlata. Leo probably told other people besides me. I'm sure he did."

"Yeah, but who are they, Roy?" Mickey said. Mickey was thinking of the lecture he had had earlier from Lou Russo who told him to get the name of the shooter no matter what, that Mr. Scarlata was mightily pissed that they had screwed up with Leo Santos.

"Our source don't remember the name, Lou," Mickey had explained.

"Do I have to spell it out? You make him remember," Lou Russo had said. "Even if it means you cut off everything except his tongue so he can talk and tell you that name."

As Mickey was thinking those thoughts, Rui Lobao was thinking of the money that passing on the information was supposed to have been worth. He didn't think he was in a position to inquire about it now.

He concentrated as hard as he could on what Leo Santos had said to him that time they had been floating on chemical clouds. He remembered Leo had talked about Gorilla Connors from Middleton Jail and then had said this other guy's name but said it only once or twice. He remembered that he himself had repeated the name.

Jesus, what was it?"

Champ. Something like Champ. But that wasn't it.

Or Chum.

They were almost at Revere Beach now and Rui knew they weren't going to Kelly's.

"You trying to remember, Roy?" Mickey asked. Mickey wanted to get the name from Rui himself. Lou Russo had said, "You can't get the name, you bring the sonovabitch to me."

But that wasn't the way to score points with Lou, to make him do the job you had been sent out to handle.

Mickey took a long, thin-bladed knife from under his coat. It was used to cut meat and it was very sharp. He grabbed Rui Lobao's left hand and placed the blade against the baby finger.

"You ever feed the seagulls at Revere Beach, Roy? Those suckers'll eat anything."

Rui moaned but didn't struggle. His fear paralyzed him. "Please. Jesus, I'm trying. I really am."

"Roy, you cold or something? You're shivering real bad."

Even on a cold March night cars were parked along the sea wall at the beach but when Sal found an empty stretch he pulled the Denali off the road and parked with the engine running.

"We're getting out, Roy," Mickey said. "Don't want to mess up the leather."

He pushed Rui out the door and toward the wall. An icy wind pummeled them with strong, quick gusts.

"Over you go." Mickey lifted Rui by the back of his coat and the seat of his pants to the top of the wall and jumped over to the beach with him. Whitecaps and moon glints glistened, frigid complements to the razor wind.

Mickey the Harp led Rui to a jumble of boulders next to the wall and pushed him down. He jammed Rui's left hand against a rock and pressed the knife on the baby finger hard enough to draw a trickle of blood even though Rui's blood vessels were constricted with shock and cold.

"Okay, Roy, I'm through playing. You think of that name or I'm gonna cut your fingers off one at a time and then your toes. You don't come up with that name I want you to use your imagination about what you might have left when I'm through with you."

Mickey pressed and slid the knife against the finger and blood poured freely. Rui screamed.

"One more slice, Roy, and it's off."

Rui replayed the scene with Leo Santos but couldn't think of any name beyond Gorilla Connors. Through misty eyes, he looked at Mickey the Harp and wanted to be that man's friend.

Mickey's hand moved again but the pain wasn't all that bad and Rui was surprised when Mickey held a big meaty comma in front of his eyes.

"Say goodbye to it, Roy. That's number one."

Mickey twirled the severed finger in front of Rui's face a moment as Rui stared dumbly at it.

"Want me to save these, Roy? We can put 'em all in a baggie or something. Or should I just chuck it?"

Tumblers clicked a little in Rui Lobao's mind.

"I think I'll just chuck 'em and let the gulls have a nice meal. What do they call it? Some finger food." Mickey laughed. He thought his pun was hilarious.

Mickey tossed the finger, wedged the hand against the rock again and positioned the knife.

Rui Lobao said, "Chuck."

"Huh? I did, Roy. I chucked it. Didn't you see me, you thick Portugee?"

"Chuck," Rui said again. "That was the guy's name."

"Chuck? The guy's name was Chuck? I thought you said the name was funny. What's so funny about Chuck?"

"No, that ain't it." Rui looked down at his bleeding hand and the knife ready to do some more paring. And then remembrance hit him.

He said, or, rather, almost sang with a joy that he would be spared further removal of body parts, "Chug. Yeah, that was it. His name was Chug."

Chapter Thirteen

Chug called Ellie's cell when he figured she was out of work and on her way home. He asked her to meet him at a 99 they often went to.

"I don't think we should meet at my place or yours," he said. He told her he needed to talk. So did she.

He parked a couple of blocks from the restaurant and checked carefully to see that he wasn't being tailed. When he saw Ellie's six-month old Passat that she was in love with pull into the parking lot, he got out of his two-year old Explorer that he was no longer in love with. But he had two years of payments left.

Inside, Chug pointed to a booth with no one sitting near it and asked the hostess if they could have it.

"No problem," she cooed. She looked all of sixteen and was dressed and groomed as if she expected to be discovered.

They ordered sandwiches and drinks, a draft for Chug, a diet Coke for Ellie. He could tell right away she was a bit frosty.

"El, I'm gonna take off for a few days. Not long term. Just to be on the safe side while I think things out."

She nodded. "That's probably smart but I'd be thinking more long term if I were you."

"Well, it may come to that, but believe this or don't believe it: there are things around here I don't want to walk away from. Besides you, my father, number one. I'm all he's got."

"Lot of good you'll do him if you're at Cedar Junction.

Or . . ." She let her voice trail.

"I'm really not too worried about the cops. I mean, I don't want to be stupid about it, but I figure they haven't got much to go on."

"So that means you're worried about Will Scarlet. At least you're showing some sense that way."

He told her about Leo Santos. "Don't know for sure if it was Will Scarlet who got him but—"

Ellie was shaking her head. "Ohmigod, ohmigod," she said slowly and softly, looking at Chug as though he were an alien creature.

"Frankie's pretty spooked," Chug said, knowing this wasn't going well.

"That would be Frankie Ricciardi, I assume. You taking off with him?" Ellie had met him once or twice. "Your old partner in crime. You know what, Chug, I don't think I'm too hungry."

She reached into her bag, pulled out a couple of bills, and dropped them on the table. "Here, this should cover what I ordered. You can take it home."

She started to slip on her coat but Chug reached across the table and grabbed her arm.

"El, you've got every right to be pissed but please hear me out."

She pulled her arm free. "*Pissed?* You think that covers it? The way I'd be pissed if the pizza was burned or I got stuck in traffic? See, that's it, Chug, you're trivializing what you did and your lifestyle that led you to do it. I don't want to be part of that. For chrissake, you attempted armed robbery and shot a woman. *Pissed*, yeah, I guess I'm pissed."

Her voice was low, a hiss that might erupt.

"Okay, okay. Listen to me. I'm not trivializing anything. I know exactly how bad what I did was. Now, I could turn myself into the cops, pay the price, but I'm not going to do that."

He looked at her for a reaction but saw none. She just stared him unblinking.

"But this is what I am going to do. First, I'm off everything except maybe a beer now and then.

"I told you there are things around here I don't want to walk away from. Besides my father. My old job. When they let me go, they told me I could have it back when the economy turns around. They were good to me and I think I could build on it, eventually become a regional manager. I'd be talking some real bucks then."

Ellie nodded. "And don't forget they took you on even though you'd been on probation."

That was the tie in to Frankie who had had a knack for stealing cars, first, when a kid, just for joyriding. Chug occasionally took a spin with him. Frankie eventually graduated to delivering to chop shops while Chug confined himself to just relieving cars of quality sound systems.

Both were caught. Frankie did a little time and Chug caught probation.

"When I get out of this jam, Ellie, I'm gonna turn it around. I'm serious. It won't be long. A good job. I'll be close to my Dad so's I can take care of him. God knows my brother's not part of that picture.

Anyway, I plan on having a good life and, far as I'm concerned, you're the biggest part of it."

"With just an occasional heist on the side when times are tough. Look, Chug, I'm sorry, but pardon me for being just a tad skeptical of your good intentions."

"I want to prove it. That's all I can do. But you've got to let me."

Their food and drinks arrived and the waitress left.

"Well, here we are, Chug, at the 99 just like everything's okay and aren't we having a good time. A little chow, rent a movie, and then you stay over and the next day off you go to work and off I go to work."

"That sounds pretty nice to me, Ellie. That's what I want. I want it full time."

"What's that supposed to mean?"

"You know. We've talked about marriage." He reached for her hand but she pulled it away.

"Well, the timing's off just a bit, I think. Right now I can't see me marching down the aisle and you waiting there at the altar probably with Frankie Ricciardi as your Best Man. What would he say for a toast? 'Better luck next time.'?"

After a long moment's pause, Ellie said, "I'm sorry I said that."

"That's okay. I'm deserving all of this. Get it out of your system. But I want you to come away with me, El. Just for the few day's I'm gone."

"You're not going with Frankie?"

"He can go his own way. It doesn't matter."

"Chug, you haven't been listening to me too carefully. I think an awful lot of you. You know that. That's not the question. But things aren't the same as they were a few days ago. You've got to get away to think things out, you say. I need time to think things out too."

He looked at her and thought of how stupid he had been for screwing things up with her and, worse, for putting her in a position she probably didn't get. He wasn't sure how to say what he had to say next. He hesitated and then said, "Look, Ellie, I don't want to scare you but I'm thinking that if they get my name they might try to find me through you. If you don't want to come with me, why don't you take a few days and go someplace?"

"Sure. Just like that. Talk sense, will you. I can't just take time off from my job like that. I'm okay. Anyone looks like they're out of *Goodfellas* comes near me I'll call the cops right away."

Neither had touched their food. Ellie pushed her plate away. "I think I want to go home, Chug."

He looked at his plate and mug of beer, also untouched. He signaled the waitress, mumbled something about how there was nothing wrong with the food but that they weren't feeling well. She wrote up the check and he paid, leaving a good tip.

They stood by her car in the parking lot, their breath plumes dissipating in the cold breeze. He noticed her car was clean. She must have run it through the car wash today. Somehow, that made him sad, that the little, everyday things that were part of her life he had put at risk of losing.

"Give me some time, Chug," she said and kissed him. The kiss was warm and he started to put his arms around her but instead let them drop to his side.

She got into her car and before closing the door she looked at him with welling eyes and said, "You'll be careful, won't you?"

He drove home thinking he was glad that he and Ellie had maintained separate addresses. If they found where he lived, she wouldn't be there. He wondered now whether he should go north with Frankie at all. Should he go anywhere with Frankie?

Maybe it would be good to give Ellie a little space.

He thought of Leo Santos, a guy he had barely known, actually, one of Frankie's many fine acquaintances. He thought of what had happened to Leo. Beaten to death. Leo had been a pretty rough guy, about Chug's height, which meant not tall but not short. Weighed more, though. Had to go about two-ten, not much of it fat. A guy who could handle himself.

Not much comfort thinking about that.

A little comfort, though, in the nine millimeter that had wounded Florence Scarlata stuffed in his jacket pocket. Christ, if Ellie knew he was carrying that.

He was about a half mile from home when he became conscious of a pair of headlights steadily pacing him. But this was a busy city and headlights always paced you.

Now he wasn't sure. Was there something or was he living a movie? He drove past his place and took the next left at the last moment without giving a signal, feeling a little foolish at the Hollywoodish ploy.

The lights followed. Too soon to rule out coincidence. He took another left, dove the block, stopped and waited. He unzipped the pocket the nine-millimeter was in. Nothing following so he went left again to his street, pulled into the paved over yard that served as a parking lot for the apartments and parked in his spot.

As he walked to his door, he was thinking how cold it was and how cold it would be where he and Frankie were going when he sensed a presence behind him. When he turned and saw a figure coming up fast, he reached for his pocket but the person pressed close and grabbed his arm.

"Jesus, chill it, man. We need to talk," said C. Trevor Whitehead, letting go and backing away.

"We need to talk. Get in," Lieutenant Billy Wilkins said to the Special Agent who was at the crosswalk between Faneuil Hall and City Hall. This agent was partial to an ethnic food mix and Wilkins knew he frequently strolled from his office at Government Center to Quincy Market for fatty German sandwiches followed by some baklava or a kourambiethe or two.

The Special Agent, who looked as if he were in insurance or finance of some kind, checked his watch and bent down to Wilkins who was leaning across the car seat and talking to him through the rolled down window of the unmarked police car.

The Agent pursed his lips. His distaste was obvious. He didn't much care for Boston cops and he didn't like Southerners. And he didn't like it that Wilkins obviously knew where he'd be at a particular time. It wasn't as if he came to Quincy Market *every* day.

"Get in," Wilkins said. Then he added, "Please."

The Agent, whose name was Jessup, got in. Wilkins took a few turns until he was on Atlantic

Avenue and slowly drove along past condos, shops, and parks.

"Are we sightseeing?" Jessup said. "I've got work as I presume you have."

Wilkins looked at him and smiled. "Will Scarlet. How'd you like to nail him?"

"Wilkins, you are the master of the rhetorical question."

"I mean it."

Jessup unbuttoned his coat. Wilkins had the heater on high, his Southern blood never having fully adjusted to the raw cold of a New England winter.

"Obviously, I'd like to nail him."

"Problem is, he's become cautious, huh?"

"Very. Paranoid, actually."

"Checks his home, his office, his car daily for bugs, right?"

"He does. But so did Angiulo and Patriarca for all the good it did them."

"But Scarlata's super careful, am I right?" Wilkins said. "If he's not sure, he'll even conduct his conversations outside. I mean, he's been spending a lot of time at the Prato and walking along the waterfront with his associates even when the weather's not so hot."

Jessup nodded. "It's not just that. The mob's changed. In a way, they've become more slippery. More legitimate holdings that turn a nice profit. Diversification."

Wilkins double-parked in front of Lewis Wharf, an old stone warehouse that had been converted to pricey waterfront condos.

Jessup looked at Wilkins and favored him with a slight smile. "Just Will Scarlet, huh? I'd like to go right to the top."

"Will Scarlet is the top or soon will be. Mario Cotoni's got maybe a year tops, from what I hear. Even his dough can't fight the big C."

Jessup said, "Yeah, but it's not automatic that Will Scarlet will take over."

Billy Wilkins held back an obscenity. Feds would nitpick you every time, never conceding a thing.

He said, his exasperation poorly concealed, "You wanna hear what I've got?"

"I'm all ears, Wilkins. By the way, can you turn the heater down? I'm dehydrating."

Wilkins turned the fan to low and pulled back into traffic.

"I might be onto the guy who shot Will Scarlet's old lady."

Wilkins watched Jessup's profile carefully and was disappointed by the lack of reaction.

He gave Jessup a full ten seconds and said, "You didn't hear what I just said?"

"I heard. And?"

"Whadda ya mean, 'and?' Use your imagination."

Jessup pushed the button to roll down his window. "Look, Wilkins, just lay it out. You're up to something. This is an unofficial contact so just spell it out and then I'll react."

"Okay, it goes like this. Since the big bust a few years ago when all the old mob guys took a tumble, it's been very hard to lay anything on the replacements. They watch their tracks. But now the number two man, soon to be number one, at least in the minds of *most* people who are aware of these things, has his mother shot, apparently by a punk, a nobody."

Jessup leaned over and slid the temperature lever to cool.

"Now," Wilkins said, "you tell me, are Italian boys—men—close to their mothers?"

Jessup leaned his head back and laughed. "Come on, Wilkins, you've seen too many movies. You're romanticizing. Let me guess what you've got in mind. Somehow you're thinking of getting Will Scarlet in the act of going after his mother's shooter."

Wilkins made an expression that said, Well, *excuse* me.

"That's Hollywood crap. Beneath the illegitimacy, the evil, the cruelty, you think there is a semi-noble person with a code and with deep Old-World family ties. Will Scarlet's main concern—his only concern—is power and profit. I'm not saying he doesn't love his mother but he'll do nothing to jeopardize himself."

"The word on the street is he's put up fifty grand for whoever did it."

Jessup snorted. "The word on the street. No one will ever see that money. I guarantee it."

"You don't think so?"

"Not a dime. So tell me, am I right? You're going to try to get Will Scarlet in the act of snuffing someone? You think he'd do it himself? He'll distance himself from anything like that."

"At the end, he'll be there. He'll want to see this person up close and personal and he'll want this person to see him."

Jessup shook his head. "I hope you're not forgetting that you can't get him for murder unless he commits it and you can't let him commit it without being an accessory. Besides, this person is just going to let himself be used as a lure?"

"He won't know. And I wouldn't let it get to that. We'll get Scarlata for something else. Kidnapping with the intent to commit murder. Violation of civil rights."

"'We'll?'"

Wilkins nodded. "Yeah. You and me. I'm doing you a real favor. Boston police officer and Special Agent nab Will Scarlet."

"Yeah, right. You're doing me a favor. What you have in mind is so wacko that you don't dare approach your superiors. Plus, it's probably entrapment. Look, why don't you turn this rolling sauna around and drive me back to where you picked me up. You do that and I'll do you the favor of not turning you in."

"Oh, wow, turn me in. Jeez. Yes, sir, Mr. Jessup. I didn't realize I was dealing with Efram Zimbalist, Jr. here."

"It ever occur to you, Wilkins, I might be wired?"

"Right. Sure. You might be wired on coffee, that's it."

"What is it with you? That screwed up bust mess up your mind?"

They were in the North End now, slowly trolling up Hanover Street, traffic congealed by illegally parked cars and jaywalkers taking their sweet time crossing from one side to the other.

"Well, you know, you were left in the cold when Anguilo and the boys went down. What happened there? I know you put in some time on that. Don't tell me you wouldn't like a little of the gravy. Maybe a nice promotion. Be in charge of a district office."

Wilkins braked hard to avoid hitting a couple of very Italian-looking young men who sauntered across the street in front of the car.

"I got half a mind to write up those jerks for jaywalking."

"So that's it," Jessup said. "Now the cards are on the table. You screwed up on the drug bust, are afraid of going to anyone in your department with a lunatic idea but would like to pull a coup. You see me as a disgruntled Fed who'd also like some glory as the guy who helped put the net around an up and coming major crime figure. Plus, you think you've got the perfect bait. Some piece of scum who, even if he's snuffed, no one will care."

Wilkins said nothing.

"You're a bastard, Wilkins."

"No. Will Scarlet's the bastard. How'd you just put it? Evil and cruel?"

Special Agent Jessup could taste knackwurst. It wasn't as good as when it had gone down. "Okay, so who's the shooter?" he said after a pause of several seconds.

"Well, that's part of the problem. I got a meeting set up through a snitch who's supposed to be pretty good but he's not mine so I don't know for sure yet. Might be a little shaky."

"Then what the hell are you talking to me for? Jesus, take me back."

"Before I proceed I have to know if you're with me. If this doesn't pan out, we've never talked."

Jessup was shaking his head slowly. Finally he said, "And you're going to tell him what?"

"Let him think he's gonna be part of a drug bust in exchange for immunity, new identity, and relocation."

"None of which will ever come to pass."

"Naturally."

"What if he sees right through this?"

Wilkins shrugged. "Nothing ventured, nothing gained but I think we might have a very desperate guy on our hands who'll try anything."

"What if he comes forward and says you promised him the world?"

Wilkins smiled patiently. "I say I didn't. I tell him to get lost or I bust him for armed robbery. Which maybe I do anyway."

"What about the snitch? He can corroborate."

"He won't. He just wants to kiss ass."

They were silent for a few moments and the Jessup said, "Don't jump to any conclusions, here, I'm just asking a hypothetical to satisfy my curiosity, but how do you see me fitting into all this?"

"I may need some help. Someone I can rely on. Someone I'm not working with in an official capacity."

"Someone," Jessup said, "who just walks away and never says anything if there's a snafu, like, for instance, a stiff turning up who thought he was part of a drug bust."

"Something like that. I gotta work things out still. Logistics, you know."

"One thing," Jessup said. "The stiff—if your man ends up as one—may prove to be no problem. I can almost guarantee that if Will Scarlet gets his hands on this guy there'll never be a body found. Not ever."

Chapter Fourteen

Mickey the Harp knocked on the door, a polite tap appropriate to 7:30 a.m. by someone in one of the trades. If this Chug guy answered, he'd say something like, 'Something's gone wrong with the plumbing. Landlord wants us to check all the units.'

If old Chug spooked, that was all right. Mickey would get through the door in about two seconds flat and, if Chug managed to get down the fire escape, Sal Manfredi was waiting outside.

It had taken Mickey and Sal almost all night to put a fix on just who it was with the oddball nickname. They had done some checking and questioning in the North End and East Boston, finally finding someone who had known Leo Santos, now gone to the big cocaine cloud in the sky, who knew someone in South Boston who supposedly knew everyone Leo had associated with.

So they had gone to Southie, a couple of Italian boys in Irish territory where not so legal enterprises were mainly controlled by non-Mediterraneans and where Mafioso could meet a little friction. Except that Mickey was half Irish, his mother having hailed from Southie, and Mickey knew his way around both geographically and diplomatically.

They found that Chug's real name was Robert Ellis, that he drove a two-year old Ford Explorer, and that he lived in two rooms on the third floor of a three decker, conveniently enough for them, right here in Southie.

Finding Robert Ellis hadn't been all that tough but it had consumed time and Mickey the Harp was tired and very irritable. He rapped again a bit harder and put his ear to the door for sounds of anything: snoring, showering, eating.

He heard nothing except Matt Lauer talking in the flat across the hall. He used to like the chick who had been on with him years ago, who had been an item with one of the Red Sox owners. What was her name? Katie Couric. That was it.

He knocked once more, not too loud because he didn't want anyone poking a head out the door across the hall.

Ellis's Explorer was parked outside but Mickey the Harp knew that didn't guarantee he was inside. He turned the handle, knowing full well it would be locked. From under his coat, he drew a crowbar and towel. Padding the doorframe with the towel, he wedged the crowbar between the door and the jamb next to the knob and pulled back hard. He hoped the door wasn't alarmed but his experience was that these kinds of apartments usually weren't. There was no dead bolt and he easily got the clearance he needed to push the door in. Another bit of luck: no door chain.

He stepped in, the crowbar and towel back under his coat and a ten-millimeter Glock automatic in his hand.

One room had a sofa and a couple of padded chairs, not too old, a pretty good TV, a computer, and a stereo with an iPod hooked into it.

The other room was a combination bedroom and kitchenette. The bed was made and the kitchenette showed no signs of recent cooking or eating. Mickey the Harp checked the tiny bathroom off the kitchenette before putting the Glock away.

He went back to the front room. Posters of the Sox and Patriots were tacked on the wall over the computer and a framed print of people sitting in a sidewalk café was over the sofa. It looked to Mickey like someplace in Europe, probably Paris over a hundred years ago. Looked like something a chick would put up.

Mickey had asked his source in Southie, whose name was Sean Buckley, what this Chug dude was like.

"He's okay. He's cool," Sean had said, wondering why Mickey who he knew was connected wanted to know. "Got himself into a little shit but never pulled any time far as I know. Pretty tough kid growing up, played schoolboy sports, but he's got a little problem with flake. But, what the hell, who hasn't?"

He went to the iPod and thought of lifting it but knew he had to keep the place untouched. Didn't want to spook the guy when he came back. If he came back. The guy had any sense, he'd be in someplace like in that print on the wall by now.

Mickey took the iPod out of its dock and spun the wheel to the playlists. There were two. *ME* and *EL*. Hmmm. He checked out the selections on the playlists. The *ME* list wasn't too bad but quite a few sixties and seventies stuff. Rod Stewart, stuff like that. The *EL* list was very heavy on Country and Western, the kind of stuff Mickey definitely didn't like.

He put the iPod back in its dock and poked around. Their source wasn't sure where Chug worked. Maybe one of the department stores like K-Mart or Wal-Mart except he was pretty sure it wasn't either of them. Thought he might have been laid off.

Mickey smiled at the thought of doing something like that, of being a working stiff. No wonder the guy had tried a little moonlighting except he had screwed up royally. Didn't even get any money for his efforts. Had shot Will Scarlet's mother but got no dough. The papers had made a big deal about that.

He opened drawers and looked under furniture. It would be nice to bring back the piece that shot Mrs. Scarlata. He thought that would please Mr. Scarlata if he could do that. He imagined things Will Scarlet might do with it and the guy before doing whatever else he did to him.

How the hell could someone live in a hole like this? Mickey wondered.

He looked around some more. Some magazines on the coffee table. A few copies of *Time, Sports Illustrated,* one copy of *Money*.

He went to the refrigerator and checked the freezer. A gun could be stashed anywhere. He rummaged under the frozen dinners, a package of frozen burgers and frozen rolls. No gun.

Below were the usual. A half-gallon of milk, nearly empty. A half-gallon of Tropicana orange juice, half full. Some eggs, bacon, butter. Three bottles of Bud. He checked the drawers. Three oranges, a head of lettuce, a package of celery. No gun.

Something in the sink caught his eye. Three plastic margarine tubs, each with a dollar bill floating in something. What the--?

He bent down and sniffed. The first was turpentine or paint thinner. The second nearly knocked him off his feet, something really strong that brought tears to his eyes.

He was careful with the third but it was just a dishwashing detergent. Each bill was held submerged by a little pebble. He looked carefully. No question, it was real U.S. currency.

He stared for a few moments trying to make sense of it. Then he smiled and said aloud, "Guy's into money laundering."

He opened the cabinet doors under the sink. The usual clutter of cleaning stuff, probably some of which was in those margarine tubs. No gun.

He checked the cabinets over the fridge, the closet near the bed, the bureau drawers. No gun. He was very careful not to leave signs of disturbance.

There was a small bathroom off the kitchenette with a shower. He looked in the medicine cabinet and pulled back the shower curtain. The shower had been recently used.

He checked around again, looking for anything and also making sure everything was as it was when he came in.

He checked the door and doorjamb to make sure he hadn't chipped any paint.

Satisfied, he went back out.

Now that he and Sal knew where he lived, it was just a matter of time before they got their hands on Mr. Robert 'Chug' Ellis.

Mickey knew that before he turned this guy over to Lou Russo, though, he'd have to ask him why he had dollar bills soaking away in margarine tubs.

Chug and Frankie Ricciardi crossed into New Hampshire in Frankie's '04 Mustang GT, a real loser's car, in Chug's opinion, at about the same time that the sun crossed the equator. They zipped along at a steady 75 or 80, ten to fifteen over the limit but just about what everybody else was doing.

At the last minute, Chug had decided to leave the Explorer at his place. Frankie had picked him up at 6:30, an unusually early hour for Frankie, less unusual for Chug. They had breakfast at a pancake place on Route One and made their plans.

"I say we stop in the White Mountains for a while before heading to Montreal," Frankie had said as he chewed through a pancake with chocolate chips in it. "Skiing's still great, I hear, and where there's skiing, there's babes."

Chug had an image of Frankie, a few under his belt, thinking he looked like Derek Jeter, shooting his mouth off to ski bunnies. He didn't feel like adding what Frankie might say to his list of worries.

He thought of the little guy who had grabbed his arm last night and had said to him, "We need to talk."

Chug had nearly pulled out the nine, especially when the guy added, "You're the guy shot Will Scarlet's mother."

Instead, he had grabbed him by the jacket and pulled him close. "Who the hell are you? What are you talking about?"

"Easy," he had said. "Do I look like a goddamn hit man? If I was, I would have drilled you already. Just let me talk, okay?"

Chug continued to hold him close and said nothing.

"Let go of the jacket, okay. Just let go."

"Who the hell are you?"

"Call me Mink."

"What did you say about me shooting someone?"

"Look, I know how you must feel, but don't play dumb, huh. I got a deal that can save your ass all around. Not just from Will Scarlet but also the cops."

Chug released his grip on the jacket. It was obvious this person was no physical threat.

"You gonna listen to what I have to say?"

Chug kept his eyes on Mink's face but said nothing.

"Okay, here's the deal."

When he had finished, Chug said, "Beat it. Number one, you've got the wrong guy. Number two, that's the stupidest thing I ever heard. Someone drop you on your head when you were a baby?"

"Hey," Mink said, "I don't blame you. You gotta play it this way. Play dumb, I mean. I'll give you a chance to continue to do that. I got a piece of paper with my name—Mink—and my cell number. I'm gonna go over there and put it under your windshield wiper and then I'll take off.

"This gives you the chance to pretend to me you don't know what I'm talking about even though I know you do. When I'm gone you can grab the paper and think about what I said. Do what you want, man, but I don't see where there's a decision."

Chug shook his head slowly as though he was dealing with a semi-amusing but very slow person.

"Look, one of the things you're probably thinking is that this is a setup to get you to the cops so they can nab you. But you know, even though you're pretending it's not so, that you are who I say you are. So if I was setting you up with the cops or Will Scarlet, wouldn't they be here right now?"

When Mink had left, Chug waited a few minutes, actually went into his apartment, before coming back down for the piece of paper under his windshield wiper.

Now he was slouched in the seat of Frankie's GT, the crap music Frankie insisted on playing and the loud exhaust note starting to pain his ass, while he thought and worried about Ellie Robinson.

Ellie Robinson put her notes from her one night a week real estate course on the floor beside her, switched off the lamp, and rested her head on the pillow. Voices from a radio talk show kept her company but she paid them little attention.

Mainly, as she lay in her bed, she thought of Chug. She wasn't going to cry. She'd already determined that.

She was glad her parents weren't aware of this latest Chug chapter, unless they were looking down from heaven where she was sure they were if there was a heaven. A guy with three previous DUI hit them head on with his pickup truck one night as they came home from a movie. The guy walked away from the accident, tried to run away actually, but couldn't manage that. He blew a .15.

She'd been seeing Chug about a year before they were killed. Long enough for them to become aware of his shortcomings, most of which were marched up to reinforce what they didn't really like: his probation record.

"He's been in trouble, goddamnit. You'll see what that leads to," her father had said.

Ellie had defended Chug but now her father looked like a seer.

"He won't make a commitment," her mother had said. Ellie had conceded the truth of that, although last night he seemed ready. The irony of her mother's complaint amused Ellie a little. Her mother had marshaled that as a defect in Chug while grateful for it.

She thought of the summer night they had met at some outside tables at a Quincy Market bar where she had gone with a couple of friends for some music and margaritas.

At the next table three guys made the usual moves except one of them had a gimmick she'd never seen. He gave a wink just to her and with a flick of the wrist poured his glass of beer down his throat as fast as you could pour it down a sink. Faster, maybe.

Her reaction could have gone either way. For a split second, she was leaning toward this is a real jerk. But the ludicrousness of the stunt and his expression of look what I just did followed by a big grin made her slap her knee and say, "You've gotta do that again. On me." She had signaled the waiter to go to Chug's table.

One thing led to another and he got her phone number. He called her the next night and they hit it off right away. He was a lot of fun and *promised,* when they went through discovery about one another's background, that probation had taught him a lesson. His slightly more than recreational use of coke was a problem with her but he promised on that too.

So much for promises.

She watched swaying tree-branch shadows on her ceiling and tried to concentrate on them to drive thoughts of Chug from her mind so she could sleep.

Then something suddenly intruded and jolted her. Was she some kind of accessory to armed robbery and assault with a deadly weapon simply by knowing the culprit and not turning him in? Then she felt guilty for wondering it.

She tried to concentrate, but couldn't, on the talk show where a caller was making a point about stem cell research.

She thought of the real estate course and watched the shadows on the ceiling again. She did that for a long time until they blurred and misted.

Just as she found sleep, Mickey the Harp was in Southie talking again to the person who had told him Chug's real name.

"Yeah," he was saying to Mickey, "he goes with someone from Charlestown. Her name's Ellie something, I think."

Mickey did some more checking, finally got a last name of Robinson to go with the Ellie and, best of all, got an address.

Chapter Fifteen

They stopped at a motel near North Conway where Frankie insisted on two rooms. Chug knew that Frankie, who had a thing about gays, would not want even a motel clerk who didn't know him from Adam to think he was gay.

Then they went for something to eat. Frankie parked the GT among the SUVS and Volvos, blipping the throttle a couple of times so that the Mustang's muscular exhaust note resonated, and they went into a place of bricks and beams and hanging plants crammed with ruddy-faced skiers drinking Heineken and Stella Artois.

They ate fancy sandwiches and drank Buds and Frankie made moves on a couple of wholesome blondes who at first seemed amused but then quickly tired of his Rocky act.

Outside, on the way back to the Mustang, Frankie said, "If they'd played their cards right they could've made us."

As they walked around and went into a couple of stores, Chug thought of Ellie. They poked around and Frankie smirked at the athletic, outdoorsy clothing. They walked around some, found a place that sold beer and went back to Chug's room at the motel. Frankie had bought a map of Vermont, New Hampshire, and Maine that he opened and spread on the bed.

He examined it a few minutes and then folded it. He tossed a can of Bud to Chug sitting by the TV and popped one for himself.

"I say we just cruise around and play this by ear," Frankie said.

"Play what by ear?"

"How much dough you bring, Chuggy?"

"I got about five bills, I think."

"I got about three. It's not gonna go far. Credit cards and ATMs will leave a trail. So-o-o . . . "

"No way, Frank."

"No way? Oh, okay. I know. We can get a job shoveling snow or something. Or in Montreal we can try out for the Canadiens. Always wanted to play pro. You played schoolboy hockey. Maybe you can be goalie, Chuggy, wear a mask so's no one will know who you are."

Chug exploded from his chair, grabbed Frankie by his shirt and pulled him up from the bed. "I'm through, Frank. You didn't learn anything from that restaurant job? Was a one-time deal."

Frank tried to pull free but couldn't.

"Sure, " he said. "I learned the old expression, Shit can happen, is true. But that don't mean it happens every time."

Chug shoved Frankie back down onto the bed but stood over him. Frankie's can of Bud had tipped and beer was spilling onto the bedspread.

"We keep this one real simple, Chuggy. There's a million Mom and Pop's up here on deserted roads. Saw 'em on the way up. I'll go in. You're the wheel man."

Frankie got up, slipped past Chug and went to the bathroom for a towel that he used to blot up the beer.

"Look," he said, "you gotta be realistic. We're up here a while to let things cool back home. But, to be honest, with Will Scarlet, they're never gonna cool. So what are we here for? Think things out, get our heads on. Decide where we're going. Eventually, you want to go back or go someplace else and get a job, I respect that. But in the meantime we have to eat, buy gas, pay for a place to stay. Simple as that."

Chug picked up the nearly empty beer can and threw it against the wall.

"I'll go by myself, Chug, that's the way you want it. See who runs out of dough first. I'll tell you now, Chuggy, I'm not gonna make this a way of life, though. Just a couple of jobs to see us through."

Chug plopped on the bed and leveled a gaze at Frankie. "Frank, I want to catch a little shut-eye. That okay with you? You can stay here, just don't put on the TV too loud, or do what you want."

"Yeah, sure. I'll go to my room catch a few Zs too. We were up early. We'll talk some more tonight."

Morning sunlight slashed through the window and it took Chug several moments to realize where he was. He had slept through but had had a dream about Florence Scarlata who looked at him with hurt and accusing eyes. He tried to explain to her that he hadn't intended to shoot her but then she turned into Ellie and when he reached out to her she disappeared.

He lay still for a moment staring at the ceiling. The motel room smelled of beer and it was on him too where he had lain on the damp bedspread.

He looked out the window and saw that the Mustang was still there. He went to bathroom and turned on the shower. He looked at himself in the mirror and didn't like what he saw.

He took a long shower and put on fresh underwear and socks. His duffel bag had a week's worth. He had three sweatshirts and two pairs of jeans.

He put on his hooded sweat jacket and walked outside to Frankie's room. The door was unlocked. Frank, showered and dressed, was lying on his bed watching Good Morning America.

"Guess we were both tired," Frankie said.

"I'm hungry. Let's get some chow."

They drove and quickly found a place that served hearty North Woods type breakfasts suitable for lumberjacks. They each consumed a day's worth of fat and calories and went back to the Mustang.

They sat and smoked cigarettes and watched the parade of people go to eateries and pricey clothing stores and scented candle shops.

"We stay up here long enough we're gonna end up more wholesome than old L.L.Bean himself," Frankie said. "Was he a real person?"

"I don't know."

"Okay, so what's it gonna be?" Frankie asked.

Chug flicked his cigarette out the window and looked at the snow bank, crusty and blackened with road grime.

"Come on, Chuggy. You with me?"

"No, Frankie, I'm gonna sit this out. Maybe I'll head back. Catch a train or bus back home."

"Goddamnit, Chug, you talked me into coming up here. I wanted to go to Florida, someplace nice. But, no, I come up here 'cause we're buds, we're in this together, I thought. You were right about one thing, though. Was you who shot Will Scarlet's mother. Not me. I'm in this mess because of you. I had a brain, I'd kiss your ass good-bye."

Frankie started the Mustang. "I'll drop you back at the motel. If you're there when I get back, fine. If you're not, that's fine too."

Frankie pulled out and headed back. Chug lit another cigarette, took a deep drag and said, "Okay, Frank. I'll come along for the ride. One time."

They drove south from North Conway for a while and then headed east toward Maine. Snow was piled high beside the roads, which themselves were bare. Beside the road was a stream, still partially frozen but the ribbon at the center was flowing fast, bouncing around rocks and looking cold. The mountains in the background were snowy and the scene reminded Chug of a beer ad.

They were on a clear, straight stretch, an undivided four-lane, when well ahead a squirrel skipped across the road. Frankie downshifted and stepped hard on the gas. The nose of the Mustang lifted as it shot ahead toward the squirrel which had stopped about ten feet from the snow bank. Chug saw the squirrel start to move again and then lost it as they zipped past the spot where it had been.

"Missed it," Frankie said, checking the rearview. A little smile played around his lips as the Mustang continued to accelerate.

Chug reached over and grabbed his arm.

"Slow it, Frankie. Bring it down to the limit right now."

Frankie looked at him, didn't like what he saw, and slowed down to sixty-five.

"Is something wrong with you? You got a brain in your head," Chug said. "We're both trying to maintain a low profile, we're both carrying, and you're driving this thing like you're sixteen years old. What are you planning to say to some Statie when he pulls you over? Or will you try to outrun him?"

They drove about forty minutes without seeing more than a half dozen houses. They passed no stores or gas stations. They knew they were finally in Maine when a Maine State Police car passed the other way. Frankie followed it in the mirror until it disappeared.

After another ten minutes, they crossed some railroad tracks and came into a cluster of houses, passed a lumber mill, a Texaco station and a little town of about five stores, one of which was a small variety store.

Frankie trolled by slowly. "What do you think?"

"Looks like they do about twenty bucks all day. Tell me something. You're not planning on using this, are you?" Chug said, tapping the Mustang's dashboard.

"Let's look around for something," Frankie said.

He continued his slow troll through town, past a few more scattered houses which quickly thinned to open fields and then snow-filled woods. They passed a one-floor cottage of peeling paint and general deterioration set back from the road about a hundred feet. A Subaru Outback, a few years old, was parked in the driveway back toward the road.

"That looks good," Frankie said. "You can see down the road in both directions about a quarter mile."

"You gonna be able to start that?"

Frankie patted his pocket. "I came prepared. But what if someone's home?"

"Knock on the door and if they answer just ask directions."

"To where?"

"Anywhere. Tahiti. Jesus, Frank."

"Calm down, Chuggy."

Chug watched Frankie walk to the Outback, quickly check it out, and then go to the house.

Chug could smell wood smoke and then saw it curling from a shiny metal chimney running up the side of the house. A woodpile was partly covered with a blue plastic tarp. Around the house were some barrels, a couple tipped and spilling. A bird feeder swayed from the branch of a tree and birds flew from it at Frankie's approach.

Frankie climbed two stairs to the front door and pushed the bell. After maybe thirty seconds he gave it a couple more pushes, waited another pause and then pounded on the door. Then he walked around to the back of the house and peeked in couple of windows.

He came back to the Mustang.

"I'll get in that Subaru and start it. Anyone comes, beep the horn and I'll walk out like I had been asking for directions. If it's alarmed, I should be able to kill it, but there's no one close by anyway so I don't think there'll be a problem."

Frankie took off his gloves and rubbed his hands together to warm them.

"I'll start it and you follow. We'll drop the 'stang, hit that variety store, then back to the 'stang."

Frankie went back to the Outback and opened the door. He looked back at Chug and smiled. "Sucker's not even locked."

Frank ducked into the Outback. His head disappeared for a few seconds and Chug looked up and down the road. Then he looked at the house, half expecting to see some hayseed come out the door with a shotgun. If that happened, he wondered what he'd do. Help Frankie or gun the Mustang and leave Frank behind. No, that wouldn't work. Frankie, if caught, Chug had no doubt would finger him and he wouldn't blame him. He pondered this and then after a minute or two he heard the Outback's engine start.

Frankie pulled from the driveway and Chug followed.

They drove back through the little town, past the variety store, Chug not really liking any of this, half expecting someone to wave at the Subaru thinking old Jeb or Ebenezer was behind the wheel then seeing Frankie, looking Italian and big city, and screaming for the sheriff or whatever kind of hick police they had up here.

But there was no one around to give the Outback a second glance.

They drove about a mile before Frankie pulled into a little rest area.

"We'll leave the 'stang here," he said when he came up to Chug.

"Frankie, I don't think this is too smart." Chug eyed a bumper sticker on the Outback. I'D RATHER BE BOWLING.

"Yeah? Why's that?"

"We leave this here, some Statie rides by and is checking it out just when we come back. Could happen, you know. Then what? Oh, excuse us officer, we're in a hurry because we just knocked over a little variety store back there in East Dunghole, but it really doesn't count because all we got was seven dollars and thirty-two cents. Oh, plus, we took a box of Twinkies. Here, my man, here's a Twinkie for looking the other way."

"So where do you want to leave it?"

Chug thought about it, let out a stream of air, and shrugged. "Guess this'll have to do."

"Okay, pull back as far as you can. Just don't get the tires in the snow or we'll never get out."

Before he got in the Subaru, Chug went to the rear bumper and pulled the bumper sticker off. It came off in pieces and he had to work at it for a few seconds, his fingers getting cold.

They rode back to the variety store, Chug at the wheel. He drove past the store, did a U-turn, came back and pulled up in front. There was still no one about. Chug was thinking the seven dollar thirty-two cent haul might have been an over estimate.

Frankie pulled a ski mask from his pocket that he bought in North Conway. "I'll go in, keep my face from them while I check things out and then put this on."

Chug watched him walk to the store and then looked at his watch. He sat and waited and thought of Ellie. Waves of guilt washed over him. He waited some more. He checked his watch again. About five minutes since Frankie went into the store.

A pickup truck drove by in the direction they had found the Subaru, the driver giving him the once over. He watched the truck in the mirror, saw it slow and then pull over and stop about a hundred yards down the road.

He looked back at the door to the variety store and then in the mirror again at the truck.

It made a U-turn and headed back toward him just as Frankie came out of the store.

Frankie got in and said, "Move it."

Chug took off at a normal clip. "Slow and easy's the way, Frank. You don't have a posse after you."

He checked the mirror again. The truck was about a hundred feet behind, going their speed.

Frankie said, "You want to know what happened?"

"Tell me."

"I think we did all right. We'll count it later. One old guy in there. He was real good. Practically messed his pants."

Chug thought of his father. He wondered if they were letting him wear his pants at the nursing home.

"I told him not to go near the phone for five minutes."

"Oh, you told him and you think he won't."

"He was practically crying."

Chug checked the mirror again. The truck was still about a hundred feet behind. He jerked his thumb backward. "I think we picked up some company."

He told Frankie how the driver had eyed him and made a U-turn to follow.

"Pull over and see what he does."

Chug pulled to the side of the road and stopped. They looked back. The truck stopped, paused a moment and then did a quick turnaround and sped back the way it had come.

"He's going for the cops," Chug said. "Good thing there's probably no cell phone reception around here."

They watched the truck disappear then made it back to the Mustang, sitting by itself, nothing in sight.

Chug spread the road map on his lap as Frankie now drove, careful to stay about two miles over the limit.

"We've gotta get off this road, Frank. They'll be watching it in both directions, especially this way. There's a left coming up here. Take it. It goes through a couple of small towns and then hits a road that'll get us back to North Conway."

Frank took the left, a narrow, winding country lane, thick woods on both sides. At a straightaway, clear in both directions a couple of hundred yards, Chug said, "Pull over."

He pulled the nine-millimeter from his jacket pocket.

"Let's have yours, Frank."

"Cut it out, Chug."

"Come on, Frank. We can't be stupid. We've gotta dump these. If we're stopped . . ."

"Chug, we didn't just rob Brinks. They're gonna look but this isn't that big a deal."

"We're not in the big city, Frank. They probably go nuts when there's a rabid raccoon on the loose up here. Come on, give me your gun."

"Frank handed him his gun, a nice Browning nine-millimeter, a little too easily Chug thought. He figured he probably had a backup at the motel.

Chug wiped down both weapons and got out of the car. He looked in both directions on the road, and one at a time threw each gun into the woods where they sank into the snow.

The roundabout route added an hour to their time and they got back to the motel in the early afternoon. They counted the money in Frankie's room.

Six twenties, nine tens, seven fives and sixteen ones.

"Two-hundred-sixty-one bucks," Frankie said. "One-thirty-fifty apiece."

He counted some bills and handed them to Chug. "Here. I owe you half a buck."

Chug took them and stared at them a moment before putting them into his pocket.

"I gotta take a leak," Frankie said, "then we'll get something to eat."

Chug nodded and sat on the bed while Frankie went into the bathroom. One-hundred-thirty dollars and fifty cents and one very frightened old man. He had never felt more stupid in his life.

Chapter Sixteen

Lieutenant Billy Wilkins was thinking how nice it would be to kill two birds with one stone. He had even doodled two stick-figure birds on a little pad on his desk and put Xs over their eyes.

There were some problems, though. How to do it at all was the major one, of course, but assuming that it could be worked out, there remained the difficulty of killing little bird without screwing up the chance of getting big bird.

Big bird was getting Will Scarlet in the act of being the death angel swooping down on his mother's tormentor. Here, there was maybe a problem within a problem: the main character in all this drama hadn't shown up yet. True, it had been only a couple of days since he let the word out. Ryan Donovan told him that his snitch, Mink Whitehead, had contacted the guy. Wilkins wondered whether Will Scarlet had already gotten to him.

Or maybe the guy saw the scheme for the nonsense it was. What was it Jessup had said? "That screwed up bust mess up your mind?" No question that the failed bust bothered him. Maybe he wasn't thinking straight. Still, in the end Jessup had gone along. Sort of. Never flat out said he was in. Playing his cards close to the vest.

Billy Wilkins looked at his doodle again.

Assuming this person *hasn't* been run through a garbage disposal piece by piece by Will Scarlet, and assuming he makes contact, Wilkins thought, little bird would be to somehow use this guy to get Ramon Mendez and the boys.

Which was just what that little snitch C. Trevor Whitehead had originally suggested. It was a stupid idea, it could screw up the larger objective, and he shouldn't even think about it, Wilkins knew. But it was intriguing.

He imagined himself on a cable cop show or, maybe, if it all worked out, he could write a book about it, like *Serpico*. A few details might have to be altered to protect certain people, like himself, but it could be done.

He thought of an early retirement to a life of ease. Maybe he could even go back South and get away from the pain in the ass Boston winters and the irritating Boston accent.

Before he could do that, though, he'd have to sell the charms of Georgia to his South Boston wife whom he met when he was stationed at Fort Devens and who was still in love with her girlhood neighborhood and who still clung, he thought, to her mother too much.

He drew a circle around one of the birds on his doodle pad and then a circle around the other bird. Then he drew a line that connected the two circles.

He brought his mind back to Whitehead's original idea,

Ramon, Philippe, and the snake brothers—Wilkins clenched his teeth as he thought of *them*—had mainly supplied several of the Boston area colleges with drugs. Both students and professors.

Would Ramon and company be interested in expanding, let's say to U-Mass Amherst, or into southern New Hampshire? Mink Whitehead had said that the shooter was a known user and buyer. No need to establish a cover in that regard. But the problem was that he was small-time. So, even though it wouldn't make sense for a small fish to make a big buy, what if he could be presented as a go between?

Billy Wilkins doodled some aimless lines around his dead birds and concentrated. He fashioned some ideas, some links, and thought they might be made to work. Hell, the months he had spent getting close to Ramon and Philippe had gone down the toilet. That goddamn Philippe had gotten onto him somehow.

So maybe something quick and simple would work.

But . . . the main thing was to net Will Scarlet.

But before he could do anything he had to make contact with whoever it was that shot Will Scarlet's mother.

Billy Wilkins doodled some whirls and swirls, wrote the word Georgia a couple of times, then crumpled the paper and chucked it into his basket.

Entering the dark silence of the booth triggered a wash of recollections and feelings. Chug wasn't sure how long it had been since his last Confession. At least ten years. The last time he had been inside a church was at his mother's funeral.

Frankie was back at the motel watching game shows on TV and Chug had taken the Mustang to pick up some chow: subs, chips, and some cake or cookies. Frankie had a bit of a sweet tooth and was partial to various Oreos.

Chug could hear the person on the other side of the Confessional and tried not to listen. He had seen her go in, an old lady wearing a kerchief.

He breathed in the church smell. Bless me, Father, for I have sinned. I'm not sure how long it's been since my last Confession, except that it's been a long time. And here are my sins. Where do I begin?

He remembered the profound innocence of boyhood confessions. I lost my temper three times, I swore ten times, I had impure thoughts many times. Hard to put a number on that. For your penance say five Our Fathers and five Hail Marys. Now make a good Act of Contrition.

"Did you go to Confession?" his mother would ask.

"Of course," he would say.

His mother would rub his head, mussing his hair.

"Tomorrow, you go to Communion and you'll be in a perfect state of grace."

Then she would kiss him and say, "And if, God forbid, you should drown or get hit by a car or something, you'll go straight to Heaven."

He could hear the priest absolving the old lady on the other side of the Confessional of her sins. Chug wondered what kind of sins she could possibly have. If she dropped dead now, she'd go to heaven. Or did she have to receive Communion first? Someone could do her the biggest favor of her life by shooting her dead right now. Send her to heaven. You'd think that would be a good thing to do. Send someone to heaven. But it would be a sin, not to mention a crime.

Chug wondered whether Florence Scarlata had been in a state of grace when he shot her. She probably was now. A priest was sure to visit her in the hospital.

The priest was finishing and Chug felt the Confessional closing in on him and the futility of talking to anyone, even a priest, about what he had done. He felt guilt but mainly he felt stupidity.

Absolution was not to be found here in this box talking to a stranger. He pulled the curtain aside and stepped out at the same time as the old lady on the other side.

He drove back past the partially frozen stream with the snowy mountains in the background, past the scattering of houses. He crossed the railroad tracks, drove past the lumber mill and Texaco station. He parked across from the variety store and felt in his pocket for the envelope he had filled with two-hundred and sixty-one dollars.

He crossed the street and went into the store. He looked around and saw a couple of kids thumbing through the magazines but no other customers. He pulled a large bag of chips and a package of Double Stuff Oreos off a shelf and went to the counter.

"Do you sell submarine sandwiches?" he asked the old guy seated by the register.

The old guy looked up at him through tri-focal glasses. "Just already prepared ones. They're over there behind the sliding glass."

As Chug looked at the selection of subs, from the corner of his eye he noticed one of the kids slide a magazine under his coat. He stared at the kid hard and shook his head. The kid stared back, gaze defiant, then quickly yielding. He mouthed something at Chug and then with his friend did a hard guy swagger from the store.

Chug picked out a couple of subs and came back to the old man. He put his subs, chips, and Oreos on the counter. He looked at the old guy as he rang it up. He felt like talking to him, maybe saying something friendly or comforting but couldn't think of anything that wouldn't sound stupid. Lottery scratch tickets hung in rows to the old guy's left and behind him.

Chug paid for the groceries, handed him a twenty and said, "Give me twenty one-dollar tickets, please."

When the man turned from him and reached over to count the tickets, Chug took the envelope from his pocket, leaned over the counter and dropped it on the chair.

"I can put this thing on automatic pilot," Sal the Dogcatcher Manfredi said. He took both hands off the Denali's steering wheel and folded his arms across his chest to demonstrate. They were on a short straightaway beating a path from Chug's place in Southie to Ellie's place in Charlestown.

"You can put your hands back on the wheel, is what you can do," Mickey the Harp said. He was in no mood to banter. Anger and frustration clenched his teeth. But fear was maybe even stronger and it clutched his stomach.

He was angry and frustrated that he couldn't find this Chug guy and also frustrated that Lou Russo wouldn't let him try to find him through the broad.

"You go to the broad and what's she gonna do first thing you're gone? She's gonna warn him. It don't take an Einstein to figure that," Lou had said.

"So what do you do to stop her? You gonna snuff her? That ain't smart."

Mickey the Harp was confident he could get what he wanted to know from the broad and at the same time make her realize it would behoove her not to make any phone calls or anything like that. That would be the word he'd use, too. *Behoove.* It had a nice sound to it and she'd know he wasn't some dumb schmuck wop you could say things to you didn't mean.

If Lou Russo was partly the source of his frustration, he was also partly the source of his fear. The other source, of course, was William Scarlata. If he didn't get this guy pretty soon, Lou Russo was going to be mega pissed off, William Scarlata was going to be mega pissed off, and Mickey the Harp might have to look for honest work someplace that hired the handicapped.

So back and forth he and Sal went, from checking out Chug's place to checking out his girlfriend's.

Just yesterday morning, when she was at work, they had gone inside to check out her place. It had been a bit tougher to get into than Chug's was. She had a dead bolt. It was Mickey's experience that most broads living alone did. It took a while and they scratched up around the door a little but the door and the frame were stained rather than painted and they came back with some scratch hider and did a pretty good job.

She was very cute, judging from the framed picture of a guy and a chick on the dresser in her bedroom. The guy—had to be Chug, unless the picture was of a sister and brother-in-law or something—looked fairly rugged but nothing Mickey couldn't handle.

It was interesting checking out a chick's place, seeing what she had. Going through her drawers, as it were.

In the bathroom, they had found his and her toothbrushes and birth control pills, which were to Mickey among the more interesting things.

The apartment was neat and clean. She was good looking and wife material too. Kept a nice place. Mickey wondered if she could cook.

Some books and notebooks on real estate. Mickey thumbed through them. He wouldn't want to sell homes or anything else, for that matter. Had to paste on the big phony smile and spill out a line.

There were a couple of closets and Mickey checked them out carefully.

They had left, making sure that everything was put back where it had been. It seemed obvious that the guy wasn't staying here and he wasn't staying at his own place.

So where the hell was he? Mickey knew that if he were this guy he'd have gotten his ass a long way from Boston and William Scarlata. But the thing was his South Boston source said Chug had been seen around, at least two or three days ago.

They pulled over and took position across from Ellie's and about four houses down. It was still cold out enough that Sal kept the engine and heater running.

"Where you think the guy is, Mick?" You think he took off to Florida or Arizona someplace?"

Mickey the Harp rubbed his jaw and tried to look wise. It wasn't all that hard to feel smart sometimes when you were with Sal.

"I don't think he's that far, Sal. Matter of fact, I bet he's not far at all. Something else, too. I think he's coming back right here soon."

"Yeah? Why's that?"

"Some of his clothes are in her closet."

He thought of the photo of the couple on the dresser. You couldn't tell for sure from a photo, but they both looked in love.

"Plus," Mickey said, "she uses birth control pills. Looks like she's right up to date. Maybe she's fooling around but somehow she don't seem the type."

Mickey put his head back. "So we'll wait, Sallie. I figure pretty soon either he'll come here or she'll lead us to him."

Chug called Ellie's cell phone from Beverly Depot, which was a restaurant as well as a train station about twenty miles north of Boston. She had just gotten home from work.

He had eaten his sub and chips with Frankie and told him he was going back. "I made a mess, Frankie, and I've gotta handle it. Mainly, I have to square things with Ellie."

He had figured on a bus trip back but was able to hook up with a couple of college kids going as far south as Beverly.

She seemed less frosty as she talked with him and for a moment, as he watched couples eat, bent over red meat and red wine, making intimate conversation, he entertained the idea of asking her to meet him here.

But then she said something that drove out the image of prime rib and a bottle of wine.

He got the next train to Boston and the last thing he told her before he hung up was to be extra careful.

She was waiting on Causeway Street in the Passat. When he got in, they said Hi and kissed quickly.

"I'm not positive," she said, continuing what she had told him on the phone, "but I'm pretty sure. Some things looked like they weren't put back quite right. It's possible it's my imagination, that I'm just looking for things like that."

"Nothing missing?"

"No. I checked carefully."

They were stopped at a light and when it changed she said, "Where should I go?"

"I don't know. Just drive."

Chug swiveled around and checked behind them but saw only headlights.

"Don't go to your place yet. Maybe just drive by it."

Ellie drove to Charlestown, past the Bunker Hill Monument and then past her place.

"Now what?"

"I don't know. Let me think."

"In the meantime, are you going to tell me where you've been? It couldn't have been far."

"It wasn't. I don't think it would matter where I went. Look, Ellie, I was worried about you by yourself and I'm worried that being with you may not be such a hot idea for you either. So, if I have to pick one, I figure I'd rather be around you."

He looked at her. "But I guess I'm still not figuring in how you feel."

She said nothing. They were on Rutherford Avenue now heading west.

"Want to go to your place?" she asked.

"Can't do that either."

"What are we going to do, Chug, ride around the rest of our lives?"

Headlights glared close from behind. Chug swiveled and saw something large—an SUV—start to pull beside them.

"Head for the bridge," Chug said. "Run the light."

Ellie looked to her right and saw the large shape trying to force her into some Jersey barriers. The light for the left turn to the Mystic River Bridge was red but she ran it causing a Dodge Caravan to nosedive.

She rowed the Passat's gears skillfully as she accelerated into the long term.

Chug looked to the rear. Their pursuer was wallowing around the turn, unable to match their pace.

Ellie rocketed down through the tunnel and then up the bridge over seventy but on the straightaway the SUV was coming up fast.

"Slow down a little, Ellie. Let' em almost catch up and then take the off-ramp to Chelsea. Don't get in the right hand lane. Wait 'til the last second to make the turn."

Chug hoped she'd be able to judge how fast she could go into the turn and not lose control.

They were moving down the hill about sixty with the SUV almost on them. The cut-off to Chelsea was just ahead.

At the last minute, Ellie hit the brakes and pulled hard to the right and they slewed close to the guardrail on their left.

Chug watched the SUV shoot past the turn and caught its brake lights flash as it tried to slow.

"He'll back up. Just get off the bridge and get lost." Chug felt his throat pulse and heard his voice, loud and strained. He thought of the Colt he had thrown into the snow.

They got off the bridge and, for a few minutes as she drove, he thought they were home free until he saw headlights coming up fast. Ellie saw them too, downshifted to third, and punched the gas.

"Don't try to outrun him, Ellie. Out dodge him. Let him get up close and then take a quick left or right."

The SUV was less than a hundred feet back now. Ellie watched it in the rearview and when it got close she timed oncoming traffic and sharply cut across it to a side street on her left. The SUV pulled over to the right and nose-dived to a stop. Chug saw it U-turn, bulling its way through traffic on both sides.

They sped down the side street, the Passat's engine revving willingly.

"Take that left coming up. Quick." Chug checked behind as Ellie fishtailed around the corner. Too late. The SUV's headlights, on brights, were stabbing the darkness and sliced across the Passat's rear window just as they turned.

Ellie ran two intersections, barely pausing at each, and took the third left as the SUV gained, getting close enough for its lights to bounce up and down on the Passat's dash and headliner.

Ahead, traffic was stopped at the lights. Ellie squeezed between the line of stopped cars and oncoming traffic. She paused at the lights and then forced her way through the crisscross traffic to the scream of horns and tires.

Chug looked behind and saw the relentless SUV taking advantage of the path Ellie had created.

At fifty, Ellie up shifted to fourth but wasn't losing the SUV.

"Chug, what should I do? I can't lose him." Ellie's voice and face were tight.

Chug was considering telling her to stop so that he could get out. They were after him, not her. As he thought about it, the idea gained merit. On foot, he stood a better chance of losing them than if he stayed with the car.

Ahead, on the right, a strip mall glowed. That was the chance.

"Pull into the mall. I'll get out. You keep going. Don't go home. Go to one of your girlfriend's. Debbie's or Laurie's. I'll call you later."

Almost tipping, she spun into the mall but she shook her head as if to argue. Behind them, the SUV bounced in appearing to Chug as he watched to almost bottom at the dip. It was close and he'd have to get out on the fly.

He was about to say, Slow down and then get out of here, when he saw the police cruiser. It was parked ahead at a donut shop. A police car never looked so good. He pointed to it and Ellie nodded.

She ran through the rows of parked cars, brushing back bulge-eyed shoppers. When she skidded close to the cruiser and stopped, she leaned on her horn and flashed her brights at the two cops sitting inside the donut shop hunched over coffees.

Behind them, the SUV stopped when it caught up, paused for a few seconds' assessment like a predatory animal deciding whether to close for the kill, and then jack rabbited away.

Chapter Seventeen

Chug would have known him to be a cop as soon as he walked into the bar even if he hadn't been told to watch for a guy wearing an Atlanta Brave's cap. He had cop written all over him despite the plain clothes: corduroy pants, ankle-high boots, a windbreaker, and the baseball cap with the letter A on it. It was the way he looked around, the way he carried himself that cops have.

Chug was on a stool at the bar. He gave a little signal with his hand and Billy Wilkins walked over and sat beside him.

"Bobby?" Wilkins said.

Chug nodded, looked at Wilkins a moment, sizing him up. He was about six feet and pretty well built, tough-looking face, weather-beaten, with deep vertical grooves running down on each side of his mouth. Sandy hair was parted on the left. He could have been in a cowboy movie.

Chug said, "If we're gonna talk, I think we should go someplace else."

Billy Wilkins nodded. "That makes sense but, you know, I'm kind of thirsty. How about that corner booth? No one will hear a thing we say."

He got a couple of draft beers and they moved to the booth and sat facing each other.

"First off, I'm gonna say up front that what I hear sounds like a crock to me," Chug said. "I think someone's yanking my chain but I gotta take a chance. My back's to the wall."

"Yeah, I'd say it is," Billy Wilkins said.

"Oh, by the way, can I see some ID, a badge or something."

Billy Wilkins showed Chug his badge and then a Boston Police Department ID with his picture.

"Okay?"

"Yeah, the ID looks okay but I don't get it. This Mink guy spun a story that to me doesn't add. I want to hear you say it."

"Glad to. Credit Mink Whitehead, by the way. It was his idea from the start. Tell you the truth, at first it made no sense but when I thought about it I figured it could be made to work, with modifications."

"What kind of modifications?"

"See, Bobby, I think we need to put everything on the table here. Find out exactly what Mink told you and then what I have in mind. But, first, back to Mink for a second. He found out who you were. I don't know if you know it, but Will Scarlet put a pretty good price on your head. Mink could've collected but instead came to us."

Chug looked at his beer a moment and then at Billy Wilkins.

"There are a few things I don't get. One, let's say after I hear what you say I don't go along? You're not just going to let me walk out of here. I mean you're a cop and I . . . at least you have reason to think that I . . ."

"This is about trust, Bobby. This is good that we're meeting like this."

"Okay, but what I also don't get is—how can I put it?—the trade off. According to Mink, you can set me up with a new ID and relocation, all things that could look pretty good right now. But, for what, a little help in some kind of drug bust? Doesn't seem like the kind of thing that would be done, especially for someone involved in what you think I was involved in. To be honest, I smell something that doesn't smell too good."

"Well, I said a minute ago, let's put our cards on the table."

"Good idea. But something else first. You're not wired by any chance, are you?"

Billy Wilkins stood, removed his windbreaker and handed it to Chug. "Check it out."

Then he patted himself down and said, "You want to go in the men's room, I'm willing."

Chug handed him the jacket.

"Okay. Cards on the table. I told you what Whitehead told me. I didn't get too many particulars, though. So I want to hear what you've got to say, especially those modifications."

Billy Wilkins took a taste of his beer and then smiled at Chug.

"Okay, Bobby, I put a lot of time into busting up a gang that's supplying high quality stuff, coke mainly, in all its variations, but actually they handle a lot of heroin too, to college students in and around Boston. Of which, needless to say, there are many.

"These guys are no good and I thought I had them. There was supposed to be a big buy but at the last minute it soured and my cover was blown."

"What was your cover?"

"I was a cop on the take, on their payroll. I was the guy who would tip them to any police activity that might interfere with their plans, who kept them from taking a fall."

"But they got onto you. How?"

"That I'm not sure of, Bobby. One of them is a real shrewdie, though."

"Call me Chug. No one calls me Bobby."

"Chug? Why do they call you that?"

Chug picked up his beer glass, put it to his mouth and flicked his wrist. "I chug fast," he said when he put his glass down.

"Jesus," Billy Wilkins said, "that's slicker'n shit down the toilet. If you were a baseball pitcher that'd be a one-fifty mile an hour fastball."

"Yeah, and I'd be making twenty mil a year instead of being the shit that might go down the toilet."

"Twenty mil easy. Where'd you learn how to do that?"

Chug shook his head. "You know, keg parties, things like that. We'd have chugging contests. I practiced a lot. That's just one of the productive ways I spent my youth. I mean, I could have gone to college—well, maybe a community college—or gone into the military but I had my priorities. I set my sights high and became a world-class chugger, a real career path, you know what I mean?"

Billy Wilkins nodded. "Aw, what the hell. We all do stuff. What's that expression about youth being wasted on the young?"

"I think that *is* the expression. But I gotta tell you, I did worse than just waste my time practicing this useless skill."

"I won't lie to you," Billy Wilkins said. "I know all about it. I ran a quick check on you. But, I'll say this, you're minor league as far as a rap sheet goes, if that's any comfort. Hell, probation. Not the best thing on a resume, but it's small potatoes."

"Yeah, minor league. *Until.*"

"Yeah. Speaking of, want to tell me who was in on that with you?"

"In on what?"

"Yeah, okay. Stupid me. But I had to ask."

"You know better."

"Worth a try. But, anyway, back to what we were talking about. Mink Whitehead comes to me and says he knows who shot Will Scarlet's mother. He says this guy's probably pretty desperate to get away from Scarlet and would be willing to do anything within reason to get set up in a deal similar to witness protection."

"This is bullshit," Chug said. "Witness protection's Federal, though, right? And it's for turning information against major crime figures from everything I've heard. Not for helping out with some drug bust."

"Hear me out. The key here is *similar* to witness protection. Basically the same provisions. It can be done."

"How's that different from someone just taking off on their own? Changing their name?"

"Well, just one example," Billy Wilkins said. "What about a Social Security number? How are you gonna do that on your own? You can't get by without one."

Billy Wilkins took a long pull on his beer. It tasted very bitter.

"I still don't get where I come in."

"Well, Mink tells me this person who shot Will Scarlet's mother is a known user and buyer on his own. That true, Chug? No offense, but you do some recreational using?"

Chug shrugged his shoulders.

"Mink figures that's the in you have to these guys I was trying to bust. Problem is, though, you're too small time so I figure you've got to be a go between. That's the modification. You're going to know someone with deep pockets who wants a lot of stuff for college students out in the western part of the state or in southern New Hampshire. Not all that complicated, actually. Keep it simple is the way to go."

Billy Wilkins took another pull on his beer. "Of course, there's no such person with deep pockets but it will never get that far. That's about it. What do you think?"

"I think you're full of shit."

"Sorry you feel that way, Chug."

"But, you're here and you haven't cuffed me on suspicion and armed robbery and assault with a deadly weapon so maybe I have to give you some kind of benefit of the doubt."

"The fact that you're here talking with me means you've already done that."

"Still, you know, I think I'm going to need something more official. At police headquarters with the police commissioner present. Statements made, guarantees given. That kind of thing."

"That's later. Right now, we're just setting things up. You don't want too many people knowing what's going on. Not even cops. Somebody says something, an innocent comment, not meaning anything, and things get screwed up."

Billy Wilkins gently punched Chug's forearm resting on the table. "You want another beer, Chug?"

Chug shook his head.

"Mink says that when you called him you seemed pretty upset and wanted to meet with me right away. Here in Chelsea, of all places. Mind telling me why?"

Chug told him of the chase over the bridge.

"When they saw the cruiser, they took off. I told the cops I didn't know who it was, just some guys harassing us, a case of road rage.

"I told Ellie to go to a girlfriend's. We maintained cell contact 'til she got there with no one following her. I walked over to this bar from the strip mall, called Mink, who called you. And here we are."

"And here we are."

"Tell me something," Chug said. "How come the Braves hat?"

"I'm from Georgia originally."

"The Braves are from Boston originally. Long before my time, though."

"I know that, Chug."

"Thought I picked up a little touch of Southern accent."

"Been here a while. Lost a lot of it. Now it's a South *Boston* accent."

"Cut it out. I'm from Southie."

Billy Wilkins picked up his beer glass and made a little toasting gesture with it.

"Okay, Chug, the thing now is for me to get things set up all around including making sure you're satisfied. In the meantime you gotta go someplace where you're safe. Got any ideas on that?"

"The Lynn Elks. I've got a buddy in Lynn who can put me up at the Elks there. I've done it in the past. Any chance of a lift?"

Billy Wilkins gave Chug a ride to the Lynn Elks. On the way, Chug called his friend to set it up.

As Chug got out of the unmarked Crown Victoria, Billy Wilkins said, "Chug, in case you need to get a hold of me, I'll give you my cell number. It might be a good idea if you gave me yours too, if you don't mind."

He handed Chug a piece of paper from a pad on the dash and a pen.

He took the paper back from Chug and said, "Hang in there. Things could happen fast."

As he drove back to Boston, Billy Wilkins thought about the wrinkle he had hoped wouldn't happen: that Will Scarlet would ID who had shot his mother. Of course, it *was* possible that whoever had chased Chug and his girl over the Mystic River Bridge wasn't connected to Will Scarlet, that it *was* a case of road rage, but the chances of that were as likely as the Braves coming back to Boston.

Still, it wasn't a fatal flaw by any means. Fatal to his plans, anyway. As far as Chug was concerned, any number of contingencies could prove fatal.

Too bad. The guy was kind of likeable. He was no dummy. He most definitely smelled a rat but the situation he had gotten himself into made him clutch at any straw that might give him an out.

Billy Wilkins thought that maybe he should forget about Ramon Mendez. Forget Philippe. Forget the snake brothers, forget killing two birds with one stone and just concentrate on using Chug to net Will Scarlet. Maybe he would.

But there was till time to think that out a little. He just had to be careful not to lose the stone, one Bobby 'Chug' Ellis, while he was planning.

He thought of Chug swilling the beer as fast as you could pour it down the drain. Hell of a talent. Too bad it wasn't marketable.

Chapter Eighteen

"I hear you went to college," Billy Wilkins said.

C. Trevor Whitehead nodded. They were sitting in Billy Wilkins's office.

"Where?"

"B.U. It's a factory."

"Ryan Donovan says you know a lot of people in the local college circles. As well as other circles."

"I've got a broad perspective," C. Trevor Whitehead said.

Billy Wilkins nodded. "That's going to be the connection. If you'll help out."

"I don't have a clue to what you're talking about."

"Sure you do. Our mutual friend is willing to cooperate. A tip of the hat to you, by the way." Billy Wilkins could tell that C. Trevor Whitehead was glowing a little inside from the praise.

He stoked the fire a little. "I would really be obligated if, as I say, you could help out a little. No risk to you, I want you to know."

"I'm all ears, man. So far you haven't said a thing, though, except to pat me on the head."

"The drug bust that went south involved the guys that supply the Boston area colleges. That includes the big schools where a lot of people are sucking up a whole lot of stuff besides Shakespeare and pi r square. That translates to a big market. Students and faculty. I don't mean they supply directly. They supply the dealers."

"Easy to follow so far," C. Trevor said. "Hey, you mind if I borrow one of your smokes?"

He helped himself to Billy Wilkins's open pack of Marlboros.

"What I got in mind is that these guys open some new territory. Out west, maybe. Amherst area. There's what, four or five colleges out there?" Billy Wilkins said as he grabbed a Marlboro too.

"Or the North Shore area, maybe even southern New Hampshire."

Mink Whitehead nodded. "So, like where do I come in?"

"Okay. What I need is somebody definitely connected to the college scene. A student, a professor, even a former student. It can't be you because it's too high a chance that you're known to occasionally cooperate with the cops."

"Where's our boy come in? The shooter."

"He's going to be the one who knows an entrepreneur who'd like to market the goodies to the academics in a brand new territory. He can't be the entrepreneur because he's already known as a small-time buyer and user."

"So you want me to supply someone who could be the entrepreneur?"

"No. I want you to supply someone who could be the connection between the guys I'm after and our boy. Calls himself Chug, by the way. Did you know that?"

Mink Whitehead blew a stream of smoke at the ceiling. "The guys you're after. Are they Mob?"

"No."

"I don't get it. I thought the Mob controlled all that kind of traffic."

158

"Things are changing. They control a lot, maybe most, but definitely not all. They'd like to"

"They must be pissed at these other guys."

"Pissed? Yeah. I'd say they're pissed."

"Why don't they do something?"

"Like what? Drive by and spray them with Tommy guns like the old movies? Things have changed. These new guys are tough and fight back, for one thing."

"Spics?"

Billy Wilkins shrugged. "Probably could call them spics. See, if you can supply someone, I'll set him up with one of the distributors that the guys I'm after use."

"Sure sounds like a lot of go-betweens before you get to who you want," Mink Whitehead said.

"That's the way it is. Makes things seem more authentic and it's harder for them to trace back. I need that go-between. It's too risky for our boy to make direct contact."

"Jeez, I don't know. I mean, you're the cop, but this whole thing seems like, what's the expression, a house of cards."

Billy Wilkins blew some smoke. C. Trevor Whitehead blew some smoke.

Billy Wilkins said, "Hey, it's never easy and it often doesn't work. But you try. You came to me with a guy in trouble and an idea. I appreciate that. Time isn't exactly on our side. Remember, if Will Scarlet gets hold of this guy, it's all over. So what I got in mind is a quick shot. What the hell, give it a go. Nothing ventured, nothing gained."

"But this guy Chug will be taken care of, win or lose?"

"Best we can." Like you give a rat's ass, Billy Wilkins thought.

"So what do you think? Do you know someone who could be the go-between? They'd do very little and there'd be no risk. I'd put them in touch with one of the bad guys' distributors. Mainly, I just want someone who's got some kind of real connection to college people. They'd check that far,"

C. Trevor Whitehead nodded.

"I can give you some time but not much. Like I say, we don't have forever."

"No need," C. Trevor said. "I think I know just the guy."

When C. Trevor Whitehead had left, Billy Wilkins sat and doodled the two birds he wanted to kill with one stone. He thought of Mink Whitehead's question about the Mob being pissed with anyone who might intrude into what was traditionally their business. He smiled a little as he thought how, if things worked out, Will Scarlet would think he was the one killing two birds with one stone.

Even though the weather had finally warmed a little, Tilly Tillotson was shivering and wondering how the hell he had let that goddamn Mink set him up in something like this. The little package of quality goodies Mink had given him was how. Definitely A-1 stuff that hadn't been cut about a million times with sugar or starch and a promise of more where that came from. That it came from a police evidence room Tilly didn't know.

Tilly was standing on Tremont Street in front of a parking garage across from the Schubert Theatre trying to look cool instead of cold. His contact was a dude named Sabeel Biggs who would be coming from the Schubert very shortly and crossing over to the parking garage. Mink had said Biggs would look like he should be playing wide receiver for the patriots except that he'd be dressed like a banker or lawyer, very conservatively pinstriped as if he very white instead of very black.

Attached to his arm would be a honey, very blonde, and he'd get into an all white 7 series BMW. Tilly had already located the Beamer angle-parked so that it took two spaces and wouldn't be scratched or banged.

For about the tenth time, Tilly rehearsed in his mind what he was supposed to say to Biggs. He was supposed to say, as Biggs got into his car, "Excuse me. Mr. Biggs?"

Don't approach too fast, Mink had warned, and keep your hands where he can see them.

When he had Biggs's attention, he was supposed to say, "Henry Gonzalez said I should speak to you."

Then he and Mink had gone through all the contingencies that could happen next, from Biggs telling him to get lost to telling him they'd meet later.

Tilly had nearly balked at the whole arrangement but Mink had confided he was working through a cop who had set everything up and had told Mink what to tell Tilly.

"Don't worry. Everything will be cool," Mink had said.

Easy for him to say, Tilly thought. He wasn't the one shivering his butt off out here, waiting to meet a badass black stud built like he ought to be playing pro football.

"The cop tells me the name Henry Gonzalez is the key," Mink had said. "Old Sabeel won't be able to resist it because Henry used to be the road to some heavy-duty scratch even though now he's doing long time at Cedar Junction."

Sabeel. Where the hell did they come up with names like Sabeel? Tilly wondered. He pondered that a few moments.

The theatre was letting out now and Tilly felt he had to pee. People, all dolled up, real ladies and gentlemen, an evening of theatre and dinner, probably at some place really fancy place, but he'd bet a lot of them would probably end the night snorting a few lines up their nose, which was what Tilly felt like doing right about now.

He'd gone to some theatre now and then when he was in college mainly to show he had a little culture but he could never understand its attraction. You want drama, go to the track. Chow wasn't bad there either, you want to make a night of it.

Jesus, he was coming. Had to be him. Even the topcoat was pinstriped, but like a tiger's stripes, it did nothing to hide the muscles rippling underneath. Sabeel spent some serious time at the gym.

The blonde was gorgeous. Centerfold material. Some kind of shiny dark fur and legs longer than Italy.

Tilly mentally checked his hands, making sure they were at his sides in plain sight. He had practiced a smile several times but he was sure it looked stupid and if he used it Sabeel would think he was an idiot. That would probably be all right, though. At least he won't see me as a threat and shoot me.

Sabeel Biggs and his gorgeous blonde friend passed by Tilly talking softly and smiling, a little wave of cologne and perfume following them. Probably trying to act like he understood the play, Tilly thought. The blonde didn't look as though she'd be any help on that score. No doubt, anything Sabeel said she thought was smart.

Tilly turned and followed at a discreet distance, even though he'd much rather be going the other way.

Like a perfect gentleman, Sabeel let the girl in the passenger's side and, as he came around behind the BMW, Tilly walked up to him

He pasted on the smile and then erased it, knowing it looked idiotic, feeling the way he felt as a little kid and had to pose a smile for the photographer.

"Excuse me. Mr. Biggs?"

Sabeel Biggs leveled a glance at him and Tilly was again reminded of a tiger, this time one about to leap for his throat. Without a word, Biggs went to the driver's door and got in.

Keeping the door open and his eye on Tilly, he nodded a barely perceptible nod. Tilly stood dumb.

After a moment, Sabeel Biggs said, "You got something you want to say to me?"

Tilly couldn't remember what he was supposed to say. He was conscious only of having to pee. Finally, he blurted, "Henry Gonzalez says I ought to talk with you."

Sabeel Biggs assessed the skinny, anemic-looking bird standing about ten feet from him. Mink had told Tilly to dress half decent and he had worn his leather jacket, not a bikey type, but a nice one he had bought out of the trunk of a car in the parking lot at Wonderland for fifty bucks. The guy said it was worth at least three bills and Tilly believed it.

He had complemented the jacket with a pair of Dockers, stylishly pleated, and a pair of H.H. Brown Watermocs he had bought in an outlet near L.L. Beans during his student days at the University of Lowell. He felt he looked pretty sharp.

"How do you know Henry Gonzalez?" There was a slight emphasis on *you* as if, Tilly felt, Sabeel Biggs meant to say, how does a goony bird like you know someone cool like Henry Gonzalez?

Tilly shrugged. "I know him. I wasn't in the can with him. Just visiting. We go back."

Sabeel Biggs crooked a finger and beckoned Tilly to come closer. He was sitting sideways on the BMW's, the door still open.

"What do you want to talk to me about?"

"Business."

"Business? What kind of business?"

"Marketing." That was the word Mink had said the cop said to use. Sabeel Biggs would get the message. It was like talking a code. Like something you saw in the movies. Still, Tilly inwardly acknowledged you couldn't just come out and say, 'Selling drugs.'

Sabeel Biggs examined Tilly carefully, the little smile gone from his lips. "When did Henry tell you to talk to me?"

"About two weeks ago. Just before he got sick." Mink had told him that Henry Gonzalez had a stroke, was unconscious and, according to the cop, probably wouldn't recover or, if he did, the doctors thought the odds were he would be brain damaged and be unable to let anyone know he didn't know Tilly.

Tilly thought of the words 'probably' and 'odds were.' They had seemed pretty reassuring when Mink said them but standing in front of Sabeel Biggs Tilly now found them flimsy.

But Sabeel Biggs nodded and Tilly found fresh comfort.

Maybe things were going okay. He wanted to, but didn't dare, sneak a direct peek at the blonde's legs. The fur coat had hiked up, exposing quite a lot of thigh that, to Tilly, looked longer than the home stretch at Rockingham.

"Henry's not going to make it, from what I hear," Biggs said.

Tilly nodded and tried to look solemn.

"Two weeks ago, huh? What took you so long to look me up?"

Tilly noticed that Sabeel Biggs didn't particularly talk like a black, actually didn't talk like one at all.

"Well, that's part of what I want to talk to you about. I had to work some things out."

Sabeel Biggs closed the BMW's door, started the engine, and lowered his window. Tilly figured he was just going to take off and leave him standing there like a dummy, which, actually, would be fine with Tilly. Despite feeling a little more at ease, he still wasn't thrilled talking with a guy who looked as though he'd rather watch you convulse on cyanide than watch a play, even though he was dressed like a banker.

"What's your name?" Sabeel Biggs asked. Tilly could see his hand resting on the blonde's knee. The fingers were large and powerful, encrusted with rings. The leg was long and white.

"Howard Tillotson." Had to go with the real name, Mink said. It was part of the plan and don't worry about any problems. Tilly knew if he had seen Sabeel Biggs ahead of time, he never would have agreed to the plan, quality goodies or not.

"Tell me, Howard Tillotson," Biggs said, his voice lingering over the individual syllables of the name as if trying it out, "how'd you know I'd be here tonight?"

Tilly smiled. "Opening night. Henry said when I looked you up I'd be sure to find you at opening night at the Schubert. He described you. Here I am."

"Okay, Howard, tell you what. I gotta get Miss Swenson, here, home and all tucked in safe and sound."

Tilly saw him give the knee a squeeze, then the hand slid up and down a little. He could swear he heard Miss Swenson purr.

"You give me a number where I can reach you and I'll get back to you tomorrow, the next day."

Tilly was able to get a peek at the long legs as Sabeel Biggs wrote down his cell phone number.

When Biggs drove away, Tilly first very badly had to pee and then he very badly wanted some of the stuff from the bag that Mink had given him.

"Things are almost all set," Billy Wilkins said.

Special Agent Jessup scrunched in his seat like a man about to be told something he doesn't want to hear, his head turned away from Billy Wilkins as they drove along Storrow Drive in an aimless route that allowed them to talk.

But he was listening anyway.

"The first fish took the bait," Wilkins said. Or at least the first bait, he thought.

Jessup turned his head so that he was looking straight ahead. He tried to concentrate on the bank robbery case he was working on, or *should* be working on right now instead of riding around with this transplanted redneck, listening to a wacko scheme that might make pretty good video movie.

But the thought of landing Will Scarlet was very enticing.

"Who's the first fish?"

"Sabeel Biggs. Know him?"

"No."

"Works for Ramon Mendez."

"I know him. What's the deal?"

"Our shooter was touted as a guy who's got a connection to someone with big dough who wants to be the steady supplier of dope up north. To all those college kids snorting it up between classes. This supplier can't get enough right now, business is so good."

"Who's this supplier?"

Billy Wilkins shrugged. He was driving about forty miles an hour in the center lane. Cars passed him on both sides, doing fifty or sixty, some giving a little tap of the brakes when they recognized an unmarked police car but then figuring unmarkeds seldom bothered with speeders.

"Beats me," he said. "There's gotta be someone up there dealing, though."

Special Agent Jessup swore. "Wilkins, are you going senile? You taking dope yourself, are you?"

Billy Wilkins feigned looking hurt. "Chill it, Jessup. You're too uptight. That's the problem with you Feds. Everything's gotta be like a military plan, right down to the letter."

"Okay, so your shooter wants to make a connection between Ramon Mendez and Company and some fictitious drug runner somewhere up on the North Shore. You mind if I ask a couple of questions? You know, just to satisfy my uptight mind?"

"Fire away."

Without giving a signal, Billy Wilkins got into the left lane to make a turn to Kenmore Square. He cut off a Mini Cooper whose driver, young and pretty, leaned on the horn and whipped them the finger.

"That's the problem with the world today," Wilkins said. "Broads are like guys. Aggressive as a bastard."

"First off," Jessup said, "why's this guy—our shooter—going to do this? I mean, within our little fiction."

"He wants a little piece of the action, naturally. But, wait a minute, there's something else. Things work out, I tell you. He'll reveal to Biggs who he actually is. I mean that he's the guy who plugged Will Scarlet's mother. Word's out, apparently, on his identity and Biggs may recognize the name. So, he's gonna present himself as a guy in a real bind who sees a chance to make a quick hit, get some up-front dough, and gets a chance to get as far away from Will Scarlet as possible. Reality, you might say lends credence to his story."

"It ever occur to you that Biggs might turn him over to Will Scarlet to collect that supposed fifty grand?"

"Could happen but I doubt it. Biggs is too tied into Mendez and, besides, there's no love lost between Biggs and the guineas."

"Okay, so our guy meets with Biggs and Biggs is going to believe him just like that and set up a meeting with him and Mendez?"

"Not 'just like that.' He'll check around, find our guy is who he says he is, that's he's bought a little dope himself from time to time."

"But he doesn't know anyone who'd have the kind of dough to buy big-time from Mendez. For chrissakes, Wilkins, this is really stupid."

"Yeah, but Biggs doesn't know who our guy knows and who he doesn't know."

"Don't you think he'll ask who this buyer is?"

"Of course. But naturally our guy won't say. He wants to talk direct to Mendez."

Special Agent Jessup scratched his head and scrunched deeper into his seat. "And Mendez is going to buy all this?"

"Well, I'm sure he'll be skeptical and cautious. But I'll tell you what else he'll be. He'll be curious. I know the man. He'll be curious enough to check all this out."

"You mean enough to meet with our man?"

"I think so."

"Yeah, but then what?" They meet and our guy's got nothing to back up his story. No connection, no dough."

Billy Wilkins smiled. They were stopped at a red light on Commonwealth. "That's as far as it has to go. Because if things go as planned, guess who comes swooping in at that point?"

Special Agent Jessup looked sharply at Billy Wilkins who was still smiling and nodding his head slightly.

"Right-t-t-t. Will Scarlet. Well, probably not Will himself, but some of his merry men. They take out Ramon, at least that's what I'm hoping. And please don't give me a church lecture. There's no loss to the world there. If we can't get Ramon legally it wouldn't bother me to see Will Scarlet plow him under permanently."

Jessup started to speak but Billy Wilkins cut him off.

"They'll scoop our boy to take him to whatever Will's got planned for him but you and I will be following close behind. At an appropriate point, when old Will is present, we'll call in some troops of our own, nail Will in the act and become heroes. Fame and fortune will be close behind. Not to mention the satisfaction that comes from making the world a better place to live in."

"I'm sure that's your major motivation," Jessup said.

"Whatever. But it *could* work. And if it doesn't, what's the loss?"

The light turned and they rode in silence until they hit the Public Gardens.

"I suppose this is stupid to ask," Jessup finally said, "but how does Will Scarlet know about the meeting?"

"Why, naturally, we make sure he gets the word. Through appropriate channels, of course."

They were on Boylston when Jessup said, "I don't know. It's too iffy."

"Jessup, what the hell isn't?"

Billy Wilkins turned left onto Charles.

"By the way," Jessup said, "where is our boy?"

"He's safely stashed away."

"When's he meet with Biggs?"

"Tonight."

Billy Wilkins drove south on Route One with Chug in the front seat beside him. He had just picked him up at the Lynn Elks.

He went over Chug's story to Sabeel Biggs. About how he was a buddy of a guy named Howard Tillotson who knew a Henry Gonzalez. Henry suggested that Biggs was the man to see to help an up and coming gold miner who was already pretty familiar with some territory just waiting to be developed. "It's pretty simple, Chug. The idea tonight is to get Biggs to agree to set up a meeting with his guys."

"And you want me to tell him my name and that I'm the guy who shot Will Scarlet's mother. What do you think, I'm soft? You know something, I'm liking this less and less. I *must* be soft."

"Chug, listen to me, Will Scarlet already knows your name. You know that. This gives a little urgency to your situation, makes it believable that you need the dough this deal will net you."

Billy Wilkins stole a glance at Chug who had slunk into a pout on his seat.

"Believe me, Biggs won't turn you over to Will Scarlet. He'll be much more interested in the possible big connection you represent. If I thought for a minute he might do that, I'd call the whole thing off. Remember, I'm after these drug guys first and foremost."

Billy Wilkins lit a cigarette and offered one to Chug who shook his head, no.

171

"In any case, I'll be close by. Naturally, Biggs won't know that but if there's *any* trouble we'll come swooping in to protect your ass.

"Right."

Billy Wilkins looked at Chug.

"Do I detect sarcasm there, Chug? You don't think we'll protect you?"

"That remains to be seen. The way I look at it, cops are like bees, not wasps."

"Huh? Like bees. What the hell you talking about?"

"Well, you know, both bees and wasps can sting, but if a bee stings you, it dies. It's a one shot deal. But a wasp can sting and sting and sting. It doesn't have to worry like the bee, that if I sting this guy I'm gonna die."

Billy Wilkins made an expression. "What the —"

"A cop even draws his gun, he's got to write a report. He shoots someone, doesn't even kill them, there's all kinds of red tape. He goes on administrative leave, gets counseling, all kinds of stuff that makes him think real hard about using his weapon. So, he's like a bee in that sense. He doesn't *die* if he fires his weapon, but he's got to think real hard before he does."

"Boy, I gotta tell you, that is one wacko analogy. You're saying if we see you in trouble, we won't react, won't use our weapons if we have to because we'll have to file a report?"

Chug shrugged.

"Yeah," Billy Wilkins said, "in a way, you're right. We're not like the wasp. It's not the Wild West where we can just gun down endless people."

"I'm just saying I have to wonder how much you'd put yourself out for a guy—can I be truthful here?—for a guy you must see as a lowlife."

"Thanks a lot."

They rode in strained silence for a few moments.

"When will I get those guarantees I mentioned I wanted? Meet with the commissioner? Have someone besides you confirm all this good stuff I'm supposed to get out of this. No offense, but I'm still not liking this too much, as I guess you can tell."

"I understand your concerns, Chug. I really do. That'll happen. Let's just get through tonight. It's the first step. The first step that'll let you get off to a fresh start."

They drove in silence, each with his thoughts. Billy Wilkins wondered what Chug's were. He thought of the wasp and bee analogy that Chug had made. It made a certain sense. Then he thought of Chug's words: *a guy you must see as a lowlife.*

Billy Wilkins stole a glance at Chug and, as he did, felt the sweat begin to trickle on his forehead and under his arms.

Chapter Nineteen

The ICU nurse drew the curtain around the bed, enclosing William Scarlata and his wife with his mother who had just quietly died. She had been improving the last couple of days and her death hadn't been expected. William and Sylvia Scarlata had dropped in for a morning visit.

William felt as though he had just been punched in the stomach. It was as if he couldn't breathe, as if some essence of feeling were compressed deep inside. But then the compression let go and everything flooded out. He fell onto his mother and cried like a little boy. Still crying, he kissed her and stroked her hair.

"Mamma, mamma, ti voglio bene. Ti voglio bene."

Then he stood and hugged his wife who comforted him.

They drove to Bernardo Tranfiglia's funeral home where William Scarlata picked out a very expensive casket and arranged for his mother's wake and funeral.

Before he left, William Scarlata pulled Bernardo Tranfiglia aside and reminded him that he still wanted his services about that 'other matter' more than ever now.

"I promise you, Mr. Tranfiglia, it won't be long."

This time Special Agent Jessup initiated the meeting. He was waiting on a bench at Quincy

Market. The sun was bright but the air wasn't quite warm enough to bring large numbers of the noon crowd outside.

Lieutenant Billy Wilkins sat beside him. Pigeons patrolled expectantly.

"We're looking at murder one," Jessup said.

Billy Wilkins knew what Jessup meant but played dumb.

"Huh? He said.

"Cut the crap, Wilkins. You know what I'm talking about. Florence Scarlata died this morning."

"Oh, that. Yeah, I heard. Hey, did you eat?" He gestured with his thumb toward the food court. "Want to grab a bite?"

"I didn't call you for a lunch date. Your player is now facing murder, as you well know. I presume you'll come to your senses and act on that."

"Yeah, I'm going to act on it. Same act as before. Things are moving along. First meeting was last night. Everything went without a hitch. Sabeel Biggs played a little hard to get but he'll bite. Believe me, he'll bite."

Special Agent Jessup made a face as though he had just tasted something unpleasant. "You're a law enforcement officer. You know the identity of a man who has just committed a murder. You don't act on that, I will."

"Jessup, will you cut it, please. Think of the greater good, if that makes it any easier. Think of your career. Think of anything you want, but make sense, will you?"

Billy Wilkins lit a Marlboro and flipped the match at a pigeon who checked it out and then backed off indignantly.

"Nothing's changed," he said. "We still got a golden chance at Will Scarlet. If anything, our chances are better. He'll be less cautious. He'll do anything to get the guy who killed his mother. But the thing is, you and I will get him and improve the planet."

Billy Wilkins stood and stretched elaborately. He looked up at the March sun now getting high.

"Jessup, stop pretending you're in a movie playing some kind of incorruptible FBI agent. It's too bad about Florence Scarlata. It really is. She was probably a nice lady. But her son is most definitely not a nice guy. This isn't a movie. This is here. Now. And we've got a chance to put a very bad person away."

Special Agent Jessup made a little mock clap of his hands. "Very nice speech, Wilkins. Who was that, Russell Crowe?"

"You with me on this or not?"

Jessup kicked at a pigeon.

"Come on. You with me? Yes or no."

Jessup just stared at Billy Wilkins.

"I'm taking that as a 'yes.' Okay, there is something I'm going to need you to do and probably pretty soon. Our guy's getting antsy about guarantees, assurances. Wants to meet with the Commissioner or someone to confirm that we're giving him a new life, a new start."

"So, the shit's hitting the fan. You can't do any of that, can you, Wilkins?"

"Well, no, I can't but I'm thinking I can do something just as good to put his mind at ease. I'm thinking that if a certain incorruptible-looking FBI agent flashed his credentials and backed me up Bobby 'Chug' Ellis would be mightily reassured."

The unpleasant taste in Special Agent Jessup's mouth got worse. He looked at Billy Wilkins almost beseechingly.

"If things work out, Wilkins, and this guy survives, what *are* we going to do with him?"

Billy Wilkins squinted at the sun. In Georgia, this time of year, it would be brighter and hotter. "Couple of smart guys like us, Jessup, we'll think of something."

Mickey the Harp and Sal the Dogcatcher sat like cowed schoolboys waiting for a birching from the principal. They were in the back room of a bakery in the North End. They breathed freshly baked bread, warm and homey, but were barely aware of it.

"What pisses me off," Lou Russo was saying, "is that you had him. You get someone in your sight, you don't let them get away."

"Lou, I understand that," Mickey said, being the spokesperson for himself and Sal, who, he felt, wasn't any too sharp. "They pulled up right to the cops, though."

"So you took off."

"Well, yeah. I didn't want to hang around in case they came out with the cops."

Lou Russo didn't say anything. He stared at Mickey in a way that made Mickey very uncomfortable. Mickey wanted to add, What do you think I shoulda done, take out the cops?"

Instead, he said, "We went back to the broad's place and waited there a while and then over to his place to check that out."

"See, that's your problem, Mickey, which I'm beginning to see. You think everyone's as stupid as you. You chase this guy over the bridge, through Chelsea, and you think he's gonna go back to his place or the girl's?"

Mickey said nothing. He was trying to think of a way to blame Sal, but that wouldn't work because he outranked Sal and the responsibility had been his.

He felt like telling Lou Russo to find the guy himself. He really didn't appreciate being called stupid, especially in front of Sal who'd probably start to think he was smarter than Mickey.

"So what have you been doing?" Lou asked.

"Well, like I say, we've been checking out his place and the broad's. We figure he'll show one place or the other eventually."

"Yeah," Lou Russo said. "Very eventually. You'll be gumming your food before he shows up at those two places."

"Geez, Mr. Russo," said Sal the Dogcatcher Manfredi, who didn't quite rank high enough to call Lou Russo 'Lou,' "what should we . . ."

Sal let the sentence trail when he noticed Lou Russo's expression.

"What should you do? I know what I should do. I should do the thing myself and I just may. Right now Mr. Scarlata's thinking only of his mother's funeral but in a couple of days he's gonna have one thing on his mind and that's getting the bastard who killed his mother."

The mention of William Scarlata's deceased mother brought a little respectful pause and downward glance from the three men.

"What should you do?" Lou Russo repeated. "Tell me everything you know about the girl. What's her name?"

"Ellie Robinson," Mickey the Harp said.

"Where does she live? Southie?"

"No. Charlestown."

"Let me ask you something," Lou Russo said. "A broad isn't home, where does she go? She has a fight with her boyfriend—which in this case don't apply— or she's in trouble or something, where does she go? She goes running back to Mummy and Daddy. Am I right?"

Mickey felt himself nodding but said, "Her parents are dead, Lou. We found that out. She's got no family around here."

"Very *good*," Lou Russo said, a little heavy on the irony. "You guys are better detectives than I thought. Okay, so she's got no family, who's she go running to?"

Mickey shrugged. "A friend?"

"Right. Get your asses back to Southie and Charlestown and find out who her girl buddies are. Do you know where she works?"

"She works for a dentist, Lou. No one we talked to knew which one."

"Dig a little harder. See, the key to finding him is gonna be through her. Find her and you find him. Or you lean on her to find out where he is."

Mickey thought it best not to remind Lou that's what he wanted to do all along but that Lou had vetoed it.

As if remembering that, Lou Russo said, "The thing now is to find this guy no matter what, understand what I'm saying? Mr. Scarlata ain't gonna take 'Oh, we tried but we can't find him.'"

Frankie Ricciardi heard the news of Florence Scarlata's death on the late night television news in his motel room. He had eaten a pizza and had consumed four cans of beer and suddenly they felt like a heavy congealing mass in his belly.

He lay on the bed and pondered the ramifications of what the news had said. Now he was involved in murder but that didn't bother him nearly as much as thoughts of William Scarlata's vengeance.

He cursed aloud, a long, steady stream of invective, most of it directed at Chug. For shooting Florence Scarlata to begin with. And then for taking off and going back home. For what? To square things with Ellie. Jesus. What a loser.

But if William Scarlata had been pissed off before, he'd be a maniac now. Frankie was sure he'd get a hold of Chug sooner or later and when he did he'd have no trouble finding out who was with Chug at the shooting. If he didn't already have his name. And even though Frankie hadn't pulled the trigger, Will Scarlet would want his ass too. There would be no escape. No matter where he went, Frankie knew that sooner or later Will Scarlet would get to him.

Things looked grim but Frankie felt there was one possible out. He packed his things, considered skipping out without paying his bill but thought better of it. Gotta play it cool and straight now.

After leaving the motel, he gassed up and headed back to Boston. Tomorrow he'd make a phone call to a certain bakery he had heard about in the North End and keep his fingers crossed.

It was a shame in a way he had to head back. He was starting to like it up here in snowdrift country. If he stayed much longer, he'd probably turn wholesome, start eating oatmeal for breakfast. He had even gotten excited when he saw a moose by the side of the road as he had driven around earlier in the day. He hoped he didn't hit one as he drove back to Boston.

Sabeel Biggs cruised along the waterfront savoring the late morning sunlight straining through the BMW's tinted glass and refracting off Boston Harbor to his right which looked pretty clean as far as he was concerned.

He had an FM station tuned to classical music: Mozart, Chopin, a lot of strings and harpsichords so that you thought you were back in the days of the Boston Tea Party. Actually, he was trying to cultivate a taste for that kind of music. It, his pinstriped suits, and the Beamer were a passport out of his boyhood Roxbury, much better ones than the usual, a bullet in the head or chest or some hard time at Cedar Junction.

He was doing okay. Not as well as if he were playing for the Sox, Pats or Celtics at five million a year, give or take, but all right. As far as strength and body were concerned, he felt he had had the ability to make the grade in the bigs (Biggs in the bigs made him smile) particularly in football, but he could never hack the schooling even if it was nothing but a farce for athletes.

The only thing that wasn't quite right was his digs. He had a condo in the South End and he wasn't complaining. Bricks and old beams and gas lamps. Hadn't seen a cockroach the whole time there. True, a lot of artsy types and gays but they didn't particularly bother him. What he wanted, though, was to live on the waterfront in one of those old done-over warehouses with security in front of the parking lot and sailboats tied up at the wharf.

He had an awfully attractive image of himself looking out the window at his Beamer, his boat, and Boston Harbor, Chopin or Mozart playing softly in the background, and one of his blonde-haired, long-legged friends leaning her head on his shoulder.

The problem was that money-wise he wasn't quite there.

But just maybe a window of opportunity, as they say, was opening. And Sabeel Biggs prided himself on seeing opportunity and seizing it.

At first, when he had talked to the guy who said he shot William Scarlata's mother, he thought he was being put on and had listened with skepticism and amusement. But then, he wondered, what the hell would be the purpose of a put-on?

He claimed he was friends with the first guy—what the hell was his name?—Howard Tillotson, who knew a lot of students at Lowell and other points north, himself having been a student at Lowell. And those students, pressured by exams and interviews and all the kinds of things Sabeel Biggs was grateful he had avoided, just couldn't get enough quality candy to escape the pressures.

Near Lewis Wharf now, Sabeel Biggs pulled over to gaze and to feed his fantasy for a few moments. He wasn't far from Will Scarlet's territory, just around the corner, actually.

Sabeel Biggs had checked the guy out. Robert Ellis, AKA Chug. Apparently, he was who he said he was and there was no particular reason to doubt he had shot Florence Scarlata. Doubtless, he was scared silly and wanted to make some quick money to get away from Boston and Will Scarlet.

What Sabeel Biggs had in mind was to help the guy out, to set up a deal between his big buyer—if one existed—but not with Ramon Mendez. Why let Ramon and Philippe, that fatty, suck up all the dough? They didn't even know how to use it. Look at the way they lived. Look at where they lived. Sabeel figured they had enough to *buy* the waterfront.

No, maybe it was time to say bye-bye to Ramon and move up. Of course, the little problem of getting the big stash of goodies had to be dealt with but Sabeel Biggs figured he could handle that. He had plenty of friends from Roxbury who wouldn't mind helping him move in on and cutting out those spics from Miami.

First thing, though, was to meet again with this Chug guy and find out who his big buyer was. After that, either throw old Chug a bone to help him escape or throw him to Will Scarlet. Sabeel Biggs had no love for William Scalata but it wouldn't hurt to be on his good side. Not to mention the fifty large that supposedly Scarlata would pay to get this guy.

He continued to gaze for a few moments at the old granite warehouse, now a high-end collection of condos. Soon the boats would be tied alongside and, maybe, with some shrewd moves and a little luck, he, Roxbury's own Sabeel Biggs would be setting sail from here.

He smiled as he savored his dream and the classical music playing softly on the Beamer's stereo.

Chapter Twenty

Florence Scarlata's funeral was one of Boston's biggest in recent memory. The line at the wake had been over an hour's wait and it and the crowd at the funeral had been a mini who's who of the business, crime, law enforcement, and political communities, among others, in alphabetical order.

If those crowds' size and variety were any indicator, the old-time Mob still packed considerable clout and there were some who felt a twinge of nostalgia. In a way, it was as if a certain type of structure and order were yet intact.

William and Sylvia Scarlata, along with Lou Russo, were back at their home on the water at Nahant. It looked right across at the Boston skyline. The after-funeral collation was held at one of William's restaurant, and it had been sumptuous.

Lou Russo and William Scarlata sat in a family room whose floor space was greater than that of most homes. Large potted plants were spaced about and oriental rugs were scattered over expensive tiles imported from Italy. One wall was entirely bookcase and many of the titles were classic and many of the bindings were leather. Most of the books were unread. Mounted on another wall was a huge HD television. It was watched often.

A third wall contained a rack of wines sent directly to him from a villa in Tuscany. William Scarlata and

Lou Russo were drinking red wine from one of those bottles.

"I thought the Cardinal's eulogy was very nice, Will," Lou Russo said.

"It was very nice," William Scarlata said. He thought of the frequent, large donations he made to the archdiocese. "But it was easy to say nice things about my mother. She was a saint."

His voice cracked and he dabbed at his eyes with a deep blue handkerchief.

"Had an interesting call at the bakery this morning, Will," Lou Russo said after a pause of several moments. "Guy said he was in the robbery but wasn't the shooter. Very sorry about what happened to your mother and wanted to help out. Gave me the name of the shooter."

William Scarlata looked at Lou Russo closely and let him talk.

"We went round and round on the shooter's address, the name of his girlfriend, where she lived and all. I told him this was all old news and that we were about two shakes from nabbing his pal. This guy was so scared and wanted to help out so bad I could practically smell him over the phone.

"I told him he wanted to help out he had to come up with something else, like where this guy might hide out."

"He give you his name?" William Scarlata asked.

"Yeah. Eventually. I had to get real soothing. Told him I appreciated what he was trying to do. That we only wanted the guy who pulled the trigger. Said, 'Mr. Scarlata would be real grateful to anyone who could help him find the person who shot his mother.'"

"This is taking a long time, Lou."

Lou Russo was thinking that it wasn't that long, really just a few days, but knew better than to argue.

"I know, Will, but I think we're practically there. This guy told me our man is an Elk but spends most of his Elk time in Lynn where he's real close friends with the bartender and caretaker there."

"Well, you gotta check that out obviously and you gotta check out this caller."

"Mickey's taking care of it," Lou Russo said. He sipped his wine and looked out at the sky, just beginning to get dark. The days were getting longer.

He hadn't told William Scarlata that Mickey and Sal nearly had the shooter but had lost him in Chelsea. He couldn't believe that for some reason the guy was staying around here. But as long as he did that, it was just a matter of time.

"I guarantee you, Will, the bastard's practically delivered."

Chug heard of Florence Scarlata's death while listening to two guys at the Elks bar drinking rum Cokes and arguing the relative merits of Coke Classic versus the Coke variations.

One of them mentioned the old tale of how if you put a nail or a coin or something metal into a glass of Coke it would dissolve overnight.

That got Chug to thinking he might be onto something, that maybe Coke was what he was looking for to wash the ink out of a dollar bill. Be something if Coke was the ticket.

That's what he was thinking about when the television news showed footage of Florence Scarlata's funeral that morning. When he saw that, he couldn't think of anything for several minutes.

Then he went to the back room where he had a cot and a locker. He lay on the cot and stared at the ceiling. His ears rushed with sound and his face felt hot. He pictured Florence Scarlata as she looked when he had shot her, shocked and sagging, an old lady horrified, fearful of death.

For some reason even though he acknowledged she might die, he had thought she wouldn't. A water-stained ceiling tile, blotched and bloated, sagged over his face. Florence Scarlata stared at him through it and he stared back.

Florence Scarlata's shocked, accusing face after a while became the face of the seal he had killed when he was a kid. He had been with his brother and parents visiting friends of his mother and father in Marblehead on the North Shore. Later in his life he had come to realize the visit as far as his parents were concerned was more to let other Southie friends know there were connections in Marblehead than to actually see Mr. And Mrs. Coffey. Chug knew that his father was bored with the visits because he used to joke that the Coffeys weren't very stimulating.

The Coffeys lived near a beach and Chug and his brother, after a decent interval of being seen, naturally went to the water. It had been in April during school vacation week, too cold for sunbathers, but a group of early teen boys was gathered near something at the end of the beach. The Ellis brothers—Chug remembered he had been eleven—went to see what the boys were looking at.

The seal was lying half on its side, messy with seaweed and litter. It wasn't very big, probably just a young seal, but it was dying. Occasionally, it tried to raise its head to look at the circle of boys.

Chug had seen seals at the aquarium a couple of times and they always looked happy, doing tricks or just thrilled with ceaseless swimming. They were like dogs, Chug thought, friendly, eager to please. They even looked like dogs with their big, soft eyes and pointy whiskers.

One of the boys picked up a rock the size of a baseball and Chug wanted to stop him, looked at his brother Jimmy to see if two big-city kids should take on a bunch of blonde-headed, freckle-faced Marblehead sissies, dressed as though they were about to step onto a sailboat, looking as though they knew all about rigging, tacking, and other things nautical.

The stone hit the seal on the side but it was only a lob and the seal didn't even raise its head. The supply of rocks at this end of the beach was infinite. They were worn round and smooth by the ocean so that they were pounders rather than cutters or tearers.

Quickly, the Marbleheaders were into it, as though they were at a job, hurling smaller, high velocity stones and seeking out heavy two-handers that you tossed like a basketball.

Chug wasn't sure how long the pounding had gone on when he picked up a stone the size of a bowling ball. He pushed through the circle and raised the stone over his head. For a moment, his eyes and the seal's locked and then he smashed the stone down onto the seal's face.

The Marbleheaders gathered around him, clapping his shoulders, hailing him as a hero.

"Jerks," he had said, about as strong an epithet he had used when he was eleven and still innocent and still called Bobby.

Sal the Dogcatcher caught a dog just as she was coming out of a joint in Revere near the beach. He was on his way to pick up Mickey and the two of them were going to the Elks in Lynn to check out a tip.

Sal made a half-hearted toss of the net at the girl. Half-hearted because, one, her dogdom was extreme even by his standards and, two, this was an important mission even though the tip didn't sound any too hot to Sal. Mickey had called him on his cell and said Lou Russo wanted them to check the Lynn Elks. Okay, but Sal could picture what would happen. They'd go barreling up to Lynn and then Mickey would say something like, Cool it, Sallie. We sit here, get the lay of the land first. We can't just go barging in, grab the guy and haul him away.

Which made sense, Sal figured, so why not give the girl a shot. He wasn't going to spend the night with her. That was the advantage with dogs.

A close up of her face almost made him boot the Denali. She was one of those little dogs with the smushed in faces and teeth always showing. Sal couldn't think of the name of the breed. Sal liked to do that: attach the breed of dog to the girl. He'd had greyhounds, skinny, nervous girls with pointy faces; sheepdogs, fat hairy girls with shapeless legs but ever so friendly. And lots of mongrels, girls kind of nondescript but just out and out homely.

Somebody once told him that Ben Franklin had been a dogcatcher. Old Ben had said go for the homely ones because they'd be so grateful.

That tickled Sal. Imagine, someone like Ben Franklin, a guy you read about in history books, talked about in school, going after the bowwows. Sal grinned when he thought about it. He could be anywhere, he'd think of Benjamin Franklin in the sack with some colonial type of ugly with all those petticoats or whatever they wore, and Sal would grin and maybe even start laughing to himself.

Sal checked himself in the mirror. There was no way he had to settle for mutts. When you get down to it, I'm a pretty good-looking guy, he thought.

This one sure was grateful, as she well ought to be. Came right up to the Denali just as friendly as could be.

She had pasty, blotchy skin and her hair didn't look any too clean. But it was mainly the teeth that almost made Sal tromp the gas.

Pekingese? Pug? Was that it? More like the wolf man. Sal hoped she didn't bite.

Chug got his bartender friend to give him a ride to the T station at Wonderland where he took a train to Government Center.

He walked over to the Common and sat on a bench near Tremont Street. He punched Ellie's number.

"It's me," he said when she answered.

She didn't say anything and he waited a long pause.

"You still with me?" he said.

"I'm still here."

"No. I don't mean that. I mean, are you still with me?"

"Wait a minute. I've got to go outside."

A long pause, muffled background noise.

"Where are you, Chug?"

"I'm sitting on a bench near the Common and I'm feeling about as low as I can feel. I-I just saw about the funeral on the news a little while ago and I'm wondering if you're still with me."

Another pause.

"Ellie?"

"I don't know. I'm really kind of confused right about now, Chug. I really am."

"Where are you, Ellie?"

"I'm at Laurie's. I told her there was something wrong with my plumbing. I don't know how long I can string that out. Where are you staying? Where did you go the other night? I've been worried out of my mind and now this."

He could tell she was close to losing it and wondered whether to tell her about the deal with the cop. He decided not to. He still had too many doubts and questions.

"Ellie, I've been thinking a lot about us. About you and me. We've had some good times, Ellie. I want to have a lot more good times."

He heard her sniff but she didn't say anything.

"Going to ball games. The Sox, the Pats. Going to the Garden to see the Bruins and Celtics. Those were great times, Ellie."

He paused, waiting for a response.

"Huh, Ellie? Weren't those great times? Remember the time we . . ." He left the sentence unfinished.

191

"We've had a lot of fun, Chug."

"Going out to eat or to the movies or just hanging at your place or mine. All that means an awful lot to me, Ellie. More than I can tell you."

"It means a lot to me too, Chug."

"We're going to have a lot more good times, Ellie. We've got a lot of time ahead of us. We've had a setback, that's all. My fault there. No doubt about it. I've pulled a major screw up but I'm gonna set things straight."

"Chug—"

"I've just got to know that you're still with me."

Another long pause.

"Ellie? Come on. Say you're still with me."

"I've gotta go, Chug. It's going to take me a minute or two to get my act together in front of Laurie. She'll probably wonder why I'm—why I'm a little teary. What am I gonna say? That my toilet is still clogged?"

He called Billy Wilkins's cell number and got his voice mail. He swore but left no message.

He wasn't sure which area Billy Wilkins worked out of. He'd mentioned a drug bust. Where? Could be anywhere in the city. Probably not Louisburg Square but could be practically anywhere else.

He spent a few minutes thinking about Ellie and then about his father. Then he wondered about his brother Jimmy now out in California selling Toyotas and doing all right but too busy to come back to see his father.

He tried Billy Wilkins's number again and this time he answered.

"It's me. Chug. Can we talk?"

"What's on your mind, Chug?"

"What's on my mind? Well, let's see. I was just watching the news and I saw something interesting. Kind of sad, but interesting. I imagine you know what I'm talking about."

"I surely do."

"Are you on duty now?"

"No. I'm at home. Wife's out. Kids are away at school. Just me and Fred."

"Who's Fred?"

"My cat. I don't tell too many people I like cats."

"Yeah, that'll be our little secret. Okay, so what happens now? Things changed?"

"You mean about our arrangement? No. Nothing's changed. We go ahead as planned. You've got another meeting with Biggs and then the important one."

Chug ran his hand through his hair and then down his face.

"Look, maybe I'm slow, but I don't get it. Old lady Scarlata got planted today so it strikes me that you, a cop who has reason to believe he might know who shot her, should be acting on that instead of some stupid drug bust. I know I've voiced these concerns before but she was still alive then."

"Chug, Chug, look, you've just said it. 'A cop who has reason to believe.' You've never flat out told me anything. Let's say, for the sake of argument, I bring you up on charges. What do you do? Why you plead innocent, don't you? Or a plea will be entered for you.

"Let's say it even gets to trial. Now, what does the Commonwealth have against you? Do we have a weapon? Far as I know, we don't."

Chug thought of the nine-millimeter Colt under snow in the woods of Maine.

"Do we have any eyewitnesses who can positively make you? I recall the descriptions saying the two perps had mustaches and both were kind of heavy set. You're clean shaven and have a little heavier than average build.

"Do we have any DNA, any prints, any anything? What we have, Chug, is a guy more afraid of a really pissed off Mafioso who's been known to do some mighty awful things to people who didn't even really piss him off the way the person who killed his mother did. Yeah, I'd say this guy has every reason to be more afraid of Will Scarlet than he has of the law.

"So am I spelling it out clear enough, Chug? This guy scratches the law's back and the law scratches his. Happens more'n you'd think."

Chug paused a second as a couple, holding hands sat near him. They touched foreheads and rubbed cheeks and smiled lovingly at each other.

Chug got up and moved to another bench.

"All right, Wilkins. Now it's my turn to spell things out. When I saw the news about Will Scarlet's mother, I came right into town. Took the T. I'm sitting in the Common right now freezing my ass. I wasn't thinking straight. I had in mind to go straight to the station where you work, the only problem being I'm not sure where that is. I was gonna say, okay, I want those guarantees, those assurances I mentioned to you and I want them now.

"But then I thought, you can't do that because now you're a goddamn *murderer* and you can't go into a police station making all these demands.

"So I'm glad I talked with you on the phone. But I still want those guarantees."

"Well, Chug, I told you we can do that and we can. I've got someone you're gonna meet and talk with who'll set your mind at ease. But right now, we've got to figure where you should go."

"I'll go back to the Elks."

"No. Better to keep you moving around. Tell you what. Give me twenty minutes, a half hour, and I'll pick you up by the Park Street T station. I'll be in my own vehicle. A Ford Ranger pick up. Dark blue."

As best she could, Ellie wiped around her eyes and put on a normal face. She sat back down at the counter in the apartment at Orient Heights of her friend, Laurie Wojcik. They had ordered take out.

Ellie worked her food around a little with her fork, took a mouthful and chewed for a long time.

"What's the matter, El?"

"I'm okay. It's nothing."

"Damn plumbing, huh? Nothing worse in the world. It'll break your heart." Laurie said it with a smile and touched Ellie's arm lightly.

Ellie smiled but her eyes were filling.

"Come on. Open up. Is it Chug?"

Ellie nodded. "Kind of."

"Look, I know it's none of my business, but is he fooling around on you?"

Ellie put her fork down and went into the bathroom.

When she came out, Laurie said, "You all right?"

"Yes. I'm all right."

"You can stay here as long as you want. That plumbing situation will work out. Everything works out eventually. Want to watch TV, catch the news?"

Ellie shook her head. "How about we just rent a video? A comedy. I could use some laughs."

"We might be talking really big time," Sabeel Biggs said. He regretted using the expression 'big time' or any play on his last name. He didn't like his last name and often thought of going with something completely Muslim, something that went with Sabeel, which his mother had read in a novel, but never got around to it.

"How big?" Tyrone Moore asked.

"I'm not sure. Could be a good market, though. That's why I want you to get your ass down to Newark to see your friend. Get a price. Get a lot of prices on various quantities and a time frame on delivery so if things pan out we can move right away."

Tyrone Moore wanted to comment on 'time frame' and 'pan out,' wanted to tell Sabeel Biggs to stop trying to sound like a white yuppie, like he wasn't black and from Roxbury. But, even though one look at Tyrone Moore could cause bladder and bowel failure in anything from a pit bull to a Cape Buffalo, he didn't dare. Sabeel Biggs could cause the same effects in him. Although old Sabeel had pretty much purged the Roxbury from his manner of speaking, he was still just about the toughest, meanest dude Tyrone had ever known.

They were sitting in Sabeel Biggs's BMW, parked on Blue Hill Avenue, the Beamer looking as congruous as Chardonnay in a paper cup. Tyrone

Moore caressed the leather absently and figured the car went one-hundred-twenty big ones easily.

"Uh, what you figure a flight to Newark and back cost?"

"Jesus, here," said Sabeel Biggs, taking a billfold from inside his banker's suit coat. He handed Tyrone some bills. He had changed his plan a little, trying to see whether he could set up a big buy at a price he could afford before meeting Robert Ellis's, AKA Chug, big buyer from up north.

Tyrone Moore smiled. "I can take a limo from the airport with this."

Her meant it as a little joke, as a little ego pumping for Sabeel Biggs but Sabeel wasn't smiling. Tyrone Moore had known Sabeel Biggs a long time, had survived growing up in Roxbury with him, neither one having a Daddy to provide a steady hand, both having Mommas who tried but were overwhelmed. Both knew friends who bled to death on the streets and each had siblings who were ultimate victims: one of Sabeel's brothers was shot in the stomach as he was walking home one fine summer's evening (they never found out who did the shooting) and took two days to die in the hospital. And one of Tyrone's sisters did herself in accidentally by injecting too much into her vein.

Even though they went back a ways, Tyrone hadn't seen much of Sabeel in the last few years. But he knew Sabeel sure had graduated from the nickel-dime street corner dealing they had engaged in. And it wasn't hard to figure that Sabeel was thinking of doing some more graduating, getting himself away from those spics or whatever they were he was working for.

Tyrone wanted to broach the subject and was trying to think of a roundabout, tactful way. Sabeel Biggs might talk like Whitey and look like a goddamn lawyer but he was pure Roxbury inside and about the only person Tyrone would never mess with.

Tyrone also wondered exactly what his own role was, other than knowing a brother in New Jersey who had access to some pretty good quantities of supposedly high quality goods.

"I'm gonna get a firm fix on this buyer," Sabeel was saying, "and if things work on my end and they work on your end, we might be able to set up a real good thing."

Tyrone went for it. "You say, 'we'?"

"How'd you like a car like this? I got me this car working for some guys who, believe me, ain't any brighter than you or me. Not as bright, actually." He thought of Philippe. "One of them's pretty smart but he's got his head in the clouds and his face always stuck in a book. I cannot figure him out."

Tyrone's hand caressed the Beamer's dash. "I know you doing okay, that's for sure."

"I got me a nice place in the South End. Lot of faggots but they don't bother me as long as they don't try nothing, know what I'm saying."

"I hates faggots."

"But, hey, I figure there's more if you're at the top. A lot more." Sabeel's eyes got dreamy. "Ever see one of them Bentley Azures? There is one car. Not even sure exactly what it goes for. Over three-hundred thou, I know. Imagine that." He threw his head back and laughed.

"Might even take me some sailing lessons. Or better yet get a big ass boat and hire a crew of white college kids to sail the sucker. Pay 'em in dope."

Tyrone Moore was smiling wide and nodding his head.

"So what I need, I need for you to get us a price— a good price. Let him know that this could be long term if things work out. I want you to fly down tomorrow morning, talk to this guy, and be back tomorrow night. Then I need you to line up a couple of dudes for muscle in case they're needed. Not that they will be, but you never know."

Tyrone Moore was feeling a little fluttery. It sounded as if Sabeel was thinking of setting himself up as some kind of drug kingpin, a role the wops held and, for the past few years, the spics or Columbians. Some of the brothers might think they had overcome, and maybe they had some, but it was still a white world. Your skin black, Tyrone was thinking, and you only go so high, Barack Obama or no Barack Obama.

He had a vision of Sabeel and himself opening up new territory and the goddamn guineas or spics spraying them like out of a scene in "The Sopranos" as they sat all duded out like a couple of stockbrokers at the Ritz.

He said, "Uh, buying the amounts you seem you thinking of come to a whole lot of dough."

"That right? You let me worry about that, okay?"

Tyrone nodded reasonably as though he hadn't been worrying at all. He caressed the Beamer's leather again. Sure be nice to move around in this. He had an Acura RSX which was okay, big, fat exhaust pipe sticking out from under the rear producing some pretty cool exhaust sounds, but there were only about ten million others like it in Roxbury.

"One other thing," Tyrone said, hoping Sabeel didn't boil, "you set yourself up as some kind of distributor—I mean at the top, you know what I'm saying?—and certain people are going to get royally pissed off."

Sabeel Biggs yawned. "That's why I want you to line up a little muscle. We can handle the spics, no trouble. This is our territory up here, not theirs."

He toyed briefly with telling Tyrone that he had the guy who killed Will Scarlet's mother but decided not to. Instead, he just said, "As far as the I-talians are concerned, I think I've got some insurance.

Tyrone Moore smiled, revealing one gold tooth embedded not too far back. He stroked the Beamer's leather again and had visions of being Sabeel Biggs's right hand man and graduating from an Acura RSX to something nice like this. Not too sure that he'd go with all white, though. He looked at Sabeel Biggs.

"Insurance?" he said. "What kind of insurance?"

Sabeel Biggs smiled. "Never you mind. Insurance or at least a way to build up some good will. And I'm going to cash it in real soon."

Chapter Twenty One

Under orders from Lou Russo, Mickey the Harp and Sal the Dogcatcher picked up Frankie Ricciardi as he was getting out of his Mustang. They had followed him from his home near Maverick Square in East Boston to where he parked in Chinatown where he hoped to catch a little amusement.

Frankie had allowed himself to feel fairly off the hook since talking on the phone to the paisan who said Will Scarlet only wanted the shooter of his mother. A diet of Mob movies made him confident that Will Scarlet probably had a sense of honor and commitment to keeping his word.

Mickey had covered for Sal and told Lou that they had arrived at the Elks real early but their target had already scooted. Mickey's mood wasn't made any better when Sal confessed that it was the doggiest of dogs that made him late.

"It's just a matter of time 'til we get the sonovabitch," Lou Russo said, "and I know how we'll do it. I don't like to, but you do what you have to. In the meantime, Mr. Scarlata's going out of his mind so we'll give him something 'til the main event."

He couldn't believe Frankie gave his real name. Probably afraid he'd eventually get caught and was trying to build up good will. He checked out the name, found the address and sent out Mickey and Sal to pick him up. Could be the name the caller gave him was of someone innocent but that would be that person's bad luck. The thing was to give Will Scarlet something that would hold him over.

As much as he didn't want to because it might cause complications, Lou Russo was now prepared to use the one enticement he was pretty sure would work and bring their boy in: his girlfriend, Ellie Robinson.

From the sounds and smells, Frankie Ricciardi was pretty sure he was somewhere near the waterfront. They had shoved him into an SUV and made him lie with his face buried in the seat while they drove for ten or fifteen minutes. But he couldn't be sure of the time.

Could be somewhere near the Black Falcon Pier or the North End or Charlestown. He was in a small portioned off corner room of some kind of old warehouse probably. The walls were granite like the warehouses that had been converted into expensive condos. There was a boarded window. The other two walls, forming another L, were cheap paneling.

He had been here all night since they had picked him up at about nine p.m. Now the sun had been fusing through the spaces between the boards over the window for a couple of hours anyway. He hadn't slept at all and stronger than his fatigue was the stink of his fear.

Without explanation of any kind, they had thrown him into the room and locked the door, leaving him to his imagination. He had tried to explore the room but the darkness was almost total. He had bumped into a couple of folding metal chairs and a big metal desk and a locked file cabinet.

Finally, he sat on one of the chairs, once or twice his shivering nearly out of control. They had taken his wallet but he knew it wasn't a case of theft. They had taken his cigarettes and matches.

They came into the room at 8:30. There were three of them. Two he recognized from the fleeting glimpses he got of them last night. The third was an older, squat, heavy-set bald guy. He looked kind of friendly and Frankie felt a ray of hope.

The bald guy sat at the desk. One of the younger guys told Frankie to get up and took his chair. Frankie stood, looked at them and shivered.

"I gotta piss real bad," he said.

"That so?" the older guy said. The three of them stared at Frankie for several seconds. Finally, the older guy nodded to the others who led him out of the room to a small toilet where they stood and watched him. As much as he had to go, he was unable to relieve himself.

One of them said, "Hey, you playing games with us?"

Frankie was as close to crying as he had been since he was about five years old.

The other one said, "Mickey, this guy's full of shit, I think, but he ain't full of piss."

They laughed at that.

Mickey said, "Maybe he don't like us staring at him."

Frankie's eyes stung with frustration and humiliation. Just as Mickey put his hand on his shoulder to lead him back, Frankie felt himself dribble and then gush.

"Whadda ya know?" Mickey said. "The guy really had to go, Sal."

When he finished, they led him back.

Mickey and Sal sat with the metal chairs turned around and their arms resting on the backs. The bald guy was leaning back in his chair looking at a copy of *Playboy*.

Frankie stood and shifted from foot to foot. He wanted to look at his watch but didn't because he knew it would evoke a response. They were waiting for something and whatever it was, he felt, was probably not going to be good for him.

The bald guy flipped shut his *Playboy* and tossed it to Sal. "Here, Sallie, check out the stuff in here. Not nearly as nice as what you get, but not too bad."

The three of them laughed at that. Frankie snuck a peek at his watch. Ten to nine.

As he continued to stand, the three others ignored him and made small talk amongst themselves about sports. Frankie wondered whether to volunteer any comments but decided the best course was to keep his mouth shut.

About five minutes later, another man walked in and Frankie recognized Will Scarlet from his pictures right away. Fear clutched him but he allowed himself some hope. The person he had talked with on the phone (probably the bald guy, he figured) had said Mr. Scarlata would be grateful to whoever helped him find the shooter. You're on your own, Chuggy, Frankie thought. You got me into this mess. There'd be no end to his cooperation.

The bald guy got up and took Sal's chair. William Scarlata took off an expensive topcoat, revealing equally expensive suit, shirt, and tie and sat at the desk.

He regarded Frankie evenly for a few moments, his face giving nothing. Finally, he said, "Your mother alive?"

Frankie felt his knees wobble. He nodded.

"You love your mother?"

Frankie hesitated and gave an almost imperceptible nod.

"What's the matter with you?" William Scarlata asked, his voice a slash. "That a hard question? You love your mother or don't you? You gotta think about it?"

Frankie's head swirled. He felt words crowd into his mouth and stumble out. "No, yeah, love my mother. Of course I do."

"My mother was the greatest woman ever walked the face of the earth," William Scarlata said. His voice was soft and even.

"You probably feel the same way about your mother. Am I right?"

Frankie felt himself nod his head dumbly but said nothing.

There was a pause of several moments. Frankie tried to marshal some coherence into his mind.

Then William Scarlata's voice slashed again. "*Figlio di*-you killed her. You didn't deserve to breathe the same air as her."

"Mr. Scarlata, please, I didn't kill your mother. Honest to God, I—"

"You were there, you sonovabitch. She goes to a restaurant for a little relaxation with friends and y - you two-bit . . ."

William Scarlata's voice trailed. He sat drawn inward for a few minutes. He looked at the bald man and said, "Lou."

Lou Russo got up and stood in front of Frankie. "Anything else you can tell us about your friend?"

"I told you everything I could."

"Yeah, we appreciate that," Lou Russo said. "You said he'd be at a certain Elks. Mickey and Sal here checked it out and guess what? He wasn't there."

"I-"

"Shut up. I'll tell you when to talk and when you do it better be interesting."

Lou Russo turned and paced a little circle.

He came back to Frankie. "I'll tell you something else we appreciate. You might be lying to save your sorry ass. What's to say you didn't pull the trigger?"

Frankie stood mute before the enormity of the accusation.

"You got nothing to say?"

"I—"

Lou Russo's fist smashed into Frankie's gut. Frankie doubled over and went to his knees.

Lou Russo brought the metal chair he had been sitting on over and set it behind Frankie. He helped Frankie to his feet and sat him in the chair.

"Where else you think your pal might go?"

Frankie shook his head.

"We know where he lives, we know where his girl lives. We know she works for a dentist. You know which one?"

Frankie drew in quick gulps of air. It took him a moment to find his voice. Finally he stammered, "Yeah, yeah, I do. It's Winters. Dr. Winters. In Brookline, I'm pretty sure."

Lou Russo shot a glance at Mickey and Sal.

"Very good. Now, what about your buddy? Where's he work?"

Despite the nausea from the punch, Frankie was starting to feel hopeful again. "He works part time for a florist. Bradford Bothers."

"What about family? He got family around here?"

Frankie shook his head. "His mother's dead. His old man's in a nursing home, I don't know exactly where. He's got a brother in L.A. That's all I know. Honest to God."

"Well, that's pretty good. You've been very helpful and we really appreciate that."

Lou Russo reached down, put his hand under Frankie's chin, and lifted his head up. With his other hand, he patted Frankie's head.

"You know, it's nice you've been so helpful but you know something else? On the other hand, it really sucks to see a guy turn on his friend to save his ass even though that friend, in this case, is a real shit. And we still don't know, don't *really* know that it wasn't you who pulled the trigger."

Frankie turned his head and looked straight at William Scarlata. "Mr. Scarlata, I'm real sorry about your mother. I really am. But I swear to God, I wasn't the one who shot her. It was Chug. Bobby Ellis."

"Actually, Frankie, we know that," Lou Russo said. "Can you think of anything else we should know about Chug that'll help us find him?"

Frankie shook his head and tried a slobbering smile at Lou Russo and William Scarlata.

Lou Russo nodded to Mickey and Sal who each grabbed one of Frankie's arms and led him off to another part of the warehouse where it had been a while since Lou the Butcher had practiced his skills.

"I want to see this, Lou," William Scarlata said as he walked with Lou Russo and they ignored the pleadings stumbling from Frankie Ricciardi's mouth.

Chapter Twenty Two

"Son of a *bitch*," Tilly Tillotson said out loud after he hung up his cell phone in the smelly two-room apartment he shared with a colony or two of cockroaches in Somerville. But it was handy to downtown Boston, Suffolk Downs or even the highway to Rockingham if he could coax his rat's nest of a car to make the trip or suck someone into giving him a lift.

Sabeel Biggs had been on the other end. Tilly felt as if lines were being drawn snugly around him. He had even been able to feel Sabeel Biggs's power through the telephone.

He had let Mink suck him into this just by dangling a little candy in front of his face. He regretted that he had ever told Mink he knew someone who knew who shot Will Scarlet's mother. Not to worry, Mink had said. Just set things up, get them going, and you never see Sabeel Biggs again. Well, talking with him on the phone was practically as scary as talking with him in person. At least seeing him in person might mean you'd get a peek at the kind of gorgeous babe that apparently hung out with Sabeel Biggs, the kind of babe that Tilly would kill for.

Sabeel Biggs wanted Tilly to get hold of this Chug guy *tout de suite*. That's what he had said. Toot sweet. Like he was trying to be funny or cool or sophisticated. Chug had never given him his number. Left it that he'd get in touch with Biggs.

The problem was, of course, that Tilly didn't have the vaguest idea who Chug was, let alone *where* he was. But he couldn't tell that to Sabeel Biggs. Tilly had the feeling that if things soured it would be him who Sabeel Biggs would come looking for. He thought of those big, powerful hands on the blonde's leg stroking lovingly and then of those same hands wrapped around his throat not so lovingly.

Okay, time to put the ball right back in Mink Whitehead's court. Better hustle to get hold of Mink because Sabeel Biggs said he wanted to hear from Tilly or Chug by tonight if possible. Tomorrow at the latest. Toot sweet.

Billy Wilkins had things worked out. Sort of. He had a snitch of his own who could get the word to the people who would inform William Scarlata that the man he was looking for was about to get involved in a deal with Ramon Mendez to scrape up enough cash to escape William Scarlata.

If all went to plan, Will Scarlet would send his troops storming in to sweep up Chug and maybe, with any luck, as an offshoot, so to speak, mess up Ramon and his cohorts. At that point, Billy Wilkins would have to play things by ear depending, among other things, on whether Will Scarlet himself was present.

But the tricky part. The tricky part was knowing where and when Ramon and Biggs would arrange for Chug to meet with Ramon. He and Jessup could follow Biggs's Beamer but that didn't allow any time to notify Will Scarlet. Maybe they'd meet at Ramon's place near Huntington Avenue but maybe not.

All this meant attaching a bug and, since this wasn't a departmental operation, getting the bug could be a little hairy. Could be done but, Billy Wilkins figured, why risk your own ass if you could risk someone else's?

That's why he was going over all of this with Special Agent Jessup as they sat parked in his car near the Congress Street Bridge which in a month or two would be crawling with tourists gawking at and climbing on 'The Beaver' and imagining the patriots throwing tea into Boston Harbor.

"Absolutely not," Special Agent Jessup said.

Billy Wilkins controlled his exasperation. They must have a course in being a pain in the ass at the FBI Academy, he figured.

"Look," Wilkins said, "you've got more autonomy than I have. I'm a small fish. I want some special equipment—a bug, whatever—I gotta go through about fifty-five channels whose immediate reaction is 'no.' But you, you're pretty near the top, I hear. Somebody wants something, they come to you."

"Out of the question."

"Besides," Wilkins continued as though Jessup had said nothing, "you stuff is state of the art. And we only need it today. One shot. No risk. Biggs won't be suspecting a bug 'cause no money's being passed on his end or anything. Mendez might but at that point Will Scarlet's troops will be moving in and then you and I plus the back ups I'll call in."

Jessup smiled the patient, sad smile of one dealing with dense child. "See, that's another thing. These back ups. You don't have that arranged."

"Naturally, I don't have that arranged. If everything goes according to plan, then we claim later this was something we got wind of recently and were working on quietly because we weren't sure we really had anything. If it works out, there won't be any fallout. We'll be heroes."

He paused to let 'heroes' sink in. A stiff breeze buffeted the car. Across the bridge, a jumble of high-rise crowded against the water like wall of mismatched columns of bricks, steel, and glass.

"If things somehow get screwed up, we jump ship. No one gets hurt except maybe Robert Ellis."

"Who's wearing a piece of federal government equipment. That I have to account for. Not you."

"Look, how about this. Ellis talks to Biggs. We find the where and when. Ellis goes into a gas station, a restaurant or something to take a leak and drops the bug. He talks into it to tell us where."

Jessup was shaking his head in that little way that made Billy Wilkins want to strangle him. Jesus, talk about uptight.

"There's still the matter of those back ups that you haven't arranged for."

"Jessup, I'm a *lieutenant*. I call for back ups, they'll be coming out of your pores in about ten seconds."

Billy Wilkins looked at his watch. "What do you say? I gotta get our Mr. Robert Ellis set up and I gotta make sure my lines to Will Scarlet are operational." He figured Jessup would like the term 'operational.'

"Speaking of," Jessup said, "where is Ellis?"

"He's squirreled away in a motel on the Southeast Expressway. When you meet him, don't forget you're gonna be the higher authority on all the assurances he's looking for."

"Who's paying for the motel?"

"Who the hell do you think?"

"My, my. You *are* enthusiastic about this, aren't you?"

Special Agent Jessup sat silent for a moment and then said, "You never said anything about my providing a bug."

His voice lacked animation and Billy Wilkins knew he had him. But he had known that all along. Jessup had his own little visions.

"Oh my God," Jessup said, "I ought to have my head examined. Drop me off. At three o'clock I'll be at the crosswalk in front of City Hall. Drive by and I'll have what you want."

Billy Wilkins resisted the urge to pat Jessup's head. He pulled into traffic just as Lou the Butcher was finishing with Frankie Ricciardi.

Ellie Robinson checked the appointment book. She had just eaten her lunch of a tuna sandwich, apple, and a can of diet soda. Naturally, she had brushed and flossed afterward.

Mrs. Sanford was due in at one. She was nearly done and at thirty-seven she'd have a gorgeous new smile.

Then Jeff Cusack, a nice-looking guy Ellie thought despite a couple of angled teeth that eventually Dr. Winters would eventually set straight.

Then the stream of after-school kids.

Then back to Laurie's and eventually what?

"Are you still with me?" Chug had asked her.

Well, that was the question, wasn't it? It was just a hell of a lot easier to concentrate on this afternoon's appointments.

"This is Special Agent Jessup, Federal Bureau of Investigation, Chug. He and his office are working on what we've got going with you."

Chug sat on the motel bed and looked at Special Agent Jessup. He looked to Chug like a loan officer at a bank. He couldn't picture him holding a ten millimeter in both hands and yelling, "Freeze."

"Agent Jessup," Billy Wilkins said, "this is Robert Ellis who's agreed to cooperate with us in breaking up that drug trafficking network."

"For considerations," Chug said.

"For considerations," Billy Wilkins said.

"And assurances of those considerations," Chug said.

"Naturally," Billy Wilkins said. "I think Agent Jessup's presence here, Chug, can ease your mind a whole lot for now."

Billy Wilkins sent Special Agent Jessup a signal with a little flip of his hands and a raising of his eyebrows.

Jessup pulled out his ID and showed it to Chug who got up from the bed to look at it.

"Feds in on a lousy drug bust?" Chug said. He shook his head as he looked Special Agent Jessup up and down.

"Not a 'lousy drug bust,' Chug," Billy Wilkins said, "if by that you mean locally confined. This is interstate trafficking. We're most definitely not talking a nickel-dime operation here."

Chug sat back down on the bed. "I still don't see any guarantees. I'm doing nothing 'til I get something concrete that I feel I can take to the bank."

He stared at them, his chin jutting at a take-a-stand angle.

"Well, we don't have anything right now, at this moment, in this goddamn motel," Billy Wilkins said, anger rising in him and staring back. "So, if the two of us aren't good enough for you, then you can walk if that's what you want. You're on your own. Except, let me remind you, that a full-fledged police investigation into certain felonies will begin."

"Yeah, but you yourself said last night that you've got nothing."

"Nothing? Nothing provable at this point but we have a hell of a head start, don't we, seeing that we don't have to go running around trying to find *who* did it. All we have to do is come up with something proving he did it."

Billy Wilkins held Chug's stare.

"So what's it gonna be? You call it."

Chug said something softly.

"What's that?" Billy Wilkins said. "I didn't hear you."

"I said, now the cards are really on the table, aren't they? But I'm in a corner so I guess it's going to have to be all right. But I sure as hell would hate to think that somehow you guys are screwing me over."

"Okay. That's good. That's showing some sense. Now we just got word that Biggs wants to meet with you tonight at seven to set up a big meeting with his boss, the guys we're really after. But we're not sure where that will be and we'll follow but there's always the chance we'll lose you so that means you'll have to wear a bug. Agent Jessup will go over that with you."

"A bug?"

"Yeah," Special Agent Jessup said. "Here it is."

He took a calculator from his coat and gave it to Chug.

"Just put it in your shirt pocket and speak normally. You won't have to raise your voice."

"Will I have to stand close to him?"

"Normal distance. You won't have to violate his space or anything. But most of the time you be beside him in the car."

"Now here's the deal, Chug," Billy Wilkins said. "That thing looks like something anyone might carry. Biggs will have no reason to think you might be wired but the others might. Probably not but they might. Even if they see it, it probably won't matter but why take chances so we want you to try to drop it off somewhere, like in a men's room, before Biggs takes you to the big fish but after he tell you where you're going."

Chug looked at the calculator and shook his head.

"You say this is something anyone might carry. No one carries these. For chrissakes, cell phones have calculators."

"You know something, Chug," Agent Jessup said, "most people don't even know there's a calculator on their cell. Just say you wanted a calculator to maybe figure out percentages or something in any deal you could work out with Biggs."

Chug looked doubtful. "Okay, what if he doesn't say where we're going?"

Billy Wilkins looked at Jessup. "Then you keep it. Just try to drop into the conversation in a nice, normal way where the hell you are. Matter of fact, you should probably keep it anyway. Never know. Biggs could say you're meeting at the Swan Boat lagoon and then end up behind Fenway Park just to be sneaky."

Billy Wilkins stared down Jessup who appeared on the verge of rebellion probably over the bug.

"We'll drop you off by South Station. Take the Red Line to Park Street then pick up the Green Line to Kenmore Square. Walk down to the corner of Commonwealth and Mass Ave, the side toward Boylston Street and he'll pick you up in that big white Beamer of his."

"There is just one little thing," Chug said. "I don't have any cash to give this guy. What's he gonna do, let me take a bunch of samples on credit?"

"No," Billy Wilkins said. "What you're gonna set up tonight is one more meeting. Tonight's a feeling out process. Your man up north is definitely interested in some very large quantities. He can pay. So you set up a 'good faith' meeting. You specify a quantity and he gives you a price. You let him arrange a time and place. This lets your man check quality and will show Biggs's boss you can come up with the money."

"And I'll be able to do that?"

"At the time. Through us."

Chug fingered the calculator. "Why is it I have the feeling that somehow you guys are screwing me over?"

"Beats me, Chug. I'd say we're the best friends you got right now," Billy Wilkins said. "Come on, let's get this show on the road."

Chapter Twenty Three

Ellie Robinson walked to her car in the little lot near Dr. Winters's office. She was grateful it was now light out when she finished work. She hated the early dark even more than the cold of winter.

As she approached the car, she didn't notice the man coming behind her and when he clasped a hand across her mouth and twisted her arm up her back so that her shoulder jolted with pain, she thought she was about to be raped and it couldn't be happening in daylight.

Suddenly an SUV bounced up in front of her and she recognized it from the chase over the bridge into Chelsea. The back door opened and she was shoved inside. The man squeezed in beside her.

The SUV swung past her car and out of the lot and Ellie knew she wasn't going to be raped.

This was about Chug.

The white Beamer swung to the curb and Chug got in and sat on fine leather and heard classical music playing on the car's stereo. Sabeel Biggs smiled at him, a white toothed, friendly smile as though he were a car salesman bringing about a fine car to demonstrate to a well-heeled potential customer.

"Fine evening, isn't it?" he said. "Everything okay with you?"

Chug looked at Biggs and gave him a nod and got right to the point. "Where are we meeting with your guys?"

Sabeel Biggs pulled into traffic and headed down Massachusetts Avenue. He drove for a few moments, a little smile moving his lips as he tilted his head and seemed to concentrate on the music.

"Ah, business, business. Always such a rush. It's a terrible master."

Chug looked at him, the powerful athletic body swelling under the expensive suit, thinking that this guy works too hard at dressing and talking in a way that says what you see is not what you get.

"Ever been to Symphony Hall?" Sabeel Biggs asked. "It's just down here to the right."

Chug saw Biggs look at him as though actually expecting an answer and as though the answer mattered.

"No. No, I've never been there."

Like you give a rat's ass.

"You should go some time. But I can tell that you want to get to the matter on hand and I don't blame you, given your circumstances. Hell of a thing, I imagine. I mean the bind you're in."

Sabeel Biggs glanced at Chug and gave him a sympathetic smile. "I assume you've heard of Mrs. Scarlata's passing. That just worsens things, doesn't it. Will Scarlet's apt to be a tad pissed off at his mother's killer. I mean, even more than he was."

"Look, if it's all right with you," Chug said, "I *would* just as soon get to the matter on hand, as you put it."

"Naturally. I understand. Let me say just this. Will Scarlet's a scary guy but he's no different than anyone else. What I mean is that he's not Superman. People hear 'Mafia' and they think *The Godfather, The Sopranos,* and so on. They build them up to be more than they are. I'll tell you what their advantage is over ordinary people. They don't worry about consequences the way other people do. They've got no conscience."

Sabeel Biggs put his head back and laughed as though he had been privy to something very funny.

"Yeah, that's interesting," Chug said. "So Will Scarlet puts his pants on one leg at a time like everyone else. Hell, I hadn't thought of that. Not to worry. But can we get down to business?"

"Let me ask you this, if you don't mind," Sabeel Biggs said. "What'd you use? A nine? Maybe a ten? Probably one or the other, am I right? For my money, a nine doesn't quite have the punch you might need in some circumstances. Although it would be plenty for an old I-talian lady. You still have it, I wonder?"

Chug felt the heat climbing up under his collar.

"You're one funny bastard. Anyone ever tell you that? I mean, what's your act? I know you're a badass dude, all roided up, ripping out that suit and all. But what's the bit talking like you went to Harvard or something, talking about Symphony Hall? You trying to prove they can take the black badass out of Roxbury *and* take Roxbury out of the badass?"

Sabeel Biggs smiled and laughed. "Oh, dear, you're hurting my feelings and here I am just trying to establish a little rapport before settling down to business. Normally I carry a .44 Magnum, just like Clint Eastwood, although it seems to me old Dirty

Harry had a Smith & Wesson. Mine's a Ruger. Care to see it?"

Sabeel Biggs pulled his suit jacket back revealing the butt of a very large revolver.

"I have several others as well. I've got a nice Glock nine-millimeter, I've got a Sig-Sauer, a Beretta, a Colt or two. Oh, yes, and I've even got me a Street Sweeper shotgun. Ever hear of that? Something for every occasion."

"That's great," Chug said. "You're packing a regular cannon and you're a gun collector. A real close friend of the NRA. Very impressive. Hey, look, why don't you pull over and I'll hop out. We've got business but seems to me you want to play around. Go to Symphony Hall, take in a little highbrow music and culture. Maybe after you can go to the Museum of Fine Arts and browse around and then go to a shooting range and blast away with your goddamn .44 Magnum. Then some other time we can get down to business if we're both still interested."

"Oh, I've gone and done it, haven't I? Made you cross. But you're right. Let's get down to business. Here's what I'm thinking. You don't care and I'm sure your connection equally doesn't care who supplies him as long as the stuff is good and the price is right and the supply can be steady and reliable. Am I right?"

"What are you talking about?"

Sabeel Biggs thought of the conversation he had had with Tyrone Moore when he called from Jersey. Things could be worked out down there and Sabeel felt as though he might just be on the threshold of something very good, if this dude sitting beside him wasn't full of shit.

"What I'm talking about is that I don't see the need for your man to go to anybody but me. I can get him all he wants and I can beat—I know I can beat—anything the people we were scheduled to meet can quote you."

Chug groped for something to say. This wasn't going according to plan. Wilkins wasn't after this middleman or distributor although obviously one doing quite well for himself.

"Ah, there's Symphony Hall," Sabeel Biggs said, pointing to the right like a tour guide. He smiled as though he had pleasant memories of nights spent at concert.

"So, what do you think?"

Chug looked at him. "Hell, I don't know. Naturally, I'm looking—my man is looking—for a good price on quality stuff but—"

"But what? Your friend, Howard Tillotson, got my name from a mutual friend, Henry Gonzalez, as the person to see if you want to do business. Now, Henry happens to know I'm doing well and I am. But, I figure you gotta keep moving. I can supply your man everything he needs. End of story."

"So we're not meeting with your people."

"No we're not. Nothing's set up. I don't see a problem." Sabeel Biggs looked at Chug, smiling the car salesman's smile.

"Do you?" The smile snapped shut. On the radio, a baritone was singing in Italian.

"Tonight was going to be just to set up a 'good faith' meeting," Chug said. "Discuss terms, prices. Then next time, I buy a quantity, to show you the dough, get some stuff for my man to check out. If you were thinking of doing something tonight, I don't have a dime on me."

Sabeel Biggs smiled again, a big reassuring smile. Sir, we didn't expect you to pay cash tonight for this fine automobile. Let's discuss—haggle, if you want to call it that—but be assured that you came to the right place. We'll beat anybody's price.

He said, "We're even. I don't have anything on me but some talcum powder I use after I shower. The ladies love it. Come on, we'll drive around some more and talk. Maybe we'll go over to the North End and see if we can find Will Scarlet so you can extend your apologies and sympathies."

Sabeel Biggs slapped Chug's knee and threw back his head and laughed his deep bass laugh that resonated as though it came from an echo chamber.

"You did fine. You did just fine," Billy Wilkins said to Chug. Sabeel Biggs had done a rambling tour of the city almost as though he had been trying to elude a tail, except that it was done in an unhurried way. In the end, Chug requested to be dropped off at the corner of Beacon and Charles by the Public Gardens.

Chug watched Biggs drive down Beacon and then walked down Charles to the crosswalk between the Public Gardens and the Common. In less than a minute, Billy Wilkins's car pulled up and Chug got in.

As Billy Wilkins drove, he and Chug went over Sabeel Biggs's pitch to Chug. Special Agent Jessup sat stone-faced.

"Goes to show you, doesn't it," Billy Wilkins said, "that there's no honor among thieves, or, in this case, drug dealers."

"So what happens now?" Chug asked. "By the way, the guy thinks he's a real comedian."

"Yeah, we heard."

Chug shook his head. "Yeah, Mr. Sabeel Biggs works hard at being a lot of things he's not."

Billy Wilkins nodded. "Okay, so we've got to think about what's next," he said. His voice was composed and hid his anger and disappointment.

"I don't know that there's a hell of a lot of thinking to do," Special Agent Jessup said. "Seems to me that it's time to fold the tents."

Chug leaned toward the front seat. "What the hell you talking about, 'fold the tents'?"

"He doesn't mean anything. It's just talk. We've had a little set-back and we've got to think it out."

But as he drove, Billy Wilkins felt a little laugh well up inside him. What the hell, he thought, I'm in this far. Why not three birds with one stone?

"Shakespearian," Special Agent Jessup said. "Or operatic. But totally wacko. But that's good because it makes me see things clearer, the way I should have all along. I'm out."

"Jessup, Jessup," Billy Wilkins said slowly as if now Jessup were the dense child who couldn't comprehend. But he couldn't think of anything to add to enlighten him.

Chug was safely back in his motel and the two men were burrowing beneath Boston in one of the Big Dig tunnels that had cost enough to fund a trip to Mars.

"You've got a flair for the dramatic, I'll give you that," Jessup said, "but give it up. As a matter of fact, anything happens to that poor guy, I'll have your ass, just in case you're thinking of going through this on your own."

"Give it a rest, Jessup. You want out? Fine. Get out, but don't threaten me. Just don't. And don't forget this 'poor guy' shot a woman in the commission of attempted armed robbery and that this woman has died as a result of her wound."

"Then bring him in as I suggested originally. We're going over old ground here, Wilkins."

They rode in silence a moment, each assessing the other's strength and purpose. When they pulled out of the tunnel, Wilkins said, his voice now conciliatory, "Maybe trying for all three is a bit much."

"You think?"

"Yeah, Scarlata's the big fish. We want him no matter. Looks like we're stuck with Biggs. I just thought that maybe we could also tip off Mendez."

"Yeah, I know. You said. Not only does Scarlata come zipping in when you tip him about Ellis meeting with Biggs but now you want Mendez to do the same to get his faithless underling in an act of betrayal. And then, all according to some totally goofball scheme you concocted in your deranged mind, Scarlata whacks Mendez and Biggs, thus ridding the world of a couple of bad guys, and then either kills Ellis or drags him off to some awful fate. Except that we, you and I on our white steeds, save Ellis and put William Scarlata away in a dungeon."

"All right, all right, all right. We forget about Mendez."

Billy Wilkins lit a cigarette and cracked his window an inch. From the corner of his eye, he checked Jessup. "Well?"

"Well, what?"

"What do you mean, 'well what'? Things are the same now, if we give up on Mendez. Just one of the players has changed. It's now Sabeel Biggs instead of Ramon Mendez. And that shouldn't matter to you. I'm the one who wanted Mendez. Scarlata's the only one who interested you all along."

"Biggs wants to see the buyer. How do you plan on handling that?"

Same as before. Ellis sets up the meeting. We tip Will Scarlet. The scenario plays out as we've planned all along. There doesn't have to be a buyer."

Billy Wilkins pulled the car over. They were on Atlantic Avenue. He waved his arm in a sweeping motion to his left, toward the North End.

"There it is. Will Scarlet territory. He's probably there somewhere right now if he's not looking this way from his home in Nahant, a home the two of us, salaries combined, could never even dream of owning. I mean, you wouldn't mind if he made his money in some nice honest way, like ripping investors off or swindling retirees, but we both know how he came by his wealth."

Billy Wilkins looked directly at Special Agent Jessup.

"So, you know what I'm gonna do? I'm gonna turn around and head back to that motel. I'm gonna set things up and get the ball rolling. It's gonna happen, Jessup, with you or without you and it's gonna happen as soon as I can make it happen. Maybe tomorrow night."

Billy Wilkins sipped on his cigarette. "So what do you say? You with me or do you want to get out here?"

Lou Russo had no taste for this. He eyed Ellie Robinson sitting straight in the same metal chair Frankie Ricciardi had sat in not so long ago. He could tell she was scared but doing her best not to show it.

He almost felt sorry for her. Pretty thing. Wholesome looking. Nice teeth that she had revealed when she grimaced once or twice.

He had never hurt a woman before. Hitting or anything like that and, when he ordered Mickey and Sal to bring this one in, he hadn't thought ahead to what he was going to do specifically. The realization that he would eventually have to kill her actually came as a surprise to him and he knew he was being careless for not having planned more thoroughly.

Maybe if he had made Mickey and Sal wear nylon stockings over their faces or ski masks he wouldn't have to kill her. But she had seen their faces, his too, and there was nothing to do about it.

The mask routine was alien to him, though. Terrorists or two-bit punks who robbed gas stations wore masks.

Lou Russo was sitting behind the metal desk, had arrived about twenty minutes ago. Mickey and Sal had brought the girl in a couple of hours earlier. Mickey was sitting in the other metal chair and Sal was standing behind the girl.

Lou Russo was grateful that at least the girl was not blubbering. She wasn't even sniffling. And she hadn't done any begging when he put a few questions to her for no particular purpose except to say *something,* maybe just to put her a little at ease. If she were at ease, he figured, she might be a little more cooperative.

To himself, he admitted that if this were a guy he wouldn't care if he were at ease or not. As a matter of fact, he would have done everything to make sure a guy wasn't at ease.

As he looked at the girl, he remembered Frankie Ricciardi and thought of something. "You have to go to the bathroom or anything?"

Ellie nodded.

Lou Russo looked at Mickey and Sal a moment and then said, "Come with me."

When she shut the door behind her, he said, "Don't lock it. If I hear it lock, I'll bust the door down."

Lou Russo thought about the lack of cleanliness of the bathroom and felt a moment's embarrassment. Maybe he'd get Sal to clean it up.

Ellie Robinson sat on the toilet and assessed her situation. Beyond its being very bad, she didn't know what to anticipate. The two guys who had picked her up said practically nothing while they drove her to the old warehouse and while they sat her inside and waited with her for the older bald guy to arrive.

As for the older man, he appeared ill at ease to her. He had asked her a few questions that seemed to go nowhere and had pretty much avoided eye contact.

As she relieved herself, she became aware of the filth and stink of the bathroom. She had run the water in the sink to cover her noise but the danger and degradation of her situation almost burst from her and she had to strangle incipient sobs. She was determined not to show weakness.

She looked around. The bathroom was windowless but she couldn't picture herself performing any movie-like escape crawling out a window if there were one and he'd hear her anyway. There was nothing she could use as a weapon unless you counted the filthy-looking toilet brush wedged into the corner beside the toilet. She wondered why it was filthy since the toilet didn't look as though it had seen a brush.

At the sink, she washed her hands and checked herself in the splotched mirror of the medicine cabinet. She was about to shut off the water when she thought of something. She turned the faucets full force to make as much noise as possible and gingerly tugged at the medicine cabinet door.

It popped open with a squeak and she held her breath waiting to see whether the man would open the bathroom door.

Inside, was a bottle of rubbing alcohol, a box of bandages, a bottle of mouthwash, a bottle of aspirin and what she was looking for. It was one of those old safety razors where you had to unscrew the top to get at the blade. It was crusted with hardened soap and looked as if it had last been used during World War Two.

She had taken the top off and was removing the blade when Lou Russo opened the bathroom door.

He had her dead to rights, the crusty old Gillette in her left hand and the blade in her right. For a moment, their eyes locked and then Lou Russo said, "What'd you have in mind, shave your legs or slash your wrists?   Probably slice me across the throat, huh?"

Carefully, Ellie placed the blade back into the razor, tightened it down, and put the whole thing back into the medicine cabinet. Then she turned and eyed Lou Russo steadily. She said nothing.

"You got guts, I'll say that," Lou Russo said, nodding his head approvingly. "But what you had in mind wasn't smart. You slice me and you got the other two to get past. And they ain't gentlemen, either one of them, I'll tell you. Believe me, you want me around."

She walked back in front of him into the room where Mickey and Sal sat. They eyed her, like pack animals, she thought, anticipating what she didn't want to think about. She returned their look steadily for a moment, felt her eyes start to fill and had to look away.

"What do you want?" she asked. She had tried to avoid the question, fearing the response it might provoke, it seemed to have a will of its own and rather surprised her when she asked it.

"You were wondering, huh?" Lou Russo said. "Figured you might be. It's your boyfriend we want, but you probably figured that too. Am I right?"

"No. You're not right. Not at all. You're wrong. I don't know what you're talking about."

"What we're talking about is your boyfriend. The guy with the weird name. What's that mean anyway, Chug?"

Lou Russo looked at Ellie evenly, not expecting an answer. She held his gaze.

"He's a hard guy to locate. We figured you could help us find him." Lou Russo continued to stare at

Ellie trying to break her with his eyes, unsure whether to proceed with force or diplomacy. He knew he was no diplomat.

"Look, we're gonna get him sooner or later and, really, it's no big deal. We just want to talk. We know he's not at his place. We know he's not staying at your place and neither are you."

Lou Russo tried a friendly, reassuring smile.

"We know he's been staying at an Elks but took off from there lickety split. So he's gotta be somewhere. We just want to know where."

Lou Russo was back behind the desk now. He looked at Sal sprawled in one of the chairs and said, "Sallie, give the lady a chair. Whadda I gotta do, send you to finishing school?"

He came from behind his desk, took the chair from Sal and said gently, "Come on, sit down. You want a coffee or anything? Something to eat?"

Ellie remained standing and looked Lou Russo straight in the eye. She was about an inch taller. He didn't like standing close to women who were taller than he was, which was fairly often.

"I'll tell you what I want," she said. "I want you to let me go. What the hell do you think?"

Lou Russo had backed away from her a few inches. He nodded at the chair. "Come on, sit down."

Ellie tested the moment by standing a few seconds and then sat down.

"That's good," Lou Russo said. "That's better. Let's just talk like civilized people. We can do that much, huh?"

He sat behind the desk. He looked at the ceiling, at the maze of wires and pipes.

"It's cold in here. It's hard to kick in the heat, though," he said to Ellie as though they were in a social context.

He looked at Sal. "Sal, whyn't you go out and pick up some coffees and sandwiches."

Sal left, giving Ellie a look and a grin, and Lou Russo said, "So where'd he go? He staying with some friend? He go out to California to his brother?"

"Look, I know you won't believe this, but I really don't know what you're talking about."

"You're right. I don't believe it so why don't we just cut through the bullshit, pardon the expression, and help us get in touch with old Chug. That's all. We just want to meet with him and then we give you a ride home."

Ellie laughed a short humorless laugh. "'Pardon the expression.' That's really good. I can see I'm with a gentleman. Not to worry and all. Sorry, but I can't help you."

Lou Russo shrugged. He looked at Ellie's purse on the desk in front of him where Mickey had put it.

"Sorry," he said, "I don't like going through other people's things."

He opened the bag, rummaged a second, and pulled out her cell phone. He hit the menu button, selected phonebook, scrolled, and quickly found 'Chug.'

He smiled at her, pushed the button, and put the phone to his ear. "If you won't help us get to him, maybe we can convince him to come to us."

Then he said, "Mickey, get her out of here for a few minutes. But treat her nice."

Chapter Twenty Four

Chug wasn't paying attention to the show on television, something about shipwrecks. Instead, he was thinking about his ride around Boston with Sabeel Biggs and Special Agent Jessup's comment about folding tents. He was quickly coming to the conclusion that it was time to head for distant places. But only with Ellie.

He was thinking of her when his cell phone rang. He checked the screen and said, "Hi, I was just thinking about you."

"Oh, I doubt it," a male voice he didn't recognize said and quickly added, "By the way, Ellie's fine. For now. Whether she stays that way depends on you."

Chug's ears rushed with sound as he sat on the edge of the motel bed and rocked in short, quick motions.

When he said nothing, the voice asked, "Aren't you gonna ask who this is?"

"Who is it?"

"Okay. That's better. This is someone calling from your girlfriend's phone, as obviously you can tell. We want to meet you and talk."

"I'm listening," he said.

"Well, that's good. So I'll spell it out for you, make it short and sweet. It's pretty simple. You tell me where you are and I'll have someone pick you up."

"You said Ellie's okay. Let me talk to her."

"In a minute."

"No, no. no. Right now. Let me talk to her right now."

"Listen to me carefully. You're not calling the shots here. Take a deep breath. I'll let you talk with your girlfriend in a minute."

"Who are you?"

"You don't need to know my name. I'm not gonna play games with you. I'm calling about a certain woman you shot who died. We want to discuss that with you. In person. Now, you take a minute, let this sink in and I'll put Ellie on the phone. Then, we'll talk some more."

Chug sat through two minutes of waiting that seemed much longer. He shut off the television set with the remote.

Then Ellie spoke on the phone. "Hi. Listen, I'm fine. I really am."

Her voice was steady and calm.

"Where are you?"

"I don't know. They've got me in some building but I'm okay. Got me as I left work."

"Ellie, I—"

"Okay, you heard her. She's fine. Now you're gonna tell us where we can pick you up."

As Chug's mind raced through possibilities, there was a rap on his door.

"Wait a minute," Chug said into the phone. He covered it with his hand, went to the door, and cracked it.

Billy Wilkins stepped in and Chug said into the phone, "I'll call you back in a few minutes. So just cool it."

Chug clicked off the phone and Billy Wilkins arched his eyebrows inquisitively at it.

"Hey, thanks for trying to help me out," Chug said, "but things just got real complicated."

Sabeel Biggs was breaking bread or, more accurately, crumbling a donut and working on his first cup of coffee for the day at a donut place called Zeke's between the South End and Roxbury. It was just after ten, an unusually early start for him to be up and about.

Normally, his day started around noon with an eclectic lunch at the rotunda at Quincy Market where he'd fill his flat belly with various ethnic samplings from the many food stalls that lined both sides of the market. His plate often ended up a veritable United Nations of food.

He was up early, though, because he had a deal going down for Ramon at 11:30 in Chinatown and he liked to allow plenty of time to get his head on straight. You go into a buy or a sell with fuzz in your head and you could easily get screwed or worse.

So, he had arisen at eight o'clock, gone to the gym for an hour and a half of pumping some serious iron and was now, freshly showered and smelling sweet, planning his day at Zeke's.

With a little luck, he'd be out from under Ramon and on his own if the setup with the guy he was with last night came to anything. Chug was a little spooky but Sabeel felt things were going to work. He felt on the verge of bigger and better things.

He was considering a second donut when Nappy Williams walked into Zeke's, spotted Zabeel, and joined him at his little table.

"Sabeel," he said. Nappy Williams was a squat man who should have looked rugged. Instead, he looked like a broad balloon that has lost a lot of its air.

"Nappy. Long time. Being a good boy?"

"Only way to be. With the man watching me, have to be a good boy," Nappy said.

"How long you been out?"

"Be five months next week."

Sabeel Biggs regarded Nappy Williams with conflicting feelings of affection and distaste. Originally, they were from the same neighborhood and Nappy had been a pretty cool guy at one time. But he had taken a few tumbles and ended up pulling some hard time at Cedar Junction. Cool guy, Sabeel figured, but a loser like so many who came out of Roxbury. No way that would ever happen to him. You had to be stupid to end up at Cedar Junction.

"You want a donut or anything? Cuppa coffee?" To Sabeel Biggs, Nappy looked as though he probably wanted some nose candy. He was doing a lot of sniffing as if he had a cold or hay fever. No flowers or trees blooming yet but Nappy could have a cold. Too bad. Nappy wasn't going to get any freebie coke out of him. He was lucky to get a donut and coffee.

Sabeel got a couple of donuts and coffees and sat back down.

"Those your wheels out there?" Nappy asked, jerking his thumb in the direction of Sabeel Biggs's BMW sitting proud and white in the parking lot.

"Yup." Don't ask me for a ride anywhere, you shitbum.

"You doing well. You always a smart guy, Sabeel."

"Yeah. It's the breaks, is all, Nappy. So tell me, how they treat you at Cedar Junction?" Sabeel Biggs inflected the words 'Cedar Junction,' the name the state had given to the state prison at Walpole because the citizens of Walpole felt a stigma attached itself to their community if it shared a name with a prison.

Sabeel figured that apparently the citizens of Concord didn't have similar feelings about *their* community having a prison in its midst sharing the name and Concord was pricey, prestigious and historical as all hell what with the Minute Men and the Revolution starting there.

"Like shit. Everybody get treated like shit."

Sabeel Biggs dug into his coffee and donut. He wanted to get away from Nappy as soon as he could. Besides not sounding too good, Nappy didn't look too good, like he might have AIDS or something. Probably wasn't hard to pick up AIDS at Cedar Junction.

"Too bad about Henry Gonzalez," Sabeel Biggs said, mainly just to make conversation. "Had a stroke, I hear."

"Yeah, I heard that too. About a month after I got out."

"I thought you told me you got out five months ago."

"I did, man, I did. I got out just after Halloween. I heard Henry got sick a couple of weeks before Christmas. Real messed up. Couldn't talk. Practically a vegetable, know what I'm sayin'?"

Sabeel Biggs swallowed some donut and thought of his conversation with Tilly Tillotson who had said he talked with Henry Gonzalez, what could it be? Less than a month ago.

'Course Nappy Williams could easily have his calendar screwed up.

"You sure it was before Christmas?"

"Hell, yeah, I'm sure. Cuckoo Collins—you remember him?—got out after New Year's. I ran into him right after that big snowstorm. He told me. How come you asking?"

Sabeel Biggs pushed the rest of his coffee and donut aside.

"Just real interesting, is all."

After Ellie had talked with Chug last night, they brought in a cot, pillow, and blankets and then left her alone. Quickly, she determined there was no way out and so she used the cot and managed a few hours' sleep.

One of the goons came in about 7:30 and let her use the bathroom. To her surprise, he behaved himself. Must be under orders from the bald guy, Ellie figured.

Around mid-morning, Lou Russo brought Ellie a McDonald's breakfast. It wasn't what she'd usually eat, an egg and ham in a roll, but her stomach juices were churning away and, despite her resolve to take nothing from them, she tore into the food greedily. There was also juice and coffee.

While she ate, Lou Russo sat and read the morning *Herald*. When she finished, he handed her a new toothbrush and a small tube of toothpaste. "Thought you might want this. You got a nice smile."

Ellie looked him in the eye. "You guys are beautiful. You really are. A piece of work. You kidnap me, stick me in this hole, but you try to act like a goddamn gentleman. You feed me, give me a toothbrush. What am I supposed to be? Grateful? Gee thanks for telling me I've got a nice smile, kind sir. Stick it."

As she spoke, she regretted her words. No point in antagonizing them. The point was to stay alive and healthy as long as possible. And she did want to brush her teeth.

Lou Russo held her cell phone in his hand. "We're still waiting to hear back from your boyfriend. We were talking last night and he cut me off. Said he'd call right back but he hasn't. I've called him but all I get is his voice mail. I've left him a message to call. Stressed just how important it is for everyone concerned that he gets back to me. So far, nothing."

Lou Russo smiled at Ellie. "So for now, I guess, we're back to square one. Any ideas how we can get hold of him?"

"You mean *where* you can get hold of him. Sorry, I don't have a clue."

"If you did, you'd tell us, right?"

"Oh, absolutely. Get this over with as quickly as possible. I could watch you break his knees with a baseball bat for starters and then . . ." Ellie's voice faded with her stoicism.

She considered another strategy. She had noticed guns strapped under the arms of the two goons. Maybe when they came back she could get at one of them. She knew nothing about guns but if she got one she'd point it and keep pulling the trigger. No negotiating. Just pull the trigger and keep pulling it, blow the bastards away and run.

She dismissed that as hopeless fantasy. Certainly as long as she kept acting like a defiant bitch. The thing to do was to try to get them to let down their guard.

She looked at Lou Russo. "I'm sorry. I appreciate the food. And the toothbrush. But I really don't know where Chug is. He took off and wouldn't tell me. Probably to protect me as much as himself."

Lou Russo nodded and smiled, trying to project warmth, friendliness, and understanding.

"See. That's what I mean. He thinks he's gotta protect you and himself. He's got it wrong. Mr. Scarlata's not that way. Oh, sure, at first he was pissed when his mother got shot and now he's grief stricken but he knows nothing will bring his mother back. Mainly, he just wants to know that the person who shot his mother cares, know what I'm saying? He just wants to look that person in the eye and have them see how much he's suffering. He figures that's enough."

Ellie nodded and felt like telling Lou Russo that he was a very poor actor.

"So I guess what we've got to do," Lou Russo said, "is wait a bit for him to call or until he answers when I call. Then I'll let you talk to him again 'cause he's gonna call. There's no way he's just gonna let you sit here. Not if I read the two of you right. Couple of nice kids got themselves into a little scrape but that can be worked out.

Lou Russo got up, came over to Ellie, and patted her hand.

"Come on, let's go to the bathroom so you can brush your teeth."

William and Sylvia Scarlata were eating lunch and watching the noon news in their private room at the

Sailor V restaurant on Route One, north of Boston. Sailor V was one of Will Scarlet's legitimate enterprises. Its specialty was seafood at very reasonable prices and it was always crowded. He had seen the name on a boat in the Bahamas. Sylvia had explained the play on words to him—c'est la vie—and he thought it would make a good name for a seafood restaurant. Sylvia often wondered whether he had built Sailor V just so he could use the name. Sometimes he did things like that.

Will Scarlet was eating a swordfish steak and Sylvia a lobster salad, the lobster caught in the cold waters off Maine. Will Scarlet refused to buy locally caught lobsters because he thought the water was too polluted. That was the extent of his environmental awareness or concern. The menu made a big thing of it, though, saying that Sailor V served only lobsters caught in the clean, cold waters off the Maine coast.

Sylvia was saying something about getting away to someplace sunny and warm, that it would be good for both of them. She was beginning to think they'd never find who shot Florence Scarlata and she was also beginning not to care although she'd still like to spit in the bastard's face just before Bill did whatever he was going to do.

But her husband wasn't listening to her. He was concentrating on what the newscaster was saying. The anchor, a handsome black woman, was saying something about a missing woman.

Then a shift to a brief taped interview with a dentist who explained that a young woman who worked for him hadn't reported for work that morning and that her car had remained in his parking lot overnight.

To Sylvia Scarlata, her husband's interest in the incident seemed beyond what he would normally show in such a story.

She probed a little. "What's that all about, Bill?"

Will Scarlet gave his wife a tight-lipped shake of the head and she dropped the question. Usually, she could read his mood but this time she wasn't sure. Bending back to her lobster salad, she thought they probably wouldn't be getting away to anyplace warm and sunny very soon.

Lieutenant Billy Wilkins hit the hammer as he sped down the Southeast Expressway. This was damage control of the first order and he had everything going: his headlights strobed, blue light pulsed from his mirrors and inside the car's grille, and his siren wailed. Traffic scampered to the side like frantic wildebeest from a charging lion.

He could feel everything slipping away. His plan and all that it might bring him was in danger of dissipating before his eyes, like vapor that you try unsuccessfully to control with your hands.

Last night, he thought he had done a nice job of calming and restraining Chug who wanted to charge out of the motel, cast himself at Will Scarlet and save Ellie Robinson in dramatic self sacrifice.

He had told Chug not to call back or to answer if they called him.

"We've got to think, we've got to plan," he had told Chug. "I know you're worried about Ellie but, believe me, they won't touch her. They want you and she's bait. She's no good to them except healthy.

"Just stay put except you can go down to the Burger King about five minutes away for breakfast tomorrow. I'll be by and let you know what we have."

One thing Billy Wilkins didn't know whether he himself had was Special Agent Jessup. Jessup had seemed to bail out last night after the switcheroo by Sabeel Biggs. Wilkins hadn't talked with him since and knew the Ellie Robinson development might be enough for Jessup's final defection.

The only thing that Wilkins felt he had going for him now was that Will Scarlet and his men didn't know that a cop knew about Ellie. But given all the circumstances, Billy Wilkins didn't know how he could leverage that.

But just fifteen minutes ago, Chug had called him on his cell, told him he had a message on his voice mail about Ellie and wanted to do something now.

"I'll be there in twenty minutes," Billy Wilkins had said. "Hold tight."

He cut the lights and siren about a couple of hundred yards from the motel and pulled in quietly.

In his room, Chug was like a man who had just burst his restraints. He shoved his cell phone into Billy Wilkins's hand.

"Here. Listen to this message."

Wilkins put the phone to his ear, selected the message and listened.

"Okay," he said when it had finished. "That doesn't change a thing. He's trying to get you to do something stupid. Like charging out of here and running to them. I told you, that's not gonna do Ellie or you any good. He's bluffing. He won't hurt her. What we've got to do is play for some time."

"Hey, they've got Ellie someplace and she can't stay like that. This is my fault. Not hers. I'm gonna do whatever it takes to get her out of this. Christ, I was just watching about her on television."

Billy Wilkins sat by the little table near the window. Outside, traffic thrummed by on the expressway.

"Chug, let me spell this out. The way things are right now, if they get hold of you, you're a dead man. That's a given. By the way, I think I recognize the voice that left the message. Lou Russo. Will Scarlet's right hand man. Not a nice guy."

Billy Wilkins paused, framing his words.

"Once they have you, you figure they're just gonna let Ellie go? 'Hey, El, no hard feelings, huh? Sorry about your boyfriend but you know how it is. And you *promise* you won't say anything to anyone and you wont ID us? Okay, there's a good girl. Off you go.'"

"So, what are you saying?"

Billy Wilkins laughed a humorless laugh. "What am I saying? I'm saying what I already said to you. We've got to play for a little time. Sit tight and think."

"You said, 'the way things are right now.' What do you mean by that?"

Billy Wilkins let out a stream of breath. "Well, they don't know that I know about Ellie. They don't know about you and me and Agent Jessup. That's something that maybe we can play for her release. But we don't want to jump into that without first figuring out how to get you off the hook with Will Scarlet."

Billy Wilkins felt like a man drowning, being sucked under by a relentless whirlpool, but one of his own making.

"Well, then, that's the ticket," Chug said. "We've got to get that started. I don't care if that means the drug bust deal is off as far as any help I might have got out of that is concerned. You gotta get moving on this and get Ellie out of there. Far as I'm concerned, that's all that matters."

"That's right. Ellie safe. You safe. The new life, all we've gone over. That means more than ever we've got to stick with the plan."

Billy Wilkins lit a cigarette.

"I know you're finding it hard to think straight, but you gotta trust me, Chug. I want you to call Biggs, tell him your buyer wants a meeting as soon as possible."

He put a hand on Chug's shoulder.

"We're gonna get Ellie out. But we gotta be smart, not stupid."

Chug pulled away and Billy Wilkins thought he might bolt.

"Come on, Chug. Stay with me on this."

Ordinarily, Tilly Tillotson would have felt like King Shit tooling around in a big ass Beamer, cocooned in leather and listening to a super quality stereo playing what sounded to him like Mozart or Beethoven.

Instead, he felt like shit.

When he got the call from Sabeel Biggs, Tilly had tried to think of a quick reason he couldn't meet with him. Something like, "I'd love to get together but I'm scheduled for open heart at Mass General in about an hour."

Sabeel Biggs was, to Tilly's surprise, driving in a very civilized fashion in keeping with the music and the conservative business suit he was wearing. Tilly knew it was racist, but he would have given four to one that Sabeel Biggs would push the beamer to Mach 1, listen to some godawful rap, and dress like a pimp. Of course, he had seen him before in a suit but that was when he was with that gorgeous blonde with the legs that started just a little south of her shoulders.

Biggs had called him as he was making plans for the evening which didn't involve a hell of a lot more than maybe going out for one of his favorite suppers: a Big Mac, some fries, and a strawberry shake. Then pick up a video, maybe a Charles Bronson or a Clint Eastwood. He'd seen them all at least once but you never got sick of Bronson or Eastwood. Bronson, Eastwood, and a couple of brewskies.

Unfortunately, he was riding around listening to boring-ass music with an individual who very definitely did not bore him. You get honest, Tilly admitted to himself, this guy scares the bejusus outa me. Goddamn Mink.

Real accommodating, Biggs had picked Tilly up near his place in Somerville before he had time to eat. But he had lost his appetite and, anyway, he'd never admit to this guy that he ate at McDonald's like some little kid all excited about Ronald McDonald or the Hamburglar.

Biggs had said he just wanted to tie together some loose ends about this Chug deal. Why with me? Tilly had wanted to ask but didn't dare. He hated when people talked about 'loose ends' like what they wanted to talk about wasn't really important to them. It usually was.

"Howard Tillotson, my man," Sabeel Biggs said, his resonant voice stepping over the separate syllables of Tilly's name in a put-down way that pissed Tilly off, "if you'll reach into that glove compartment you'll find a little bag of some very high quality stuff."

When Tilly did nothing, Sabeel Biggs persisted. "Go ahead. Be my guest. If it was wine, it'd be a bill a bottle. At least."

Tilly thought, this ape wants to give me some candy, why the hell not?

It was a zip-lock plastic bag, about a quarter of a cup, sitting on top a little mirror and a couple of straws.

"Actually, Howard, whyn't you wait a bit? I know a little spot we can pull into. We'll have ourselves a couple of sniffs and then talk."

They headed north out of Somerville and were near Wellington Circle. Sabeel Biggs laughed and pointed at a restaurant. "You know, it was right over there that our boy Chug popped Will Scarlet's mother."

He laughed some more and hooked a left by Wellington.

"Can you imagine doing anything so dumb? Shooting the mother of a Cosa Nostra boss. Not that the guineas are what they used to be, but still."

Tilly smiled. It *was* amusing. He was also glad to be sharing some camaraderie with this terror he was riding around with. Where the hell *were* they going? You want to talk, you have to ride around? Maybe that's the way people like Sabeel Biggs operated. Some kind of ritual the way some people have to have a cup of coffee or a couple of drinks and cigars before they get down to business. With Biggs you rode around in a big-ass Beamer a while, listened to classical music, did a couple of lines, and then talked. Welcome to the world, Tilly told himself.

Tilly was beginning to warm to the situation. This guy was actually kind of a cool character. Built like one of those pumped up guys on the cover of a muscle magazine, muscles and veins popping all over the place, but dressed like someone from State Street, riding around in a BMW, and listening to Brahms. No one would make fun of him about the music.

Tilly could think of a couple of people he knew he wouldn't mind seeing him with Biggs. Tilly'd give them a look that said, screw with me and you screw with him.

They were riding through an area with woods on both sides of the road now. Tilly had been here before a couple of times. A small zoo was nearby. The woods were really thick. Just out of Boston and you'd think you were in Maine. Wouldn't surprise Tilly to see a moose walk across the road.

Sabeel Biggs slowed the Beamer down, pulled off the paved road onto a narrow dirt road that wound around a bit until progress was stopped by some boulders about fifty yards in. There was a little maneuvering room and Sabeel Biggs deftly turned the car around in three quick moves.

As Tilly sat and massaged the plastic bag, a small alarm buzzed in his head. This wasn't reading right. It was one thing to ride around and sort things out by talking, but sitting in the goddamn woods to sniff some snow with Mr. Universe wasn't his idea of a night out.

Biggs killed the engine and, with it, the concerto in A minor that had been sweetening the car's air. The two men sat through a moment's silence.

"Well, go ahead," Biggs finally said. "Open the bag and let's breathe some bliss. Better get the other stuff out of the glove compartment, though."

Tilly did and they set up by the glove box light. He looked at Sabeel Biggs quizzically when he finished, hardly able to see the man with the light off.

"It's dark as a bastard here," he said, feeling foolish for making the observation.

"Yeah, Sabeel Biggs said. "Black as a nigger's ass."

He laughed a deep laugh that to Tilly sounded like the almost echo chamber laugh of some black guy who did commercials.

"Hey, Howard Tillotson, I'm smiling now. That light up the night for you? Can you see my teeth? I got big white teeth. But, shit, all us black guys got big white, bright teeth. Isn't that right?"

The alarm in Tilly's head was buzzing pretty steadily now.

"Here, let's just open the glove compartment back up. That'll give us enough light. Go ahead, Howard. You start. Don't wait on me."

Tilly sat, scrunched in his seat, starting to shiver a bit.

"You rather have some crack, Howard? I got crack. Some meth, maybe some horse. Whatever you want, I got."

"No. I don't do any of that stuff. It'll kill you."

"Smart man. I don't do it myself. Actually, Howard, I don't do any of it. That's for the losers. I just sell it."

Sabeel Biggs leaned back in his seat, getting comfortable as though he were home about to watch some TV and maybe have a drink.

"Oh, Howard," he said suddenly, "I was wondering. Henry Gonzalez. He ever get that big, hairy mole on his cheek removed? He always said he was gonna have it taken off. It sure was an ugly looking sucker. First thing you noticed when you talked with Henry. Am I right?"

Tilly's heart did a drum roll. He tried to remember all he had had to learn about Henry Gonzalez. He couldn't remember anything about a hairy mole. Would the cop and Mink have told him about the mole? They probably would have if it were a distinguishing feature. But maybe it was just a small mole. Maybe there was no mole. Or maybe there *was* a big goddamn hairy mole.

One thing was sure. For some reason, he was now being tested about Henry Gonzalez.

"Mole?" Jesus. He was sure he had squeaked the word.

Sabeel Biggs laughed. "Yeah. You know. That big mole with the hair sticking out of it. You wanted to at least cut the hair off for Henry."

"What mole? I don't remember any mole." Hell, Tilly figured, if Henry Gonzalez had a mole he hated with hair sticking out of it, he would have cut the hair out himself.

"Goddamn," Sabeel Biggs said, "I must be losing my marbles. Who the hell am I thinking of? Must be someone else."

Sabeel Biggs was smiling but Tilly didn't feel comforted. The sonovabitch did have big white teeth.

"Anyway, Howard, go ahead. Enjoy."

Tilly's heart was beating nearly out of control and, under the circumstances, he sure didn't want any coke. As it was, he thought he might have a heart attack.

"You said you wanted to talk about Chug." Change the topic, Tilly thought. Get things moving. Anything to get the hell out of here.

"Yeah."

Big pause.

"So what's the problem?" Tilly asked.

"No actual problem," Sabeel Biggs said, still kind of smiling but not too broadly.

Another pause. Suddenly, talking with Sabeel Biggs had become like playing ping pong with someone who can't or won't return the ball, Tilly thought.

Absently, he pressed the plastic bag he was still holding unopened.

"I'm just thinking about Henry Gonzalez," Sabeel Biggs said. "He was good people. A real nice guy, don't you think?"

"Yeah." Can't go wrong with that answer.

"Cancer sucks."

"Henry had a stroke," Tilly said, hoping Mink hadn't screwed up the information he had given him.

"Yeah, but he had cancer a long time before that. Always had to piss but could hardly. Doctors told him they got it but, you ask me, that's what led to the stroke."

Tilly mumbled a little all-purpose syllable. The conversation wasn't slowing his heart rate and Sabeel Biggs's smile wasn't lighting his life.

"Enough talk of cancer and strokes," Sabeel Biggs said. "Open that bag."

As Tilly squeezed the bag a little and then bent his head to open it, Sabeel Biggs wrapped his big hands around his throat and squeezed hard and quick. Tilly gurgled and thrashed.

Sabeel Biggs let go one hand, opened Tilly's door and shoved him out before the lying bastard messed on his leather. Outside, with Tilly lying on the ground, he squeezed until Tilly stopped thrashing.

He stood and looked down at Tilly lying limp and angled on the cold, matted leaves. "You really knew Henry Gonzalez, you would have known about his cancer. They cut it out of his cheek—big ugly thing—not so long ago. Too late, though. It had spread."

Using his handkerchief, Sabeel Biggs put the plastic bag in Tilly's jacket pocket, got back in the BMW and drove out.

Just a minor change of plans was all this was. He'd make things work out. Gotta go with the flow. Start a little business of his own anyway through the Newark connection set up by Tyrone Moore. He wasn't really worried about Ramon Mendez, especially if he got some help from the wops.

Chug had called this afternoon and said his buyer was anxious to meet with Biggs as soon as possible and Sabeel agreed on tomorrow. That gave him time tonight to check out Howard Tillotson first who turned out to be full of shit so what did that say about Chug?

Sabeel Biggs wasn't quite sure but he was pretty sure there was no big-time buyer from the north.

Didn't matter. Whatever the scam was, Sabeel Biggs wouldn't let it evolve the way Chug and whoever he was involved with planned. He had a plan of his own for Chug.

Just Sabeel Biggs, Robert Chug Ellis, and William Scarlata.

Time to make a phone call.

From the BMW's excellent sound system, *Sheep May Safely Graze* by Johann Sebastian Bach played a pleasant counterpoint to Sabeel Biggs's thoughts. No doubt about it, he was really getting to appreciate this kind of music.

Chapter Twenty Five

Billy Wilkins stayed until Chug made the phone call to Sabeel Biggs. Chug then spent most of the rest of the afternoon lying on the bed, surfing through the television channels, but not seeing anything.

Around 4:30 he walked to the Burger King and chewed through his food quickly, barely tasting a thing.

He walked back to the motel, surfed through the television channels again for twenty minutes, finally settling on a news story about the terrific spring training the Red Sox had had and how promising the regular season looked.

He concentrated on interviews with a couple of players and tried to lose himself in thoughts of baseball at Fenway Park. He found himself thinking of games he watched with his father, stories his Dad told him about players from his era and the years of perpetual frustration.

He thought of times with Ellie in the bleachers, the air sweet with summer and filled with noise and his life happy and warm with her.

He clicked off the television and called a taxi.

It was nearly dark when the cab dropped him off at the end of his street. He knew most of the cars that were normally parked along the street and he kept sharp watch for anything strange, especially an SUV.

He stood across from his apartment. Lights were on in the units on the first two floors and in the unit across the hall from his on the third floor.

His explorer sat where he had left it, looking undisturbed.

He thought of the gun he had thrown away in Maine and wished he had it. But he didn't and that was that. But there were some things in his apartment he could use that would have to do.

He looked around again and went to the front door, unlocked it, and climbed to his apartment. He could hear the television news from the Donlin's unit across the hall.

No sense in putting his ear to his door. Anyone inside would be quiet. If they were there, they were there. What the hell.

He unlocked the door, went inside and let his eyes adjust to the dark broken only by the dim light from the streetlight.

He tuned to the quiet sounds of his refrigerator and the hum of the little electric clock. He stood still for several moments trying to sense anything alien.

A car passed by outside and its headlights made a wave of light across his ceiling.

Ellie had said she thought someone had been in her place. He wondered whether anyone had been in here.

He went to a cabinet where he kept a flashlight and used it to probe about.

He looked around and everything seemed as he had left it. From the knife rack by the sink, he took a carving knife, a murderous-looking thing, with an eight-inch blade. He ran it back and forth a few times on the sharpening rod and then wrapped it in a towel and stuck it under his belt.

Quickly, he examined the bills in the tubs in the sink. The ink was still untouched.

He opened the door under the sink and pulled out the jug of muriatic acid. Then he found a plastic spray bottle he had kept window cleaner in. He emptied it, rinsed it, and filled it with muriatic acid.

He tested the spray into the sink, adjusting the nozzle to a stream, working the plastic trigger. Probably good for ten or twelve feet but much better up close. Jesus, the stuff opened your sinuses.

Then he took out his phone and punched Ellie's number.

Bernardo Tranfiglia sat slumped in his fine leather chair in the office of his funeral home, feeling like a man on the verge of total calamity, like someone about to be crushed between the proverbial rock and hard place. It wasn't right that a man of his age and stature in the community should be in this situation.

He had already taken a pill from the bottle in his desk drawer and an ever so discreet pull from another bottle to wash it down but his nerves still jangled and he debated either another pill or another pull. Had to be careful with that stuff, though. And mixing was bad.

Retirement was indeed looking more than just good. It was an imperative when this awful situation was over.

In a way, though, he'd miss the business his grandfather had started, his father had nurtured, and he'd made into a North End empire of sorts. He had made a more than comfortable living from the dead.

This office reflected the degree of that comfort and Bernardo Tranfiglia's taste. Big mahogany desk. Red leather chairs and sofa. Dark paneling, built in, not nail on. Oriental rug that had cost a fortune. Fine brass lamps. The whole effect was Beacon Hill Wasp rather than North End Italian.

He had a triple going now. Armando Raucci in the front room. Eighty-five years old and went in his sleep just the way everyone wants to go.

Angelo Spinale in the middle room. Fifty-seven. A brick mason. Worked hard all his life but too much butter, cheese, and fatty meat. He went quick, too, but not the way everyone wants. Nine-thirty a.m., clutching his chest and turning blue over a stack of red bricks.

One of the newcomers to the North End, a thirty-four year old yuppie in one of the side rooms. Piled her Acura into a bridge abutment on 128 while commuting home. Talking on her cell phone and not wearing a seatbelt. A real mess. They'd done their best patching up her face but in the end the only way to go was closed casket.

In his head, Bernardo Tranfiglia tallied the receipts from these three and sighed. Tough giving up that kind of income.

You pay for your sins, I suppose, he reflected. Not that he ever did anything really wrong. The favors he had done for William Scarlata in the past had, after all, involved people already dead. And who in his right mind could refuse Will Scarlet anything?

Oh, some might talk high and mighty, but just let them sit across a desk from Will Scarlet, look him in the eye, and say, who the hell you think you're talking to? Get out of my office right now or I'll call the cops.

Bernardo Tranfiglia smiled bitterly as he thought of cops. If Will Scarlet was the rock the cops were the hard place. Or at least one of them.

He glanced at the Chelsea ship's clock on the mantle. 6:30. He should be downstairs and visible but it certainly wouldn't do to have the smell of what was in that bottle on his breath. He patted his pockets for some mints.

There was a dreadful irony about the situation he was in. The cop—the hard place—had called that afternoon, had told him to be ready to get word via one of his trusted channels to Will Scarlet that his mother's killer was going to be involved in a drug deal sometime tomorrow. Specifics of time and place would follow soon.

Bernardo Tranfiglia mulled the significance of this intrigue between a cop and a Mob boss but except for his own role he was actually beyond caring.

When he had done the cop's bidding, and he supposed he had had no choice, he knew he would be setting the rock—Will Scarlet—in motion and he'd have to do his much worse bidding: to bury some poor soul alive.

Yes, you pay for your sins, he thought. In this case the sin of trying to cover all bases and getting involved from time to time over the years with the goddamn cop Billy Wilkins.

Against his better judgment, Bernardo Tranfiglia took another pill and a pull.

"This is how it's going to be," Chug told Lou Russo after they put Ellie on and she told him she was all right.

"It's 6:30 now. At 7:30, you drive around the Common, just keep driving 'til I tell you to stop. I'll be on the phone to you the whole time. Stay on the streets that go around the Common."

"Hold it, hold it, right there," Lou Russo said. "You want to see your girlfriend nice and safe, her pretty face still pretty, you do what we say."

"What do you say we get to the bottom line, stop jerking each other around," Chug said. "It's me you want. Not her. She's the bait to get me. I understand that. But I'm gonna tell you something, if you want me you'll listen to what I have to say. There's gonna be no other way."

There was a pause and then Lou Russo said, "Go ahead. Let's hear what you have to say."

"You drive around the Common. At some point, I'll tell you to pull over. You let Ellie out of the car. Naturally, someone's got a hold of her. One person. I'll be nearby. I'll tell you where I am and wave my arms. We walk toward each other. I'll signal to whoever has Ellie to let her go. If he doesn't, I'm gone and we start all over again."

"You're dreaming. We let her go and you're both gone."

"No. I'll be close enough so that whoever has Ellie can get one of us but not both."

"No way. Definitely no way. We tell you where we'll meet. We have your girlfriend standing by the car. She waves to you, shows you she's okay, you come up to the car and we let her go 'cause you were right about one thing. It's you, not her, we want to talk to. And, by the way, that's all we want to do. Talk."

"Sure. Okay, I'll say it one more time. We will do this the way I say. If that doesn't work for you, I'll hang up, give you some time to think about it, and call back later.

"If you still don't agree, I'm prepared to go to the cops and turn myself in. But if I do that, I also tell them about the woman missing from the dentist's office. How Will Scarlet's guys took her.

"That's probably what I should do but I figure the other way, I get to see her go and it makes me feel a hell of a lot better."

He didn't add that he also planned on not being taken himself, that he'd give himself a fighting chance to get away with Ellie. If she'd go with him. But first things first and the first thing was her release.

"So what's it gonna be?" he said.

A long pause and Chug repeated the question.

"I heard you. We'll try it your way."

Lou Russo clicked off Ellie's phone and wondered just what the hell was going on. First, there had been a call that afternoon from Carlo Fuccione who was always a reliable source. Carlo said he had a solid tip that the shooter was going to be involved in a drug deal sometime tomorrow, exact time and location not yet known but he was pretty sure he'd have a firm line on that in time for Lou to be there.

Lou Russo had long ago stopped questioning Carlo on his sources because he was so reliable. Even if he had, Carlo wouldn't have told him the lead came from Bernardo Tranfiglia. Not that Carlo would have reason to suspect anything shaky about Mr. Tranfiglia and he certainly didn't know the lead had been fed to Mr. Tranfiglia from a cop named Billy Wilkins.

Then, just before Chug's call, there had been a call to the bakery from a spear chucker from the sound of his voice although he didn't talk like one who said he was going to meet with the man who shot William Scarlata's mother. He was pretty guarded but said he'd get back later. He wasn't interested in any reward but did hint about future considerations.

It sounded to Lou that the chucker was involved in the drug deal but was playing some kind of angle. The funny part of the whole thing, though, was how would a two-bit loser like the guy who shot Florence Scarlata have the scratch to be involved in any kind of dealing? Must be a small deal. Didn't matter.

Lou Russo figured they'd get the guy on their own tonight, but if there was a screw up he had an insurance policy. Two of them.

Chug knew that except for a general description of him that they might have gotten, they really didn't know what he looked like. But they probably would be looking for a thirtyish man dressed like a thirtyish man of blue-collar tastes.

So he changed from his jeans and sweat jacket to some stylish chinos, button-down shirt, and a nice corduroy jacket. He put on a pair of New Balance running shoes that he never used for running but he might tonight. He wondered what Ellie was wearing on her feet. Sometimes she wore sneakers to work.

He fit the knife and spray bottle as comfortably as he could under the jacket and then called for a cab to pick him up at the end of his street.

As he walked to where the cab would meet him, he considered calling Billy Wilkins but decided not to. He still had hopes of success tonight and meeting with Sabeel Biggs tomorrow to secure whatever Wilkins would do for him. He hoped Wilkins didn't come out to the motel and find him missing.

He had the cab circle the Common once and then drop him off at the corner of Charles and Beacon. It was 7:20. Lou Russo had said they be in a platinum STS Cadillac sedan. There would be just the one car, Lou Russo had assured him but Chug thought that was unlikely. Probably they'd have cars on all four streets. Maybe even guys here and there on foot.

He walked up Beacon quite certain they were already in position. He kept his face straight ahead, not stiffly, and checked about just by moving his eyes. He walked the pace of a man who knows where he's going, trying to appear neither anxious nor furtive.

He had his cell phone to his ear as though he were already in conversation like just about everyone else walking a city street. It wouldn't do to whip the phone to his ear if they called him. He even talked meaninglessly into the phone and gestured with his arm. "Yeah, it is a nice evening and I'm having a hell of a time."

And, in actuality, it *was* a nice evening, cool and pleasant, a nice night for a walk, for a young man to meet his lady friend, do a little shopping, maybe, then dinner, perhaps at Legal Sea Food, then dancing someplace afterward.

But that wasn't in the cards for tonight.

In front of the State House, he crossed Beacon to Park Street and then down to Tremont. At the foot of Park, he crossed Tremont and walked toward

Boylston. He continued his conversation, occasionally nodding and gesturing.

He already had Ellie's number selected and pushed the call button.

Lou Russo answered. "Yeah."

"Where are you?"

"We're on Charles. Almost at Beacon."

"Let me talk to Ellie."

He heard Lou Russo curse under his breath as he handed the phone to Ellie. He wasn't used to taking orders except from one man.

"Chug?"

He wanted to reach through the phone to hug her.

"You okay?" he said.

"I'm okay. Are you okay?"

"Ellie, we're gonna be fine. Just hold that thought."

Lou Russo's voice came back. "Okay. Now what?"

"Where's Ellie sitting in the car?"

"What the—"

"Where's she sitting?"

"Back seat. In the middle."

"I want you to make a loop around the Common in that platinum Caddie of yours. Drive slow and make sure Ellie is visible. Then I'll tell you where to pull over."

"Yes, sir, Mr. Chug," Lou Russo said, heavy on the irony. "How many miles an hour you want us to drive?"

Chug clicked off but kept the phone to his ear. He crossed Tremont to the Common and walked slowly back in the direction he had come. He wanted to be facing the Cadillac as it approached but he also wanted to be able to fade a bit into the Common so that Ellie didn't see him.

He saw it come to the foot of Park Street and then turn right on Tremont. He talked into the phone, maintaining his bogus conversation in case any William Scarlata operatives were circulating nearby on foot. "Yeah, we'll send out for Chinese, that sounds good."

He turned left onto a path so that he was not very visible from the street and then turned so that he could see the car.

It rolled past slowly. Two men in front and two in the rear with Ellie sitting between them.

He watched it all the way until it turned right onto Boylston. Staying in the Common, he picked up his pace and headed toward Beacon Street.

It was time for a test.

He selected Ellie's number and pushed the button.

When Lou Russo answered, he said, "Where are you now?"

"Boylston. Headed toward Charles. Did you miss us?"

"At Charles, pull around the corner on Beacon and stop. I'll be nearby. I'll tell you when to get Ellie out of the car and we'll make the exchange. Remember, one guy gets out with her."

"Got it."

Chug walked quickly to the steps that led out of the Common by the State House, walked to the other side of Beacon, and then down the hill toward Charles.

He kept the phone to his ear, maintained his imaginary conversation but kept alert for activity near the intersection of Charles and Beacon.

He wasn't too far down the hill when he saw the Denali SUV pull up about one hundred feet from the intersection and double park. He peered intently and, across Charles by the Public Gardens, he saw a couple of guys loitering a little too casually. Maybe they were just a couple of guys and maybe the Denali was just one of the endless supply of Denalis.

But maybe not. Maybe they had flunked the test. Better count on it.

He took a right onto Joy Street and walked up a few feet so that he was out of sight. He pushed the call button on the phone.

"Where are you?" he asked Lou Russo when he answered.

"We're just about to turn onto Beacon."

"Okay. We'll try it again. This time without the reinforcements."

"What are you talking about?"

"I'm talking about the extra people you've got spread around. Let me say it again. This is how it's gonna work. Ellie gets out with one person. I identify myself, come pretty close, I signal him and he lets her go. Then I come to you.

"If I see extra people, it's off. I scoot and go to the cops and I mean it. So, are we agreed?"

There was a pause and Chug could almost feel the slow burn on the other end.

Then the voice spoke. "Yeah, yeah. Okay. Where we going this time? Let's move this show."

"This time pull over on Tremont Street. Across from the Park Street station. Wait 'til I call you."

Chug waited in the shadows of Joy Street a minute or two until the Denali rode up the hill and disappeared. He wanted to step forward to where he could see which direction it took but couldn't risk the Cadillac being close behind it.

In another thirty seconds the Cadillac drove past and he slipped out of the shadows and crossed to the Common.

Ellie sat between Lou Russo and another man she hadn't seen before they got into the Cadillac going on an hour ago. He was a good-looking guy in a swarthy, sinister kind of way and she could sense a wiry athleticism in him. She could also see the butt of a gun under his coat. The bald guy called him Mario.

None of them said much to her or for that matter to each other and she had said nothing except when she talked with Chug on the phone. Her phone.

Despite her situation, she was aware that she hadn't bathed or groomed properly since, what was it, just over twenty-four hours ago. She knew she probably didn't smell any too good, not that she cared if she offended them.

She considered going for Mario's gun but rejected that as foolish. At least at this point. But if it came to it, she'd sell herself as dearly as possible. Her nails were sharp and she knew how to kick but she conceded she didn't have much of a chance.

She fought a little battle with tears, defeating them before they spilled.

They had been riding along Charles Street between the Common and the Public Gardens when her phone rang again.

The bald guy told Chug where they were and then said, "What are you talking about?"

And then a moment later, "Yeah, yeah. Okay. Where are we going this time? Let's move this show."

Quickly, he put her phone away and took out another. "Get your asses over to Tremont Street near the Park Street station," he said into it. He punched another number and said the same thing.

Then he looked at Ellie and smiled. He patted her knee paternally and said, "Relax. You'll be fine and so will he. Believe me, we just want to talk."

As he came through the trees and benches, he could see the Cadillac parked where he had said. He couldn't see the Denali but people on foot could be anywhere. He'd have to chance it.

He pushed the call button.

"Okay," He said. "Get Ellie out of the car. One person with her. When I see that I'll tell you where I am. I'll wave to identify myself. This person and Ellie come toward me. I'll wave again, he lets her go and that's that. He doesn't let her go or I see other troops moving in and I'm off."

He resisted saying, 'Capeesh?', and instead said, "That's clear?"

"Yeah. You shoulda joined the Army. Been a general."

He waited a moment, checked around and then stepped out of the cover of the Common and onto the broad sidewalk.

A fairly tall guy with his arm linked through Ellie's as though they were a couple stood on the sidewalk by the Caddie. He looked athletic, as though he had been selected for his speed.

Chug spoke into the phone. "Have them cross Tremont. I'm standing across from you by the Common."

He raised his arm and waved it.

Arms still linked, Ellie and the guy moved toward him, jaywalking through traffic.

As they approached the sidewalk, he waved and yelled, "Let her go."

The athletic-looking guy hesitated and then released Ellie. She started toward him but he pointed toward the T station and said, "Move it, Ellie."

The athletic-looking guy looked from Chug to Ellie and then sprinted toward her.

She was running now toward the station and yelled, "Chug, be careful. There are others."

He looked around, saw two guys moving fast toward him from his right along the sidewalk. He saw the plan now. The guy who had held Ellie let her go just to keep him in place for the few critical seconds it took for reinforcements to get to him and then he would go for Ellie.

Ellie was almost at the T station but the athletic guy was closing fast. Chug ran straight for him, saw him start to reach under his coat, and body checked him hard as he had done countless times before on the ice in his hockey-playing days. They both went down on the sidewalk.

Chug tried to get at his knife but couldn't quickly and the man was getting to his knees. Chug swung hard and landed a right on the man's jaw. He heard him grunt and he swung again, this time landing a blow on the side of his head. He swung two more times and the man stayed down.

He got to his feet and saw the two other men closing in on him through a gathering crowd. They were coming fast and he reached under his jacket and got the knife out just as one moved in on him.

He slashed with the knife and felt it rip through fabric and strike flesh. The man yelled and backed off but the other came at him. He slashed again and the second one backed away too.

He turned and ran toward the T station but now all three were after him. He knew they'd be on him before he could get to the station. He switched the knife to his left hand and pulled the spray bottle out. He waited until they were within four feet and aimed for their faces, squeezing the trigger and spraying from one to the other.

They yelled a chorus of curses and cries but kept coming. He flung the bottle at the closest and swung the knife quickly in a wide arc all the time moving toward the station.

Then he saw the Denali pull right onto the sidewalk. Two men came out and sprang for him. He turned and sprinted for the station, got about five feet and someone had him around the waist trying to bring him down.

He slashed with the knife, felt it strike, and then he was on the ground and lost the knife. He struck out with his fists and knew he was landing blows.

A punch to his belly took his wind and then another to the side of his jaw flashed lights but he felt no pain. Now they had his arms and legs pinned and he felt himself being carried through a parting crowd of amazed, questioning faces.

Before he was flung into the rear seat of the Denali, he noticed that its license plate was smeared with something. Someone jumped in beside him and thrust a gun into his side. Then the Denali bounced off the sidewalk and sped down Tremont Street.

Quickly, it pulled to the side of the street and he was jostled out and into the back seat of the platinum Cadillac sedan. Chug knew he was near Chinatown. Sirens pulsed in the distance.

The man with the gun was in the back seat with him and a bald man. Two men were in front. Chug saw the Denali head westerly while the Cadillac went easterly. Both blended into traffic and moved along at an unhurried pace.

Chapter Twenty Six

William and Sylvia Scarlata were at home watching a show on the big-screen television and drinking some of their red Tuscan wine when Lou Russo called.

"We got him," Lou Russo said.

William Scarlata exhaled a long breath, put his glass of wine on the coffee table and smiled. He looked at Sylvia and flashed a circle made of his forefinger and thumb.

"Hang on, Lou," he said.

He got up, patted Sylvia's shoulder, and walked with the phone to his private den. The walls were covered with framed, autographed photos taken at William Scarlata's various restaurants of famous people from sports, music, and movies shaking his hand or draping an arm over his shoulder.

"Lou, this is great. I'm not second-guessing you but when I heard on the news about the girl I was ripshit. It's not my style but it worked."

"Not my style either, Will. You know that. But you do what it takes. Could be a problem there, though."

Lou Russo explained how Ellie got away.

"I got guys looking for her right now, Will. She might try to go to the cops but I don't think so. I think she's gonna try to protect the boyfriend.

"Something else, Will," Lou Russo added quickly. "Don't know what it means and right now it don't matter but I got a couple of calls that our guy was gonna be in a drug deal tomorrow so we might have got him anyway. But you know what they say: a bird in the hand."

"Yeah. Where are you now, Lou?"

"We're practically at the warehouse."

"Okay. Good. Hold him there. I'll be there within an hour."

Bernardo Tranfiglia was busy being visible, being the comforting presence as he briefly looked in on the three mourning families when his son Paul told him that he was wanted on the phone. His heart fluttered when Paul said the caller was William Scarlata.

He went to his office and had the desk drawer with pills and bottle open before he picked up the phone.

William Scarlata wanted things ready to roll. Was there a funeral for tomorrow? he had asked.

Unfortunately, from Bernardo Tranfiglia's point of view, there was. Three, in fact.

They had talked for a few minutes and Bernardo knew exactly what was expected of him. He'd have to have his sons in on this one. There was no way he could trust anyone else.

It was a question of timing. Things would have to move fast.

In the morning, after the bereaved left the open casket and filed outside to the cars that would take them to the funeral Mass, Armando Raucci's body would be removed and stowed until it could be taken to the crematorium. Despite William Scarlata's airy assurances that there would be no problem on that end, Bernardo Tranfiglia's fat fingers trembled a bit as he thought of the potential security problems involved.

Then, into the casket would go the person who, Mr. Scarlata said, would be brought to the funeral home sometime that night. This person, Mr. Scarlata said in soothing, reassuring tones as though he were the comforting funeral director, would be securely bound and silenced. If need be, he would be sedated to absolutely guarantee that he could neither move nor make noise.

Bernardo Tranfiglia's entire body trembled as he imagined the funeral Mass in full progress and somehow the person inside the casket being able to scream or move his body. Or maybe it would happen at the gravesite as Father Tullo said the final prayers and family and friends bid farewell.

Bernardo Tranfiglia's hand slipped into the open drawer and found the bottle.

The whole thing was completely unthinkable but even more unthinkable was saying no to William Scarlata.

Maybe the most unthinkable part of the whole nightmare was something William Scarlata absolutely insisted on. He wanted holes drilled through the bottom of the casket to allow air to seep in.

That would have to be done tonight after the wake. One break on that, though. Armando Raucci could stay in the casket. He wouldn't mind if the drill came up and bit him a couple of times.

Sabeel Biggs got a call from Ramon Mendez as he was driving through the theatre district which he frequently did just to absorb its ambience of bright lights, limos and elegantly dressed people. It was nice to know he was part of it.

He had been about to call Mr. Full-of-Shit Robert Ellis to arrange a time for tomorrow's supposed deal with the big buyer who Sabeel by now was convinced didn't exist. Then get the time and place back to Will Scarlet.

His conclusion that Chug was part of some kind of set up was a disappointment even though he was relieved he had bumped into Nappy Williams before he got caught in it. But he was feeling better about it now. Wringing that silly-ass Howard Tillotson's neck had been a real purge.

Then it occurred to him that if Chug was part of some kind of set up it wouldn't do to involve Will Scarlet. No percentage in that. He'd have to think that one out.

Ramon told him he had a quick, unexpected deal. A chance for Sabeel to pick up some easy big money. The best kind.

For a moment, Sabeel toyed with telling Ramon to find someone new but thought better of it. No sense burning bridges until you knew for sure you had made it to the other side and would never need to come back.

"Nine-thirty," Ramon said. "Usual place under the Common. Luis or Miguel will be there. Get the stuff and they'll tell you where it's going. But you can wai' until tomorrow on that."

Sabeel was going to meet a lovely, lithe fair-skinned young lady at ten but he decided to shower and spray himself after he met Luis or Miguel Orantes. Just being near either one of them made him want to wash up.

They were in the room in the warehouse where Frankie and Ellie had been kept and when Chug's cell phone, which was in his pocket, rang, Lou Russo said, "Whose phone's that?"

""It's mine," Chug said. His voice was loud and defiant.

Lou Russo stared at him a moment. "Give it to me."

He snatched it from Chug's hand, stared at the screen and handed it back to Chug.

"Just say, 'hello.'"

"Kiss my ass."

The guy with the gun standing next to Chug whacked the side of his face.

Lou Russo took the phone back and said, "Get him out of here."

When Mickey the Harp took Chug at gunpoint from the room, Lou Russo pressed the talk button and said, "Yeah."

There was a pause and then a voice said, "Who's this?"

"It's me. Chug. Who's this?" Lou Russo said, keeping his voice soft and low on the theory that doing so would make him sound more like Chug.

There was another moment's pause and then Billy Wilkins clicked off.

Sabeel Biggs killed some time tooling around until 9:30 when he wheeled the big Beamer into the parking garage under Boston Common, one of several rendezvous spots he had with Ramon Mendez enterprises. He was anxious to get the pickup over with quickly and get away for the evening with his lady friend.

He checked the Beamer's clock and cruised slowly. Ahead, in the middle of a row, well away from exit doors so there would be less chance of anyone surprising them, was the beat up van used by Luis and Miguel.

He wondered who it would be tonight. Sometimes it was just one of them. Sometimes both.

He pulled into an empty spot between a Honda Accord and a Dodge Caravan, kept the engine running and waited. Usually, they gave it a couple of minutes before coming to him.

Some kind of wind instrument that Sabeel Biggs couldn't identify played slow, solemn music. An oboe or a bassoon, he thought. He had bought a book that identified all the classical instruments, their history and sound qualities, but had made little headway yet. When he went to Symphony Hall—and he planned on doing that soon—he wanted to be knowledgeable.

As he sat, he thought the thing to do was to set up a deal with Chug and kayo him right in the car. Then take him to Will Scarlet gift-wrapped. Or maybe just forget the whole Chug deal.

He was pondering that when out of the corner of his eye he caught Luis Orantes walking from the van. He had on a heavy coat and a navy watch cap. Sabeel knew that under the coat would be tonight's delivery. The coat was heavy enough for you to take a walk around the North Pole, Sabeel thought. But that's about all it was good for. Spic probably bought it at Walmart or picked it up at a Morgie's.

Sabeel sighed. He'd be glad to get out from under these guys too.

Luis and Miguel Orantes watched the white BMW roll past them. The sounds of Bob Marley filled the van but much less loud than usual so as not to attract attention from anyone passing by.

Luis felt under his coat, a subconscious gesture, to make sure he was ready. He let Bob Marley finish, exchanged a look with Miguel, and got out of the van.

As he approached the BMW, he checked around. No one in sight. Then he and Sabeel Biggs locked eyes. He didn't much care for Biggs. For one thing, he knew that Biggs inwardly sneered at all of them: Ramon, Philippe, Miguel and himself. Even though Biggs worked for Ramon and Philippe, he thought he was smarter than they were. But he sure wasn't smarter than Philippe.

For another thing, Luis was afraid of Sabeel Biggs. Who the hell wouldn't be? He was afraid right now. But he knew that's why Ramon and Philippe had taken Biggs on board. He was well connected locally, he was cool under pressure, and people were afraid of him. Better to have the kind of guy no one would mess with on your side.

He went to the passenger's side and opened the door. Jesus, what kind of music was that?

Biggs leveled a gaze that made Luis Orantes mighty glad it was a .44 Magnum he pulled out from under his coat and shot Sabeel Biggs through the head with. The driver's window shattered and turned red.

Luis looked at the exploded head of Sabeel Biggs and said, "You think you smart. Tha' Philippe, he knows someone in New Jersey too."

After he clicked off his cell phone, Lieutenant Billy Wilkins once again zipped down the Southeast Expressway with his lights flashing and siren bipping. He knocked at Chug's door and then went to the motel office. Yes indeed, the clerk in the office had seen a cab pull up at Mr. Ellis's unit, oh, around 5:15 or 5:30.

Billy Wilkins headed back but in silent mode while he tried to figure where to go and what to do. Maybe the smart thing was to do nothing. Let things play out and let Mr. Robert Ellis meet whatever fate he would meet.

He tried to put himself in Chug's mind and knew his chief concern was his girlfriend. So, what would he do? He'd respond to that message on his cell phone and try to negotiate Ellie's release. Which meant he didn't have a prayer.

Did he still have access to the gun he had used in the robbery? Would he get it and try to shoot his and Ellie's way to freedom? Then Billy Wilkins thought of something that made him suck in his breath. Frequently, Will Scarlet's Nahant address was in the papers.

Would Chug be impulsive enough to try to invade the Nahant fortress, think he could somehow get into Will Scarlet's home, point a gun at Mrs. Will Scarlet and bargain for Ellie Robinson's safety?

As he drove, Billy Wilkins, like all cops, paid at least subliminal attention to the steady dispassionate flow coming from his police radio. In the radio transmission going on now was something about an incident near the Park Street T station that had occurred earlier at some time while he was out of the car.

He tuned in on what was being said and then flipped on lights and siren as he headed toward the Common.

When he got there, two marked cruisers and an unmarked detectives' car were on the sidewalk and the cops were talking with people and taking notes. Crime scene tape marked off some blotches on the pavement that looked like blood.

"What do we have?" he asked one of the detectives, a guy named Snyder that he got along with pretty well.

Snyder looked at Billy Wilkins quizzically a moment but then said, "Not sure, Billy. Seems about four or five guys ganged up on one guy who from what I'm hearing gave a pretty good account of himself. Wailed one of them with his fists, used a knife on a couple of others and got them pretty good, looks like."

Snyder waved his arm at the splotches on the pavement.

"Sounds like it was over a girl. One of them was chasing a girl and the lone guy tackled him. The girl ran into the T station. We're checking on that. So far, no sign of her."

Snyder looked at Billy Wilkins a moment as if he wanted to ask him why he was here but instead said, "But here's a funny one. Check this out."

He went to his car and returned with a plastic squeeze bottle holding it with a pencil wedged under its trigger.

He held it up for Billy Wilkins's inspection.

"Take a whiff but be careful. It'll knock you on your ass."

Carefully, Billy Wilkins sniffed the bottle's nozzle.

"What is that?" Snyder asked.

"Hydrochloric acid. Muriatic acid. Same thing. They use it in swimming pools. Awful stuff if you're not careful."

"Well, the lone guy had this and sprayed the other guys with it. Got 'em good, too, the witnesses say. They were screaming and rubbing their faces. Tell me this. What the hell would a guy be doing walking around with a knife and a spray bottle filled with acid?"

Billy Wilkins shrugged.

"So what happened to the guy?" he asked.

"Like I say, he gave a pretty good account of himself but they overwhelmed him. Two of the guys dragged him off to an SUV. A Denali, dark blue. License plates obscured by paint or mud or something. They take off with him. The other guys go stumbling off into the Common. We can't find them. Must have had a car parked someplace."

Detective Snyder scratched his head and laughed. "Hey, Billy, you want to handle this? This is a crazy one, huh? Any ideas?"

"Beats me, Snyder. Jesus, we get all kinds, don't we?"

It wasn't much more than the proverbial hop, skip, and a jump from the Park Street T station to the North End but in Boston, Billy Wilkins was thinking, with its goddamn cow paths for streets, and despite some improvements after the Big Dig, nothing was a hop, skip, and a jump or a stone's throw or a piece of cake or any other expression you'd care to use that implied easy.

But what the hell was the rush? What did he have? Probably nothing, when you got right down to it.

He didn't feel that way, though. As a matter of fact, in his heart of hearts, he knew Will Scarlet's men had nailed Chug and had taken him off to Never-Never Land. It was unlikely that he'd ever be seen again, his fate a mystery known only to a wood chipper or the worms or the fish or a cement mixer which poured a funny mixture into some bridge abutment somewhere.

It wasn't supposed to have been this way. He and Jessup were supposed to have been poised in place to make the big rescue and send Will Scarlet away for a long, long time.

So now there'd be no commendations, no write ups. What the hay. Still, he was headed for the North End because who knew what he might stumble on?

He was almost to Atlantic Avenue when a transmission on the radio caught his ear.

"What the hell?" he said as he flipped on his flashers and siren and headed back to the Common.

Less than five minutes after Luis Orantes shot Sabeel Biggs, the owner of the Honda Accord parked next to the white BMW with its engine still running and the wind instrument that Biggs couldn't identify still keening solemn music returned to his car and a sight that would rob him of sleep for three nights.

His 9-1-1 call was relayed and dispatched and Lieutenant Billy Wilkins picked it up on his radio. He was pretty sure who the black man was whose brains were now strawberry jam on the shattered window of an all white BMW.

Mickey the Harp bounced Chug off the warehouse wall but he bounced back, kicked Mickey's knee and when Mickey bent forward, he landed his right fist in Mickey's gut.

Sal the Dogcatcher moved in and tried to pin Chug's arms but Chug broke free of his grip and lunged for the gun strapped under Sal's arm. Chug knew, or was pretty sure, that his advantage was that they wouldn't shoot him because he was being saved for something else.

His only chance was to get at one of their guns.

He grappled with Sal but now Mickey the Harp was on him too and the two of them forced him to the cement floor. Sal straddled his waist while Mickey kicked his legs and then moved up and kicked his arms and shoulders.

Mickey then dropped to his knees and stuck the barrel of a ten-millimeter into the left side of Chug's neck.

"Give it up," Mickey said.

Chug's right arm was free and he swung it up at Sal's jaw but could get no momentum. When Sal tried to pin the arm, Chug humped up with his body and toppled Sal off.

He heard a string of trite, terrible curses from Mickey and then lights flashed as the butt of the ten-millimeter slammed into his jaw.

He blinked and grunted and drove his right elbow into Sal's face as he came at Chug and then, ignoring the gun in Mickey's hand, he drove his right fist at Mickey and caught him above the left eye.

As Chug rose to his knees, Sal, from behind, grabbed his belt and pulled him back down while

Mickey came in and kicked and punched, landing blows to his face and chest. He felt his nose open up and warmth gushing out. Then Mickey's knee found his jaw and he sank to the floor.

Breathing hard, Mickey the Harp and Sal the Dogcatcher stood over him and eyed him warily for a moment.

"Jesus, he's a tough sonovabitch," Sal said, straightening his mussed clothing.

Mickey straightened out his clothing too.

"Okay," Mickey said, still breathing hard. "Let's get him out of here. Lou and Mr. Scarlata are at the funeral home. They're waiting for him."

Bernardo Tranfiglia had just finished drilling the air holes in Armando Raucci's casket and was pretty sure he had nicked Mr. Raucci only once when they came to the back door. When he answered, flushed and a bit sweaty from stress and exertion, he faced William Scarlata and Lou Russo.

"We have someone we'd like to be alone with, Mr. Tranfiglia," William Scarlata said. "You got a room we can use?"

For a moment, Bernardo Tranfiglia stood uncertain. Refusal wasn't in his mind but he wasn't sure of William Scarlata's immediate purpose.

"A room," Mr. Tranfiglia," Lou Russo said. "We need a goddamn room. You know, to get this person ready. You and Mr. Scarlata have already discussed it."

"Oh, yes. Yes." Bernardo Tranfiglia oozed some more sweat and felt his pressure, already making his head feel strange, squeeze a little higher.

"We can go down to the embalming room."

Bernardo Tranfiglia watched Lou Russo, a man he had met on one or two occasions and feared almost as much as he feared William Scarlata, gesture toward an SUV idling in the parking lot with its lights on.

"Mr. Tranfiglia, you show us how to get down there and then you go upstairs or something. We'll call you when we need you," Lou Russo said.

"Certainly. Straight down the hallway here." A pause for breath. "Last door on the left.. There's an elevator. It goes right down. There's a phone there. Just pick it up when you want me. I'll be in my office."

When Bernardo Tranfiglia had left, Mickey the Harp and Sal the Dogcatcher led Chug into the funeral home from the Denali. His arms were bound at the wrists in front of him by rope and tape.

Lou Russo and William Scarlata looked at the three of them.

Lou Russo said. "What the hell happened?"

Chug's nose still slowly dripped blood and his left eye was swollen. His face was splotched and bruised.

Both Mickey the Harp and Sal the Dogcatcher were bumped and cut in the face and carried themselves as though they had been in a hockey brawl.

"Sonovabitch didn't want to come with us," Mickey said.

William Scarlata stepped forward and stared at Chug but said nothing. Then he turned and led the way to the elevator.

In the embalming room, they paused and looked about.

Two stainless steel tables with sides raised about three inches were set side by side. One end of each table was slightly elevated. In the lower end of the tables was a drain hole and under that a slop sink. Each sink had a hand-held shower nozzle.

On shelves above each table were large opaque plastic buckets partially filled with fluid. Hoses were coiled from each bucket.

On the wall beside the buckets was an anatomical chart of the human body.

One wall consisted of a Formica shelf with white cabinets above and below it. It looked like a 1960s kitchen.

"What's that smell?" Sal the Dogcatcher said. "Smells like something I smelled in high school.'

"Smells like you smelled in high school, Sallie," Mickey the Harp said. "Matter of fact, you still do."

"Put him on this table," William Scarlata said, indicating the closer of the two tables.

Chug broke from Sal's grip and swung his bound arms in an arc at his head.

"No you don't," Mickey the Harp said and bumped Chug into the table and then slammed him up and onto it. Chug twisted and churned off the table but fell to the floor and hit it with his head. He lay still.

William Scarlata muttered something in Italian and then said. "Get him on the table and tie him to it. Tie his feet together. You brought stuff to do that, didn't you?"

From under his coat, Mickey the Harp pulled two packages of clothesline, one of nylon rope and the other plastic covered.

They lifted Chug to the embalming table and laid him flat.

He stared at them through dazed eyes.

William Scarlata bent over him, looking at him closely. "Good. He's gonna be okay. I want him awake."

He looked at Mickey and said, "Tie him up right now. Start at his ankles and go up to his waist. Pull the rope tight as you can. Then tie some rope around his arms and right around his body. Go under his back and over his chest. I don't want him to be able to do anything but move his eyes and breathe. When we put him in the box, we'll stuff the space between his legs and chest with blankets so he can't thrash."

He stepped aside and gestured to Mickey the Harp. They watched as Mickey bound Chug as William Scarlata had directed.

When Mickey finished, William Scarlata looked at Chug again, saw him try to focus.

"I hope you heard what I just said, my friend. *Carogna*. But in case you didn't, I'm going to spell it out for you. I want you to know exactly what's going to happen to you."

He grabbed Chug's face and tilted it toward him.

"You are in a funeral home. This is where they get the bodies ready to put in the casket. Right now, you might be lying on the table my mother was on, God rest her soul. But there's a big difference. You're alive. She was dead because you, you piece of shit, you killed her."

William Scarlata's eyes filled, his face got lumpy, and his mouth worked.

"I loved my mother. She was the greatest woman ever walked the face of the earth."

He paused and rubbed his chin and under his eyes with his hand. Then he looked at Chug again.

"Upstairs, right now, is a casket which we're gonna put you in and which is gonna be buried tomorrow. But the thing is, you're not gonna be dead when they plant you."

He looked Chug steadily in the eye and spoke slowly and softly. "You're gonna want to scream but you won't be able to. You're gonna want to bang the casket with your hands or feet so someone will hear you. You won't be able to do that either."

William Scarlata folded his arms across his chest and rocked slightly on his feet.

"But let me tell what you will be able to do. You'll be able to breathe. And you'll be able to hear it when they shovel dirt on the casket. You'll have time to think about what you did to my mother. You'll be able to think about how long she lay in that hospital bed and suffered."

William Scarlata looked at Chug a long moment. "You got anything you feel like saying?"

"Yeah," Chug said. His tongue was thick and he was groggy. "You can believe this or not believe it. I'm very sorry I shot your mother. It was unintentional. I still feel sorry for her. But now more than ever because she must have really suffered having a psycho like you for a son."

After Billy Wilkins stared briefly at Sabeel Biggs's exploded head and thought how you can't plan on anything, he headed back to the North End.

If he couldn't salvage his plan because of the now missing Robert Ellis, the now deceased Sabeel Biggs, and the now AWOL Special Agent Jessup, then maybe he could still salvage Robert Chug Ellis himself. He smiled as he thought of Chug chugging, swilling a mug of beer practically in the blink of an eye.

Maybe looking for Chug wasn't exactly like looking for a needle in a haystack. For some reason, Billy Wilkins couldn't stop thinking in clichés. Hop, skip and a jump. Piece of cake. Blink of an eye. Needle in a haystack.

Life sucks and then you die.

He also couldn't stop thinking of Georgia and wishing he was there. He hummed a little tune about the red Georgia clay.

The reason it wasn't a total haystack was because he knew places in the North End that had been Mob hideouts, stashaways, and fortresses over the years. Places used by Milano Corso, Gennaro Anguilo and later by Junior Patriarca and others now either dead or guests of the taxpayers. Places also used by William Scarlata and Mario Cotoni since they had filled the void. Places where maybe they had taken Robert Chug Ellis before they did what they were going to do to him.

Damn, it would have been easier if Chug hadn't bolted, if he had stuck to the plan. It would have worked. He knew it would.

He thought of the article in *Time*.

Water under the bridge or over the dam or whatever the hell the expression was. No use crying over spilt milk. Damn it, he couldn't stop thinking this way.

He rode past warehouses. No parked Cadillacs or GMC Denalis. No lights in basements.

He rode past a couple of pizza places that dealt in more than pizza. Saw nothing.

He rode past the endless restaurants of the North End and savored the smell of garlic and olive oil that spilled from them onto the streets.

He rode past a bakery that everyone knew made more than canolis and bread and Italian pastries. But tonight it looked as innocent as a rectory.

Time to throw in the towel?

Maybe one more time around.

Nothing ventured, nothing gained.

Ellie sat and bounced and watched her reflection in the opposite window. No eye contact with the other passengers, especially on the Orange Line, parts of which were pretty tough.

Probably no one wanted to make eye contact with her either because she knew that right about now she looked pretty tough herself.

Tough in the sense that what would you make of a woman dressed in fairly nice but wrinkled clothes with hair that hadn't seen shampoo or a brush in a while and who looked as though she hadn't seen a lot of sleep lately?

She was damned lucky to have gotten on the train. She had had no money, had to beg five people before a woman shoved some bills in her hand, all the time frantic *they*'d catch up to her.

Now she felt guilty for not staying with Chug and didn't know what to do. But what could she have done?

She put her head back and let it bounce against the glass behind her. She could fall asleep right now, bouncing like this, with her stomach and head churning.

She wondered if she should go to the cops. She didn't know what to do.

Suddenly, she started crying. Deep wracking sobs that finally broke through the indifference of her fellow passengers.

The man sitting next to her got up and changed his seat.

Chapter Twenty Seven

Chug lay on the stainless steel table and tried not to dwell on what William Scarlata had said to him. But it was a losing battle that overwhelmed everything else, even the pain in his arms and legs from the rope that was wound around them and was cutting off his circulation.

Buried alive. Everyone's worst fear. For a mistake.

He wondered how long he'd last. There couldn't be much air in a casket but Will Scarlet had said he'd be able to breathe. He made calculations and felt his mind twist in rebellion. The concept was beyond imagination.

He forced the thought from his mind and thought of Ellie and wondered if she had gotten away. What would become of her? But he had given her a shot that maybe she wouldn't have had if he had followed the cop's plan. Never know now.

Will Scarlet and the bald guy had left but the two who had brought him here in the SUV—they had to be the same two who had chased him and Ellie through Chelsea—were sitting on a couple of folding chairs not paying him much attention. One was reading the *Herald* and the other was cleaning his nails with a penknife.

The one reading the *Herald* put his paper down and said, "Hey, I got a question for you."

Chug looked at him and then looked at the ceiling.

He stood over Chug and said, "Hey, look at me when I'm talking to you. I was in your apartment. Your girlfriend's too. See, it was just a matter of time until we got you. But, anyway, I was wondering, what's with the money you got soaking in those little tubs?"

Despite the situation, Chug laughed.

Mickey the Harp looked at him a moment and said, "So, you gonna tell me or just lie there and laugh?"

"Guy's rude, Mickey," Sal the dogcatcher said. "Hey, don't you know it's not polite to laugh at someone who asks you a question?"

Chug thought of something weak but he had nothing else. Houdini couldn't break out of these ropes.

"Yeah, I'll tell you. Couple of nice guys like you two. I was conducting an experiment. An experiment that could lead to easy big money. Here's the funny part. I found what I was looking for too late. I already stepped into the mess that landed me here."

Mickey rolled his eyes dramatically. "Owww. Hear that, Sallie? Easy big money. Jesus, you gonna let us in on it?"

"Hey, you asked and I told you."

"You hurt his feelings, I think, Mickey."

"Oh, I'm sorry. I didn't mean to hurt your feelings."

Chug turned his head and wondered about Frankie Ricciardi. Frankie was headed to getting caught, and probably pretty soon, in some gas station job and would end up doing more time. But I'm the smart one. I'm here on an embalming table being prepared for my burial.

He thought he was going to lose it.

He turned his thoughts to his father and felt his eyes fill.

"Aw, you made him cry, Mickey. Come on, don't cry."

"Here's what I think, Sallie. Guy's found a way to get rich. I'll take a guess. He's gonna let us in on it if we let him go."

Sal went along. "Wow," he said, dragging 'wow' out, giving it a couple of extra 'o's. "Sounds like a good deal. Let's untie him now."

"He had dollar bills soaking in soap or something. I thought maybe he was into clean money. Guess I was wrong."

Mickey looked at Chug. "So is that it? Was I right? We let you go and and you let us in on this?"

Chug thought, is this what you do when there's no way out? Try anything, no matter how stupid because nothing matters more than living or buying yourself some time when you face something that'll make you scream and scream just thinking about it.

He knew he was on the edge of panic and that it was preventing him from thinking straight. Despite himself, he was slipping into a place where he'd try anything. Except beg. He wouldn't beg. Not yet, anyway. But when they closed the cover, he conceded he'd probably become a screamer and a shitter. The only thing, he wouldn't be able to scream, Will Scarlet had said.

He looked at Mickey and, despite knowing he was just setting himself up for more ridicule, said, "You got a twenty?"

Mickey gave him a look.

"A twenty? Oh, yes, sir. Right away, sir. What do you want to do, send out for pizza?"

Sal was convulsing. Mickey was a comedian.

Mickey dug into his wallet. "A twenty. I've got a lot of twenties. I'm a rich man."

He stood close to Chug and held up a twenty.

"I can make a twenty you couldn't tell from that," Chug said. "Or a fifty or a C note."

"Sure you can."

Mickey looked at Sal and gestured at Chug. "*Lui e` pazzo.*"

Sal was grinning. This whole thing was very funny, especially how this guy was going to end up. But it was really funny to see what he'd do or say to try to avoid his fate.

Despite inwardly kicking himself, Chug found himself saying, "The trick's the paper. It's impossible to get paper like real money."

"And you know how," Mickey said.

"I know how," Chug said. "I know how to get the ink out of paper money so you've got plain paper. But it's still got those threads and other things in it. You know what I mean? Then all you do is use one of those super photocopiers and shoot a twenty, a fifty, or a hundred onto it. You can't tell it from the real thing."

Mickey shook his head and walked away. "Give me a break. The new bills got all kinds of things in them."

"It took me a long time to find out what would wash out that ink. I tried everything. Bleach, detergents, acid. Nothing worked. Nothing would get that ink out."

Chug heard his words and voice, the sounds of stupid desperation.

Mickey turned and looked back at him. He made a mock-dramatic drum roll. "Nothing worked . . . until!"

Chug looked away.

"Come on. Don't be like that," Mickey said. "Tell us."

Sal laughed out loud. Mickey was a riot.

"I found out what would take out that ink. It's a combination of things."

"Tell you what," Mickey said, "you tell us and we'll try it out. If it works we'll tell Mr. Scarlata and maybe he'll be so grateful he'll let you go."

Chug felt himself slipping into a quagmire of futility. He thought of an old black and white movie he had seen once on television where some guy was getting sucked under by quicksand and everything he did made it worse until finally only his face was above the surface and then just his mouth letting out one last scream.

Mickey came back over to the table. "So what did you think we were gonna do? Go running to Mr. Scarlata with a stupid story like that? He'd laugh his ass off and then carve ours off. Or let you go because you promise to tell us your great secret way to make perfect funny money?"

Mickey looked down at Chug a moment, shaking his head and smiling. "I'll give you this much. It's a pretty creative story, though."

For a few minutes there was silence except for the rustling of Mickey's newspaper and then Sal said, "Mickey, you yourself said you saw the money soaking. Why would anyone do that? I mean, you couldn't make up a story like that."

"Forget it Sal. Use your head. You want to help this guy, go say a few prayers for him."

The SUV and the platinum Cadillac in Bernardo Tranfiglia's parking lot made Billy Wilkins's heart do a little jig. Of course, Cadillacs and SUVs parked behind a funeral home were pretty ordinary except that usually the Cadillacs were black and a more conservative model. Some funeral homes used SUVs for picking up the departed but at this time of night Bernardo Tranfiglia's vehicles were probably in the big garage at the end of the lot.

Also, the way they were parked wasn't right. If Mr. Tranfiglia left any of his vehicles out at night, Billy Wilkins felt they'd be parked side by side near the garage in a nice formal, orderly way.

These two looked as though they had come into the lot from the side street entrance and parked randomly, the SUV angled behind the Caddy.

It was after wake hours but a light glowed in the office room. Basement windows were blocked. You wouldn't want kids or anyone peeking in to watch what went on down there.

Billy Wilkins drove around the corner and into the parking lot. The SUV was a dark blue Denali but its tag had been cleaned if it was the same one that Snyder had told him about. It wasn't a hearse tag.

The tag on the Caddy wasn't livery. He thought of calling in for registration checks but decided not to just yet. Both vehicles bore a dealer's name who Billy Wilkins knew was financed by the Mob.

He wrote the registration numbers down, pulled out of the parking lot, rode around the block, and parked down the street a bit and across from the funeral home where he could watch the SUV and the Cadillac.

"Tranfiglia, you fat sonovabitch," Billy Wilkins said aloud, "what the hell are you up to? You're supposed to be helping me."

But, of course, that little arrangement was down the tubes or, to be more precise, splattered all over the window of Sabeel Biggs's BMW.

Bernardo Tranfiglia, Billy Wilkins knew, played both ends. He'd been cooperative with Billy Wilkins and a couple of other cops over the years, going back to the days when Wilkins had been with Vice.

Mr. Tranfiglia's specialty in bodies, it seemed, had extended to live ones as well as dead ones. Live, young, pretty female bodies who worked out of an apartment building Bernardo Tranfiglia owned in the North End. The business had just been started and Billy Wilkins and Bernardo Tranfiglia both, knowing an opportunity when they saw it, made a deal.

Mr. Tranfaglia would get out of the 'escort' business in exchange for Billy Wilkins not making a bust. There was a double advantage to Bernardo Tranfiglia if Billy Wilkins remained discreet. Not only would Mr. Tranfiglia, a respected business man, avoid an embarrassing encounter with the law and risk losing the business of old Italian ladies, but more important, he would avoid the ire of the younger Italian men who controlled, or thought they did, all of that sort of enterprise in Boston.

And, of course, there would be future considerations to Billy Wilkins. After all, Bernardo

Tranfiglia had access to the pulse, as it were, of the North End in a lot of ways. Future considerations like acting as a conduit of information from and to the non-Irish illegal power structure of Boston, which these days meant William Scarlata.

And those were William Scarlata's vehicles parked behind the funeral home. Billy Wilkins would bet on it. That dark blue Denali chased Chug and Ellie Robinson over the bridge and into Chelsea and scooped up Chug by the Park Street T station.

Chug was now somewhere in that funeral home.

Billy Wilkins thought it out. Somehow, Bernardo Tranfiglia was to be the disposal service. That wasn't hard to figure. Cremation, maybe. That had been done before. Very effective way to get rid of a bod although certainly there were no cremation facilities inside the funeral home.

But why was Will Scarlet still inside? That wasn't hard to figure either. Right now poor old Chug was probably having his fingernails pulled out with pliers or suffering some other unspeakable agony while William Scarlata watched and felt as though he was buying retribution for his mother.

Billy Wilkins thought of his options. Right now he was probably in the very situation he had been aiming for since Mink Whitehead had told him he could get the name of the man who shot Will Scarlet's mother. Here was his chance to nail Will Scarlet and get that write up and all the attendant glories that would come from putting away a major organized crime figure.

Except for two things.

One, he was *probably* in the situation. His plan had been based on the certainty of catching Will Scarlet in a trap he had set. And although he was nearly certain the blue Denali was the one that had made off with Chug, he wasn't absolutely certain Chug was in that funeral home. They could have him stashed someplace else.

Billy Wilkins knew he was in the murky world of probable cause here. He had good reason to believe he knew where a person abducted near the Boston Common earlier that evening was being forcibly held and in danger of bodily harm. But he didn't have a warrant and any explanation he gave to obtain one involved all sorts of things about his relationship with that person that he wasn't anxious to divulge.

Likewise, he couldn't call for backups without giving complicating explanations afterward and running the risk of looking like a fool if he was wrong.

Two, he didn't have Jessup, goddamn him. That's who he needed.

He sat and smoked a couple of cigarettes and watched, waiting for what he wasn't sure.

As he was about to light a third cigarette, he saw William Scarlata and Lou Russo walk to the Cadillac and drive away. Even though it was dark, he recognized both men by size, shape, and walk.

He waited a few more minutes while he smoked his cigarette. The Denali stayed. He gave it another half hour and still the Denali stayed.

To Billy Wilkins that meant Chug was still alive and that he was in the funeral home.

He fished in his pocket for the little notebook he kept with phone numbers. On his cell phone he punched the home phone number of Special Agent Jessup who was such an uptight bastard, Billy Wilkins felt, that he was probably tucked in for a long night's sleep.

Special Agent Jessup wasn't tucked in but was, in fact, reading a book about planting a perennial garden. He loved gardening and damned if one day he wouldn't do beds of perennials, maybe even an herb garden. The problem was that with his job he lived in apartments or condos and had to settle for window plants.

When he took the phone from his wife, he listened to Billy Wilkins and felt a faint throb start at his temple.

He thought he had washed his hands of Billy Wilkins and his insane scheme. A Southern Boston cop. Maybe that's why the whole Wilkins plan was so dumb. The blend of redneck and Bostonian produced a mutant intellectualism. He had a busy day tomorrow and didn't want to spend even a few minutes talking to this maniac let alone the entire night which was what Wilkins was suggesting.

Against his will, he listened some more and finally found himself saying, "Yeah, yeah. Give me a half hour."

It took Jessup the half hour plus five minutes from the time he hung up to drive from his suburban condo into the North End and meet Billy Wilkins. They sat in Wilkins's unmarked Crown Victoria and watched the funeral home parking lot. The Denali was still there.

Billy Wilkins filled Jessup in on the incident by the Park Street T station and the shooting of Sabeel Biggs under the Common.

"So you're not even sure that he's in there," Jessup said, his voice rising as he pointed at Bernardo Tranfiglia's funeral home. Over the phone, Billy Wilkins said he had tracked down Chug to where to where he was being held by Will Scarlet.

"Jessup, I'm as sure as I can be. I mean I didn't actually see him but it adds up."

"So we've got a goddamn mess on our hands. Or you do, I should say, because I'm going back home and get a good night's sleep."

"Hey, I can walk away too."

"You had any brains you would before you have to start explaining things you don't want to have to explain."

Jessup opened his door.

Billy Wilkins said, "What about the poor bastard in there? I mean forget about the original plan but I think now we should at least think about him a little."

"You're in a bind, aren't you Wilkins? You can't call in the troops. You can't get a warrant. What the hell *are* you going to do?"

"I figure they've done to him what they're gonna do short of killing him. Will Scarlet will be back for that. My theory is that Will and Lou Russo will be back in a little while. They went somewhere to set something up. They and their soldiers will come out with Chug to take him to wherever to administer the kiss of death. Or maybe he already *is* dead. He comes out, dead or alive. Then we call in the troops and move in like originally planned."

"And you and I, who don't normally associate, just happen to be riding by and see something suspicious. I'm going home. Good night, Wilkins."

"We were consulting on a case. There's gotta be something we could be consulting on, a couple of conscientious law enforcement officers like us. Use a little imagination, will you. And, yeah, a bizarre incident occurred by the Boston Common, we have a description of the Denali and lo and behold, there it is and some guy being led forcibly to it."

Special Agent Jessup ran his fingers through his hair. He felt the special kind of fatigue bred of a late hour and tension building up.

He said, "Let's say all of this happens, everything goes by script. Then what? Chug looks at us and says, probably in front of witnesses, 'what about our little deal?'"

Billy Wilkins lit a cigarette, cracked his window, and blew a stream of smoke out.

"This has been the weak part of your plan all along, Wilkins. No, I take that back. This has been the dirty rotten bastard part of your plan. We nail Will Scarlet. Chug, if he lives, looks to you for salvation, for a new life, but you'll just shrug your shoulders and play dumb and let him take the fall for shooting Will Scarlet's mother. Because it'll surely come out that he was the guy who did the shooting."

Billy Wilkins took another drag.

"I'm right, aren't I?" Special Agent Jessup said.

"Come on, Jessup. Give me some credit, huh?"

"Ohmigod, for what? For being a heartless sonovabitch?"

Billy Wilkins took a couple of deep drags on his cigarette.

"Jessup, why don't you go back home and get your eight hours' sleep?"

Jessup looked at his watch. "That's long gone anyway."

They waited through the night, nodding occasionally, staving off the cold by running the heater once in a while, and sparring verbally.

Twice, a patrol car drove past and the cop behind the wheel nodded at Billy Wilkins.

"That's great," Jessup said. "We'll just say we were driving by and saw a crime in progress. That uniform will go along with that, huh?"

"Aw, Jessup, relax."

At 6:30, Billy Wilkins directed Jessup to the bakery to get coffee and donuts. "Might as well try some of Will Scarlet's products. They say the stuff that comes out of that bakery is actually very good."

He fished into his wallet. "Here. Treat's on me."

"Damn right it is," Jessup said.

When he returned from the bakery, Jessup said, "Will Scarlet himself waited on me. Said he'd been cooking donuts and bread all night. Nice guy."

They sipped and munched and watched the funeral home. The Denali was still there but Will Scarlet and Lou Russo hadn't returned.

At 7:45 Jessup said, layering his voice with irony, "Wilkins, I work for a living as I presume you do. Day shift. After such a refreshing night, this is going to be a real fun day."

"Let's give it just a bit more. Those guys don't live in there."

"Yeah, they were probably waiting for broad daylight to drag a body or struggling body out."

Billy Wilkins inwardly conceded that Jessup had a point. He had dealt with this stupidly but didn't know what else he could have done.

As he started the engine for another blast of heat, the first people arrived. They parked in the lot behind the funeral home. Two cars, a Toyota Avalon and a Buick LeSabre.

Nine people dressed for mourning left the cars and went into the home via a side door.

Two minutes later, Sal the Dogcatcher came out and moved the Denali to the rear of the lot.

"That's Salvatore Manfredi," Billy Wilkins said. "He's one of Will Scarlet's boys."

Over the next several minutes, more cars arrived and parked in back under the direction of one of Bernardo Tranfiglia's sons who lined the cars up and gave each driver a white magnetized funeral tag to put on their car's roof.

"Must be a nine o'clock funeral. Family and friends saying the last goodbye," Billy Wilkins said.

"Great," Special Agent Jessup said. "I think I'm about to say my last goodbye to you."

"Hello," Billy Wilkins said. "Look who just arrived."

A platinum Cadillac pulled into the parking lot and backed in beside the Denali. A rested looking William Scarlata and Lou Russo got out and went into the funeral home.

"Who's that with Will Scarlet?" Jessup asked. "Friar Tuck?"

"That's Lou Russo. He's a sweetheart."

"What the hell is this all about?" Special Agent Jessup sat up alert and brushed donut crumbs from his jacket.

"Interesting, huh?" Billy Wilkins said.

At 8:40 three men came from the funeral home and went to the garage. From it, they drove out a flower car, a hearse, and a long Cadillac for the deceased's family.

Five minutes later, mourners returned to their cars, sat and waited with engines idling and headlights on. The hearse drove around to another door away from view.

Jessup looked at Billy Wilkins. "You know what I think, Wilkins? I think Will Scarlet lost a cousin or a friend. And I think you've lost your marbles and I've lost a night's sleep for nothing."

Once when Chug visited his father at the nursing home, he found him with his arms and legs tethered to the bed. He nicely controlled his rage when he talked with the supervisor but let him know exactly how he felt about that kind of treatment.

The supervisor told him that it was for his Dad's own good, that he was going through a spell. But he never found his father that way again.

But right now, it was the way he himself was. His arms and hands, his legs and feet were tethered as if he were some piece of livestock to be slaughtered. He wondered who would visit his father. Probably not his brother. Ellie would if they didn't get to her.

Throughout the night he lay trussed and listened to his guards snore. He had tried not to think. His limbs were numb and he wondered if they were permanently damaged.

Then he remembered the play *Our Town* his English class had read in high school. There was a part where one of the characters dies but is allowed to re-live one day in her life. She comes back to the day of her twelfth birthday but seeing her parents and her brother young again is more than she can bear and drives her to tears.

Before she returns to her grave, she takes a final look around and says farewell to the world, farewell to ordinary things. Chug remembered the line. *Goodbye to clocks ticking, hot coffee, sleeping and waking up.*

Chug remembered his teacher going on about the significance of all that and how it meant nothing to him then. Now it did.

He pondered the lines from the play and thought a long time about high school. Some good times there, actually.

Finally, his guards woke and talked. After a while, a heavy man came down with coffee and pastry for the two guards. He refused to look at Chug. Maybe a couple of hours later, as best he could judge, Will Scarlet and Lou Russo returned. So this was it.

Will Scarlet looked at Chug a long, silent moment. Then he gestured at Sal and Mickey. "Take this guy to the bathroom. Make sure he goes."

When they carried Chug into a small adjoining bathroom, he said to Lou Russo, "Wouldn't want anything leaking out of that casket or it stinking up the church."

They had to loosen his bonds a bit in the bathroom but any thoughts of fighting were dashed when he discovered he couldn't stand and could barely move his arms. When they propped him on the toilet seat, he immediately released.

He looked at Mickey and Sal and said, "Here's to you."

When he finished, they retied his bonds, if anything pulling them tighter than before. Then they brought him back out.

On the table beside the one where he had spent the night, lay a dead man, nicely dressed in suit coat and tie but no pants.

On the table where he had spent the night was an empty open casket.

Mickey the Harp patted the casket and smiled at Chug.

"Hey, there's your new home. What do you think? Looks pretty comfortable to me."

Lieutenant Billy Wilkins and Special Agent Jessup watched the hearse come back around and the parade of cars leave the parking lot. Less than a minute later, Will Scarlet, Lou Russo, Mickey, and Sal came out, got into their two vehicles and drove out, not following the funeral procession.

"So where's Chug," Special Agent Jessup asked. "He was never inside that funeral home, Wilkins, you moron."

Billy Wilkins gave Jessup a wilting look.

"Jessup, chill out, will you. You wait here or come with me if you want. I'm going inside and have a chat with my friend, Mr. Tranfiglia. I didn't see him leave either. Just his sons."

Jessup checked his watch and ran his hand over his stubbled face. "Okay, I'll go in with you. Maybe at least I'll get a laugh out of this. Then I'll sneak home for a quick shower and shave. Good thing I've got some seniority."

"Good thing you're with me, Jessup. Anyone sees you looking like that or gets a whiff of you, they'll call the cops."

Chapter Twenty Eight

Bernardo Tranfiglia sat on the chair Mickey the Harp had used and stared at the withered body of Armando Raucci lying on the metal table.

Mr. Raucci's thin hair had gotten mussed when they took him from the casket and his eyeglasses had been knocked a little askew. His skinny old legs stuck white and hairless from his suit jacket. He had on a white shirt and a dark tie. A pin that Bernardo Tranfiglia couldn't identify glinted from his lapel.

Bernardo Tranfiglia patted Mr. Raucci's hair and adjusted the glasses. He was trying to come to grips with what he had done. He knew he had just seen the devil. Bent forward in his chair toward Armando Raucci, he looked as though he was praying.

William Scarlata's men had squirmed the trussed up person into the casket, stuffed his mouth with cloth, and taped the mouth shut but not before he managed to clamp his mouth down hard on Mickey the Harp's hand, drawing blood and a scream.

Then they stuffed blankets between the man's torso and the casket lid so that he couldn't thrash. As Bernardo Tranfiglia closed the casket, he lost his fight to avoid the man's eyes.

Worse, he knew he would lose the fight to ever forget what he saw in those eyes.

For now, he had to think of getting rid of Mr. Raucci. In a way, that problem was a blessing that allowed him temporarily not to think of the eyes.

William Scarlata had said to cremate Mr. Raucci. Easy for him to say, as though that process meant simply to stuff the poor old man in one of the fireplaces upstairs. Cremation could be done but that meant arrangements and confidences. And the greasing of a few palms. But that could come from what was in the envelope William Scarlata had given him. It contained the fifty-thousand dollars that had been rumored to be the reward William Scarlata had offered for his mother's killer.

The buzzer and light signaled someone at the upstairs front door. For now, he was the only one left at the home except for Mr. Raucci and the other two upstairs awaiting their own funerals later that morning.

He took the elevator up and opened the front door knowing he looked as though *he* were in mourning, a look that for once was genuine.

"We've got to talk," Lieutenant Billy Wilkins said to him. Bernardo Tranfiglia noticed that the police officer and his companion, whom he didn't recognize, looked as harried as he pictured himself. The world was in grief or turmoil.

They sat in the paneled office. Recognizing a man in agony, Billy Wilkins launched a frontal assault.

"Mr. Tranfiglia, I want you to tell me what went on here last night. I don't want any bullshit. I know Will Scarlet was here and I got very good reason to believe the person he thinks shot his mother is still here."

Bernardo Tranfiglia started to protest but Billy Wilkins bore in. "Look, we go back, you and I. I'd like to keep this informal and, if I can, keep you out of trouble. But if I have to I can have a court order here in ten minutes and more cops than you'd like to think of pouring all over the place. At the least, it'd be bad for business."

He jerked a thumb at Jessup, hoping Jessup wasn't about to have apoplexy. "Federal," he said.

Bernardo Tranfiglia looked at the two men and crumbled in his chair. Water oozed from his eyes and skin. He wanted a priest.

"I'll burn in hell. I made a pact with the Devil and I'll burn in Hell for it. That man—that Will Scarlet—he makes you do things. He has no soul. He'll kill me but I don't care."

They let him blubber for a minute and then he told them, purging himself, holding nothing back.

He ran a large handkerchief over his face and patted his eyes. His hand shook as he opened the drawer and pulled out two bottles.

"I'll never forget his eyes. He is a brave man. A brave face and brave eyes but there was something else in those eyes. I'll never forget those eyes as long as I live. May the Blessed Virgin help me."

Smothering his revulsion, Billy Wilkins said, "Where's the funeral?"

"Saint Agnes."

"Where's the burial?"

"Walnut Grove."

"How much time?"

Bernardo Tranfiglia looked at his watch. "The Mass. The procession drives slow. Graveside prayers and all. People leave and the cemetery crew moves in." He shrugged. "Two hours?"

"How long can he last in that casket?"

Bernardo Tranfiglia shrugged again. "He made me drill large holes in the bottom of the casket, right up through the lining. I think enough air will get in."

Bernardo Tranfiglia mopped his eyes.

"Can you believe such a man . . . such a thing? It is beyond . . ."

His voice trailed. He looked at them.

"I will burn in Hell and William Scarlata will burn beside me."

"Goddamnit, so how long can he last, Mr. Traanfiglia?"

"Mr. Scarlata wanted the poor bastard to be alive when they . . ."

Bernardo Tranfiglia had to pause. He took a pill from one bottle and a pull from the other. Billy Wilkins thought the man was going to lose it.

"The bastard wanted him alive when they shoveled the dirt onto the casket. I drilled a lot of holes. They were large. I knew he would check them. Unless the poor man has a heart attack, he'll probably have enough air until they bury him."

"One last thing, Mr. Tranfiglia. What's the name of the person whose funeral this is supposed to be?"

"Armando Raucci," Bernardo Tranfiglia said, hoping they didn't question him about what was to become of that old man.

Billy Wilkins and Special Agent Jessup left Bernardo Tranfiglia slumped behind his desk.

"Well, what do you think, Jessup, did you get your laugh?" Billy Wilkins said when they got back into the unmarked Crown Victoria.

"You and I will burn right along with that pathetic thing in there and Will Scarlet," Special Agent Jessup said in voice that sounded strained.

"Okay, right, but the question is, what are we gonna do? Whatever it is, we might have two hours. Emphasis on *might.*"

"Question? There's no question. You call in your troops, we go to the church, and see if that poor sonovabitch is still alive."

"I'll chalk that up to lack of sleep, Jessup. You Feds should get out into the nitty gritty police world and pull all nighters a little more often. You get used to not sleeping and still can keep your smarts about you.

"Now use your college-degree head and think about what you just said. I'll say this, we might get that big write-up but we wouldn't like it."

Wilkins started the car. "I think I know what we've gotta do. First we've gotta save Mr. Robert Ellis. How complicated that'll be depends on Will Scarlet."

After getting on the Orange Line, Ellie Robinson rode all the way to Forest Hills, turned around and rode aimlessly for a long time, falling asleep, waking, making train changes and random turnabouts. She got on the Blue Line and headed for the North Shore. She got out at Orient Heights with the thought of going to Laurie Wojcik's house, thought better of it, and, using the last of her money, headed back to town. When she was convinced no one was in pursuit, she got off at Government Center as though places of various governmental agencies could provide refuge even at night when manned mainly by custodians.

She walked toward Tremont Street, shivering and exhausted, past where she had run into the T station, where Chug had blocked the guy chasing her.

She thought of him and didn't know what she felt. Yes she did. She felt the old feelings and wept.

For a moment she toyed with the thought of going into the Common and sprawling on a bench until either the bums, the cops or the cold got her. Instead, she turned off Tremont and headed toward Washington Street.

The streets were lonely and mean looking. The few people she passed, if they eyed her at all, eyed her curiously. This was the time of night when eye contact could be a dangerous signal.

The wind keened and whistled and a siren pulsed faraway. She saw rats in an alley by a dumpster, bold now in the gloom, not furtive, as they feasted on something that they had beaten the street people to.

She found a place that sold coffee and muffins. Its light splashed onto the sidewalk and she walked in. Behind the counter, a man sipping a coffee regarded her warily. She knew she looked as though she were there just to suck up the heat.

When she remembered she had no money, the smell of the coffee became unbearably delicious. She and the man exchanged a stare before she went back out to the street and the cold.

When she reached Washington Street, she stood aimlessly for a minute and then turned south. She stopped and tried to force herself to think rationally for herself and for Chug, to come up with a concrete course of action. She didn't know what had become of him but because she was safe for the moment *she* could do something.

She leaned against the metal security gate stretched across a storefront. She concentrated on having the rational thoughts and the sensible course of action. She knew she wasn't far from sliding down the grate and sprawling senselessly on the sidewalk.

She thought of Chug and wondered whether fear, fatigue, and cold had stolen her common sense. Should she have gone straight to the cops? Should she go now? Of course she should. They weren't looking for him in connection with the shooting of Will Scarlet's mother.

She had to find a cop.

A large, dark car came toward her moving slowly, searching. She tried to draw into the grate as it passed in front of her. When it slowed, she saw two men look and size her.

When it stopped, she watched the glow of its brake lights and then the white reverse lights snapped at her.

"Jesus," she said as she stumbled into a hobbled, slow run.

They drove past Saint Agnes's, eying the parked cars lining the sidewalk. Billy Wilkins rode around the church and through the parking lot in the rear.

"We're looking for the silver Caddy and the Denali. Probably not here, but you never know," he said.

"All right," Special Agent Jessup said. "So what's the plan?"

"Simple. We now go out to Walnut Grove Cemetery and wait for the burial. When everyone's cleared out, we see Bernardo Tranfiglia's sons, let them know we know what's going on. They keep the cemetery crew away while we let Chug make like Lazarus. We whisk Chug away, get him medical attention if he needs it, and they bury an empty casket."

"What if he's dead?"

Billy Wilkins shrugged. "Let's deal with that then."

"What if Will Scarlet's out there watching the whole procedure?"

Billy Wilkins lit a cigarette. "That's the tricky part, huh? See, at this point I think we just want to save Chug, don't we? If we can make Will Scarlet think he's buried him, then Chug can take off with his girl and start a new life. And we don't want him serving any time either. What he's going through now is punishment enough for any sins he's ever committed."

"Including shooting a woman?"

"Give it a rest, Jessup, will you?"

"No heroics for us, huh, Wilkins? That stupid plan you had about collaring Will Scarlet is all gone. Why I listened to you I'll never know."

"Ah, we're on the side of the angels, Jessup. What'd that character say in *A Tale of Two Cities*? I remember reading it in high school and thinking how cool it was. 'Tis a far, far better thing I do than I have ever done.'"

"Yeah, just before he went to the guillotine. I think I know the feeling."

The darkness was total and was exceeded only by his fear. He opened his eyes and closed his eyes. It made no difference, none at all. He had never known such darkness except maybe when he was in his mother's womb.

He had a sense of various movements, the casket being lifted, slid, positioned. Then the motion of being in a car. A hearse, he knew.

Slid, lifted again, more movement. But for a while, now, no motion.

Just darkness like he imagined eternity must be like. And the sound of his breathing through his nose which still hurt from his fight in the warehouse. He tried to make the breathing sound loud but the soft cloth of the lid was pressed into his face and they had stuffed and taped his mouth tightly.

He couldn't feel his hands and feet.

He tried to make growling noises and to squirm but could not do that either. Then, he remembered they had injected something into him just before they shut the cover and it had taken his strength but left him his awareness and his fear.

His pulse was heavy in his ear, heavy and loud enough surely to be heard outside.

And now another noise came from outside, penetrating the casket. More a feeling than a noise. A vibration. Was he dying? No, he was still breathing.

He held his breath. Maybe he could hold it until he died. He would welcome death. Nothing could be worse than this.

Then he knew what the vibration was. He was in a church and the organ was playing, vibrating the metal casket. The last sound the dead heard. Except for the dirt being shoveled onto the casket.

He tried to scream. He tried to move but could do nothing except listen to that vibration.

When he died, if there was anything at all to what they used to tell him in Sunday School, he would go straight to heaven.

Purgatory couldn't be as awful as this.

Wilkins and Jessup stopped at the Walnut Grove caretaker's office and Billy Wilkins went inside. He asked for directions to the Armando Raucci burial site and came back to the car.

They drove the narrow cemetery road, through thickets of stone monuments. Even though the calendar was closing in on April, the air was still cold and the sky looked brittle and chilled. But the sun was high and some of the trees and shrubs were hinting of spring.

Ahead, at the end of a long, straight road on the side of a hill they saw the canopy and a discreet distance from it behind some tall, bare shrubs were parked the truck, backhoe, and crew who would move in to lower the casket and throw on the dirt.

Billy Wilkins took a right and drove to the top of the hill where they could watch and wait for the funeral procession.

"Back in Georgia," he said, "in the back woods country where I grew up, I used to hear some of the stuff the Klan would pull. They were before my time but if you can believe what you hear, if it was half as bad as people used to say, it was pretty awful. I mean, some of those good old boys . . ."

He shook his head. "But I don't remember anything as cruel or sick as this."

"Hell," Special Agent Jessup said, "we knew Will Scarlet's done some pretty sadistic things but you're right, this goes beyond anything I've ever heard of. It's sicker than sick. It's depraved."

"I heard a story about him once that I didn't believe," Billy Wilkins said. "Now I'm not so sure. You know how they say that with the Mob it's strictly business when they whack each other? I think with Will Scarlet it's personal."

"Anyway, the story goes that one of his guys wasn't turning in all of his receipts to Will and Will caught him. They took this guy in Will's big assed powerboat, he's got one of them boats will do about fifty or sixty, and put him in some kind of net and dragged him around behind the boat.

"They'd drag him some, then stop, bring the guy up to let him recover a bit and then do it some more. Took a couple of hours, if the story's true, for the guy to die. I don't know if he drowned or if hypothermia got him. Supposedly, Will Scarlet thought the whole thing was pretty funny."

"You know," Special Agent Jessup said, "I really wanted to nail that bastard for something which is why I'm here, I guess. But now he's going to get away with even this."

"Yeah, Bernardo Tranfiglia can talk about burning in Hell but, I'll tell you, he'll never say a thing about any of this. And his sons won't. And I guess we're now in the position where we can't. But I remind you, Jessup, if we get Chug out alive and Will Scarlet doesn't know about it, I'll settle for that."

They waited and fidgeted. Billy Wilkins smoked and Jessup dozed. After twenty minutes, Billy Wilkins nudged Special Agent Jessup. He pointed to a platinum Cadillac parked on a road away from the

Raucci gravesite canopy but where it commanded a good view.

"That's Will Scarlet."

Jessup sat up and rubbed his eyes. He squinted and stared.

"You sure it's them?"

"Yeah. They pulled up a couple of minutes ago. Lou Russo got out to throw a coffee cup in the trash barrel there."

"I guess we can't get them for littering," Jessup said. "So now what?"

"They wait, we wait," Billy Wilkins said. He looked at Jessup. "Jesus, Jessup, you look like hell."

Chapter Twenty Nine

After what seemed much longer than it really was, the funeral procession, led by a cemetery truck, came slowly and solemnly along the narrow road.

The hearse and the flower car positioned themselves near the gravesite while the remaining cars, twenty of them, waited patiently for the set up, most with headlights still glowing, their running engines puffing small clouds of vapor into the air.

The priest talked with Bernardo Tranfiglia's sons while pallbearers arranged flowers near the grave.

"I can't begin to imagine what it's like for that poor devil in that coffin," Special Agent Jessup said as they watched. "If he's still alive."

They sat and watched the graveside ceremony. The frail old widow was comforted and supported by sons and daughters and their wives and husbands. A handful of elderly friends clung to the circle and wondered about their own time. The priest helped Armando Raucci gain admission to Heaven.

In their platinum Cadillac, William Scarlata and Lou Russo also watched without speaking a word. William Scarlata's gaze was intent as his head nodded from time to time as though giving approval.

The priest finished and friends and family came closer to the casket. Some touched it, some draped long-stemmed flowers on it. Reluctantly, they parted and shuffled back to their cars.

The flower car and hearse took their leave and the family boarded the Cadillac limousine driven by one of Bernardo Tranfiglia's sons. The other cars, occupied by friends and family, likewise took their leave.

As soon as the gravesite was clear, William Scarlata's Cadillac pulled down to it. Wilkins and Jessup watched him walk to the casket and bend down so close it looked as though he was kissing it.

He lingered a long moment and then returned to his car.

Even from the distance, Wilkins and Jessup could see his broad smile.

He had slept for a while, or something which was a deformed, evil relative of sleep. Whatever it was, even though it provided a respite from conscious awareness, it substituted nightmares he had never known, swirling mixes of demons and snakes and worms and horrid insects that he couldn't fend away. He tried to scream but couldn't, both in reality and in his mind.

When he returned to the nether world of total black and of the soft fabric pressed into his face, it was merely the other side of a terror that revolved and refused even a moment's mercy.

He willed himself to die and then had the horrible thought that maybe he *was* dead and that this was his eternal fate, his punishment for the sum of his sins.

For a time he was aware of motion, mainly slow and steady, some soft stops and starts, then being lifted and positioned again.

Voices. One voice, actually. A solemn voice. Meant to comfort but no comfort to him.

Then, for a while, nothing. He couldn't measure time.

Then another voice. Just near him. Speaking clearly, a pronouncement of evil and triumph, and vengeance.

He knew whose voice it was and even though it was the voice of the Devil he knew he wasn't dead or in Hell.

Yet.

They watched William Scarlata and Lou Russo drive away.

"Okay," Billy Wilkins said, "one of Tranfiglia's sons is driving the hearse, the other the limo. We gotta get one or the other before the crew moves in."

They looked and already the truck and backhoe were moving forward to bury the casket.

Billy Wilkins exceeded the cemetery's fifteen mile per hour speed limit by a lot as they sped to the main gate. Grave markers blurred by on either side of the narrow road.

When the hit the public street, he popped his blue lights and siren.

"They had to go back this way," he said

"You hope."

They vanquished traffic and saw the limo. Billy Wilkins flew past it.

"I'd rather get the hearse. Too complicated to talk in front of the Rauccis."

"Jesus Christ, Wilkins, there's no time. That guy's gonna be buried alive."

"Two minutes. If we don't catch it in two minutes, I'll get the limo," Billy Wilkins said. He found it difficult to talk, as though he'd just been climbing or running.

They ate the two minutes and more.

"Sonovabitch, Wilkins, go back for the limo. Or just go back to the cemetery. This is unconscionable."

Billy Wilkins wrestled with that and started to slow when they saw the hearse.

It pulled to the side and he stopped behind it.

He ran to the hearse, flashed his shield at Bernardo Tranfiglia's son and said, "You come with us. Don't argue. We know about the casket you just left back at Walnut Grove."

Clement Tranfiglia's mask of sympathy and concern, frozen by habit onto his face, changed to defiance.

"I haven't the slightest clue what you're talking about."

"Yeah you do. I'll say it one more time. Turn this thing around. You hear me? Do it now."

"Screw you. You want to talk with me, you talk through my lawyer."

Billy Wilkins glanced around. Traffic was slowing and looking as it always does when a police car makes a kill. This time the curiosity was higher because the prey was a hearse. The lion had taken a hyena.

Billy Wilkins ran to the passenger's side and got in.

He pulled his revolver and stuck it under Clement Tranfiglia's chin.

"Now listen very carefully, you sorry sack of shit. You're gonna turn this goddamn thing around and follow us. We've talked with your father. We know everything. We're trying to keep this unofficial. Everything works out and they plant an empty casket back there and no one will ever know. And that means Will Scarlet too. And that means you and your brother and father can continue making a good living.

"You don't do it that way, we're going back and opening that casket anyway. Now you think about it really fast. Which way's it gonna be? You still want to talk with your lawyer?"

Clement Tranfiglia's defiance stood its ground a moment and then crumbled. He pulled his head back and eyed the revolver. This cop was a madman.

"Put that gun away. Please. I'll follow you."

They U-turned and headed back to the cemetery. Billy Wilkins pushed the Crown Victoria as hard as he could. The engine pinged and rapped and he thought the car was going to throw a rod or stall. He cursed the maintenance crew.

"Keep your eye on him," he said to Jessup. "Make sure he doesn't try to pull a fade."

Special Agent Jessup obediently swiveled in his seat and wondered if this was his last day as an FBI agent.

In the cemetery, Billy Wilkins stopped and ran back to the hearse.

"Okay. You go ahead. Talk the burial crew into stopping. Come up with something. Tell them to get lost for a few minutes. We'll be behind where they won't notice us but where we can see. If worse comes to worst, give a wave and we'll come in."

Clement Tranfiglia stared at Billy Wilkins.

"You are out of your mind. What in hell am I going to tell them?"

"I don't know. Use your imagination. Tell 'em you mistakenly left some ring or something that the family wants."

Clement Tranfiglia looked at his watch. "Jesus, it's too late. They've buried him."

Billy Wilkins banged the fender of the hearse with his fist. "Move it. Go."

They followed and as they approached the gravesite Billy Wilkins and Special Agent Jessup felt as though they had died.

The truck and crew had finished their work and all that remained was a pile of flowers.

And now he was going down, down. Shaky, jerky movements but no mistaking it. Sinking. A spiral to hell.

He hit bottom and time stopped.

Seconds, minutes, hours. He would never have believed tracking time would be so beyond him.

He thought of his mother when he was a little boy and how she comforted him when he was hurt or afraid. Soon, maybe, he'd be with her again and she could comfort him. He thought of when he had stood beside her casket at her gravesite with his brother and father and how they had tried to comfort each other.

Memories of his boyhood flooded his mind, of summer days in the small back yard his family shared with two other families who lived in the same triple decker, the air filled with glorious sunshine and blue sky and bird song, of playing ball with his father and brother, of going into the house afterward for a dinner of beef and potatoes his mother cooked or maybe hopping into the Chevy and heading someplace that served fried clams. His father would let him and his brother have a small sip of his beer while his mother shook her head disapprovingly. His mother always drank rum cokes but she never let her boys have a sip.

After the meal his mother and father would smoke cigarettes and they'd all walk along the beach if the clam restaurant was near a beach.

His reverie snapped shut when the first dirt crackled on the metal roof just over his head. He knew it would soon be over and he might have smiled if he could move his mouth.

The night before, Ellie Robinson had slumped against the back door of the car. In the front, the two men wrinkled their noses in disgust at her smell, so incongruous in one whose prettiness showed despite her tangled hair and smudged face. They smiled knowingly anyway as they drove. Just a short ride and they'd be rid of her.

When they put her in the back seat, they said, "Sure, sure," to her prattling but then she gave out and they thought she had died. She had been running pretty hard. Or had been trying to.

But she wasn't dead. She wheezed and shook a little and had no fight left in her as her head bounced against the car window. They could see her eyes fill and small tears running crooked trails down her face.

At one point, they thought they heard her say, "I love him. I love him so much."

Not far to go and she'd be off their hands. They had other things to do.

The three men stood at the grave. Billy Wilkins clamped his hand to the back of his head and looked about unseeing.

Then his eyes focused on the yellow backhoe swaying slowly along the road as it headed for other work.

He grabbed Clement Tranfiglia by his expensive black coat and pointed. "Go get him. Tell him . . . tell him what I said. Tell him you buried something that the family wants. It was a mistake and it's embarrassing as hell to you and your father. Christ, it must happen sometimes. You just want the dirt uncovered and it'll only take a minute. Slip him a twenty if you have to."

"Aw, you . . ." Clement Tranfiglia looked at Billy Wilkins in disbelief.

Billy Wilkins shoved him into the hearse.

"Wilkins, it's over," Special Agent Jessup said as they watched the hearse in incongruous pursuit of the backhoe.

"We blew it. Just pray a lot now and go to church. Try for forgiveness."

"He's got air," Wilkins said. "I'm telling you, he's got a few minutes."

They watched Clement Tranfiglia talking to the backhoe operator.

Come on, come on," Billy Wilkins said. "Move it."

It did, lumbering back toward them like some large swaying beast.

"What are gonna do when we open that casket and that guy's sitting on his backhoe taking it all in?" Jessup asked.

"I don't know. Come on, let's get out of sight."

328

They sat in the Crown Victoria and watched the backhoe eat the dirt. Filled only a few minutes previous, it was loose and was an easy meal.

When the operator finished, he and Clement Tranfiglia talked a moment and the backhoe lumbered away. Billy Wilkins drove down to the grave.

Clement Tranfiglia climbed into the open grave and worked the lid of the coffin. As they watched, Billy Wilkins almost reached out to hold Special Agent Jessup's hand.

Bending and leaning his expensive coat against the dirt wall, Clement Tranfiglia raised the lid.

And it was now almost impossible to breathe and for that he was joyous. But his body couldn't stop the mechanics of trying to draw in what little air remained.

The noise of his tortured respiration grew beyond any logical bounds and filled his metal and cloth world. It was heavy and rhythmical and soon he knew it wasn't coming from him.

Was it the demons from Hell?

When the lid opened, the light blinded him and he drank in limitless air.

He couldn't see the three men bending toward him through his tears and the all-encompassing light that he thought was God.

Chapter Thirty

His recovery, in the back seat of the Crown Victoria, was surprisingly fast. At least physically. Billy Wilkins wondered whether Chug's mind would ever be the same. Or his own.

"Come on, let us take you to a hospital," Billy Wilkins repeated. He and Jessup had already said that several times.

"No. I'm all right."

His head lolled a little but he repeated, "I'm all right."

"You have your hands and feet checked at least."

"They're feeling better. They're gonna be all right."

They drove without talking for a while. Billy Wilkins lit a cigarette and offered the pack to Chug.

"No. I just want air for now."

Chug looked out his window, the light still paining his eyes, but just a little now. The streets were still grimy on the sides with winter sand and debris that the street sweepers would soon pick up. Trees were mostly bare and cars were dirty. To Chug, it all seemed pretty nice.

"I'm sorry I screwed up the deal. But they got Ellie."

They had already been over this, too, but Billy Wilkins knew Chug needed to rehash it, as though he were saying penance.

"I mean I had to do what I thought was best for Ellie."

"We understand that," Special Agent Jessup said. "You're a very brave man."

"So what happens now?"

Billy Wilkins avoided Jessup's eyes as he spoke.

"Well, the deal we discussed is off, naturally. I mean the money part, the new IDs. But, in a way, you got what you wanted. Will Scarlet thinks you're buried and dead by now. The bastard will probably visit the grave once in a while to gloat. He wants Ellie but he'll eventually forget about her as time passes.

"So, what you've got to do—you and Ellie—is start a new life somewhere. You can always change your name legally, if you want."

After they had carried Chug to the car and massaged his hands and feet and had seen that his breathing was stable and his mind not deranged, Wilkins had radioed in with inquiries about a missing Ellen Robinson.

He was informed that a young woman with that name had been picked up by two patrol cops the previous night running up Washington Street in a panic and near collapse. She was brought to District A-1 Station. She, like Chug, declined medical attention but had asked if she could remain at the station for a short time during the morning.

Wilkins asked if they would hold her for just a short time longer.

"I think we can drop the charade, Wilkins," Chug said. "That deal was never gonna happen, was it? You were playing me for some purpose of your own but I was kidding myself too."

"Now, that's not true, Chug."

"But, hey, believe me, no hard feelings. You guys pulled me out of that hole. I can't even begin to tell you . . ."

Billy Wilkins flicked his cigarette out the window.

They rode in silence some more.

"What about my father?" Chug finally said. "I can't leave my father. He's in a nursing home. I guess I can take him with me. Sorry. I'm just rambling. I gotta think things out."

Billy Wilkins looked at Chug via the mirror.

"Maybe this will make you feel better. No one knows about this except us and the Tranfiglia's and believe me they'll never say a word. We were lucky that backhoe guy took off. Tranfiglia thinks he thought he was up to a little grave robbing he had forgotten to perform back at the funeral parlor and that he'd get a nice big payoff if he was discreet."

They dropped Jessup off at his car.

He shook Chug's hand and a look passed over his face as if he were about to deliver a speech. Instead he said, "The best of luck to you."

Then he looked at Billy Wilkins.

"It's been a trip, Wilkins. No offense, but next time I see you I'm going the other way."

Billy Wilkins flipped Special Agent Jessup a salute.

"Aw, Jessup, that's no way to be. We make quite a team, you and me, I think."

Chug looked at both of them hard for a moment but said nothing and as they drove away through the North End, he slid out of sight in the back seat.

"Now we go get Ellie?" he said when he came back up.

"Now we go get Ellie."

Billy Wilkin's and Chug's gaze met in the rearview. They exchanged a smile.

"So there's a whole country out there, Chug. Got in mind any places you'd like to go? I'll tell you, Georgia's mighty pretty if you can take the summer heat."

"I don't know. I'll have to talk with Ellie. I don't even know if she'll come with me. I'm not the safest guy in the world to hang around with."

He looked out the window at the late-morning traffic and the Boston skyline as though he had never seen any of it before.

"Damn traffic," Billy Wilkins said.

"Looks pretty good to me."

Wilkins caught Chug's eye in the mirror again.

"Yeah, I imagine it does."

After a pause, Billy Wilkins said, "You know, Chug, my Daddy used to say that every experience, good or bad, no matter *how* bad, either, was a learning experience. We could take something from it, you know what I mean?"

Chug was quiet for a moment and then said, "Yeah, well right now the only thing I'm sure of is that when I die I want to be cremated."

Chapter Thirty One

It was a hurt that couldn't go unanswered. Chug was sure that he would never fully recover. Sleep would never be the same. Nor dark rooms or confinement. He wondered whether he'd ever be able to attend a wake or funeral again.

He had more than paid for shooting Florence Scarlata and now Will Scarlet owed him. So did the avuncular Bernardo Tranfiglia. Chug had gotten his name from Billy Wilkins.

He and Ellie were reunited in the back seat of Billy Wilkins's Crown Victoria. Wilkins had gone into the station to get her and remained outside the car, walking a distance away for a few minutes to give them time alone.

Then he drove each of them to their places and stayed outside on watch as they went in and packed what they needed.

At each stop he was confident they had gone unnoticed.

Then he drove them to a motel near the airport.

"Thank you," Chug said. "I guess we're square, huh?"

"We're square. You've got your chance for a new life. Take advantage of it. Watch yourselves."

When Billy Wilkins drove away, Ellie said, "What was that all about? Being square?"

"I'll tell you sometime."

They went into the motel and took long showers and then lay on the bed and slept throughout the rest of the day and night.

In the morning, they breakfasted at the motel and then went back to their room where for the first time they talked over what had happened to them. Chug simply said he had broker away from the attackers at the Park Street station and had been trying to stay away from Will Scarlet.

Ellie ran her hand over his bruised face and cried a little.

"What happened to your wrists?" she asked, gently touching a cruel groove left by the ligatures.

"Actually, they did get me. They had me tied for a while."

"Pretty tight I'd say."

"Very tight."

"Your ankles too? I noticed you're limping."

She kissed his wrist. "Are you going to tell me about it?"

"I will. But not now. The important thing is I got away and you're here with me. But I've got to keep going, Ellie. I want you to go with me."

She nodded. "I want to go with you. I know that now."

They took stock of what they had, money and credit cards, and talked about where they might begin a new life.

"I've always wanted to go out West," Chug said. "Plenty of open space, fresh air and mountains. Montana or Wyoming. Someplace like that. Someplace where the sky stretches forever over your head."

"I think that sounds just fine."

"I'm gonna bring my Dad."

"I wouldn't have it any other way."

For three days, Chug and Ellie clung to each other. They spent a lot of time just lying on the bed while she slept and he kept his eyes open grateful for the sunlight by day and the streetlights at night, staring at the ceiling to keep it from closing over his face. Even the whine of jet engines from the nearby airport was an affirmation of his senses.

On the afternoon of the second day, Chug walked to an area that bordered one of the runways and watched and listened to the planes as they slowly wheeled into position and then suddenly jolted into their acceleration that flung them heavenward. He watched them as they climbed up and up and followed them until they were lost. He raised his arms and squeezed his fists as if celebrating their escape from the boundaries of land.

His hands and feet hurt him a lot more than he had let on to Billy Wilkins and he wondered for a while if they were permanently damaged. But, as their pain left him, it was replaced by a searing need to get even. Vengeance crouched in his psyche beside the malignant memory of being buried alive.

He savored various ways and means of exacting payment. The best, of course, was imagining Will Scarlet being lowered alive to his grave. But he could imagine only that part of his revenge, not the means to begin it or carry it out. Besides, it was too horrible a fate to inflict on anyone, even one who had done it to you. It comforted him somewhat to think he was a better person than Will Scarlet.

He knew if he got a gun he could get to Will Scarlet. He knew how to get a gun and, hell, if a president can be shot, anyone can be shot. But he surely didn't want to shoot and be shot or be caught and put in prison and lose Ellie.

He went through various methods of revenge, thought about them, and then discarded them one by one as not right for this reason or that.

On the fourth morning he drank coffee while Ellie slept, and reviewed all that had happened since he shot Florence Scarlata. He remembered Mickey the Harp asking him about the money he had soaking in various things.

As he thought about that, a plan slowly began to weave itself in his mind. He poked lots of holes in it and admitted it was filled with sticking points and unknowns and dangers. But he liked it and wanted to make it his final shot.

He checked the Yellow Pages and wrote down a couple of addresses. He thought it through again, going over everything.

After showering and shaving, he dressed in the suit and tie he had brought from home. He checked himself in the mirror.

Still a little bruised but not too bad.

Then he woke Ellie.

She looked at him quizzically, taking in the suit and tie.

He kissed her and smiled.

"I won't be long. Stay by the phone. I'll tell you about it when I get back."

Then he called a cab

He was back by early afternoon. He had had a busy morning going to the places he looked up in the Yellow Pages, observing and asking lots of questions.

While Ellie watched, he worked a paper cutter. He had bought it and a package of high quality paper at a stationery store.

"Want to tell me what you're doing?"

He winked at her. "Getting ready to go out West. I've got a good night's work and then we get things squared away."

"A night's work?"

"Yeah."

"Tonight?"

"Yep."

"Can I come?"

"Sorry. I gotta do this alone. It's gonna be on the job training."

This time he took a cab to Revere, and had the cab drop him off about a block from a place that specialized in photocopying.

It was 11:30 and the street was deserted. It was the fourth photocopy place he had had the cab drive him past that morning and he selected it for its relatively isolated location and the alley that an alongside it. And, he had gone inside for a visit and a chat.

Well before he got to the alley he checked around as he walked and when he was beside it he stepped in.

From his backpack, purchased that morning along with the paper cutter, special paper, heavy duty wire cutters, and sundry other items, he took a dart with a rubber cup on its end. He spit into the rubber cup and placed it on the window. He rubbed the cup around the glass a little until it formed a tight bond. Then he took out a glasscutter and cut a circle large enough for his arm to fit through.

He had never done B and E before but he knew guys who did and had listened attentively when they discussed their trade. What he was doing was a fairly rudimentary procedure.

The circle of glass was excised neatly and obediently clung to the dart. He pulled it free and added it to the litter in the alley.

Now he pulled two pieces of alarm wire from the pack and stepped onto the boxes he had been using as a ladder. He reached through the circle and attached the alligator clips on the ends of the wires onto the alarm connections at the top of the window.

He reached down, unlatched the window, and swung it open. The wires he had added kept the circuit unbroken and the alarm didn't sound. He was grateful the place didn't have a sophisticated alarm system.

He pulled himself up and over the window ledge and dropped to the floor. He winced as his feet protested even that short drop. Thank you, Will Scarlet. But if things work out, you'll be getting a small payment back.

There was a security light on so he'd have to be watchful for patrolling police cars and hope for the best.

He went to the copy machine, turned it on and let it warm up. That morning, he had a couple of things copied but that hadn't been the purpose of his visit. He observed, asked questions and got the name and model of the machine.

After that, he had his cab drive him to a place that sold the same machine and, nicely dressed up, had pretended he was interested in buying a couple for his business. He got the salesman to show him all about the color copier, especially all about loading the paper.

When the machine was warmed up, he set to work.

About an hour into his work, a police cruiser rode by slowly and then stopped. He crouched low and waited for the cops to come to the window and flash their light in. If they saw him, it was over. He certainly couldn't outrun anything faster than a person with a walker.

He had felt that because the copy machine was at the rear of the store he wouldn't be visible without a dedicated scrutiny. He had also felt that to his advantage was that this kind of place was an unlikely target for a break-in. No cash and the valuable stuff, the copy machines, were too big to remove easily.

He was cursing himself for being stupid, for risking freedom with Ellie and letting Will Scarlet win after all when the cruiser pulled away. What had they stopped for? His heart was ticking pretty fast as he went to the front window and looked out. A skunk ambled up onto the sidewalk and the cruiser moved on.

He went back to the machine and continued his work. Another hour and he was done. It had been a tedious trial and error procedure.

He loaded up his backpack with what he had copied on the machine. He put everything back the way it had been and left by the window he came in. In the morning, they'd scratch their heads. There had been a break-in but goddamn if they could find anything missing. Not even paper.

Probably, they'd phony up some stuff for the insurance claim. No wonder premiums were so high.

It took him twenty minutes to get a cab that dropped him off a short distance from William Scarlata's bakery in the North End. It was 2:15. The night air was cold and his breath feathered in front of him.

The bakery was on a street corner and he walked the now quiet neighborhood to it. He was counting on the alarm system being nothing too complicated. Maybe there wouldn't even be one. William Scarlata, he felt, was probably quite confident that no one would be foolish enough to break into a known Mob front. Even if they did, anything inside was probably not of any real value to him.

He went to the rear of the bakery. The glass on the door was covered with a wire mesh that he cut through with his wire cutters. He cut the entire glass piece, removed it and placed it on the ground.

He peered in, flashing his light around the doorframe looking for alarm wires. There were none. The only lock was an old slide bolt. He unlocked the door and walked in.

Inside, he was greeted by the wholesome aroma that perfumes all bakeries. He knew he'd have to work quickly because bakery people were famous for starting their work during the wee hours.

There was no light inside except that which filtered in from the street. He used his flashlight but kept its beam on the floor. He went to the cash register. Probably locked or empty but it wouldn't matter to his plan.

He tried the register anyway and it snapped open revealing a tray of bills and change. They were so cocky and this money so petty to them that they didn't even bother to secure it.

He took some of the bills from the tray and stuffed them in his pocket. From the backpack he took the fruits of his labors at the photocopy store, crisp tens and twenties.

Jesus, they looked good. Actually, with a quick exam, they looked perfect. But some of the technology of the new bills couldn't be photocopied. A careful examination would reveal the shortcomings. And the paper, although pretty damned good, wasn't the same as that of real currency. Still, at first touch it had the right feel and he knew it could be passed with a high success rate.

He mixed in with the tens and twenties still in the register several of his freshly made phony ones, crumpling them a bit before he put them in.

He wasn't certain of the penalties for manufacturing or possessing counterfeit money. At one time he had read that it was life for more than ten counterfeit bills. But he had also researched it online and found conflicting but vague information.

Whatever those penalties might be, William Scarlata, as owner of this place, was going to have to do some convincing explaining and use some pretty good lawyers. And federal officials, Chug felt, were probably looking for something to tag him for and would push their hardest. At the least, it should cost him something and be damned inconvenient. At the best, from Chug's perspective, Will Scarlet might take a fall.

If Will Scarlet served some time for this, Chug told himself he'd visit him and give him the finger. Maybe the bastard would drop dead thinking he had just seen a ghost.

Chug went to the kitchen. He checked around the ovens and refrigerators. On a shelf was a stack of boxes of cupcake papers. He took a couple, emptied the papers into his backpack, and filled them with bogus bills. He put the boxes back at the bottom of the stack.

He emptied a box filled with bottles of spices and replaced the bottles with neat stacks of tens and twenties. He put that box under similar boxes.

He went back out front, opened the counter under the register, took a couple of doughnuts and left.

It had been a long time since Bernardo Tranfiglia had handled a middle of the night call himself. Michael, who manned the phone downstairs, buzzed him.

Bernardo Tranfiglia had been sleeping fitfully the last few nights since he had looked into the face of that lost soul just before he had closed the lid over him.

"Sorry to wake you, Mr. Tranfiglia," Michael was saying, "but I got a guy on the line wants you to handle things personally. His wife just passed on."

Bernardo Tranfiglia looked down at the snoring Mrs. Tranfiglia and got out of bed. He spoke softly into the portable phone.

"Michael, why does this person have to deal with me personally at this hour?" His voice was thick with troubled sleep.

"I know, Mr. Tranfiglia, but he said if it was too much trouble he'd go to Bertone's. So I felt maybe you'd want to talk to this guy yourself."

Better not to lose business to Bertone.

"I'll talk to him."

Bernardo Tranfiglia went to the extension in his upstairs office.

"They just called me from Mass General," a distraught voice informed him. "My wife just passed on. Was in a car accident a week ago."

"I'm so sorry to hear that," Bernardo Tranfiglia said. "And you want us to handle the arrangements?"

"Yes. She always said she wanted to be shown at Tranfiglia's if possible."

"I'll send someone out to the hospital immediately. Of course, I'll need some information first. Then in the morning you can come in to—"

"Oh, I know, but I want to come in now." The voice caught. Bernardo Tranfiglia recognized a crier, someone who wanted to talk. He ought to palm this guy off on his parish priest. But then he thought of Ralph Bertone getting this business. Besides, he was awake now, anyway.

"Where are you now, sir?"

"I live just around the corner."

"Why don't you come by in say, ten minutes? You can give me the particulars and, if you want to tonight, I'll show you our line of caskets."

This might work out, Bernardo Tranfiglia thought as he hung up. Someone distraught enough to call in the middle of the night would probably go for an expensive casket.

Chug had his baseball cap pulled low and knew that Bernardo Tranfiglia didn't recognize him as he was led into the paneled office.

Bernardo Tranfiglia smiled a smile of sympathy and said, "Now then, Mr. . . . ."

"The name's Lazarus," Chug said as he took off his hat and returned the smile.

In about a second, Bernardo Tranfiglia's smile was replaced by a look that Chug thought might signal a stroke or heart attack.

Yes, Mr. Tranfiglia, it's me. Your son didn't tell you, I guess. He probably won't tell anyone which is what you should do."

Bernardo Tranfiglia sagged in his chair.

"I've risen from the dead, Mr. Tranfiglia."

Bernardo Tranfiglia found his voice. "He made me. You don't know that man. He made me . . ."

"I understand that. I really do. Will Scarlet's a scary guy. I wonder if I wouldn't have done the same thing if I were in your shoes."

They sat for a few moments, Chug smiling at the hyperventilating Bernardo Tranfiglia.

"Well, I suppose in a way I shouldn't really be surprised," Bernardo Tranfiglia managed to say. "You know, I told a police officer, A Lieutenant Wilkins. Oh my God, what's . . ."

"Relax, Mr. Tranfiglia. You're in no trouble with Lieutenant Wilkins or Will Scarlet. And I guess you probably want to keep it that way."

Bernardo Tranfiglia nodded. "Oh yes." He desperately wanted to reach into the desk drawer for his bottles.

"But I, Mr. Tranfiglia, *I* want one thing. I overheard something interesting when I was in . . . when I was in that situation. Funny, in a way I could hear better.

"Anyway, what I heard was Will Scarlet say he was gonna give you the fifty grand reward he put out on me."

Bernardo Tranfiglia's breathing eased a little.

Consideration of money always steadied him. He began to shake his head to indicate no.

"He gave me nothing. Do you think I'd do such a thing for money?"

"I don't believe you, Mr. Tranfiglia. I think he did give you the money. But let me spell it out for you.

"First off, you do not want Will Scarlet to know I'm not buried in that cemetery. He'll think you screwed up but probably worse than that he'll see you as a witness who might start screaming to save his own neck. You understand what I'm talking about here, don't you, Mr. Tranfiglia?"

Bernardo Tranfiglia reached into his desk drawer and took out the bottle of pills. He unscrewed the top and popped a pill into his mouth, which he barely managed to swallow dry.

"Second, Mr. Tranfiglia, as you know, the cops do know what happened because you told them. Billy Wilkins knows and that federal guy knows. But they're willing to let it ride, which is a whole other story we don't need to get into. But, if I push it, they'll do something."

Chug was pushing his luck here but the popped pill told him that he was in a good position to do so. He wasn't clear on exactly why Wilkins was looking the other way on certain things although he could guess. And he knew he really couldn't do much pushing without going over Wilkins's head and bringing out his involvement in the shooting of Florence Scarlata.

Bernardo Tranfiglia started to say something but Chug waved him down.

"Let me finish. Third, you've got an empty casket buried out there. What if the family of whoever was supposed to be in that casket got wind of that? Let's say it was presented to them that maybe you were donating bodies for medical research—whatever— and put an empty casket into the ground. Who knows what they might do? They might want to have that coffin dug up. At the least, it would be awful bad for business."

"You can't do any of this without Will Scarlet hearing and knowing you're alive," Bernardo Tranfiglia said.

"You're right. And I don't want him to know. I want things to be like they are. I want to get away and never come back. That's why I need the fifty thousand. I don't get it and I probably have to stick around for a while, which is dangerous.

""Dangerous for both of us, let me remind you, because if Will Scarlet knows I'm alive he's gonna be coming to see you to find out why. I can run. I've got nothing to lose. Where are you going to run to? You've got a nice business here you don't want to leave behind."

They looked at each other.

"And fourth, Mr. Tranfiglia, I figure you owe me. Simple as that. Whether Will Scarlet gave you the fifty grand or it comes out of your pocket. Do you have *any* idea what it was like in that . . ."

They looked at each other some more. Bernardo Tranfiglia stared into Chug's eyes. Remembering.

"Come on, Mr. Tranfiglia. What the hell's fifty thousand to you? Think how you got it.

When he got back, Ellie was watching a movie whose age and status were appropriate to four a.m.

"I couldn't sleep," she said when he kissed her.

"Here, have a donut." He pulled the donut from his jacket pocket. He sat on the bed and watched her chew.

"Any good?"

"It's very good. Didn't you have one?"

"I did. It was delicious."

He smiled at her. "What do you think of this?"

He opened a manila envelope and took out stacks of fifty-dollar and one-hundred-dollar bills.

Instantly, her face contorted in anger and she started to get out of the bed.

"Chug, you didn't—"

He grabbed her arm. "Ellie, listen to me. I didn't do anything wrong to get this money. I swear on anything you want me to swear on."

"I said I'd go with you to wherever you want to go. But wherever we go, you and I are both going to get jobs, work hard, be law abiding, get married and have a family. There will be no other way. Say it."

"Wherever we go, you and I are both going to get jobs, work hard, be law abiding, get married and have a family. There will be no other way."

"Okay. Where did you get this money?"

"This is the best part, Ellie. I got it from Will Scarlet in a roundabout way. Of course, Will doesn't know I've got it."

"Chug, Chug, come on. This is Ellie."

"I swear it's the truth. And I'll tell you all about it. Very soon. But first, I'm tired as hell. I want to try for a couple hours sleep and then I've got one last phone call. After that, we get ready to head out West. After we find a place to settle, I'll come back to get my Dad and bring him out so he can be near us.

He tried to sleep but couldn't. Bakeries open early and he was worried that the help might somehow filter out the bills he had put into the register before he could complete his plan

He showered and made coffee from the service in the room.

While Ellie was showering, he dialed 4-1-1 and got the phone number of the Boston field office of the Secret Service.

He called the number, got an agent and said he believed he had been given a bogus bill as part of the change he received while shopping at the Soft 'n Fresh bakery in the North End.

"Your name, sir?"

"I'd rather not."

"When did you receive the bill?"

"Yesterday."

"How do you know it came from this bakery?"

"I remember they gave me a ten. It's the only ten I have in my wallet."

"Why didn't you report this yesterday?"

"I wasn't aware then. I was just counting my money this morning and I noticed it then."

"Why do you think it's counterfeit, sir? Does it look counterfeit?"

"No. I don't think so. It looks real. I guess it's the paper mainly. Doesn't feel quite right."

"Okay. Are you an expert on currency, sir? Do you work in a bank?"

"No. I'm not an expert and I don't work in a bank."

Chug tried to keep exasperation out of his voice. He could tell Ellie was finishing her shower. He didn't want her to hear this conversation.

"I'm afraid we need more, sir."

"What do you mean, you need more?"

"You say you think you got a counterfeit ten from this bakery but you won't give us your name and we don't have the ten. Sir, if you give us your name or come to our office and let us see the bill, we'll check it out. What sometimes happens, sir, and I'm not saying that it's the case with you, is that someone's got a grudge against someone, they say they picked up a funny bill at their store."

Chug thought of the glass and wire mesh he had cut through at the back door of the bakery. Will Scarlet would use that to claim the phony money had been planted but he doubted it would stick. But there was nothing he could do about it now.

"Look," Chug said, "we both know who owns that bakery. I don't want to get into any trouble with him. But I'll tell you, and I should have said so right away, this isn't the first time I got bills from that place I thought were funny."

"Well, sir, we appreciate the tip but I wish you'd come to the office and bring the bill with you. It would be in complete confidence."

"If you were to see the bill you'd check out the bakery?"

Ellie had the hairdryer going now.

"We'd like to see you too but if the bill is bogus we'd follow up, yes."

"I'm gonna get that bill out to you. I'll send it by cab. It'll be there within a half hour."

"Okay, put some paper around it and put it in an envelope. Have the driver leave it at the front desk. Put my name on the envelope. It's Rice."

Chug got the address and wrote it on the manila envelope.

He called for two taxis and sent one on its way to Agent Rice and he and Ellie took the other to the North End. He had it park in front of a deli where it commanded a view of the Soft 'n Fresh bakery. On its front the deli said *Negozio di Salumerie.*

He told the driver to wait, that they were going into the deli for a few items.

On the sidewalk, Ellie shot him a quizzical look.

"I don't want the driver to think we came here just to watch the show."

"What show? What are you talking about?"

"Come on. We'll go in and get a few cold cuts or something. There should be a show down by that bakery in a few minutes. I hope. I'll explain later."

"Seems there's a lot of things you're going to explain later."

He squeezed her hand and hoped the taxi had made its delivery, hoped that Agent Rice would act, and soon, and hoped Will Scarlet would take a fall. He was counting on Will Scarlet being such a delectable target that the Feds would act even if certain protocols weren't followed, like an accuser not wanting his identity revealed. Maybe they'd just like to push Will Scarlet around a little and see what fell out of his pockets.

They went into the deli and while Ellie picked out a few items he watched out the window. He was beginning to think he was a fool and would have to settle just for the fifty thousand. No, not just that. He was alive and he had Ellie. That was everything. Revenge on Will Scarlet would have been nice but now he thought it wasn't going to happen.

He watched Ellie select some items. Yes, he had all that he would ever want in her.

He looked out the window again and saw a plain-Jane Ford pull up in front of the bakery. Two men who might have been central casting's Secret Service agents got out of the car and went into the bakery. In less than five minutes, one came back out and got back into the Ford.

Chug waited for Ellie to finish and led her to the cab.

"Show might be in progress. Let's wait a few minutes and see what happens."

She shook her head and smiled. "You're being mysterious."

When they got into the cab, the driver said, "Guess there's some excitement going on down there." He pointed at the bakery.

"Oh?"

"Yeah, down at that bakery. You know who owns it?"

"No. Who?" Chug said.

Three more plain-Janes arrived each toting four men who scrambled quickly inside.

A crowd had gathered on the sidewalk.

"Believe me, you don't want to know."

Chug squeezed Ellie's hand again."

"Those don't look like city cops," the cabby said. "They look like the G to me. Someone's in deep, I think."

"Who is it?"

The cabby put his hand beside his mouth and spoke in a hushed voice. "You know who Will Scarlet is?"

"That bakery?" Chug said, pointing. "No kidding?"

Ellie gave him a knowing smile and started to say something but he pulled a slice of prosciutto from the bag and fed it to her. He took a piece for himself.

"Oh, this is good," he said.

He offered a slice to the cabby and said, "Would you take us to Logan, please. We have a flight to catch.

About The Author

William L. Story has taught English, creative writing and various other writing courses. He has published three previous novels and co-authored two others. He enjoys reading novels of crime and particularly enjoys the works of Elmore Leonard, Robert Parker, Nelson DeMille, Michael Connelly and James Lee Burke. His current primary hobby is most things Italian: the food, the wine, the people, the country and, of course, the language. He has taught himself a smattering of *la bella lingua* and is able to stumble through a conversation. He enjoys traveling, especially to Italy. He lives near Boston with his wife Marie.

Books by William L. Story

DOMINO SPILL
CEMETERIES ARE FOR DYING
FINAL THESIS
SALEM'S SECRET
co-authored with Robert E. Cahill
CAPE COD'S SECRET
co-authored with Robert E. Cahill